Ann Mann has enjoyed an eclectic career in show business and the media. As a singer, she made numerous broadcasts on television and radio in the sixties and performed in some of the top cabaret spots in the West End of London. She has produced and presented over a 1,000 programmes for TV and radio, worked for Walt Disney and Hammer Films, and lectured on musical theatre and Irish Literature. She has also written articles for major newspapers and other publications. Currently she is working on a film screenplay.

The best secrets should always be shared

IMPERSONATOR

ANN MANN

Matador
5 Weir Road
Kibworth Beauchamp
Leicester LE8 0LQ, UK
Tel: (+44) 116 279 2299
Fax: (+44) 116 279 2277
Email: books@troubador.co.uk
Web: www.troubador.co.uk/matador

ISBN:
978-1848765-856 (SB)
978-1848765-917 (HB)

British Library Cataloguing in Publication Data.
A catalogue record for this book is available from the British Library.

Featured song lyrics:
"You Don't Have To Say You Love Me" (Wickham/Napier Bell/Curci Edizoni)
"Eleanor Rigby" (Lennon/McCartney/Sony/ATV Music)
"Norwegian Wood" (Lennon/McCartney/Sony/ATV Music)
"You've Got To Hide Your Love Away" (Lennon/McCartney/Sony/ATV Music)
"Today Has Been A Lovely Day" (Roberts/Rossi/Parsons/Peter Morris Music)
"Wimoweh" (Traditional/South African)
"Good Timin" (Ballard jr. Tobias/United Artists Music)
"Just Like A Woman" (Bob Dylan/B. Feldman)
"Waterloo Sunset" (Ray Davies/Carlin Music Corps)
"Fire Down Below" (Washington/Lee/Universal Music/ Shapiro-Bernstein)

Typeset in 11pt Aldine by Troubador Publishing Ltd, Leicester, UK
Printed and bound in the UK by TJ International, Padstow, Cornwall

Matador is an imprint of Troubador Publishing Ltd

For Hopper and The Brute

*With special thanks to Sarah Molloy of A. M. Heath, Hilary
Johnson, De Beers of London, Jan and Mickey Morgan,
Olivia Landsberg and other good friends.*

They know who they are.

"A pity beyond all telling is hid in the heart of love...."

W. B. Yeats.

SOUTHERN RHODESIA
OCTOBER, 1966

Elizabeth watched the school bus pull away and trundle down the hot, dusty road, waving at Marion and Chloe in the back seat as they crossed their eyes and blew huge, pink bubbles which collapsed and sagged on to their chins. She laughed, but something inexplicable, something heavy, tugged at her stomach, making the walk home difficult and different on this end of week day.

The ribbon on one of her plaits came loose and she stopped to tie it. Why? Normally, she wouldn't bother. Patches of sweat clung to her armpits through her thin school dress. She stopped again and sniffed at them, her freckled nose curling in disgust.

"Yuck!" she said out loud. "Must wash..." She said to herself.

Teatime was likely to be hard going, due to the blazing row she had had that morning with her mother. Well, what was the point of great-aunt Margaret giving her a brand new bicycle for her birthday, a shiny, red Raleigh with three speeds, if she couldn't ride it to school occasionally?

"Not safe." Her mother had told her without further explanation. "Things aren't safe."

She knew something was wrong when she saw the jeeps, and the boss-boy and his assistant who had been employed on the farm as long as she could remember being roughly pushed into them. She stood still, as though rooted among the ploughs, harrows and rusting machinery, as the tallest of the policemen saw her and shaded his eyes with his hand.

"Why isn't he sweating?" she thought, irrationally. His neat khaki shirt and shorts looked freshly pressed, although the veins

1

protruded from his forehead, and his fine, sandy hair needed cutting.

"That's the girl – the daughter!" He moved towards her. "Don't come any closer, sweetheart."

But now the breath was charging back into her body and her limbs were working again. Running past him through a posse of scattering chickens, she managed to escape the outstretched hands of his two deputies and reached the open kitchen door where she rooted once more.

"Hey." He was beside her, his voice gentle but his fingers digging into her arm. "You don't want to go in there."

Her father lay at an angle that wouldn't have been possible in life.

The gunshot had sprayed his brains across the primrose-coloured wall, and she slowly inclined her head to examine the pattern. It looked like a heart. A big, red heart, its definition only marred by the pearl-shaped droplets which had spread out from the perimeter and come to rest on the cream-painted skirting board.

Her mother's shoe was beside where her father's head had been, and, next to her mother's bent leg, the Singer sewing machine, still tangled with the dress she had been working on that morning. Bright blue glazed cotton, dotted with small, white daisies. They had chosen the material together in Jones Brothers in Salisbury last week.

"Mummy..."

But she didn't get to see any more of the woman who had been her mother. Mrs. MacLeod from the next farm, her round face distorted with shock, her apron still covered in flour from the day's baking, gently led her away.

"Come with me, Elizabeth... Come with me..."

LONDON
OCTOBER, 1966

Jack Merrick drained the last comforting measure from a Napoleon brandy, took a final puff on his favourite Montecristo cigar and made a mental note to try and lose some weight before Christmas.

Still, he felt discreetly confident and well-groomed today in a manner which only Savile Row can bestow on its devotees, creating an impression of strength from broad shoulders set in his six foot two frame.

It seemed the time had now come to deliver the speech over which he had been toiling for half the night, and which he considered to be the down side of what was otherwise proving to be an extremely pleasant afternoon.

"Ladies and gentlemen, may I have your attention, please?"

The scarlet-coated Master of Ceremonies with the questionable toupee cracked his gavel sharply down on the table, narrowly missing a Waterford crystal wine glass and eventually encouraged the two hundred or so luncheon guests assembled in the Grosvenor House banqueting suite to a tapering silence.

"We are gathered together..." He continued, adopting a gesture of prayer and drawing a polite titter, "...To pay tribute to a man to whom so many owe so much. Someone who has recently, and quite properly, been awarded the Order of the British Empire for services to show business."

Ignoring the tentative ripple of applause – because that wasn't the right place for it in his script – the M.C's voice now rose to a powerful boom.

"I am sure that his many friends and colleagues who are here today, would like to join with me now in raising their glasses in a toast to our Guest of Honour, not only a talented theatre producer and director, but probably best known to us all as that most successful impresario and agent to the stars, Mr. Jack Merrick. Jack Merrick, OBE!"

With a dramatic flourish, acquired from years of hosting similar events, he cued the assorted celebrities and professional associates to their feet as Jack remained seated, wondering, as he had for most of the day, just how he had arrived at this point in his life, surrounded by such distinguished and gifted people who were paying him tribute. Honoring him for doing a job he enjoyed and which, although he considered he had performed it competently, certainly did not seem deserving of such lavish praise.

"To Jack..."

"Jack..."

The toast completed, people re-took their seats noisily, amidst cries of "Speech, speech," which forced him reluctantly out of his chair. He had, during the last thirty seconds, decided to abandon what he had written, and to render words of thanks which would be short, sweet and to the point, then he would get off, allowing himself and others to pursue the obligatory mixing and mingling, plus some serious afternoon drinking.

"Thank you, Arthur. And my thanks to everyone who has made this honour possible. You know, it's a well-coined phrase, almost a cliché, but a theatrical agent is only as good as the people he represents, and I have been very fortunate in working with some of the best in the business. This..." Further reaction was produced as he held up the distinctive golden medal hung on a ribbon around his neck for inspection. "...Belongs to all of you. For your talent, support and friendship."

He ran his hand over his thinning dark hair, then noticed a quiet late-comer wearing a full length-mink coat silhouetted in the doorway.

"As I look around this magnificent room at so many familiar and loyal faces, I count my blessings that this wonderful business of ours has brought us together and, if I was asked for any wish

4

in the world right now, it would simply be to continue to do what I love doing, for many, many more years to come. Thank you all. From the bottom of my heart."

The crowd rose to a spontaneous standing ovation and Jack was surprised to find that he was on the verge of tears, although there was no time to examine such mystifying feelings of emotion. People were soon at his side, pressing his hand and beaming with the appearance of true sincerity in what he knew was all too often a self-obsessed and insincere world.

"Jack, darling." Shirley Bassey, the owner of the mink, kissed his cheek affectionately. "Congratulations."

"Hello Shirley. I thought you were in the studio recording a new LP?"

"I am. But I've played truant for five minutes to come and see you."

"Thank you so much. I appreciate it."

As the singer wafted back through the crowd which appeared to part biblically to allow her passage, Jack was unexpectedly thwarted by the appearance of a pair of identical blonde twins, resplendent in their matching Pucci silks and expensive, designer jewellery and whose faces he knew, but whose names, he silently confessed, did not spring readily to mind.

"Hello, ladies," he offered pleasantly, knowing this was the safest means of address.

"Mr. Merrick, congratulations." One of the sisters shimmied forward to plant a sticky kiss on his lips, then as she stepped back leaving him speechlessly covered in Yardley's "Pink String", she nudged her twin and giggled.

"Oh, look, Angie. He's blushing. Isn't that sweet? I always find shyness so appealing in a man, don't you?"

Rescued from a repeat performance by someone tapping his arm, Jack was suddenly conscious of an urgency of tone. One of the hotel staff, a blotchy-cheeked young man with a curtain of thick black hair, grown as near to a Beatles cut as would be allowed in such an establishment, spoke quickly.

"A long distance call, sir. You can take it in one of the booths in the lobby..."

Slightly unsteady from the heady combination of alcohol and compliments, Jack rose quickly and excused himself from the glamorous duo, following the messenger across the room and acknowledging guests as he made his way to the Reception area. From there he was directed towards a small, wood-paneled booth with a tiny glass window and which contained a house-phone, a pad and pencil and a low, three-legged stool.

Fully expecting the caller to be an overseas friend or colleague, possibly ringing from America to offer good wishes, he was unprepared for what followed.

"Jack Merrick speaking."

"Hold on please..." The operator's voice was faint and Jack placed a finger into his free ear to try and decipher words which came in fragments through a barrage of static.

"Mackenzie ... Solicitor ... Rhodesia...."

He tensed, cursing the poor line that existed between England and its Commonwealth neighbour. His sister and her husband lived in Rhodesia, but they knew nothing of this celebratory lunch.

"... I'm very sorry to have to tell you that Mr. and Mrs. Tarrant were brutally murdered at their farmhouse yesterday."

Instantly sober now and with cold goose flesh hitting the back of his neck, Jack sat down heavily on the small stool. "How? Who by?"

"Some black farm workers are helping the police with their enquiries," the man who sounded like a bad impersonation of Ian Smith continued.

"Mr. Merrick, were you aware that you are named as the joint next of kin of Miss Elizabeth Tarrant, together with her great-aunt, Margaret Ainsley?"

"Yes," Jack answered, running his tongue over stress-dried lips. "I suppose the Ainsleys will take care of her?"

"You were not aware that Mrs. Ainsley's husband recently died, and that Mrs. Ainsley is herself preparing to move into a nursing home?"

"No.... No... I wasn't... I see."

Had he known? A vague recollection of one of Emily's

frequent letters danced in the back of his mind. Yes, now he thought about it, she had mentioned that Samuel Ainsely had died. But Margaret? He didn't want to see where all this was leading.

"Under the terms of the will..." The solicitor's voice was monotone now. A flat, unvaried timbre that made the information he was imparting all the more surreal. "... If both parents pre-decease the minor known as Elizabeth Anne Tarrant before she reaches the age of twenty-one, then Jack Merrick or Margaret Ainsley as the only other next of kin, will be responsible for overseeing the welfare and education of said minor who will be assigned to their care until such time..."

"Wait a minute, whoa..."

He felt nauseous, as if someone had kicked him in the belly, inciting the prawn cocktail and steak au poivre he had just enjoyed to be regurgitated.

"I can't... I'm a single man – in business. Show business. I can't look after a child!"

He knew he sounded panicky. And mean spirited. After all, she was his niece, Emily's beloved daughter and his only living relative now.

More crackling silence, then he heard himself asking with a degree of embarrassment "How old is she again?"

"Fifteen. Elizabeth's fifteen."

The last time he had seen her she had been three or four. A baby anyhow.

"And where...?"

"She's alright. She's staying with friends. I suggest that you give yourself time to get used to the idea and we'll talk again tomorrow. My number is Salisbury 14327 if you wish to call me."

"Yes... Yes... Alright... Thank you. It's been a bit of a shock..."

Hearing the receiver click, his words melted into the ether, and the numbness he had been slowly experiencing now seemed to have immobilised every nerve in his body. Suddenly desperate for air, he emerged from the booth like a sleep-walker, clutching the piece of paper on which he had scratched the number and noticing that several of his guests were now taking their leave. A few saw him and tried to engage him in conversation, but the expression on his face and lack of response confused them and they simply stared as he walked across the lobby, out of the hotel and into Park Lane, which after an earlier thunder storm was now bathed in bright autumn sunshine.

Oblivious to the stiff breeze and the lack of an overcoat, Jack made his way back to the office through Hyde Park, where the usual collection of dossers, joggers, young lovers and people going about their daily business, all served as a grim reminder of the fragility which surrounded the familiar pageant of everyday life.

—∞—

So Emily was gone. Blown away by some stranger who believed it was right for a cause. What cause – he thought desperately – gave anybody the right to kill another human being, especially one as sweet-natured as his sister?

The picture of her which he conjured up now was still that of the nervous little girl, docile, religious and bookish, to whom he had made a sincere childhood promise, but which, as an adult, he wondered whether he had ever fulfilled. And yet, he had always tried to be there for her, hadn't he? Even though an enforced two years in what turned out to be inactive service for the RAF in Canada was their first real time apart, he returned to discover that she had become engaged to a young man named Ben Tarrant, whose father owned a farm in the next village on which she was working as a land girl.

Jack had never understood why Emily and Ben decided to up sticks and move to Rhodesia seventeen years ago when political rumblings were already in the wind, but assumed that it had been something to do with his sister's sudden miscarriage of a much-longed for child at six months into her pregnancy.

New beginning, new country, and eventually a new baby, Elizabeth Anne.

He had been pressurised by Emily into visiting them, but it

was not the most auspicious of trips, although the first two or three days had been reasonable enough. The farmhouse was old and comfortable, with large, shady rooms and a deep, wrap-around verandah where he would sit each evening at sundown, sipping a gin and tonic, accompanied only by the noisy chirping of the crickets and pleasantly mesmerised by the quick movements of the chameleons as they darted through the mulberry trees.

His brother-in-law, who claimed Scottish ancestry, had taken to this new life happily and easily. Ben was a big man, with a wild mop of ginger hair and a chuckle which was infectious. It had been his idea to settle here, as his father's sister, Margaret, had married a Rhodesian Scot two decades before, and had adapted well in her role as a farmer's wife. Better, Jack thought, than his own sister, who, now looking uncannily like their late mother, moved around the farm in her pale, intense way, always shaded by a wide, straw hat, and never separated from her little curly-haired girl, whom she carried everywhere.

"Do you think we have to pay for our happiness, Jack?" Emily would ask him, to which he was at a loss for a reply. "I'm sure that some day I'll have to pay for the happiness Elizabeth has brought me. We always do, don't we?"

The farm produced a few cattle, maize and a little tobacco and seemed to make them a reasonable living.

There was a dairy, a blacksmith's and leather worker's shed, plus numerous fruit trees attended diligently by Joseph, the 'garden boy', who spread his task between their farm and those of their closest neighbours.

Jack was aware of some tensions that Ben was experiencing, though these were never spoken of to Emily, for Ben appeared to want to shelter her from the smallest concern. He talked to Jack when Emily had retired for the night about his anxiety over employing a poor Boer farmhand with six children, a decision which was likely to cause hostility from his other native workers. This was so far removed from Jack's world, that he could only listen and mildly warn Ben about the politics of this action and its possible reprisals.

Then Jack contacted dysentery. Never in his life had he been so ill. In fact, death would have been preferable. His stomach and bowels felt as though they had been torn from his body and almost two stone in weight mysteriously disappeared. No-one seemed to know what had caused it as no-one else suffered, but Jack had always suspected bacteria in the water to which he presumed the others had grown immune, and, for the following fortnight he had lain in a darkened bedroom, eating only tiny portions of corn bread and sipping flat Coca-Cola till the weakness subsided and he was well enough to fly home.

He had never returned and they had never come back to Britain. Elizabeth Anne was a cute, blonde-haired baby. That was how he remembered her. And now…

"Now is the wrong time!" he startled himself by saying loudly as he pushed open the heavy front door of Merrick Management, passing an equally startled receptionist on the way into his office. Once within the familiar security of his surroundings, he sank with weary relief into the studded, olive-green leather chair and swivelled round to face the window. The sky had now turned a deep magenta and heavy spots of rain were starting to bounce off the flat roof below, where a few miserable-looking pigeons huddled together as if picking up his mood.

Now was the wrong time. But could there ever be a right time for this particular set of circumstances? He was an unmarried, forty-two year old man with a successful business to which he had been known to devote twenty-four hours a day and who, before all the excitement created by his receiving the OBE, had been cautiously poised to make a long-overdue improvement in the quality of his personal life.

Well, that particular goal wasn't going to be realised. Not in the foreseeable future, at any rate.

His head continued to spin with the vision of his fears. To be responsible for a young teenage girl. To manage her education and her finances. To have her live with him, for God's sake, in his luxury bachelor apartment in South Kensington.

He tried to remember how Emily had described her in her letters. Alarmingly, words like tom-boyish and boisterous came to mind. Did that mean that she was rough and noisy?

Was she was going to hurtle through the flat like a banshee, causing havoc amongst his priceless antiques, his Venetian glass and his oil paintings, which he had so painstakingly acquired over the years?

He shuddered, hardly aware that someone had entered the room.

Tall, thirty-eight and exuding an air of efficiency combined with a strong whiff of Chanel No. 5, Sylvia Lawrence was wearing the well-cut navy silk suit which she had bought especially for the luncheon, and her glossy brown hair was neatly woven into a French pleat.

"You're back early, I told you I could manage…" His long-time business partner trailed off then asked sharply. "What's happened?'

"My sister Emily and her husband…" He stood up and began to pace a trail between his desk and the door. "They were killed yesterday in Rhodesia. They're dead."

"My God, Jack. I'm so sorry." Sylvia was instantly at his side, her hand on his arm. "What about the little girl?"

"Elizabeth, yes. She's alive." He opened the cabinet where he kept a selection of drinks and took out a half bottle of Jamesons'.

"Would you…?"

"Please."

Jack poured a liberal amount of whisky into two tumblers and handed one to Sylvia. "She's got to come and live with me. Apparently, I'm the only next of kin able to look after her. It's in Emily's will"

Sylvia sipped her drink, for a moment uncharacteristically lost for words.

"But how…? How can you look after her?"

"Don't you think I'm asking myself the same question?"

"When is all this supposed to be happening?"

"It looks imminent. A couple of weeks."

Regaining her composure, his partner metamorphosed back into her customary organized self.

"You'll have to find her a school. Have a chat with Mark

Dover, he's got a girl around, what is she? Fourteen, fifteen?"

"Fifteen. That's a good idea. Perhaps they could meet. Become friends."

Mark Dover was a fairly new addition to the agency, solely responsible for representing night-club and cabaret performers. His wife Judy had been a dancer in the Tiller Girls famous line-up, and Jack had met their teenage daughter socially, plus on the odd occasion when she had popped into the office. She was a nice kid and seemed friendly and well-adjusted.

"Well, don't let's get ahead of ourselves." Sylvia said briskly. "Listen, what can I do to help? Tell me? You're going to have to take a few weeks off work when she arrives, so we should go through what you need to do before that happens."

This was another factor to consider and he looked around the room as if searching for inspiration. Taking time off, or rather, working from home with the frantic Christmas season fast approaching, would have been anathema up until an hour ago.

Sylvia's clear hazel eyes expressed concern while she tried to maintain some buoyancy. "It'll work out, Jack. It'll change your life, but it will work out. Between us we can keep the business running the way we always have."

If only he could believe that. He glanced at the framed photographs which lined the walls, dotted between theatre posters and featuring many of the stars whom he represented. Symbols of what seemed like a lifetime of risk-taking and negotiation. He noticed that his secretary, Lesley, had recently added two more and he moved forward to study them.

A picture of him outside Buckingham Palace after his investiture, beaming proudly as he displayed his award, and next to it a gold disc, earned by his Liverpool group, The Road Hogs, for selling three million copies of their number one hit *Mersey Nights*. The foursome had also started their musical career at the famous Cavern Club and, in Jack's opinion, were far more talented than the Beatles. But that Epstein guy was something else. With him, they couldn't put a foot wrong. Although he hadn't been given an OBE – yet!

For a moment Jack had spooled into work mode, the recent

news taking on the illusion of a bad dream that hovers at the back of the conscious mind hours after its formation.

"You know the panto in Blackpool's a sell-out?" He offered lamely.

"I do." Sylvia enthused. "That was a touch of genius on your part, getting a name like Syd Daniels to star and direct."

"I really should get up there for the opening."

"You will. Take your niece, she'll love it."

"Will she?" He frowned, suddenly jolted back to reality. "Who knows what she'll love?"

"Go home, Jack." Sylvia removed the glass from his hand and gave him his briefcase. "Go home and try to rest. You've had quite a day."

He allowed himself to be kissed on both cheeks as the door was held open for his departure. The most successful Showbiz agent in the country would climb into his red Alfa Romeo and head for his immaculate flat, which now seemed strangely at odds with the life-altering predicament that he had so suddenly and unexpectedly been presented with.

NOVEMBER, 1966

During the long flight to London, Elizabeth tried to assess the whirlwind that she had just lived through. Now, although the storm had stabilized, the initial shock and horror was replaced by confusion, with no apparent end in sight.

The flurry of people in and out of the farmhouse as soon as the bodies had been removed. People whom she knew, others she had never seen before. Detectives, solicitors, house-agents, well-meaning friends of her parents, all fulfilling their individual roles with varying degrees of ability, coupled with uneasy sympathy.

After staying with the MacLeods for the first few days, Chloe's family had taken her in, and for that she had been relieved, if simply to escape the scene of the bloodshed. Sharing her best friend's bedroom might not have been the fun it would have under normal circumstances, but these circumstances were anything but normal and this, Chloe appeared to quietly understand.

And she still hadn't cried. Tears, which should have come so easily and which she knew would bring relief, seemed to be eluding her, although they ached inside as if waiting for some specific moment to burst forth. Convinced that this moment would be the funeral, Elizabeth had made sure that all her pockets were stuffed with tissues, but, at the graveside service, when others around her wept, she could only remain an observer, feeling self-conscious and inadequate at her inability to express what was considered to be such a natural emotion.

Chloe and her mother had made sure that all her favourite food like fish and chips, fried chicken, strawberry ice-cream and chocolate milkshakes were produced in abundance by their cheerful maid, Elsa, but the three boys, usually loud and teasing, now became subdued and awkward when she was around and she longed to scream at them "Kick me under the table like you used to. I'm still me. I haven't changed."

But she knew it was useless to pretend things could be the same. Maybe she hadn't changed, but everything else had. The world had gone topsy-turvy. 'Stop it, I want to get off!' her inner voice demanded. There was a show called that, wasn't there?

Chloe's father, a quiet, serious man, whom Elizabeth had hardly ever seen smile, became even more solemn. In the evenings, after supper, he would sit in his favourite chair smoking his pipe and talk about the developing crisis in his country. "We are in a period of adjustment. Rhodesia is fighting for her life. For her identity."

He would quote some verse by the poet Yeats, which he told her was written about the 1916 Easter uprising in Dublin, and, although she barely understood it, it made her tremble.

"Is a terrible beauty to be born in Rhodesia?" she asked him.

"Perhaps," he told her, "but how many lives will it take to induce that birth?"

In lighter moments, she and Chloe played their old, familiar game of "What if?" Only now, it had taken on a deeper significance.

"What if you were to live here, with us? If mum said you could?"

Of course, that was the answer, Elizabeth thought delightedly. That way she could stay in the country which she loved and where she had grown up, go to the same school and not have to leave her friends. Two weeks ago she had been informed by the dour solicitor that her next of kin, an uncle in England, was to be her guardian and that she would be leaving for London as soon as practically possible. The solicitor explained that it was her parents' wish and had all been written down and legalised.

Now, if there were a way of getting out of it, she would be overjoyed.

"Oh, yes... Yes. Could you ask her, please?"

But she was not to know that Chloe's parents were already making plans to leave Rhodesia the following year, having more or less decided on moving to Australia where other family members had recently re-anchored.

"I'm so sorry, Elizabeth. Of course you could have stayed here. Another one wouldn't have made any difference. It's just that right now... It's difficult."

"I see." Elizabeth said, struggling to hide her deep disappointment.

"Try to look at the positives." Chloe had suggested brightly in an effort to cheer her. "Television, Carnaby Street, the Beatles!"

"Don't they live somewhere else?" Elizabeth retorted. "Liverpool?"

"I really think that England at this time will be a wonderful education for you." Chloe's mother told her gently. "And the pain of losing your parents will be cushioned a little by all the new and fascinating things you will learn and see there." She moved towards the young girl and enfolded her in a warm hug.

"I'll make you a promise," she added, with a quick glance at Chloe's father. "If we're all still here in March or April and you haven't settled, then ask your uncle to give us a call. We'll work something out. Okay?"

Elizabeth nodded vigorously. "Okay."

On the day she was to leave, the entire family piled into the beaten up nineteen fifty-five station-wagon for the two hour drive to the airport, picking great-aunt Margaret up en route from the nursing home where she was now reluctantly ensconced.

"It's alright." Elizabeth said reassuringly, taking the frail hand and knowing that she would probably never see her father's auntie again. They had been such good friends, shared so many chats and laughs, and all through Elizabeth's life she had remained a robust and energetic force. But since being told of the murders, the old lady seemed totally enveloped in a web of confusion, her vacant blue eyes were red-rimmed, and her skin, always tanned from the sun, had developed a sinister, greyish hue.

The decrepit car bumped along a series of unmade roads, before finding its speed skimming recently tarred new ones, the heat from the tires leaving a spiral of acrid steam in its wake. Elizabeth rolled down the window and breathed in deeply, needing to gather all the sensations that made up her homeland and take them with her.

Farmhouses like her own, where cattle grazed contentedly and lines of washing flapped in the breeze, were separated by lacey jacaranda trees and bursts of purple bougainvillea, only to be replaced a few miles later by stretches of withered, brown desolation. It was all so uniquely and intensely African. That special smell of dark red earth and the way the clouds formed like scales in the sky just before the rain, became a vibrant dreamscape, crystallised forever in her memory.

Salisbury airport, small for a capital city, had a fair-sized airstrip bordered by low hibiscus shrubs, and a circular windowed building on its roof where people could watch and wave to their departing loved ones as they boarded their planes.

Elizabeth, almost deafened by the roar of a plane taking off overhead, felt her first beat of excitement at the thought of travelling in something so enormous. How different to when she and her parents had on occasions flown to the Transvaal in small fourteen-seater air buses with creaky propellers.

"Hello, young lady."

She turned and found herself facing the balding, bespectacled solicitor who had come to place her in the care of the airline staff. "All set?"

"Yes," she replied quietly.

"This is Lydia." He gestured towards the perfectly made-up, well-manicured air-hostess who smiled at her kindly. "She will make sure you have everything you need on the journey."

With a heavy heart Elizabeth looked at the people she was leaving behind. This was it then. Goodbye time. Almost automatically she hugged everyone in turn and when she came to Chloe, they clung to one another with promises to stay in touch forever.

"Don't forget us." Chloe told her, starting to cry.

"Don't be silly." Elizabeth swallowed the lump that had risen in her throat and put her arms around her great-aunt who seemed unsure of the degree of sadness that surrounded her.

"What a to-do. Good-bye then."

As she stood on the steps before boarding the plane, Elizabeth shaded her eyes to try and see them through the windows, but it was hard to recognize anyone among such a sea of faces.

"I know they're there," she whispered, and waved anyway.

—⁓—

He cursed himself for his nervousness and for the fifth cigarette he had smoked since arriving at Heathrow, realising that he had been anticipating this day much like a predicted earthquake. But why should he be so scared? Jack Merrick, whose tough show-business deals were legendary on both sides of the Atlantic and who was well-known for getting results under pressure. His was the neck that was well and truly on the line if performances staged for royalty weren't polished and entertaining, and who had sat in recording studios while some of his star singers backed by a hundred musicians, took the clock ticking towards a massive bill for overtime.

He recalled the last occasion he had been at the airport. It was to greet Bob Hope, whose services he had secured for a run at the Palladium and, over the following weeks, Jack had calmly met the star's not inconsiderable demands without batting an eyelid or doubling his nicotine intake.

So why, he asked himself for the umpteenth time, should he be so goddammed frightened now?

The announcements reminded him that the plane had landed and people from the flight were beginning to spill out. Perhaps he should be holding a card with her name...?

But that was ridiculous, for not many fifteen year old girls would be coming through the barrier on their own, or, as he had been informed, escorted by a BOAC official.

He started as a young, fair-haired girl in a red coat appeared pushing a trolley, but relaxed when he saw a couple who were obviously her parents, laden down with cases and following behind.

Then suddenly she was there in front of him. Instantly recognizable; the cheek-bones were Emily's. He was amazed to see how like their side of the family she looked. She was wearing a chunky purple cardigan, almost certainly knitted by her mother, and black drainpipe trousers. But where was the blonde hair that he thought he remembered? This hair was golden-red, long and falling in soft curls over her shoulders.

He caught his breath. Whatever he had been expecting, this wasn't it. His niece was beautiful, even with the weary tension evident on her face and dark circles shadowing her eyes.

Jack stepped forward and held up his hand in greeting, unnerved by the presence of someone who seemed so familiar and yet unknown to him.

"Mr. Merrick?" The young uniformed steward smiled and steadied the luggage trolley to a shuddering halt. "Are you Mr. Jack Merrick?"

Jack nodded "Yes, yes I am."

"Here she is then. Delivered safe and sound".

The two related strangers looked at one another as Jack took the trolley from the steward and slipped a ten pound note into his hand. "Thank you. We're alright now."

"Thank you, sir."

"How was the flight?" He asked her as they made their way to the car-park, knowing that only commonplace banter could be exchanged. The main event, the one that had brought them both to this landmark in their lives, was, at the moment, to be avoided.

"Fine, thanks."

"Did you manage to sleep?"

"Yes."

He placed her two suitcases and a small holdall in the boot of the Alfa, then opened the passenger door.

"Do you like my car?"

"Mm." She answered, sounding, he felt, less than impressed.

Out of the airport and out of habit, he slammed his foot on to the accelerator then, noticing her gripping the door handle tightly, measured his speed and apologised. "Sorry, am I going too fast?"

"No, it's alright".

She glanced up at the dismal sky only just visible through the cold, November drizzle. How was she ever going to get used to this weather?

"I hope you've brought some warm clothes?"

"Yes."

But not many. Everyone had told her to pack warm clothes, but she didn't want to leave without some of the pretty dresses which her mother had made for her, or her white shoes with the two inch heels. She had a raincoat, some jeans and a few jumpers. That would have to do for now.

"The rest of your things are coming by freight, I believe? But we can buy you anything you need."

"Do you have a record player?" She blurted suddenly. "I...I mean, I do. But it might be broken when it gets here – and my records."

He smiled. "Yes, I do. I've recently treated myself to a radiogram. Quite a smart-looking piece of furniture. But my taste in music is probably not the same as yours."

She bent down to remove her shoes. "I've got a Dansette. A red one. And I love the Beatles and Petula Clark."

He lit a cigarette from a lighter which appeared out of the dashboard and which seemed to intrigue her.

"I think I can oblige. I collect more jazz than pop, but it's easy for me to get you records."

"Thank you."

She felt the atmosphere was becoming less tense, that some of the initial awkwardness was passing and she tried desperately to remember what her mother had said he did for a living. Something to do with singers and actors. She wondered if it was polite to ask.

Seeming to pick up on her thoughts, he spoke again. "I've taken a few weeks off from the office. To get you settled in. Although, I'll probably be on the phone a lot. Perhaps you'd like to come to the theatre with me? Some of my clients are opening in new plays and musicals."

"What about school?" She asked tentatively.

"I've been in touch with a couple nearby which have been recommended. They don't have any places until next term, so we can go and see them whenever you're ready."

It sounded fair enough. She yawned and tugged at her hair, winding it around her finger and recognising through this habitual gesture that she was tired and hungry.

He switched on the radio and Dusty Springfield's smoky and distinctive voice filled the warm cocoon of leather and gleaming walnut which was transporting them towards the centre of London.

"You don't have to say you love me
just be close at hand...."

She closed her eyes, luxuriating in the sound of the music. When she opened them, the scenery had changed from repetitive stretches of bleak concrete lined with boring foliage, to a bustling mélange of red, double-decker buses and black taxis, moving amongst architecture of such uniqueness which up until now she had only imagined.

He noticed her excitement and slowed down as they drove

along Kensington Gore. "That's Hyde Park, and that big building's the Albert Hall. I do wish you were seeing it in better weather."

"It doesn't matter," she whispered as, for the second time within twenty-four hours, she was absorbing a country's environment from the window of a car. But this was so very different. Wet leaves swept into neat piles by the side of the road, horses trotting through the park carrying winter-clad riders and people in Mini cars and mini skirts. She suddenly knew that Chloe's mother was right, and if she had to come and live in England, then now was the very best time.

"Well, we're here." Jack swung the car around and pulled into the forecourt of the imposing red brick building which was to be her new home.

He unloaded her luggage and she followed him in through the heavy, glass double doors where an elderly porter sat behind a highly polished desk, almost hidden by an enormous vase filled with scarlet gladioli.

"Hello, Mr. Merrick." He gave Elizabeth a smile. "You've arrived then?"

"This..." said Jack, putting down the cases, "... is my niece, Elizabeth. Elizabeth, this is Victor."

"It'll be good to have someone young and pretty in the block. Make a change". Victor came round from behind the desk. "Shall I carry the cases up, sir?"

"No, thank you, Victor. I can manage."

The Porter held the lift door open and Jack pressed the button to take them to the eighth floor.

Elizabeth gazed at the cases and then at Jack. "Don't you have a boy to do that?" She asked as innocently and naturally as enquiring about the weather.

He looked at her quickly, realising again the enormity of the task that lay ahead of him. Not only was her academic future in his hands, the shaping of her growth into womanhood, but the obvious day to day education necessary for living in this country. And, with that, went changing the habits of a lifetime.

As they entered the flat, a small, kind-faced, silver-haired woman welcomed them warmly. "You poor wee thing," she said in a lilting Scottish accent. "Come in, come in."

"This is Hannah." Jack hung his raincoat on the brass hallstand. "My housekeeper and without whom I would be a lost soul". It suddenly struck him that Elizabeth might be surprised that he employed someone who was white.

"Aach, away with you Mr. Merrick." Hannah picked up the cases with little effort. "I'll show you your room and where the bathroom is, then come through and have something to eat. I've made tomato soup, and there's some chicken casserole left over from yesterday."

Ravenous now, Elizabeth followed the spry housekeeper into an obviously newly decorated bedroom, where delicate white lace curtains hung from an enormous window, and lemon floral print wallpaper matched the pillow cases and bedspread. A bright cyclaman sat on the kidney-shaped dressing table, which was also draped in white lace, and a small china sink nestled above a louvred pine cupboard. It all looked so immaculate, so like a picture in a glossy magazine, that she seriously doubted that she would be able to stick her Beatles posters on the walls.

"Take your time," said Hannah, drawing back the bed-covers. "Come through when you're ready."

After washing her hands and face she felt revived and, because the flat was warm, took off her cardigan and polo shirt then rummaged through her case to find something clean and fresh to wear. The white cotton top which she settled on had suffered from the journey, and although badly creased, provided a welcome coolness against her skin.

It didn't take long to put her few remaining clothes away and as she sat in front of the mirror drawing a comb through her hair, she reflected that so far things could be worse, even though the homesickness she was experiencing gnawed at the very core of her being like a silent, ever-present tormentor.

Uncle Jack did appear to be making things as normal as possible, but she was realistic enough to know that this early show of cordiality could not last. There would come a time when she would do something to displease, that was inevitable, and he would have to assert his new authority at some point and tell her off. She wondered briefly what she might do to cause him displeasure.

The knock at the door made her jump and she spun around, her comb flying out of her hand and hitting the dressing-table with a clatter. "Come in."

Her uncle stood in the doorway enquiring whether she had everything she needed.

"Yes, thank you."

His eyes took in a rather battered, yellow teddy-bear which had been placed carefully against the pillows. A familiar and much-loved toy with a loose button eye that seemed to be focused on him and which he recognised immediately as having belonged to Emily.

Suddenly and unexpectedly he was filled with an overwhelming sympathy for this orphan girl, his late sister's child and he walked towards the bed, gently lifting up the bear.

"Is this Rufus?" He heard himself ask, his voice echoing in his ears as though it did indeed come from the past, through a long, misty tunnel.

She was looking at him curiously. "Yes. How do you know?"

"Oh..." He tried to contain the emotion which now threatened the appearance of normality. "Rufus and I are very old friends."

—◁▷—

When she woke it was early evening but already dark and as she clicked on the bedside light to check the clock, discovered with amazement that she had slept for nearly five hours. Pulling on her pink quilted dressing-gown that had seen better days, she opened the door and tiptoed into the hall. It was obvious that Hannah had gone and the flat was quiet, with illumination spilling from two rooms, one to her left, another to the right which she presumed to be the sitting-room. Padding towards it, she sank her toes into the thick, powder-blue Wilton carpet and looked around.

It was sophisticated, without being severe, its cosiness

accentuated by the glow from four strategically-placed table lamps and a lit alcove painted in Wedgwood blue. Inside the alcove the glass shelves held not only the very distinctive china from that same company, but vases, bottles and jars in shades of blue varying from cornflower to aqua and placed next to photographs in filigree silver frames.

A drinks bar, like those she had seen in old black and white films, curled itself into one of the corners, and a marble fireplace surrounded a mock coal fire where flame shadows flickered warmly. The three-piece suite appeared both inviting and luxurious, covered in pearl-grey velvet and dotted with deep blue cushions, while the numerous paintings which hung on the walls ranged from the stark and colourful post-modern, to more traditional Turneresque seascapes.

Shivering now, Elizabeth moved towards the fireplace, noticing that the only object which looked out of place in this well-composed room, probably because its large, teak body seemed to rest so hazardously on four crude metal legs, was a television. Only the second one she had ever seen, for great-aunt Margaret had been given a set by a wealthy friend from Johannesburg and if she had wanted to see any programmes, she had to trek the sixteen or so miles to their farm. It was all still mostly experimental though, and, she knew, on a tiny scale compared with the ones in England.

Suddenly she was gripped by a strong compulsion to switch it on, but thought perhaps it was rude to do so without asking first. On the other hand, there was no-one around to ask. Passing through the hall once again, she could hear her uncle's voice coming from his bedroom and as he seemed to be winding up a telephone conversation and saying good-bye, she scurried back and threw herself into one of the armchairs, not wanting to be discovered hovering outside. She heard a door open and close again, then he came in, reacting with mild surprise when he saw her sitting there.

"Oh, hello. Had a good sleep?"

She nodded as he went across to the bar to pour himself what looked to her like a whisky.

"Can I get you anything? A cup of tea?"

"A bitter lemon?" She answered swiftly, reading the label on the smallest bottle, and he smiled, then crushed some ice into a glass and handed it to her with the bottle, which for some reason made her feel distinctly grown-up.

To her additional delight, he turned on the television and she folded herself into the chair, completely captivated and forgetting everything else, as she watched with fascination three old women sitting at a table in what appeared to be an English pub.

Uncle Jack seemed to find the programme amusing. "Can you understand what they're saying?" He asked her.

"Not really."

He laughed. "It's called Coronation Street, set in a county up in the north of England... Let's see what else there is."

He flicked the switch and this time a tenor in a kilt was duetting with a dark-haired, full-skirted Scottish soprano against a curtained set.

"Do you know them?" She asked him.

"Yes, but I don't represent them. The woman's called Moira Anderson and he's Kenneth McKeller."

She drank cocoa and ate cheese and tomato sandwiches during the news, while Jack regularly refilled his glass. Then when the programmes closed down for the night she expressed disappointment.

"You'll grow tired of it," he said, standing up and stretching. "It's a novelty at the moment."

She didn't think she would ever get tired of it, but wasn't going to contradict him.

Leaving the sitting-room for bed, her attention was diverted by a large framed photograph on the mantlepiece, set apart from the others. A glamorous woman with long blonde hair, heavy jewellery and wrapped in white fur smiled out at her. Elizabeth turned to Jack questioningly and, to her surprise, thought that she detected irritation at her curiosity.

"One of my clients," he answered her un-voiced question casually then changed the subject. "Have you switched on your electric blanket? I think you're going to need it."

"She's very beautiful."

Her uncle looked pensive then simply said, "yes."

—⁓—

The tall young man in the brown leather jacket and tight blue jeans strolled confidently into the Rolls Royce showroom, ran his hand along the flawless paintwork of the latest Silver Shadow, then opened its door and sank into the soft leather upholstery.

Within seconds, a suave, pin-striped salesman materialised at his side and enquired in a low voice, specially cultivated for his position. "Can I be of assistance, sir?"

"How much?"

"For this particular model, sir? Nine thousand, two hundred pounds."

"And do you make them in peppermint green?"

The salesman ran his hand over his smoothly-combed white hair and adjusted his Remembrance day poppy whilst carefully considering his reply. "Sir can order this model in any colour he wishes."

"Could I have a test drive?"

In for a penny, in for nine and a bit grand, the young man thought to himself, with mounting exhilaration. The sensuous pleasure he was experiencing from just holding the smooth steering wheel, was already a turn-on. Actually being in control of this supremely powerful vehicle as it purred along the road, he was convinced would be ten, twenty times better than sex.

"Certainly, sir. If I may just see your driving licence…"

"Of course."

The young man reached into the pocket of his leather jacket and frowned. Where the hell was it? Don't say he had left it at the flat or in another coat. As he rummaged through the rest of his pockets, he realised to his anger and embarrassment, that he must have done just that, as the jacket he was wearing had recently come back from the cleaners'.

"I seem to have left it at home. But it's kosher. And no endorsements."

"I'm sorry, sir. Perhaps another day."

"But I drove here this morning. Look, that's my car outside."

The sales assistant turned his head and, as his eyes rested on a purple Mini with a psychedelic daisy pattern painted on its hood, he tried to suppress a smile.

"I'm sorry, sir."

Fuming at having put himself in such a humiliating position, the young man climbed out of the massive car, leaving the showroom in as dignified a manner as was possible.

"You'll certainly be sorry when I come back and buy one," he uttered under his breath, making his way towards the Mini, inside of which a small, white poodle was uttering a series of high-pitched barks.

Still smarting from the arrogant treatment he felt he had received, he drove at top speed across to the park in order to unleash his excitable pet for her daily exercise.

So, it had been an impetuous notion, some might say a fantasy of elegance, which had inspired him to set foot within the hallowed interior of that showroom this morning, but it was time he got a new car. Something to do his progressing career justice. Although he had to admit that even raising enough dosh for a Triumph Herald was still a long way off.

He uncoiled himself from the driving seat then reached into the back for his dog, banging his head as he finally extracted her from the car.

"Fuck! Ssh, Flora. Patience...Patience."

Flora squatted happily against the railings and he lit a king-size Dunhill, blowing a ring of smoke into the already murky London air, wondering why things seemed not to be going as well now as he had anticipated a few months ago.

After trying for nearly a year to get one of the country's most high-profile theatrical agents to come and see him perform in a witty, though ever so slightly vulgar cabaret spot in Soho, he could hardly believe his luck when Jack Merrick walked in one night, caught the early show, then invited him to dinner at Quaglino's, suggesting that he should personally represent him.

Within weeks, the agent had lifted him out of that apology for a club in Wardour Street, into an expensively produced floor-show at Grosvenor's, a respected establishment in Grosvenor Place, where well-known and distinguished personalities gathered nightly.

"Flora, come here."

A mud-caked Jack Russell was sniffing the poodle's rear end, which sent her scurrying around in delighted circles and yelping hysterically.

"Flora!"

The terrier lost interest and Flora, disappointed that the adventure was over, came trotting back, whereupon he slipped her collar and lead around her neck while grinding his cigarette into the grass beneath one shiny, brown, snakeskin shoe.

Jack Merrick was his dream ticket to recognition and a better future. A chance, in his mid-twenties, to make a name for himself in the world of show-business. To get out of that poky little flat perched above a strip-club and to have money, together with everything it could buy.

But then, just as he had been celebrating his fortunate change of circumstances, the press announced that his new agent was to be awarded an OBE, and, almost simultaneously he was impersonally informed by Merrick's secretary, that for the foreseeable future, he would be represented by another member of the agency. Somebody who had been solely appointed to look after cabaret performers.

It was more than just infuriating, it stank and he felt like a landed fish who'd been left gasping. The last thing he wanted was some also-ran at Merrick Management instead of the main man whose name guaranteed respect. Sure, he was still with the same top agency, but this was not the way it was supposed to be. When Jack Merrick picked up the phone, results happened. People listened, and were more than willing to negotiate anything from a fat pay cheque to a dressing room with a private urinal.

Insecure and disappointed, yet not prepared to give in without a fight, he had decided to call in at the office yesterday, ready to wait all day if necessary, to try and persuade Jack to reverse his decision.

To his intense frustration, he had been told that Jack was

taking time off until the New Year. Personal business, the girl had said. So that appeared to be that – there was nothing more he could do.

Suddenly, he stopped dead in his tracks. His walk with Flora had brought him to that edge of the park beside the Albert memorial, and across the road he was aware of the prestigious Victorian apartment block, near which he had parked many times while taking these frequent excursions.

Only today though, had he been reminded that this was where Jack Merrick lived, for in the forecourt was one of his very obvious trademarks, a red Alfa with the personalised number plate – JM 14.

He glanced up at the row of long windows, their glass so well cleaned that he could only see the reflection of the Beech trees which waved tall outside, and hoped that the man who, not so long ago, had appeared to take a genuine interest in his career, might notice he was there and come out to greet him enthusiastically.

He shrugged and looked away, his expectations unfulfilled. That kind of encounter only happened in the movies, but he, Laurie Christian, hadn't come this far to sink back into obscurity.

Climbing into his dilapidated symbol of the decade, he set off, determined to devise a plan.

—m—

Over the following two weeks, although it was a strange and trying time for both of them, a daily pattern of sorts was beginning to develop.

The first week had been spent sight-seeing and Jack had to admit to re-discovering and enjoying places and events which he hadn't witnessed for years and, like every Londoner, had simply taken for granted. Buckingham Palace of course he had been to recently, but to see the changing of the guard in the forecourt and the horse guards of twelve men trooping in with trumpet and Standard on the west side of Whitehall, engaged him as much as it did Elizabeth.

"Can we go now?" She asked, apparently bored by the Tower of London, until he told her the history of Tower Green, and her now enlivened interest led her to stare in fascination at the spot where those unfortunate souls had met their end on a primitive wooden block.

Jack was a little surprised at her obvious bloodthirsty interest, given her own personal experience, but when he mentioned it to Sylvia, she dismissed it, telling him that her own teenage niece loved horror films and spooky stories and that Elizabeth would almost certainly not connect anything at this historic landmark with the recent death of her parents.

"Take a photo, Uncle Jack," the young girl demanded on a second visit, positioning herself beside a pair of yeomen in their frilly, red costumes. "I want to send one to Chloe."

For Elizabeth, getting used to the early mornings was the hardest part of the day. Drowsing to the sound of steady rain and the rumble of traffic instead of a deafening dawn chorus and bright sunshine, led her to sleep in till around nine.

For him, sharing his home for the first time was more disquieting than he had anticipated. Because there was only one bathroom, he made the practical suggestion that for the present he use it first until Elizabeth started school next year, which would mean her rising earlier.

Hannah arrived at around eight forty-five and stayed until six, preparing meals, cleaning and doing the laundry, while Jack spent the mornings working and Elizabeth read or wrote letters home to great-aunt Margaret, Chloe and Marion.

Lunch was usually a bowl of home-made soup, warm rolls and some cheese, then Jack would pop into the office for a couple of hours, leaving Elizabeth with Hannah who recruited her culinary assistance as she conjured up mouth-watering cakes or, her particular Edinburgh speciality, butterscotch flan.

"When am I going to meet her?" Sylvia asked him insistently. "You really are a bore, keeping her all to yourself."

But he maddened her by his evasiveness. "Soon. Very soon," he would say, for he wanted to use this time to get to know her himself, pacing the amount of adult introductions and allowing her to acclimatize at her own speed in her new surroundings.

In the evenings they would watch television and she had accompanied him to the theatre, where she met cast members whom he represented and who, to her delight seemed interested in what she had to say, involving her in their conversations as though she was older than her fifteen years.

Today, she was sitting on the floor in the sitting-room in front of the radiogram, singing along to the recording of *Funny Girl,* a musical she had seen with Jack the night before, and which now convinced her that she wanted to be a singer.

He stood in the open doorway listening. Not a bad voice, nor a bad mimic. Her Barbra Streisand was impressive. 'Hey, come on,' he told himself with inner amusement. 'Your talent-spotting technique is inappropriate here. Elizabeth's future means university, not show-business.'

"Time to go," he said, waving the school prospectus.

"Oh, I'd forgotten." She stood up, smoothed down her skirt and removed the LP from the turntable. "I'll only be a minute."

She wiped her face with a damp flannel, combed her hair then put on her old gabardine raincoat. She was getting so fed up with her clothes. He had suggested buying her some on that first day, but hadn't brought it up since. She thought she might mention it to Hannah. Perhaps Jack would take more notice if it came from her.

St. Hilda's school for Girls was set in a quiet, leafy road just off Kensington Church Street. It was a sturdy, pre-war conversion with tall sash windows that had recently been painted, their white starkness contrasting with the old brickwork. An iron staircase doubling as a fire escape ran up one side of the building from an overgrown, weed-ridden garden, and a flaming virginia creeper, now beginning to feel the effects of winter, clung to its rust-coloured walls.

Anthea Thomas, the school's headmistress, greeted them in her office. A woman, Jack guessed in her late forties, wearing a turquoise knitted suit, which accentuated her ample proportions.

On her nose was perched a pair of small, rimless glasses, adding sternness to an otherwise cheerful countenance.

"I've arranged for our head-girl Pamela to accompany Elizabeth to one of the classrooms while we have a chat, Mr. Merrick" she told him. "Do you want to leave your coat here Elizabeth?"

"No thank you." Elizabeth said quickly, unable to believe that people could walk around without overcoats in such a draughty building.

The headmistress thumbed through the copies of Elizabeth's school reports which Jack had sent her and directed her question at them both.

"Why do you think that St. Hilda's is the right school for Elizabeth?"

"Because," Jack shifted in his chair "I have a colleague whose daughter is here – Josephine Dover?"

"Ah, Josephine. Of course. She's doing very well."

"Her father told me of your good A-level pass-rate and university entrances and the fact that you also have a reputation for excellent tuition in English literature, languages and music. As you will see from Elizabeth's reports, these are among her strongest subjects and the ones that interest her most."

Mrs. Thomas adjusted her spectacles and studied the information in front of her once again.

"You have some impressive marks in French, English essay and history."

"I'm also considering the Lycée," Jack explained. "But perhaps the French studies will dominate. I would like her to have a fully rounded education."

A knock at the door caused them to look up and a tall, strong-faced girl in her mid-teens, with dark hair swept back by two tortoishell combs, bid them good morning.

"Oh, Pamela, this is Elizabeth Tarrant and her uncle Mr. Merrick. Elizabeth may be joining us next term."

The girl smiled as Elizabeth, noticing the grey and topaz uniform she was wearing, tugged at Jack's arm.

"Same colour uniform," she whispered "...as my last school."

"Really?" Mrs. Thomas said pleasantly, overhearing. "What a coincidence. I don't expect you had the grey felt hats for the winter though, did you?"

"We wore straw boaters all the time." Elizabeth told her, not liking the thought of grey felt hats one little bit.

"Pamela, why don't you take Elizabeth to Classroom Two and we'll catch up with you in say..." The headmistress consulted her watch, "ten minutes."

Elizabeth glanced quickly at Jack, then rose and followed the older girl out of the room. When they had gone, Anthea Thomas leant across the desk and removed her glasses.

"What a terrible tragedy. How is she coping with it all?"

"Surprisingly well in the circumstances," Jack replied honestly. "She's only been here a couple of weeks. It's all so new and strange. For both of us."

"Of course. And she will be ready to start school in the New Year. That will make all the difference."

"Absolutely. And if I decide on St. Hilda's, I believe you said you had a place available in Elizabeth's age group next term?"

"I do. Am I right in assuming that it would be as a day pupil?"

Jack smiled tolerantly. "Yes, of course. We only live locally."

"Actually, that question is not as strange as it sounds. I have three pupils who live fairly locally and who board because their parents travel extensively. You're a working man with a demanding job, Mr. Merrick, and un-married. Elizabeth could stay here during the week and return home to you at weekends."

For a second, Jack hesitated, the prospect seeming an easy and convenient solution to the situation in which he found himself. Then, remembering how as a boy he had hated being a boarder, he shook his head. "No, Mrs. Thomas. Thank you for the thought, but I would feel as though I was shirking my responsibilities if I sent her to a boarding school."

"I understand." Anthea Thomas got up from her chair and came round from behind the desk. "Would you like to have a look at a class at work in Elizabeth's year?" She asked him.

"Yes, thank you."

The woman led the way down a dimly-lit hall where a worn Turkish rug was thrown precariously over old, wide floorboards and stopped beside an unsuitably modern glass door. As he looked inside, Jack could see about twenty girls, one of whom he thought he recognised as Josephine Dover, all around thirteen to fifteen years old. A tall man, with salt and pepper hair and a matching beard was communicating with them enthusiastically and to his right, standing just beside the door, Jack noticed Elizabeth and the head girl.

"It's an English class." Mrs. Thomas told him. "Let's see what they're reading".

As they entered, the girls raised their eyes in an act of silent unison and the man rose from behind his desk.

"It's alright, Mr. Jenkins...don't let me disturb you. We've just come to observe."

"Certainly. We're studying Dickens, *A Tale of Two Cities*." He pointed to one of the pupils who must have been about Elizabeth's age. "Julie, would you please continue from where we had stopped, on page thirty-five?"

The fair-haired girl whom he had picked got up and began to read with impressive diction.

" ....so expressive the voice was, of a hopeless and lost creature, that a famished traveller, wearied out by lonely wandering in the wilderness, would have remembered home and friends in such a tone, before lying down to die."

Abruptly she stopped, rudely interrupted by a rasping sound which caused the rest of the class to look up curiously and, to Jack's alarm, he became aware that his niece was being racked by an uncontrollable bout of tears. They rolled freely down her cheeks while she caught her breath in heavy sobs as a vexed Mrs. Thomas ushered both her and Jack out of the room.

"Alright. Thank you, Mr. Jenkins."

Standing awkwardly in the hallway, Jack pulled a large, cotton handkerchief from his pocket and handed it to the sobbing girl who blew her nose loudly in a desperate attempt to curb the flow. "I'm sorry... I don't know why..."

"It's alright, Elizabeth." Mrs. Thomas was at once both

soothing and maternal. "Come to my office and have some tea."

Elizabeth raised her wet face towards Jack. "Can we go back, please?"

"Of course we can," he said gently. "Mrs. Thomas, I'm sorry. It's early days..."

"Mr. Merrick, you don't have to apologise. I quite understand."

The headmistress accompanied them to the front door where a few of the little girls from the kindergarten were starting to drift out, talking excitedly across one another and waving to their doting mothers who stood waiting at the entrance, arms outstretched.

"I'll be in touch soon." Jack told her, shaking her hand. "Goodbye and thank you."

As they drove back to the flat, Elizabeth was silent, recalling with horror the dreadful and embarrassing experience which had just taken place. How could she face those girls – her future classmates – after this? And wasn't one of them somebody whose father knew her uncle? She gazed straight ahead, wishing that she had the courage to tell him she'd got her period, and also wishing she had remembered that it was due and had put on a sanitary towel.

Her tummy had been feeling funny all morning, but now the familiar stickiness which attached her pubic hair to her panties made her shift in her seat, and she willed Jack to drive as fast as he had on the day he had picked her up from the airport.

Yet she also knew that the mysterious emotions linked to these cyclical visits had been triggered by that specific passage of literature, for A Tale of Two Cities, along with other classic stories by the Brontes' and Daphne Du Maurier as well as poems by Browning and Robert Louis Stevenson, were special favourites of her mother's, read aloud at night before Elizabeth fell asleep.

As she had grown older, she soon began to realise that the central theme of each of those works depicted a fervent sense of loss, coupled with warm memories of a much-loved country, reminding her mother not just of England but of an unborn child, who, so tragically and unaccountably was to be denied its place in the world.

Today, she had heard the tears in her mother's voice as she listened to those familiar words spoken once again.

Jolted back to the present, she managed a weak smile when her uncle tried to make a joke. "If that's what Dickens does to you, remind me not to take you to see *Oliver.*"

But Jack felt inadequate. He had only given her his handkerchief and held her arm. This was the nearest he would ever get to having a child of his own and although it had been forced on him and was difficult and demanding, it was not without its rewards.

Once inside the flat, she dashed into her room, pulled a packet of Dr. Whites from the drawer and shot into the bathroom, passing a startled Hannah in the hall.

At the sight of her swollen eyes, the housekeeper threw Jack an enquiring glance and he shrugged in bewildered response.

"...I don't know. One minute we were in a classroom listening to an English lesson, the next, she was..."

"Aach, Mr. Merrick, she's a young girl who's just lost her home and her parents. Maybe she hasn't got around to grieving yet. And you couldn't be expected to know. She'll be having her monthly visitor."

That evening, still awkwardly conscious of the day's trauma, Jack and his niece exchanged little conversation as they watched *Z-Cars* and ate spaghetti Bolognese. At nine, she excused herself and went to bed where, the floodgates now having been wrenched open, she wept again and cuddled Rufus, the toy bear who had shared every night of her life.

She tried to cry quietly, but the choking sobs were difficult to control and she stuffed the corner of the eiderdown into her mouth as her body shook with painful memories. The last time she had seen her mother they had had a row. If she had only known what lay ahead, that she would never see her again, then she wouldn't have shouted and slammed out of the house in one of her typical paddies.

With the dull headache which comes when there are no more tears left to cry, Elizabeth finally drifted into an uneasy sleep, sprinkled with fragmented dreams.

In the room next door, Jack paced the floor, cradling a large whisky, his mind caught in a crossfire of conflicting emotions. Twice his hand had rested on the door-handle of her bedroom, but twice he had drawn back as though pushed by some invisible force.

If she was to experience further moments of deep unhappiness, and it was more than likely that she would, someone would have to be tactile with her. Someone would have to take her in their arms and give her a cuddle, for she would need physical affection. To his dismay, he realised that whatever talent for comfort and sympathy he may have possessed as a small boy with Emily, as an adult with Elizabeth he seemed unable to respond.

Yet was it so very different? The fear that his sister had felt when their father's cries had sliced the night into a dozen invisible pieces. And then always the unease, in case it happened again. When she had come into his room and slid into his bed trembling, while he tried to explain that it was not their father's fault. That those anguished cries simply stemmed from the nightmares of an obscene war, fought out of duty and commitment, with little thought of the tortuous aftermath on the human soul.

"Promise me you won't go away?" Emily had asked him pleadingly. "I don't know what I'd do if you went away."

"I'm not going anywhere," he had told her, meaning it, but knowing that one day things would be different. Then, realising that this might be a rash vow, Jack had decided to use a sentence he'd read in a book. "I'll always be there for you, Emily, I promise."

But however much Jack told himself that there was little difference between then and now, the plain fact was that the girl in the next room, although Emily's child, was a stranger. And, at this time, when his words to his sister had never been more tested, his sense of failing her was overwhelming.

Welcoming relief at the eventual silence that came from his niece's bedroom, Jack discovered that he now felt as tense as a drum. His neck muscles throbbed painfully and his back was killing him. It was as though he'd been placed on a medieval torture rack, similar to those they had recently seen in the Chamber of Horrors, and stretched to the limit.

What he needed was a massage, or better still, sexual release, but that at the moment was not an option. It even seemed wrong thinking about it, or indulging in any fantasies of that nature, while she was in the other room.

Feeling trapped and frustrated he lit a cigarette, poured another sizeable drink and placed *Ella sings Gershwin* on the turntable of his newly acquired radiogram.

Gazing out of the window, his tired eyes embraced the buzzing activity which was happening right below him in the capital. People were doing their own thing, going out to dinner, to parties – having fun. When would he have fun again? Sex again? It had been too bloody long!

"They're writing songs of love, but not for me..." Ella crooned and he gave an ironic laugh.

Jack had always been a believer in fate, assuming that the really big events in a person's life were predestined to happen and that the path ahead was set, so that only the diversions one took to reach that path were a matter of individual choice. He was now being forced to accept his destiny and, for the moment that destiny bound him together with Elizabeth. If that meant forgoing his own selfish cravings in order to fulfill his responsibilities, then so be it. He smiled again wryly.

The phrase "Redemption Through Abstention" came to mind and brought back memories of his strict, Catholic upbringing. Well, you know the old adage, Jack, 'Once a...'

He shook his head and tossed back his drink. This had nothing to do with superstition labouring under the guise of religion. This was about real life.

—m—

He thought when the phone rang at six-thirty that it was his alarm and brought his hand down on it automatically, knocking his whisky glass off the bedside table.

"Shit!" Raising himself on to one elbow, he peered at the

clock. What anti-social cretin was ringing him at this ungodly hour?

"Hello?" His voice was gravelly from an abundance of alcohol and nicotine.

"Hello, Jack, it's Sylvia."

"Hi...What's going on?"

"Listen Jack, I've just had a call from the Queen Victoria hospital in Blackpool."

"A hospital – in Blackpool?" He repeated, realising he sounded thicker than the London smog.

"Syd Daniels was in a car crash at four o'clock this morning. Likewise his passenger and young Master Whittington, Helen Rogers."

"Syd and Helen?" He was awake now, swinging out of bed, anxious adrenalin pumping through his nervous system. "How are they? What were they doing together at that time?"

"Best not to ask." His partner answered pragmatically. "They're okay, but they'll be out of action for a while. There's just over two weeks before they open, and Syd reckons he can still play Mrs. Fitzwarren, but Helen can't be principal boy. Not with one of her legs in a plaster cast. The main thing is we need a director like now, and there's no-one available at this time of the year at such short notice. Can you get yourself up there to take over rehearsals today?"

"Jesus!" Jack rubbed his aching eyes. "Yes...Yes, of course. Tell them not to worry... I'll be there."

As he woke himself up with a shower and black coffee, the old pantomime gag "Forty miles to London and not a Dick in sight " came to mind. But today he couldn't laugh, not even in irony.

Then he came to an abrupt halt as the cold light of day, literally, hit him. What the hell was he doing? That involuntary knee-jerk reaction to a work crisis, born out of a near lifetime of similar occasions, had made him forget everything else. So much for his philosophical musings last night. So much for guilt and for responsibilities. He had forgotten about Elizabeth.

She came out of the bedroom and looked at him questioningly through tear-encrusted eyes.

"Has something happened?"

"Yes…Yes something has, but nothing for you to worry about. Come and have some breakfast. I'll explain."

He edited the story by telling her that he was needed urgently in Blackpool. That people's working lives depended on his being there.

She buttered a piece of toast and spread it thickly with marmalade, listening, but not speaking.

"You'll have to come with me. I'll book us into a nice hotel and you can come to rehearsals. It'll be just a few weeks…"

"No, thank you." She cut across him in a surprisingly unfamiliar, grown-up voice. "I'd rather stay here, if it's okay?"

He stared at her, quite winded by her response and not hearing the front door open and close as Hannah came into the kitchen weighed down by two large carrier bags.

"… I can barely see a hand in front of my face…" She noticed their expressions and dumped the bags on the floor. "Alright, what's happened?"

Elizabeth took the lead, helping the housekeeper out of her coat and hanging it on the back of the door. "Hannah, is there any chance you can stay here for a while with me, while Uncle Jack goes to Blackpool?"

"I've got to go. An emergency." Jack said, helplessly. "Elizabeth will have to come with me."

"Aach, don't talk such nonsense." Hannah's Dresden china complexion flushed a warm shade of pink. "She can't go to Blackpool."

If it hadn't been crisis-time for Jack, he'd have seen the funny side. She uttered the word Blackpool as if it were Beirut under siege.

"She thinks it's cold here, Lord knows what she'll do up there. And I suppose you'll have her hanging around theatres and drafty rehearsal halls? You can't do that to the wee girl, Mr. Merrick."

"Well, then what do you suggest?" He knew he sounded edgy now, but God he couldn't be all things to all people and he ought to be getting on his way.

"You'll be back before Christmas?" Hannah demanded rather than enquired.

"Of course."

"Because I'm going up to Edinburgh to be with my family over Christmas."

"I'll be BACK!" He practically shouted.

Hannah looked at him disapprovingly then patted her neat, white knot of hair and slipped on a freshly starched apron. "If I can get Mrs. Richards from next door to feed my cat, then of course I'll stay here with Elizabeth," she said with typical Scottish forthrightness, moving him out of the way to get to the sink.

"You've got a cat?" Elizabeth squealed, once again childlike. "Can't it come here with you?"

Hannah threw a doubtful glance at Jack. "That's up to Mr. Merrick."

Anything for a quiet life, he thought, but asked anyway. "Will it scratch my furniture and do its business on my carpet?"

"She certainly won't do the latter. Betsy is house trained." Hannah told him indignantly. "But I can't promise about the scratching."

"Betsy!" Elizabeth repeated with delight. "Short for Elizabeth." Then, throwing caution to the wind, added "And can we go shopping?"

Again, Hannah looked at Jack, who nodded approval. "Of course."

Elizabeth ran towards Hannah and gave her a crushing squeeze, which caused the housekeeper to beam happily.

To Jack's immense satisfaction and relief, it seemed to be settled.

"Money!" He announced loudly, making them jump. "I've got to get some money." He pointed at Hannah and then at Elizabeth. "For you, and for you."

Then, leaving the teenager and the older woman bemused at such uncharacteristic agitation, he pulled his coat from the hall-stand and made a hurried exit from the flat.

The bank was not the only place he needed to visit. There

was the little matter of some personal, unfinished business which had been preying on his mind for weeks and impulsively, Jack swung the Alfa into New Bond Street, that up-town haunt of the wealthy and discerning shopper, where designer clothes, antique silver and jewellery-stores neighboured alongside art galleries and expensive auction houses.

When he returned an hour later, Elizabeth, now dressed in ill-fitting dungarees and a denim shirt, was fiercely beating eggs in a large, earthenware bowl.

He beckoned her into the sitting room.

"We'll have to have this conversation at some time, so it might as well be now." He gestured her to sit opposite him.

She saw that he was holding two large envelopes and a buff-coloured folder and presumed he was going to talk to her about money. She felt excited and very grown-up. No-one had ever discussed money with her before.

He took a green cheque-book out of one of the envelopes and held it in the air. "You have a bank account in your name at Lloyds Bank. This contains your general personal spending money, for clothes, books, records, anything like that but because of your age you can't get to it unless I'm with you. Therefore, I suggest that you receive an allowance of say... Five pounds a week, which I'll put into effect after Christmas. Until then..." He rummaged in the envelope and brought out a bundle of notes, which almost made her gasp. "I've just drawn out five hundred pounds for you to buy some things with. If you need any more let me know when we next speak and I'll arrange to get it for you."

He noticed her stunned expression and asked uncertainly. "Do you think that will be enough for now?"

She swallowed hard and smiled. "Yes... Thank you."

"Don't thank me, it's your money," he told her. "Transferred from your parents' account in Salisbury." He then opened the buff folder and spread it on his lap.

"I have opened two other accounts for you in a Building Society. One will be in the form of a trust fund and, when things are eventually settled in Rhodesia with the property and the estate, will be invested for you and won't be touched until you are twenty-one. The other is for your school fees and all expenses connected with your school, which obviously I will handle on your behalf."

He sat back and observed her pretty, quizzical face. How sad, he suddenly thought, for the golden freckles which dotted the top of her nose, were beginning to fade through lack of sunshine.

"I don't want to blind you with financial science," he told her. "Obviously everything in the flat is paid for by me and any holidays you take – we take – will also be paid for by me."

She wondered if she should say thank-you again, but remained silent as he continued.

"I have two service accounts. One is with a tailor in Savile Row who makes my suits and shirts, also an account at Harrods which you can use if you wish. Fish and meat are normally delivered from there once a week. Now, any questions?"

"No, no... I don't think so."

The vacuum cleaner began to drone in one of the bedrooms and he stood up looking at his watch.

"I've got to go."

He paused in the doorway. "Oh, and there's a black cab firm you can both use while I'm away. Hannah knows the number."

She trailed behind him as he went into the kitchen to leave the other envelope for Hannah, then when he opened the front door they both stood uncomfortably, wondering how to part.

Surprising himself, he bent to kiss her on the cheek. "Take care of yourself. I'll call you tonight with numbers where I can be reached. Otherwise, well, I'll see you soon."

She curled her hair around her finger as he stepped into the lift and waved his hand, then ran back into the sitting-room and watched as his car nosed its way into the London traffic soon becoming a crimson speck in the distance until it finally disappeared from her sight.

She suddenly felt incredibly independent. He had left her alone in London. Well, there was Hannah, but that didn't really count. She picked up the money from the table and flicked through it. The notes were new and crisp, and she wanted to spend them right now.

—⁂—

The young man was there again at five when the taxi dropped them back, after they had visited Hannah's home in the Edgware Road to pick up a small suitcase and a basket containing her feline companion.

Elizabeth had first noticed him about four days ago when she happened to glance out of her bedroom window. He was standing on the pavement opposite the block lighting a cigarette and he appeared to be gazing up at Jack's flat. When she next saw him, he was walking out of the park with a small dog and today he was chatting to the seller at the newspaper stand.

Was it her imagination, or did his eyes lock with hers as she looked towards him? Averting them quickly, she followed Hannah inside, but once upstairs she peeped around the curtains then jumped back, her cheeks burning as if caught in some guilty act. He had definitely been staring up at the window and had seen her looking out. But why? Who was he? A strange, yet familiar sensation crept up on her, a tingling excitement which she only ever experienced when possessing a special secret.

Elizabeth loved secrets. And she had always thought that they should remain just that. Secrets should never be spoken of or shared with anyone else. Chloe and Marion had never been able to keep anything to themselves and had giggled and gossiped and said things like "You mustn't tell a soul, but…" while revealing details of this and that rumour or event which they considered shocking.

Now, sitting on the bed and stroking a sleek, black cat with amber eyes, Elizabeth's mind raced back to a Christmas party at Chloe's nearly a year ago. A magical day full of sunshine, where multi-coloured balloons were hung on the trees, there was home-made lemonade and presents for all the children hidden in various corners of the large, avocado-scented garden.

Her personal 'clue', one of the many which Chloe's mother had expertly placed inside individual Christmas crackers, was 'Cock-a-doodle-do' and, as the rest of the children rushed excitedly in different directions searching for their gifts, she made her way down to where she remembered the hen-house to be, pushing overhanging leaves from her face, while the sound of voices grew more distant and the giant branches momentarily blocked out the sun. When the shadows gave way to sunlight once more, she came across a small, roughly constructed hut, built entirely from logs and where a proud, orange-necked cockerel strutted amongst an admiring band of golden hens.

Smiling to herself in satisfaction for being so clever, she stooped down and climbed inside the warm gloom, where the scent of hay was head-swimmingly sweet and a few nesting birds eyed her warily. Then, when she had become accustomed to the half-light, she noticed that in the right-hand corner of the hut, a small wicker basket had been perched on top of an upside down flower pot.

"Gotcha!" she said out loud and as her hand reached out towards the basket, to her shocked amazement someone came up behind her, pushing her forward into the soft hay.

"Got YOU!" A boy's voice chuckled and Elizabeth immediately recognised it as belonging to Simon, the sixteen year old friend of Harry, Chloe's eldest brother.

"Simon," she spluttered, trying to get up, but he had her pinned on her stomach beneath him and wisps of hay were creeping up her nose and into her mouth.

"I just want a kiss." He panted. "Come on, Elizabeth, be a sport."

"No, Simon, no." But he was stronger than she was and somehow he found her face and pressed his mouth against it. Now she could hardly breathe and squirmed beneath him in panic and confusion, feeling the hardness of what was inside his jeans pressing against her buttocks.

Suddenly, the laughing voices of approaching children floated through from the garden and Simon, as swiftly as he had hurled himself on top of her, got up and brushed himself down with an easy nonchalance.

She turned over on to her back and looked up at him. For the first time she could understand why all her school friends found him such a dish, although his looks were far too obvious for her liking. Tall for his age and wearing a tight white vest and even tighter blue jeans, the muscles of his brown arms were well-developed through working on his parents' farm. His hair, which was inky black, had been carefully trained into an Elvis quiff and his deep blue eyes now studied her in amusement.

"Give me your hand," he said, pulling her up. "Did you find your present, little girl?" Then he laughed and was gone, leaving her angry and disconcerted.

She pulled the hay out of her hair and picked up the wicker basket. Inside was a cube-shaped package covered in Christmas wrapping paper and she opened it curiously, then gazed with pleasure at what she now held in the palm of her hand. There lay a small, clear plastic pyramid containing a tiny Sphinx, which, when she shook it, sent golden dust particles swirling around the entire centre, then gradually settled down, looking for all the world like sparkling sand.

Clutching her find, she made her way back to the party, but later, when she heard Chloe and Marion discussing Simon and how gorgeous he was, while they shrieked with laughter imagining what it would be like to kiss him, she smiled, hugging to herself that special, inviolate excitement.

It would have been so easy to have told them. They would have loved to hear that he had followed her and tried to kiss her, would have pestered her to repeat the story again and again, hardly able to believe that such a rough-and-tumble character as Elizabeth would have attracted the local neighbourhood heart-throb.

But Elizabeth kept that afternoon locked away, and the pleasure that had afforded her far outweighed the pleasure of shared teenage confidences.

—❦—

"Today – has been a lovely day -
the sort of day when everything went –
the way it was meant to go.."

"Crap, crap, crap!" Laurie stopped pounding the tinny upright, banged down the lid, which made the poor instrument resonate as if in pain and threw himself on to his chocolate-brown, fake fur bedspread, which he told everyone was Biba, but was Morocco 1963 and not bought new.

Flora, who had been snoozing on the bed contentedly, was now nearly flattened by her master and whimpered in indignation.

"Oh, sorry, darling." He kissed the dog's woolly head which seemed to appease the animal. "Naughty daddy... Sorry."

Life at present was a bitch and he just couldn't seem to get on top of it.

Last night, that idiot manager of Grosvenor's had decided that his opening number in the new show should be this dinosaur of a song, instead of his own choice, a powerhouse attention grabber called *Big Spender* from a new American musical, *Sweet Charity*. That would have made a great opener and he would be the first entertainer to perform it in England.

He snatched the music off the piano to try and study it again, but gave up, wondering whether it was too early at three in the afternoon for a gin and tonic. After all, it was his twenty-fifth birthday, although apart from a large card shaped like a poodle from the boys and girls at work and another, dripping with garlands of violets and a saccharine-imbued rhyme from his aged mother in Luton, there was nothing really special to indicate such a celebratory landmark.

Instead, he picked up the small article which he had cut out of the Evening News a few nights ago and studied it again. The heading had immediately attracted his notice as it read – 'TOP IMPRESARIO LOSES FAMILY IN SHOOTING INCIDENT' and went on to report how Jack Merrick, OBE, had been bereaved of his sister and brother-in-law in a Nationalist murder in Rhodesia. But it was the last line which he re-read with fascination. 'He has been appointed ward in charge of his fifteen year old niece who was orphaned following the disaster.'

Now he knew the nature of the 'personal business' which had resulted in Jack Merrick taking time off to be at home. It also explained the presence of the young, sun-tanned girl with the boyish figure, who he had seen coming and going from the building as well as gazing forlornly, like some fairy-tale heroine, from one of the top windows.

What it didn't explain, however, was why, for the past week, there had been no sign of either Jack or his car.

Was his behaviour becoming obsessive? Laurie didn't think so. It was, in fact, quite reasonable that he should continue his daily walks in that particular area, even though it was in the vicinity of Jack Merrick's home. And, he pondered, if he were to run into Jack, accidentally on purpose, and was forced to enquire about his professional dilemmas, it was nothing less than the agent deserved, after having dumped him so unceremoniously, without even the courtesy of a phone call or a face to face meeting.

The door buzzer sounded a shrill distraction and he picked up the intercommunicating 'phone, barking irritably. "Yes?"

"Delivery for Mr. Christian."

"Okay, come up. Third floor."

Depositing a yelping Flora in the kitchen, Laurie opened the door of his flat and peered out, intrigued as to who the messenger could be. As the sound of footsteps on the stairs grew closer, he gazed down upon the unfashionably short, square hair-cut of a pale young man, younger than himself, wearing a herring-bone tweed overcoat, who tilted his head upwards as he reached the last flight of stairs.

"Mr. Christian?"

"Aye, aye. Captain Bligh, I presume?"

Immediately the words left his tongue, he felt foolish. The boy had probably never even heard of *Mutiny on the Bounty,* and that old gag which he had used a million times was lost on him.

Without altering a line of his vapid expression, the tweed-clad courier replied. "No, sir. Asprey's, sir. And I've been asked to wish you Many Happy Returns of the day."

Laurie took the waxed, logo-typed envelope from him in surprise, pretty sure that there must be some mistake, but not in the mood to argue.

Once behind the door he tore at the envelope with more force than was necessary, then stared at its contents with amazement.

It was, without doubt, the best looking cigarette lighter he had ever seen. Made of solid silver and bearing an impressive current hallmark, it felt light and comfortable in his hand and, as he delightedly flicked its clear, blue flame, he noticed with even more surprise, that there was an engraving etched on one of its corners.

His mind whirling into overdrive, Laurie sat heavily on the bed as he tried to absorb the writing. 'To Laurie, happy birthday from Jack M.'

It didn't make any sense. There was only one Jack M, but what would Jack Merrick be doing sending him an expensive birthday gift? How would he even know it was his birthday, unless he had made it his business to specifically find out?

Laurie stood up and started to pace the fourteen-by-twenty-five foot area that made up his bed sitting-room, while straining to arrange his spinning thoughts into some semblance of order.

Question: Was Jack Merrick in the habit of sending birthday gifts to his clients?

Answer: No. Not unless they belonged to that Equity card-carrying fellowship of Star Names!

Question: Could this then be a gesture of goodwill on Jack Merrick's part for withdrawing his services of promised personal management?

Answer: Unlikely. But if so, then there had to be more to it than that, surely?

The necessity for a drink having intensified, Laurie sauntered into his kitchenette, painted by his own hand in Imperial purple, opened the tiny, freezer compartment of his fridge and tipped half a dozen ice cubes into a long glass. He then poured a fair-sized portion of Gordon's on top, before adding a small amount of tonic.

He was happy to discover that his old confidence had returned, making him feel less invisible somehow, able to take on the world, although he had to admit that if his assumptions were correct, then his instincts were certainly slipping.

Could it really be that Jack Merrick had sent him a present because he wanted to fuck him? Usually, he was able to tell within minutes if someone was of the same sexual persuasion. Perhaps on the few occasions they had met, he had just been too preoccupied with furthering his career to notice a look, a gesture, anything which might have given him a clue to interest of a more personal and intimate nature.

He knew that the agent, now a personality in his own right, was unmarried, but he had heard none of the usual gossip which normally surrounded a prominent homosexual within the nightclub circles through which he moved.

Doubting now that it could be so, he once again picked up the lighter and tried to visualise Jack's physical presence. A quietly spoken, mild-mannered man was the way he would describe him, if asked. Although he knew that behind the retiring personality lurked a considerable business brain, coupled with the bottle to hold out for what he wanted in the way of a deal. Tall, with a slight proneness to overweight, but not unattractive, with deep-set blue eyes.

"I could, if pushed," Laurie said out loud, then laughed, as Flora, thinking he was talking to her, came and nuzzled his ankles.

If, and it was still a big if, his suspicions were confirmed, then that changed everything. It meant that he was now in a position to make himself indispensable to one of the most influential figures in his line of business. Time for the artiste to assume control, instead of constantly obliged to wait on others.

And God and all the saints in heaven knew that there was no control as powerful or as potent as sexual control!

"Right," he said, again out loud. He had to find out where the hell Jack was and get to speak to him. And he would start by ringing the office.

Laurie picked up the phone, then hesitated. He knew exactly what would happen. He'd be put through to Mark Dover who may decide not to tell him of Jack's whereabouts, but then neither would Jack's snooty bitch of a partner, Sylvia Lawrence. She would do what she always did so well, protecting Jack and his privacy with such fierce intensity that if he wasn't sure the woman was a dyke, or worse, completely asexual, he would be convinced that she was in love with him.

But now he didn't care, for he had all the ammunition he needed in order to sound nonchalant and relaxed. In fact, he would ask for Sylvia Lawrence, the biggest cheese at the agency, next to Jack.

He flicked the lighter with his free hand and sang the first line of *Big Spender.*

"The minute you walked in the joint..."

"Hello, Sylvia Lawrence speaking?"

"Oh, good afternoon, Miss Lawrence." He couldn't conceal the contempt in his voice as he enquired. "I need to get hold of Jack. Could you tell me where he is please?"

He heard the woman draw in her breath as she carefully chose her reply in a tone that was cooler than the ice cubes now rapidly melting in his drink.

"Mr. Merrick is in Blackpool."

"Oh, Blackpool. How interesting. What's he doing there?"

"He's directing the pantomime at the Grand. Do you wish to leave a message?"

"Yes, please. Perhaps you'd ask him to ring me? It's rather important."

"Alright. I'll tell him."

"Thank you, Miss Lawrence. Good-bye."

Sticking out his tongue at the receiver as he replaced it, Laurie then dialed directory enquiries for a number for the theatre and for the Imperial Hotel in Blackpool, the best hotel in the town and the only one in which Jack would consider staying.

If he waited for that cow to pass his message on, he'd wait forever. Better to leave his own and see what might happen.

But he realized that he would have to concentrate with every molecule that made up his brain-power when he eventually did get to speak to Jack, for in order to obtain important answers, simply from a telephone conversation, he would have to trust his ears. Nothing would distract him from listening carefully to every nuance, every variation in tone, the odd word or a breath caught in some small tremor of passion, so that at least he would know. And when he did know, for sure, then he would test the water with his plan; a suggestion which may or may not be thought worthy of consideration.

If Jack Merrick wanted to slide open the closet door and invite him in, then that was cool, and, if the hand Laurie soon hoped to be dealt was played prudently, then a new family would be formed, with himself very much at the centre of it, just in time for Christmas.

—◊—

"Okay, notes over. I want Mistress Whittington, Alderman Fitzwarren and the Cat at ten tomorrow morning. Chorus at twelve... And everyone word perfect. May I remind everybody that we open in just under a week?"

From his seat in the auditorium, Jack watched the weary company disperse, leaving the stage empty except for two scene-painters poised on ladders and touching up an old London skyline, while his new Dick was anxiously going over her songs with the pianist. He collected up his papers and stretched, realising that as usual, a small queue of production staff was forming to ask him questions and pose their individual problems which he was miraculously expected to solve. He wondered briefly whether he was getting too old for this business, but the thought was so unrealistic that he dismissed it almost as soon as it developed. This was his life – his identity. It was simply that he was tired. The stress of the past few weeks was taking its toll and it was hard to be completely focused on the job in hand, when he knew that a bored and lonely young teenager was restlessly pacing his flat in London with only an elderly woman for company.

"Hasn't she spent any of the money I left her?" He had asked Hannah bewilderedly, when she voiced some concern about her charge.

"Some of it, aye." Hannah had told him. "She bought a blouse. And some underwear. But I don't think she liked Peter Robinson's much and I don't know if I've got the energy for the King's Road."

"No, no of course not."

Of course he understood. He couldn't expect Hannah to traipse up and down the currently most popular thoroughfare in London crammed with dedicated followers of fashion.

But then last night's call proved a little more encouraging. Elizabeth's personal things had arrived from Rhodesia and she was happily playing her Beatles records, looking through old photo albums and, according to Hannah, wearing her mother's jewellery, some small and moderately valuable rings, necklaces and ear-clips, touchingly out of place with her old sweaters and shirts.

He knew though that it was unsatisfactory. He should have insisted that she came with him. At least she might have enjoyed mucking in and helping. He considered ringing her that night and putting her on the first train in the morning, but things were fraught, working up to panic-driven as the opening night loomed. At least she now had her books and her music and he could only hope that the monotony she was clearly experiencing since he left, might be partially removed.

Patsy, the long-suffering wardrobe-mistress was the first in line, her arms full of checked gingham and stiff net petticoats. "Jack, do you think Syd's put on weight or lost it since he's been in hospital?"

He wanted to shout 'How the hell would I know?' but instead said that he would find out when he visited the hospital that evening. "The most important thing is to cover his neck brace with higher collars. I'm sure you'll do it, darling."

Thank God Syd was on top of his part as he couldn't participate in rehearsals until next week. It was just so frustrating for everyone else having to work around the lanky, twenty-two year old assistant stage manager who had been standing in for the Dame in his absence, with the worrying effect that the humour, so essential in those scenes, was not yet forthcoming.

When the enquiring line had finally melted, Jack's secretary Lesley, as slender as a string bean and loyal as a puppy, plopped into the seat beside him and handed him a list of the day's messages. He glanced at the half a dozen or so names, noticing that apart from calls dealing with the production, one was from Sylvia and the other from Laurie Christian. Well, Sylvia was no surprise. She rang regularly with various things to ask and to tell. But Laurie? Ringing him here? He had obviously found out where he was from the office and Jack wondered whether he had spoken to Sylvia. She was no idiot, and her antennae had been on alert ever since Jack had signed Laurie up to the agency.

"You can get off now, Lesley. I'll see you back at the hotel."

The young woman stood up and stretched, winding her hand-knitted red scarf tightly around her neck.

"Are you sure?

"Yes, yes… I need to think over a few things… Quietly."

The heavy fire door situated near the prompt side of the stage shut with an echoing and tooth-edging clang as she left, then a silence, almost eerie, descended on the empty theatre which only a few minutes ago had been filled with the whirling bustle of show-people at work.

As Jack sat back and looked around the deserted auditorium, a wave of desperate loneliness crept up on him, as stealthily as a silent assassin and with no less devastating an effect.

For the first time, he began to reflect on the out of character impulse which had propelled him into an expensive West End jewellers' before leaving London.

He had no regrets about his action, whatever complications it may now throw up, for it was something that he'd had to do, if only to assuage the shame which had been slowly festering like a stubborn wound for months. What sort of man was he really? Certainly, not the man that others took him to be. A coward at best. A shallow human being who simply did not possess the courage of his own convictions. That alone demanded punishment.

He started to light a cigarette then, suddenly remembering where he was, replaced it quickly in its packet.

Was it really three years ago that he had finally acknowledged his inability to form satisfactory relationships with women and that it had taken one more excrutiating experience for this to at last sink in?

Thinking about it now, his nervous system contracted with that same hot spasm of embarrassment, as if it had only been three minutes instead of three years, and reluctantly the vision of the gorgeous Belinda Carey materialised within his re-awakened memory.

Not only was Belinda Carey blonde, beautiful and sexy but, unusually for a Rank starlet with acting aspirations, she had possessed a razor-sharp brain, a talent for the piano and a degree in Fine Arts. She could also quote passages from Shakespeare's heroines with the dignity and sensitivity equal to any classically trained actress at the Old Vic.

Jack knew that when she invited him back to her flat after a first-night party, that she intended to seduce him. In fact, he wondered whether Belinda had invented the Ian Fleming cliché of slipping out of a strapless Dior evening gown, revealing nothing but a perfect body and a diamond necklace.

And he had wanted to want her so much.

But although she had said all the right things and touched him in all the right places, it was simply impossible for him to rise to the occasion and, when he took his leave, muttering abject apologies, she kissed him sweetly wishing him future happiness in love.

Six months later she married an architect, moved to New York and stormed Broadway, still retaining Jack as her agent in London.

Belinda's wish for his happiness in love had not been fulfilled, although he now knew how and where to pursue his sexual pleasures, albeit within a confused and emotionally crippling sort of twilight existence.

Evenings spent in those clubs and pubs in Soho and Notting Hill, raided regularly by the police, where furtive and desperate fumblings led to frantic, one-night stands of passionate intensity, paling in the light of day and often leaving him feeling used and depressed. He would then anxiously wait for those casually encountered to be on their way, relieved to close his door, yet all too frequently relieved of the contents of his wallet.

Then, in the spring of this year, hitting him with all the force of a biblical revelation, he had fallen in love for the first time. God, when his mind formed the words now, they sounded as slushy as a Rodgers and Hammerstein song. But the emotional and physical symptoms, alternately wonderful and tortuous, convinced him that this was how it was supposed to feel.

Tentatively he had reached out, only to withdraw in panic when an envelope bearing an official seal plopped through his letter-box one morning which, until then, had started out like any other.

It had taken Sylvia to pronounce, in her usual down-to-earth fashion, that the OBE was his reward for all the many years of dedication and sacrifice, even if he didn't regard his working life in that way. And he was forced to agree that although it was not something he had yearned for or necessarily aspired to, he nevertheless was proud to have received it.

Now, if there were even the slightest hint of scandal, of any hidden, illegal skeletons, it would all have been for nought. Might as well take his hard-earned achievements and flush them down the nearest loo.

He had already been privy to the dark mutterings recently surrounding a well-known Liberal M.P., a man whom Jack had met socially and whose relentless work for charity was renowned, but who had been less than discreet on his views regarding homosexuality. At the annual seaside conference, when he had blatantly flaunted his pretty-boy lover as his new parliamentary assistant, not only had a wave of anxiety passed through the party faster than a camel on laxatives, but the anticipated honour from the Palace evaporated, along with the cinerous wisps of fog that curled around those spires of Westminster.

Somewhere a clock chimed eight and Jack stood up, once again aware there were never enough hours in his day. Certainly never enough necessary to function in the real world as well as to concentrate on what they were calling these days 'The Inner Self.'

Although he had tried so hard to avoid his feelings, he now acknowledged wearily that he wanted Laurie Christian more than ever. Even seeing his name scribbled on a note-pad, brought with it the same sweet, aching desire that he had felt during their first meeting.

The lighter had been purchased on an impulse, driven by a fierce burst of adrenalin. A feeble attempt to atone for his cowardice. But he knew that even if, on a conscious level, he had considered it as simply tying up loose ends, then somewhere buried deep within his psyche, there was little doubt he was instigating a beginning.

—m—

After he had visited Syd and Helen in hospital, heard the same old jokes and given them a blow by blow account of how rehearsals were progressing, Jack returned to the hotel for a bath and to make his calls before ordering his dinner from room service.

He tried Sylvia's office line, not really expecting to find her there.

"Still burning the oil?" He asked, marvelling once again at her dedicated work ethic comparable only with his own.

"I've been on the phone to Vegas. The Sammy Davis deal is looking good. I think another ten grand should do it."

"Okay. Let's stall until Monday, then offer seven. Anything else I should know?"

"Nothing that can't wait." There was a pause and then she volunteered in a hurried adjunct. "Oh, and Laurie Christian rang. I hope he didn't bother you."

"No, no, that's alright."

He wished her goodnight, wondering just what she would

say if she knew precisely how much Laurie did bother him.

Checking the time, Jack realized that there was a chance he might catch him at the club before his first show at ten, for he had finally decided, after much heart-searching, to invite him up to Blackpool on Sunday, when he would suggest they drive up to the lakes, find a B & B, and, if his fantasies went according to plan, would spend what was left of the day getting properly acquainted.

That at least would be safe, away from prying eyes and also from any explanations and deceptions where Elizabeth was concerned. He'd have things to do, but hell, didn't he also need some much-deserved relaxation?

The impudence of the chorus boy who answered the pay phone amused rather than irritated him.

"Oh, Mr. Merrick, my name's Chris Perry. Can I send you some photos?"

"Send them to my assistant, would you?"

"Of course, Mr. Merrick. I just saw Laurie come in. I'll get him."

"Thank you."

He waited against a background of live music and excitable voices until a breathless Laurie came on the line.

"Hello stranger."

"How are you?" Jack tried to keep his voice steady although his heart was banging so hard against his chest that he was convinced that it could be heard in London.

"All the better for speaking to you."

"I'm in Blackpool," he said stupidly.

Laurie's laugh carried the promise of shared pleasures. Deep and rich, strangely at odds with his slight build. "I know. I left a message."

Confused by such desperate longing, Jack began to blurt out his invitation, as Laurie cut in.

"Jack... Just let me say something? Alright?"

"Go ahead."

"I just want to say how sorry I was to hear about, you know, your sister..."

"Thank-you."

"And also say to say thank-you. For the gift."

"Oh, you got it. Good." The dry mouth and knotted stomach muscles had returned with a vengeance. "The least I could do... In the circumstances."

"I was hurt, Jack. I can't pretend otherwise."

"I know. And I'm sorry. I should have got to your opening. It was unforgivable."

"Do I still have to go through – what's his name? Mark Dover?"

Jack cleared his throat, trying to find the right words. "Officially, yes. Unoficially..." His sentence trailed into silence and, hoping that he had conveyed the right message, he continued rapidly. "I was wondering if you'd like to come up this Sunday? Go back Monday morning." He laughed nervously then added, "for a breath of sea air?"

There was a short pause, then a groan. "Oh God, I'd love to, but I can't."

His response was so unexpected that Jack abandoned his carefulness and heard himself enquire churlishly "Why not?"

"They're changing the show. Every six weeks, remember?"

"Oh yes." Of course he had forgotten.

"We're rehearsing for the next two Sundays with the choreographer and the band."

"Oh well..." Jack said, as evenly as he could manage. "That's show-business. There's nothing we can do."

"We'll have to wait till you're back."

Jack paused. "That will be difficult."

Another silence, then someone asking Laurie if they could use the phone.

"Listen," said Jack. "I'd better go and let you go back to work."

"Just a minute... Before you do... I don't suppose I could help you in any way?"

"That's very kind of you, but I don't see..."

"I was thinking about your niece."

"Elizabeth? What about her?"

"Just that… While you're up there… Perhaps I could go and see her… Take her to Carnaby Street or something?"

Jack gathered his thoughts together quickly. Laurie meeting Elizabeth. No, it was much too risky, wasn't it?

Laurie continued his flow, this time more confidently. "She must be fed up. Young girl, very few friends in London…"

"She has no friends." Jack interrupted. "Not until she starts school. That's the problem. She knows no-body."

"… I could help her choose some fun clothes. Make sure she doesn't get ripped off."

The turmoil which was now scrambling Jack's brain struggled for a response. Maybe it wasn't such a bad idea. Laurie was young and could be very good company. Elizabeth was plainly in need of both company and stimulation and one day's shopping would do no harm. But what if she got to find out that Laurie was homosexual? Or worse – that he was! She was so innocent, so protected. Almost certainly, she had never heard of two men doing it together.

"I'd have to ring her." Jack said, very nearly persuaded. "Let her know you'll be in touch."

"That'd be great!" People were calling Laurie's name and he yelled back, "okay, okay! I must go. Trust me, it'll be fine." His voice dropped, becoming more intimate. "And might make it easier, don't you agree?"

Jack put down the phone wondering just *what* he'd agreed to. Laurie's suggestion was so out of the blue, so unforeseen, that it had caught him off his guard and totally unprepared. He opened the mini-bar and, irritated by its lack of his favourite whisky, emptied two miniatures of Bells' into a glass and took a deep swig. Perhaps Laurie had just provided the glimmer of light for which he had been waiting. One that might illuminate the hitherto un-navigable path leading to his much longed for relationship? Although, he would never have thought to suggest it in a million years.

Picking up the room-service menu, Jack glanced at it distractedly, his appetite having deserted him. If indeed, Elizabeth got to know and like Laurie, then maybe she would accept seeing them together. It would be something she wouldn't question, regarding them as nothing more than two men who were friends.

He shook his head, the jumble of nervously hopeful emotions he had been experiencing now settling into the more familiar one of futility. Who was he kidding? Logistically, it was impossible, and he knew it. Better to nip it in the bud right now and save all the heartache and recriminations. For himself and for others.

—⁓—

Elizabeth plumped four pillows up behind her head, tucked the yellow, quilted eiderdown under her chin and proceeded to devour Chloe's letter for the third time since Hannah had first brought it in to her earlier that morning.

It was so wonderful to hear all the news from home. Her friend had loved the photos and the various postcards she had sent, particularly one featuring the London Embankment in winter, covered in a white meringue-like substance which they had only heard of or seen in films.

Chloe wrote of a school trip to the Falls, where great excitement had occurred as one of their teachers, Mrs. Lewis (she of the buck teeth and lazy eye) had, while wearing open-toed sandals, narrowly avoided treading on a small, black Mamba, a harmless-looking snake, whose lethal bite could kill within minutes.

There was news too of Simon, who had bought a motorbike and was dating the local butcher's daughter, Monica, a sixteen year old, who, according to Chloe's mother, was far too forward for her age and would probably end up in trouble!

Elizabeth smiled as images of Monica came flooding back on a tide of memories. She had always considered her the most beautiful girl she had ever seen; a Prefect in the upper year with long hair the colour of ripe, golden corn and a figure that went in and out exactly where it should. And, as she and Chloe had discovered, Monica had been the first at their school to dare to wear a bra and panty-girdle, something which had proved a source of fascination to Elizabeth and her friends, causing them to stare and snigger whenever she happened within their orbit. In quieter moments, however, Elizabeth was acutely aware of her own tiny breasts and narrow hips in comparison.

As she re-read the end of the letter, tears stung in her eyes as her friend asked if there was any chance that she could come over for Christmas. 'Do try?' she begged, in capital letters. 'We're having a big party in the garden as usual and we'll miss you.'

Chloe's mother had also enclosed a short note, hoping that Elizabeth was well and happy and telling her that she was continuing to place flowers on her parents' graves. She added that she had also visited great-aunt Margaret in the nursing home, taking her a freshly baked ginger cake.

Elizabeth wiped her eyes and folded the letter carefully, tucking it back into its envelope. She would read it again later because it made her feel sad and glad at the same time and brought the people she loved so much closer.

A knock at the door interrupted her thoughts and Hannah peeped in.

"Are you alright, hen?"

Elizabeth jumped out of bed and stretched. "Yes, Hannah, I'm up. I'll be in for breakfast in a tick."

"You haven't forgotten have you? About your uncle's friend coming at eleven?"

No, she hadn't forgotten. But she was less than keen on the prospect.

How on earth could Uncle Jack imagine that a man would have any idea of what she wanted to do in London, or what she wanted to buy?

"He's young." Her uncle had told her on the phone. But she didn't regard twenty-five as young. To Elizabeth it was practically middle-aged. Still, she considered that at least he was younger than both Hannah and Jack, so it seemed the best of her very few alternatives.

Shopping with Hannah, something which she had been looking forward to, turned out to be a nightmare. The housekeeper had led her through a series of grossly old-fashioned clothes stores, where Elizabeth had decided it was far better to keep her money than to spend it on outfits which made her look older than her great-aunt. Hannah had also taken her for tea in a crowded shop in Piccadilly, which she evidently regarded as a special treat, but where there were no young people visible, and tweed hats and flat-heeled shoes seemed to be the order of the day.

As Elizabeth dragged a comb through her springy hair, she wondered if this friend of her uncle's knew where she could get a decent haircut. It was really starting to annoy her, for it had grown way beyond her shoulders and was far too curly to be fashionable.

Her mother used to straighten it with heated tongs so that it could be plaited, but she hoped that she would never have to wear plaits again. They were just so juvenile. Uncle Jack wouldn't know about them though, so she determined that when she started school next year she would choose her own hairstyle.

Victor rang at eleven on the dot to say that Mr. Christian was on his way up to take Miss Tarrant out.

Elizabeth groaned, stretched out beside Betsy on the living-room floor and turned up the volume of *Norwegian Wood*.

"*And when I awoke, I was alone, this bird had flown…*"

She heard Hannah answer the door and greet the visitor. "Hello, you must be Mr. Christian. Come in, come in."

"Thank you. And it's Laurie." The man's voice was light, cultured. "But you can't be Hannah. Mr. Merrick told me you were in your sixties!"

"Aach, away with you, you flatterer." Hannah sounded young again, a giggling girl. Elizabeth sat up, intrigued.

When he appeared at the living-room door her heart cartwheeled with such force, that she said without thinking. "You!"

A bewildered Hannah looked from one to the other questioningly. "Have you two met?"

Laurie smiled, crouched down to stroke Betsy, then glanced

up at Hannah. "I think Elizabeth must have seen me walking my dog in the park. I often leave the car near here."

Her face was burning and she had no idea why. Surprised and strangely pleased, she got up. He rose with her and pulled a small carrier bag out of his coat pocket which he dangled before her eyes, then tilted his head towards the radiogram. "I thought you might like this. Their latest..."

Elizabeth heard her voice soar through what seemed like four octaves and she jumped into the air, causing Hannah to stare in alarm and astonishment.

"Their new one... You've brought their new one? How did you know?"

"I've made it my business to know." He told her.

"Elizabeth!" Hannah said sternly. "Whatever's got into you?"

"Oh, Hannah," Elizabeth threw her arms around the housekeeper, almost taking the wind out of her small body with one huge bear hug. "Mr. Christian's brought me the new Beatles single."

"Is that all? Thank heavens for that." Hannah sounded relieved. "Would you like coffee Laurie, or do you both want to get off?"

He looked at the flushed, excited girl who took the bag from him as if it contained stardust then removed his grey overcoat, draping it over the velvet settee.

"I think we've got time for a coffee. Someone needs to hear something rather badly."

With trembling hands, Elizabeth took the LP she had been playing off the turntable and carefully lowered the small piece of shiny new vinyl in its place. Changing the speed, she sat back down on the floor, crossed her legs and listened enraptured.

When it had finished she turned to him and whispered, "Wonderful."

Hannah brought in the coffee and, sensing that they wanted to talk about pop music, left them alone.

"I must play it again. Can I play it again?"

He laughed and raised the Wedgwood cup to his lips. "Of course you can. It's for you."

As she listened for the second time, she tried not to let him notice that she was also taking in how he looked at close quarters. Quite tall and slim with thick, light brown hair and large, grey eyes that danced with humour, but which were so expressive that she was sure they could also be capable of deep melancholy. His mouth was what she imagined writers in women's magazines meant by generous and if warm honey had a sound, then that was how she would describe his laugh. He was wearing mostly grey, except for a bright red cashmere sweater and everything, Elizabeth thought with inexplicable satisfaction, looked just right.

"Do you understand it?" He asked her and, surprised by the question, she shook her head.

"Only that it's about lonely people."

"I've heard…" He leaned forward, as if imparting a secret which Elizabeth found irresistible, "…That Paul McCartney wrote these rather sad lyrics about this woman whom he invented called Eleanor Rigby. Then, some time later, he was walking through a cemetery in Liverpool and saw a very old gravestone with the name Eleanor Rigby on it. He swears blind that he never saw it before, one of those odd things that often happen in life. Anyway, the Beatles have given her, whoever she was, her own little niche in posterity."

Elizabeth looked at him wonderingly, trying to absorb not only the poignant story but the unfamiliar words he was using. "That is strange. And sad."

He checked his watch and stood up. "I think we should be on our way if you want to do some shopping before lunch."

"Yes, yes." She clapped her hands and switched off the radiogram. "I'll listen again later remembering the mysterious, late Eleanor Rigby."

She collected her coat, wished Hannah goodbye and they squeezed together in the small lift which took them jerkily down to the ground floor.

"Do you know a good hairdresser?" She asked him, pulling a face at the sight of her reflection in the lift mirror.

He studied her, then moved forward and wrapped his finger

around one of her curls. "Yes, I was wondering about your hair. It's pretty, but it's so old-fashioned."

"Oh, I know," she said in a voice that she hoped didn't sound like a whine, then followed him across the road towards the parked car. "Oh, a Mini... And is that your dog?"

He unlocked the passenger door for her and, as she slid into her seat, her face and neck were assaulted by the vigorous licks of a highly-strung Flora.

Elizabeth giggled and tried to calm the poodle down as Laurie started the rather temperamental and cranky engine.

"Knightsbridge first, I think. To a reasonable enough hairdresser called Vidal Sassoon!"

—⁂—

RHODESIA
DECEMBER, 1966.

Margaret Ainsley wiped away the crumbs she had dropped on her lilac, brushed-nylon nightdress and counted the cinnamon doves which had been gently cooing in the pear tree just outside her window. How many were there supposed to be? Six lords a-leaping, seven maids a milking… Oh, it was so bothersome not to be able to remember. She used to sing that song every Christmas with her mother and father. Why couldn't she remember it now?

Was it two? Yes, yes that was right – two turtle doves, or were they partridges? Oh, dear… Sam would know. Sam always knew everything. But Sam wasn't here, was he? She kept forgetting.

She took a sip of tea, but it was cold and she spat it out. Oh, no! More of a mess on her nightie. Nurse would not be pleased with her this morning.

She looked closely at the calendar on the wall which had not yet been changed to December and tried to work out how many days there were until Christmas.

Perhaps her nephew Ben would visit soon with his wife Emily. She hadn't seen them for such a long time. And darling Elizabeth, such a beautiful child. If only she had been able to have a child like that…Oh well, no good lingering on sad if only's. *Que sera sera…*

Shaken out of her reverie by the door opening, Margaret's watery eyes met those of Jennifer Moore, the burly, thirty-something, geriatric nurse, who, for some reason, she seemed to see more than any of the other twenty-five nurses who worked at Chisholm House. Margaret didn't really care for Jennifer Moore; found her bossy and often intimidating. But she appeared to be in a less sour mood today, even though a slight frown crossed her brow as she saw Margaret was still not dressed, and her tone was tinged with disapproval.

"I thought you told me you wanted to dress yourself this morning, Margaret?"

"I was waiting…" Margaret said defensively, "for my pills."

The nurse began to pull the bedclothes together into something roughly approximating order. "You've had your pills, Margaret. I gave them to you earlier with your morning tea."

She straightened up and went towards the single teak wardrobe where a variety of summer dresses and skirts were hanging closely together on thick wooden hangers. Selecting a dress of beige silk with a white floral motif, she held it up for Margaret's approval and towards which the seventy-five year old nodded.

"Oh yes. That will do. I like that one."

"Come on then," said Nurse Moore. "Arms up."

The old woman obeyed and allowed the nightdress to be pulled over her head, revealing all her naked helplessness in the long mirror on the wall opposite. Then, while the nurse rummaged in a drawer for a brassiere and a pair of cotton pants, Margaret gazed forlornly at such an unrecognizable phenomenon with its brown, wrinkled skin hanging over all-too prominent bones and the now shrunken and despondent little breasts which drooped sadly above vein-ridden legs.

As she was being zipped into her dress, she asked Nurse Moore if her father's portrait on the wall could be moved nearer the bed so she could see it when she woke up.

"That's not your father," The woman said with obvious irritation. "That's Cecil Rhodes. His portrait's in every room."

"Really? He looks just like my father."

"I'm just nipping down the corridor." Jennifer Moore told her. "So be a good girl, do your hair and powder your nose and I'll be back to take you down to breakfast in a tick."

"Emily made this dress." Margaret said proudly. "That's my nephew's wife, you know."

"The one that was murdered?" Nurse Moore attempted a sympathetic look as she left the room. "Yes, that was awful."

Alone again, a wave of hopelessness and depression descended on Margaret with a dizzying intensity and she put her hand out to steady herself against the chair. Murdered? Emily? Was that really true... And if so, what of Ben?

She did remember now. They had taken her into Chisholm House shortly after she had heard the news and she had been allowed to see Elizabeth off on a plane somewhere.

The old woman began to cry. She was sick and tired of not remembering and she was sick and tired of life. Without her husband and her family, who was she now? How could this even be called a life? All her friends were dead and the people here strangers and senile, like herself.

Dropping painfully on to her bony knees, she rummaged under the bed then dragged out a small suitcase, clicked it open and peered inside.

A large leather-bound Bible stared up at her, the once bright golden cross and variegated lettering on its cover faded and disintegrated through time.

Looking at it, Margaret Ainsley's tears suddenly gave way to a chuckle as she pulled herself up from the floor and sat down heavily on the bed, holding the Bible on her lap.

"A secret, a secret, I've got a little secret..." she sang in a high, child-like voice, then with shaking fingers opened the massive book.

The pages were missing and it was simply a hollow box, a container. She carefully lifted out what was inside, peeling away the layers of white muslin in which it was wrapped and drawing in her breath as the glint of a small and silver object almost mesmerised her.

"I'm coming, Sam," she whispered. Then Margaret Ainsley picked up the loaded, antique South African hand-gun, put it against her right temple and remembered to pull the trigger.

—⁂—

"That looks fab!" Jeffery, the floral-shirted, Sassoon stylist stepped back to admire his handiwork, as Elizabeth gazed in stunned disbelief at her reflection in the huge, gilt-edged mirror.

Behind her, Flora yelped in Laurie's arms as if adding her own canine comment of approval to that of her master.

"It looks great, Elizabeth. Don't you think?"

She couldn't speak, only nod, for the transformation which had taken place was such as to make her believe that she was looking at another person entirely.

The unruly locks that she had walked in with had now been cropped a good three inches and straightened into a smooth bob, although a length of hair on the right hand side of her face had been allowed to remain long, and was trained carefully as to appear careless, sweeping across her eye and tucking in behind her ear. A colour rinse had been applied "to enhance, not eliminate" her natural shade, so that the familiar, titian-gold now seemed to be far richer, giving the overall appearance of a glossy, copper helmet.

"A touch of Twiggy with a soupçon of Quant." Jeffery dived into a series of different poses as he held up the hand mirror to enable her to study what he had created at the back of her head and she spun around in the leather and chrome chair, gradually finding her voice.

"It's nice." Her words were no more than a whisper and Jeffery pulled a face as he turned to Laurie. "I give her fabulous and she gives me nice. I'm hurt."

Elizabeth laughed then, relaxing into confidence. "I'm sorry. What I mean is I like it. I love it!"

"That's better."

"What you can do, if you want to...." Laurie suggested, surprisingly knowledgeably, "... is ask Jeffery to make you up some fake curls in the same colour if you'd like to add to your own hair for a party."

"Really?" Her momentary interest then faltered. "But I don't go to any parties."

"What?" screamed Jeffery. "A dolly bird like you. I don't believe it!"

She looked at Laurie then nodded decisively. "Alright then. Yes, please."

She had never felt on such a high. Wait until Chloe heard about the grown-up decisions that she was making. More to the point, she was being treated like a grown-up in this unreal, almost dreamlike atmosphere.

In fact, she wouldn't be surprised if it was, after all, just a dream from which she would suddenly wake, finding herself back in the farmhouse on a perfect summer's afternoon, like Dorothy in *The Wizard of Oz,* with her mother's anxious voice calling her in for tea and the familiar sound of her father whistling as he washed his hands in the kitchen sink.

And, although that would be the most wonderful thing in the world, she knew that right here and now she was as happy as she ever could be.

"Bona!" Breathed Jeffery. "I'll get them ordered right away. They're a snip at three guineas." He realised the pun he had either deliberately or accidentally made and roared with laughter. "Listen to me... Snip! Oh, I'll kill myself laughing one of these days."

Elizabeth giggled with delight, as they made their way to the front desk and Laurie took the bill from the receptionist.

"I'll look after this," he said, taking out his cheque-book.

"No," Elizabeth rummaged through the old tapestry shoulder-bag which had come over with her mother's possessions. "Uncle Jack gave me money. Here."

"Later." Laurie told her. "We'll go through it all later. What do you want to do now?"

She hesitated, unable to take her eyes off her reflection in the numerous mirrors. "Well, I could do with a new mac," she said, sliding embarrassedly into the ancient school gabardine held up for her by a skinny assistant.

"Come on then, madam," Laurie said, leading her out of the salon and towards the Mini, where he gave an exaggerated mock bow as he opened the passenger door. "Your carriage awaits."

The early mist had cleared and by the time they found a parking meter on the King's Road, a watery, December sun was struggling to break through the grey clouds.

"Please don't rain on my hair," she pleaded in a whisper, gazing up at the sky.

He heard her and laughed. "It won't rain on you. I've ordered sunshine, did I forget to say?"

She looked at him quickly, glowing with appreciation, for even if he was a friend of Uncle Jack's, she was sure he could be with anyone he chose today, rather than pandering to the wishes of some unsophisticated chatterbox of a teenager.

It didn't take her long to realise that the famous King's Road was no ordinary London street. It throbbed and pulsated with frenetic, youthful activity and it was difficult to walk in a straight line without being bumped into or pushed against, especially, Elizabeth thought, if you are staring at everything and everybody as though you have just landed from another planet.

Strains of Beatles music floated out from boutiques and coffee bars, as girls who looked like models and boys who resembled pop stars passed her, seeming like exotic, untouchable entities in their abundance. Stylish creatures that she would never get to know, let alone become one of their special circle.

A tall, elegant girl in the shortest coat of vivid lime-green, with long, pale hair, pale lips and coal-black eye-liner, drifted serenely by, even though she was wearing dangerously high stiletto heels. In one hand she held a carrier bag designed as a Union Jack, in the other a dog-lead to which was attached a perfectly groomed Afghan hound, and, Elizabeth noticed with amusement, the boy who accompanied her also resembled the look of an Afghan, but sadly, not so perfectly groomed. His shaggy hair was tucked inside the collar of his long, dirty-blonde, shaggy coat and the outfit was finished off by a pair of tan leather cowboy boots bearing a heavily embossed pattern of cactus plants.

Laurie nudged her as another lovely girl with cornflower blue eyes and wearing a black coat with a mink collar and a wide-brimmed, black hat, walked past on the arm of a mean-looking fellow in a silver jacket.

"Mick and Marianne," he said reverently, turning along with several others to look after the pair.

"Really?" Not wanting to appear stupid, but having no idea who the couple might be, Elizabeth also turned and stared at their retreating backs.

Then suddenly, she saw what she wanted. It was as though the shop window just seemed to loom up and demand her attention, for inside was displayed the most perfect confection of dazzling and outrageous clothes. Colourful and geometric patterned dresses, bright coats and shiny raincoats, all of which exceeded her wildest imagination and caused her to stop in her tracks, greedily imbibing this feast of fashion delight.

"Aah, Bazaar." Laurie breathed. "You've got good taste, girl. Come on."

She followed him in, experiencing a fusion of excitement and shyness as a young assistant tottering under the weight of a huge, chestnut beehive and wearing a white ribbed vest, offered to help them.

Not quite knowing where to begin among so many goodies, Elizabeth pointed out three dresses and a raincoat, which she tried on behind a burgundy velvet curtain then emerged, laughingly parading like a model in front of him for approval. Obediently, and because for some bewildering reason, she trusted his judgement, those towards which he shook his head she declined, accepting others from him as he handed them to her and pulling up zips, fastening buckles, choosing and discarding, as if she had been doing it all her life. In fact, the only clothes she had ever bought from a shop had been school uniform, for her mother had made everything she wore, from jackets and trousers to dresses and skirts.

When she had committed herself to the three mini-dresses, one white, one black, the other covered with multi-coloured, squirly patterns, together with a Mary Quant raincoat of flower-printed plastic, he talked her into trying on a pair of knee-high, white plastic boots. Squeezing her toes into them, she found they fitted perfectly, although secretly she was convinced that they might be hot and painful after being worn for longer than an hour.

But by now, she was so addicted to the combined buzz of the

shopping, Laurie's eyes and his laugh, that she didn't care. Flopping exhausted into a chair, she tickled his dog's neck and told him she had finished.

"Try one more thing for me." He walked over to one of the rails and selected a long-sleeved white shirt, black trousers with a slight flare, a black waistcoat and a wide, black and white spotted kipper tie.

She shrieked with laughter and shook her head. "What's that? I can't wear that!"

He moved towards her, offering his hand to pull her up from her seat, then turned her round to face the mirror, holding the outfit against her as he stood behind. Painfully aware of his proximity, she swallowed hard and tried to think of what to say, but was saved by him declaring "Unisex, it's all the rage. Girls wear their hair cropped like a boy's and some fashion styles can be worn by both sexes. Perhaps you won't like it, but I think it will make you look very attractive. Like a little boy lost."

"A little boy…" she faltered, wondering why she felt so bothered by the throwaway manner in which he used the 's' word.

He handed the clothes to the beehive who once again beckoned Elizabeth behind the curtain. Deeply unsure, she pulled on the shirt, trousers and waistcoat, but had trouble with the tie. Shoeless, with the trousers flapping around her ankles, she shuffled towards him and he tied it for her then handed her the shoes.

"It looks lovely," the assistant said in a squeaky, Cockney voice. "Doesn't it?" She directed her question at Laurie who was studying Elizabeth's expression which had now changed to favourable surprise.

"Well?" He asked.

"I don't know…" But she needed more persuasion. It was exciting and very, very different and she knew that it probably suited her temperament more than the dresses did.

"You've got just the figure for it." He told her. "You're slender – and with the new hair…"

Her cheeks were flushed as she turned to face him. "Why do you always say all the right things?"

He smiled and shrugged. "I think she wants it," he told the assistant.

They were the last people to leave the shop and, laden with bags, they wove their way through the rush-hour of a dusk-lit evening, the old gabardine now rendered a thing of the past, along with, Elizabeth reflected poignantly, her other life, which seemed further away than ever now.

The tantalising aroma of food permeated the hallway when they arrived back at the flat and Elizabeth dived into the kitchen where Hannah was examining whatever delicious wonders lay inside the oven.

The housekeeper's eyes widened with amazement as they alighted on the vision of the new Elizabeth. 'Everything shiny, from the hair to the boots,' Hannah observed silently, as she struggled to collect her thoughts.

Laurie stood beside the young girl, studying her with satisfaction. "Well, what do you think then, Hannah?"

"Goodness, gracious." Hannah pulled a pair of thick bifocals from her apron pocket and placed them on her nose for more careful inspection. "Whatever happened to the wee lassie who left here this morning?"

Elizabeth laughed and began to twirl and dance around the kitchen.

"Gone, Hannah. Gone forever. Forever and ever... Amen!"

Hannah wanted to smile, but her strong Scottish Presbyterian background reminded her that perhaps this excitable outburst was bordering on blasphemy, so she clicked her tongue and shook her head, totally bemused.

"Will you stay for supper, Laurie? It's only a stew."

"Oh, yes. Please stay." Elizabeth begged. "Please... Please!"

"Hannah, indulging in one of your stews is a temptation which I will sadly have to resist," he said then noticed the crestfallen expression on Elizabeth's face. "I've got a rehearsal at seven-thirty and I'll grab a quick coffee and a sandwich."

"Are you an actor?" Elizabeth asked, needing to know more and more about the man who had given her the most exciting day she'd ever spent.

"An actor, a singer... An entertainer, really, I suppose."

"Well, miss," Hannah interrupted, "time you got out of that mackintosh and washed your hands and face."

Elizabeth walked with him to the door, not wanting him to leave, but trying not to let him know.

"It's been fun." He told her. "We'll do it again."

"Will we?" She said eagerly "When?"

He laughed and placed the tip of his finger on the snub of her nose. "Soon. I'll ring you."

"Yes, please."

"Be good."

—⁂—

RHODESIA
DECEMBER, 1966.

Richard T. Mackenzie – the T stood for Theodore after his paternal grandfather – took his exasperation out on a bluebottle which had dared to intrude upon his office through the thin, wooden slats of his window blind and alight on the Victorian mahogany desk between his blotting pad and the brass lion paperweight.

Laying the plastic swatter to one side, he examined the flattened body of the insect and tried to work out how to remove it.

The creaking ceiling-fan above him, although having made the same irritating noise for as many years as he could remember, also became the target of his wrath and he threw it a filthy look hissing, some would say rather uncharacteristically, "Jesus Christ!"

He had worked as a general Solicitor and Commissioner for Oaths in Salisbury all of his adult life, with his father inheriting the firm from Theodore Mackenzie senior in 1942 and only this year they had brought in another full-time partner, now making three of them in total. Not surprisingly, Ian Smith's Unilateral Declaration of Independence from Britain and the ensuing sanctions had produced the effect of an increasing workload, with the nervous and bewildered white population clamouring for advice on overseas trading and financial negotiations, as well as personal and property security.

Added to which, the divorce rate was rising. Even his own thirty-year marriage was a sham and now that the kids were at college, all pretence at happy families had finally been dispensed with, his erstwhile spouse Susan having moved permanently into the spare bedroom where she could quietly read and re-read that perennial best-seller, the Bible, while he would indulge in more basic pursuits like masturbation, through seedy literature imported from Europe.

Sweating profusely now, he stuck the two forefingers of his right hand beneath his shirt collar in an attempt to loosen it, then went for the easier option and undid the top button and unknotted his tie.

Another complicated little matter had just arisen which meant dealing once again with the old country and, curiously enough, concerning the same fifteen year old schoolgirl who had recently been made an orphan by terrorists posing as freedom fighters, then shipped off to London to live with her uncle and legal guardian.

Yesterday, the seventy-five year old Margaret Ainsley, a long-time client of Mackenzie & Mackenzie and the girl's only remaining relative in Rhodesia, decided enough was enough and had methodically shot herself at a nursing-home in a local suburb, thereby creating yet another last will and testament naming the child its beneficiary. Consequently, this left him with another funeral to arrange, a further property to try and dispose of, as well as negotiations concerning a substantial amount of money in the local branch of Lloyds. In addition there was a safety deposit box, contents unknown, held in the Royal Bank of Scotland, in, of all inconvenient places, Scotland.

Although he was not without feelings for the poor girl, Richard T. Mackenzie wished with great fervour that she hadn't gone to live in England. Her parents' farm, although having been on the market for only a month, had not been viewed by any potentially serious buyer, for it seemed that the black man's fear of superstition had eerily crossed the divide, filling the white population with the dread that the stench of slaughter might still pervade its genteel structure. Not to mention the more realistic option that the same fate could well befall them.

It had been a fairly good working farm as farms in the area

went, but it was also quite dilapidated, as the Tarrants had found neither the time nor the inclination to lick the walls with paint or replace rotting windows and floorboards. Although they had not been wealthy, there had certainly been enough funds to allow for what he considered should have been a worthwhile investment for the future, whatever it might hold.

The Ainsley farm, on the other hand, was a different matter entirely and he had little doubt that it would be easy to sell. Before Samuel Ainsley died of cancer five years ago, he had had the foresight to hire a strong and honest Africaaner, Steven Van De Berg, to run the farm, alongside his trusted bossboy of twenty-five years, Tembi Dabengwa. De Berg returned home at weekends to visit his large family and bring them money and the farm grew from strength to strength, providing acres of good cultivated soil for tobacco, fruit and vegetable produce, a small, but thriving herd of cattle, equipment regularly repaired or replaced and the buildings maintained satisfactorily. After Ainsley died, his warm-hearted and energetic wife, Margaret, continued the respectful bond she and her husband had forged with De Berg and the black workers. Now, in accordance with her will, salaries would continue for one year, enabling potential purchasers to see the farm running pretty much as it always had, as well as allowing the workers enough time to find alternative employment if necessary.

The fly in the ointment, he thought, as he carefully lifted the corner of a white, foolscap envelope and slid it with great precision under the bluebottle, was that Mr. Wilson, the British Prime Minister, had recently claimed that oil sanctions were proving increasingly effective and Smith had retaliated by severing the Rhodesian pound from the sterling, therefore making the transfer of funds, relatively easy up to a month ago, now a lengthy procedure, particularly where probate was concerned and that was nobody's problem but his.

He breathed out deeply, holding the envelope at arm's length and tipping it with a certain degree of caution into his patriotic, copper waste-bin, decorated with figures of Wildebeast and fierce, spear-bearing natives.

Mackenzie opened the door to the adjoining office where a weary-looking secretary, her grey hair severely scraped back and tied on the nape of her neck with a black ribbon, was typing on a twenty-year old Olivetti.

"Can I help you, Mr. Mackenzie?"

"You'd better get me that chap in England – Jack Merrick, wasn't it? The Tarrant estate?"

The woman gave a small but audible sigh and rifled through the pages of her leather-bound address book.

"That's Elizabeth Tarrant, yes?"

"That's right."

"Shall I try him now?"

Richard T. Mackenzie checked the fading Roman numerals on the large, oval clock above the door, its heavy ticking seeming ominously symbolic of a country whose current philosophy was 'time will tell', then nodded as the call was placed to London.

—⟋⟍—

BLACKPOOL
DECEMBER, 1966

It wasn't until Sylvia pointed out to him at the first night party that the Mayor bore an uncanny resemblance to the actor playing Alderman Fitzwarren that Jack was finally able to laugh and relax. As he moved around the Green Room making sure that the guests' glasses were well filled with champagne, he could at least be grateful for the fact that the Mayor's wife, a pleasant, bird-like little woman with a shrill laugh, didn't look at all like Mrs. Fitzwarren, in other words, Syd in drag.

It had all gone off extraordinarily well considering the mishaps which had occurred at the dress rehearsal, thereby affecting the performance. The trap door had failed to open to swallow up the pirates and one of the twenty local children, hired to play the rats, decided to fight the cat a little too enthusiastically and blacked her eye, with the result that every time Dick patted and petted her, she winced visibly, making him appear to be more of an anti-hero with a tendency towards animal cruelty.

The press were gushing in their praise as they lapped up the fizz and canapes and, although he knew this might be regarded by some as small beer compared to the shows which he had put on in the capital, the experience served to remind Jack of the many complexities involved in mounting one of the oldest forms of theatrical entertainment. Now, at least, he was comforted by the fact that he could return to London, secure in the knowledge that it was going to have a successful run.

"Would you direct another pantomime, Mr. Merrick?" A

young journalist from *The Stage* newspaper asked him.

"Let's get this straight," Jack said, firmly but politely. "Syd Daniels is not only a big television star, he's a director. He was responsible for plotting the whole show. I simply stepped in when Syd had his accident."

"But have you found it as rewarding as producing in the West End?"

"I think the provincial theatres are doing very well at the moment," Jack continued as Sylvia joined them. "Our colleagues over at the Opera House are booking to capacity like us and don't let us forget that the commercial theatres in the West End are difficult to run at a profit at present."

"Thank you very much, Mr. Merrick."

As the reporter closed his notebook and drifted towards a tray of freshly renewed champagne, Sylvia took Jack's arm and led him over to a couple of chairs some distance from the general hubbub.

"I wish Elizabeth was here," she said, sitting down beside him. "Why on earth didn't you insist?"

He didn't know. All he did know was that he felt peeved and quite surprised that his niece had declined to come up for the opening night. He had thought it inappropriate to be too assertive over the telephone, so that when she had told him that she was quite happy to stay where she was, he had accepted it, wondering whether he had entirely misread her character and that perhaps she was not the curious and adventurous spirit he had supposed, anxious to experience every new aspect of her changed environment.

"I'm sorry not to have met her yet again," Sylvia persisted. "What on earth is she doing with herself?"

"Whatever teenagers do. Playing records and shopping apparently."

"Who takes her shopping?" Sylvia asked him "Not Hannah, surely?"

Jack drew in his breath and said as casually as he could manage. "No, I believe Laurie – Laurie Christian has taken her. It was quite a success by all accounts."

"Laurie Christian?" Sylvia looked astonished, then waited for Jack to offer something more in the way of a sign of his own personal interest in their recently acquired client. When it was not forthcoming, she ventured, "Is that wise?"

Jack looked at her quickly. "Why ever shouldn't it be?"

Sylvia, wondering whether she'd overstepped the mark, tried to backtrack diplomatically. "No reason really. It's just that she sounds so, well, so un-worldly..."

"And you think he'll corrupt her? Is that what you mean?"

"Jack, I didn't..."

"Forget it." He felt suddenly tense and desperate to get home, although he knew he shouldn't take his frustrations out on Sylvia. After all, she was only voicing his own concerns.

"Listen," He said, trying to make amends. "Why don't you come over on Christmas day, if you're not doing anything special? Meet her then."

"I wouldn't want to intrude." Sylvia was spiky now, hurt by his earlier defensive tone.

He leaned over and planted a peck on her Arden-rouged cheek. "Don't be silly. I'd really like you to be there."

She softened, recovering some of her natural humour. "Oh no, you wouldn't."

He laughed, responding on cue, "Ooooh, yes I would."

"Is it really that close? Christmas? I haven't done a thing."

"God, neither have I?" He had always hated it, but realised that he would have to think about it soon for Elizabeth's sake.

Then, to his chagrin, he remembered that he had been given a note from Lesley earlier on this most harrowing of days when there had been barely enough time to eat or even take a leak. The Rhodesian solicitor had rung and left a message for him to make contact regarding an urgent matter, but of course he hadn't got around to it. He assumed that it concerned some news about his sister's farm, but it would just have to wait until tomorrow, for now it was nearly one in the morning and he was exhausted.

Starting with Sylvia, he performed the long-practiced routine of goodnights and gratitudes, kisses and hand shakes then excused himself from the celebrations. Choosing to walk back to the hotel, he relished the chance to try and clear his lungs of smoke and his head of the unforeseen stresses which had come at him much like those proverbial batallions over the past few weeks.

Pausing on the seafront beneath strings of twinkling Christmas lights, Jack tucked his Burberry scarf tighter around his neck, dug his hands into the deep pockets of his cashmere coat and stared out at the dark, rolling clouds which, every so often, blackened a delicate new moon hovering above a retreating tide.

The Atlantic air was icy fresh and he breathed in great gulps of it, hoping that tonight he might be able to sleep without the aid of some recently acquired sleeping pills and without constantly playing and re-playing his fantasy re-union with Laurie. This regular scenario, invoked by hungry, yet unfulfilled desires, was now reaching heights of passion that left him as bewildered and shaken as a pubescent boy after his first wet dream.

Ever since they had talked on the phone last week and he had agreed to Laurie accompanying his niece on a shopping expedition, Jack had been beset by misgivings. Was he really doing the right thing, allowing this young girl placed in his care to be in the company of a virtual stranger?

After all, what did he really know about Laurie Christian? Only that he wanted him as a lover and that could be put down to temporary insanity. Somebody must have once loved Jack the Ripper!

A finger of pain traced a line across his forehead and came to rest between his eyes. The tension was taking its toll and he wondered, as he had wondered frequently throughout his life, whether, as a man, he was too much of an island.

Maybe it was time to open up, confide in someone about his feelings and anxieties. But who would want to listen and who could he tell? That, as they said on *Beat the Clock,* was the sixty-four thousand dollar question!

It occurred to him that perhaps it should be Sylvia and that he ought to be taking her into his confidence right now instead of internalising yet again. She had always been a loyal and trustworthy business partner and friend, proving herself capable of discretion. On the other hand, probably because he sensed disapproval particularly where Laurie was concerned, he wondered about seeking professional advice. He thought back to an article he had read in the Sunday Times written by some shrink and suggesting that to bottle up emotions could have a detrimental effect on one's physical health. Okay, so that made sense, it was all the rage in America, but it was easier said than done. Jack just could not see himself lying on a couch in some thickly carpeted confessional, lulled by the soporific tones of someone who would extract three guineas an hour from him, simply for finding out that he had preferred bottled milk as a baby.

Shivering now, he began to walk briskly, his mind still crowded by past, present and future disquietude, although he told himself sternly to get a grip. Laurie was certainly no serial killer, and Elizabeth was fine.

In Hannah's words, Mr. Christian had behaved like a perfect gentleman when he called round and had given her a lovely day; that she was ecstatic about her new look and the trendy clothes she had chosen.

His job in Blackpool was finished. Time now to continue with the one waiting for him at home and which made all other work look easy. That much he knew he owed Emily and Ben, certainly Elizabeth and perhaps, even himself.

—∞—

When Hannah rang at ten past nine the following morning to tell him that Richard T. Mackenzie had once again rung the flat, Jack knew he would have to try and put in a call to Rhodesia from the hotel. A damn nuisance, as it most likely would take ages, particularly as he had simply wanted to check out straight after breakfast and get on the road.

He hung around waiting for the lines to become free and told Sylvia and Lesley, both of whom he had promised he would take back, that he was going to be delayed.

At eleven, he managed to get through and was given the news about Margaret Ainsley. The solicitor sounded stressed, suggesting that negotiations could take a long time, but that he would send a letter of authority addressed to Elizabeth, care of Jack, for her to present to The Royal Bank of Scotland in Glasgow in order to obtain the key to a safety deposit box.

Jack ended the call, his day already clouded by the fact that he would soon have to impart this latest news to his niece. And how would she respond? How much comfort would he be to her in yet another tragic situation?

He arrived on the outskirts of London at around five, dropping Lesley off in North London and Sylvia at her home in Maida Vale, then raced towards the flat, fervently hoping that the law didn't pull him up on a speeding charge which, with the way his luck was going, seemed more than a distinct possibility.

As he fumbled for his key, he could hear music coming from behind the door – *"I look at all the lonely people…"* and, as he went inside, he blinked as she came towards him almost unrecognisable from the person he had left only two and a half weeks ago.

At a glance, he took in the short, white dress with a zip running up the length of its centre, from which a plastic ring hung provocatively above her small breasts and the tight PVC boots which looked as though they had been painted on to her long legs. Her hair was much shorter and straighter which gave her face an unusually angular look, the family female cheek-bones far more pronounced.

"Hello, Uncle Jack." She smiled and he was relieved to see that at least she wasn't wearing make-up. She appeared tired though, the shadows under her eyes having returned.

"You look stunning," he told her. "A bit thin perhaps? Hasn't Hannah been feeding you?"

"I don't mind being thin," she retorted. "Laurie says it's more fashionable anyway."

He started at the mention of Laurie's name then pulled himself together. He should have expected it, although not quite so soon. "Oh, Laurie does, does he?" was all he could think to say.

"Mr. Merrick, it's grand to have you back." Hannah said as he went through to the kitchen to greet her.

"Hannah, thanks for everything. I really mean it. I don't know what I'd have done without you."

"How did it go?" Elizabeth asked tentatively as Jack's mind became momentarily distracted by the vast collection of bowls and tins, foil and greaseproof paper which covered the work-surfaces and table, alongside a pile of mincemeat, candied peel, almonds and an icing set, all part of Hannah's long-term plan to leave them well-provided for the festive season.

"It's a great success. You should have been there." He answered, hoping that it sounded like a rebuke.

"Sorry." She used a small voice and he was gratified to once again recognize the little girl who was still somewhere inside this strange and unfamiliar, young woman.

Knowing that what he had to say couldn't be postponed indefinitely, he asked Hannah to bring tea into the sitting-room as he needed to talk to his niece.

Elizabeth followed him in sheepishly, convinced that he would want to know why she hadn't joined him in Blackpool and trying to think of a plausible reason. The truth being that there was no reason which she could give him. It was only for her to know that she had not wanted to leave the flat, just in case Laurie rang and asked to see her again.

"I'm afraid I've got some more bad news. From home." There was no easy way to tell her but she made it easier by saying quite calmly.

"Great-aunt Margaret's dead."

He looked surprised. "Yes. How did you know?"

Her brow knotted into a frown. "I guessed. She was old... And ill."

"I'm sorry." He decided to spare her the details of how her great-aunt had died. Maybe he would tell her some day, but now was not the time.

He watched her as she stood up and went towards the window, pulling the heavy drapes slightly apart and gazing into the busy street below.

Hannah brought in a tray of tea and biscuits and threw her a concerned glance.

"I'll be getting a cab home in a while, Mr. Merrick. There's a cottage pie in the oven and Elizabeth can do the vegetables. They're all peeled."

"Thanks again, Hannah. See you in the morning."

"Goodbye Betsy." Elizabeth scooped up the purring cat from the sofa and kissed its glossy head before plopping her into Hannah's arms..

Jack closed the door behind the housekeeper then poured a trickle of cream into two cups.

"She's left you some money."

Elizabeth's eyes widened. "Who? Aunt Margaret?"

"No, Marilyn Monroe. Of course, who else?" He was struck by the difference between telling a child and an adult the same piece of information. There was nothing remotely avaricious or even inquisitory about her response.

"Don't you want to know how much?"

She tried to curl her hair around her finger but remembered that it was too short. "How much?"

"Well, the solicitor says that before probate – do you remember we discussed probate?"

She nodded and bit into a chocolate biscuit.

"The sum left to you will be something in the region of two hundred thousand Rhodesian pounds."

He waited for her reaction which was to finish her biscuit and then say "You're kidding, right?"

"I'm not kidding. Now, that is without the sale of the farm which apparently should be far easier to sell than your own home and should ultimately fetch more money. The fixtures and fittings, I have suggested, are all included in the sale price and indeed the furniture, if the new tenants want it. Your great-aunt has said that you have first choice on all of her personal possessions, jewellery, paintings etc. but if there are some things that you don't want and its more than likely there will be, then they will be distributed amongst her servants. You will be sent a list in due course to study and to make a choice."

She remained silent, so he took a breath and continued.

"There is also something in a deposit box in Scotland. We will probably have to go up there at some point and collect it." He sat back, quite pleased with himself for handling the matter in such a business-like and efficient manner. Also, deeply relieved that she wasn't making a scene.

"And I'll have all that when I'm twenty-one?" She asked him.

"The money, yes. And obviously your allowance will continue to come out of the interest. The personal possessions and whatever's in this box, almost certainly you can have before then. If there aren't any stocks and bonds, that is."

"Wow!" She said, picking up another biscuit, then resisting and placing it back on the plate. "So, I'm rich."

"Yes, Elizabeth. I think we can safely assume that you are rich."

"I still need a winter coat. Is that alright?" She asked tentatively.

"Of course it is. You don't have to ask about things like that."

Jack stood up and stretched. "And I need a bath. I'm sorry about Margaret. I remember her as a very nice woman."

"She was." Elizabeth said quietly.

"You must use the money in the way you think she would have approved," he told her.

"Yes."

While she washed up the tea things and heard Jack running his bath, Elizabeth tried to think of what her great-aunt would have wanted her to do with all that money. There was a phrase she used on occasions, both in later years, rocking in her wicker chair on the verandah or, when Elizabeth as a small child, under the ever-vigilant eye of her mother, would follow her around the garden while she snipped off the heads of the last crumbling, ivory roses towards the end of a scorching summer.

"Always listen to your heart, little one. Listen to your heart."

—⁓—

It wasn't so much of a letter really, as a note. Handwritten and hand-delivered to Victor at the front desk and Jack read it once again before making his second incautious move within three weeks.

'Dear Jack, welcome back! I hear the panto is a great success. Congratulations! Could we meet? There are a few things I'd like to discuss with you. Laurie.'

That night, or rather at two o'clock in the morning, Jack convinced himself that there was no longer any virtue in the protracted, self-imposed celibacy which he had been enduring. Being a romantic at heart, he had always considered love to be the necessary nourishment for the soul. And to add strength to his conviction, what he was about to do would be done out of his own particular notion of romantic love.

He recalled that Oscar Wilde had said (although, to the writer's cost, he was to learn differently) 'that man can not be always estimated on what he does. He may keep the law and yet be worthless, or he may break the law and yet be fine.'

Spurred on by this thought, Jack slipped into a loose Aran sweater and a pair of baggy, beige cords, tiptoed into the kitchen to extract a bottle of Cristal from the fridge then paused outside Elizabeth's bedroom door before letting himself out of the flat and down to the car-park.

As he drove through Soho, he marveled once again at how many people were still milling about at that time on a winter's weekday morning. Some were the old nightclub set, remnants from the 'fifties, not as many as there used to be but still enough to keep the clubs ticking over. These were a mixture of gambling aristocrats and East End gangsters, most of whom left Murray's or the Embassy in the early hours with a showgirl in tow, generally a blonde, who would uncannily be replaced a week later by a duplicate model.

It was easy for him to also recognise those singers, dancers and musicians who had just finished their floor-shows or jazz gigs and were now ready to relax in the way each of them chose. Either by smoking a joint or two, having a Chinese and a few beers, or simply getting themselves laid.

He parked the Alfa in Rupert Street and made his way to the courtyard where he knew Laurie lived. Glancing around, he noticed that the nearby strip club was just closing, although amber and rose-coloured lights still glowed through the thin curtains, behind which the Soho working girls were selling their services.

A small, shifty-looking weasel of a man in a vividly patterned silk shirt sidled out of one of the doors and headed in the direction of Shaftesbury Avenue. He might as well have a sign with 'pimp' printed on his forehead, Jack thought as he paused outside the narrow, three storey building where Laurie rented the top floor. The lower two levels looked empty, although he had heard that there had been several raids by the police on a crew shooting pornographic films there and he noticed the deep blue of the blinds on the ground floor; a dead giveaway and invitation to anyone in the know.

His finger poised to ring the bell, Jack was hit by a sudden moment of panic. He supposed Laurie was back because the lights were on, but what if he had someone up there? Someone who, because of Jack's procrastination, had been invited to give him what he suspected Laurie would not be able to do without for long.

"Courage," he told himself sternly and pressed the bell. He could hear Flora barking and then Laurie's voice came on the intercom.

"Yep?"

Jack put his lips next to the small piece of slatted metal on the wall. "Laurie, it's Jack."

A fraction of silence then he heard him say, "Jack! Come up."

The door buzzed as he pushed it open and climbed the stairs. The light switch was the kind that if you didn't make the next set of stairs before it clicked off, you were plunged into pitch darkness. He hurried now, his Hush Puppies skimming the threadbare carpet, his eyes trying to avoid the flakes of peeling paint on the none-too-pristine walls.

Breathless, but having made it to the third floor before the light expired, Jack saw that the stripped pine door at the top of the stairs was open and the object of his desire was leaning against its frame wearing a poppy-red, silk dressing gown and smoking a recently-lit cigarette.

"Well, here's a surprise... And Cristal champagne...Lovely."

As Jack moved forward, he noticed that Laurie's thick hair was slicked back rather in the style of a Spanish dancer and his glistening chest looked as though it might have just been oiled.

Jack could only gaze at him, aware that all of the pent-up and frenzied emotions so effectively controlled over the past few months were now surfacing, submarine like, from the very core of his being. His member swelled with longing, as, still speechless, he handed Laurie the champagne before being led into the dimness of his host's bed sitting-room.

"Laurie, I…"

Finding his voice, but losing all intention of romantic foreplay, Jack tore at his sweater and slacks frantically and clumsily as he was guided him towards the fur-covered bed, where Laurie removed his dressing-gown and lay beside him. Then, as the younger man slid, snake-like, further down the bed and began to tongue his erection, Jack groaned with pleasure, but pushed Laurie's head away, knowing that he was in grave danger of spilling his passion all too soon.

"You have no idea..." Jack panted, beads of perspiration beginning to form on his brow. "How much I've thought about you...Wanted you."

"Show me then." Laurie said, turning over and presenting his perfect, upturned posterior to the older man. "Show me how much you've wanted me."

Tears of passion rose in Jack's throat as he tentatively eased himself into the amazingly lubricated opening then pumped with such voracity, that when he came minutes later in quick jerking movements, he shouted "Fuck, fuck, fuck... I'm sorry. I'm so sorry."

His body quivering, he pulled out slowly and, as Laurie turned on to his back and stroked Jack's damp face, Jack lifted his head to kiss him with tender intensity, not wanting to look at the shrunken penis now resting between his legs.

"My turn now."

Gently, but firmly, Laurie rolled Jack over on to his stomach, his fingers reaching for the jar of petroleum jelly on the bedside table with which to moisten his entry.

Jack bit his lip, tensing from the intoxicating combination of anticipated ecstasy and trepidation. There was no doubt that it would be erotic, almost certainly fierce, but there was also little doubt that it was inevitable.

Laurie raised his body then began to rub his erection teasingly against Jack's buttocks, continuing for what seemed to Jack like hours. Then, without warning, Jack felt a sharp thrust causing him to let out a piercing scream and bury his face in the pillow as Laurie began to fuck him roughly then gradually slowed to a more even tempo, until all movement ceased.

"Do you want me to stop?" He asked from a position of seemingly frozen suspension.

Jack's voice was muffled but he shook his head wildly. "No, God, no."

"You want more?"

"Yes... Yes... More."

"Say please."

Jack could no longer control the tears that squeezed through the corners of his eyes. God, what imbeciles the sex act makes of us all, he thought desperately, as he begged again.

"Please... Please."

Laurie arched his back resuming the ride, slowly at first then rising once again to a pounding rhythm. As he did so, his hand found Jack's arousal and, his sense of timing impeccable, managed to bring them both to a simultaneous and vociferous climax.

Jack, now weeping openly, turned over, and stretched out his arms cradling Laurie inside them and pressing warm, salty tears against his lover's face and neck.

"I love you...I love you."

There was silence for several minutes until hearts stopped racing and limbs recovered, then Laurie got up to un-cork the champagne, bringing back two foaming glasses from which they drank thirstily.

"I need a cigarette." Jack said, wiping his eyes with the back of his hand.

"Sure." Laurie placed two Dunhills between his lips, lit them with his new lighter then handed one to Jack. "Well," he exhaled slowly. "Wonders will never cease."

Jack regained a little of his composure. "I'm sorry about... Well, you know… The crying… I only got back last night and I think I must be overtired."

"Don't worry about it." Laurie threw his dressing-gown loosely around him and yawned. "Listen, I'm starving. I think I'll make a sandwich. Do you want one?"

"No, thanks."

While Laurie refilled their glasses, Jack salvaged his underpants from the floor where they had been so passionately discarded, then joined him in the kitchen, watching while he removed two rashers of bacon from the fridge, lit the grill and placed them carefully underneath.

Unable to resist touching him, Jack moved behind him, wrapping his arms around his waist and kissing the base of his neck.

"You were wonderful."

"Watch it!" Laurie warned, slicing through a large, white loaf. "I won't be so wonderful if I lose my fingers."

"Sorry." Jack moved away as the rich waft of sizzling bacon began to fill the small room and Laurie thickly spread the bread with creamy, yellow butter.

"Are you going to stay?"

"I'd love to, but I can't. Got to get back to the flat before the porter comes on at seven."

Laurie deftly flicked the bacon over then turned to face him.

"So – when will I see you again?"

Jack moved forward to take his hands. "Soon. I promise, very soon."

"Jack, we have to talk."

Jack smiled tolerantly. "I thought we were."

Laurie turned back again to scoop the bacon from the grill before smothering it with brown sauce and folding both pieces into the bread to make two rough sandwiches. Then, taking a massive bite, he picked up his champagne glass and strolled into the bedroom as Jack followed.

"I mean..." Laurie continued, through mouthfuls of food "...Talk properly."

Jack sat down beside him on the bed, wondering again why he found this man so irresistible. His own fastidious nature would normally despise the way in which anyone talked while eating. But then, this basic act of sensuality was also reflected in the way Laurie told jokes, laughed and made love.

"What about?" He asked, his natural caution returning.

"Lots of things, Jack. Like us, for instance. Like work, for instance."

"Okay." Jack took another sip of champagne. "What's on your mind?"

Laurie dug his finger-nail between his teeth to retrieve the piece of meat which had lodged there, then chewed on it frowning.

"Bernard Moss – from the Club. He's chosen most of my numbers for this new show and they're crap. I hate them. He won't even listen to any of my suggestions, as if he knows anything about anything."

"I'm sorry, darling, but that was in the contract. Management responsible for final content. You'll make them work, I know you will."

Laurie shot Jack an accusing look. "I obviously didn't read the small print."

He gave an exaggerated sigh then carelessly rested his hand between Jack's legs, causing the now familiar stirring. "You know, Jack, Rory Lake has just bought his own club, leased it, that is. He's calling it "Rory's" and people will go just to see him fronting his own floor-show. Isn't that amazing? He's got complete and total control."

"I know what you're saying, but it's also madness to invest that much money in the current climate when clubs are actually closing down."

"But the punters come to see *me*. Moss fills the place, sells his drink, gets his money on the door because of me. I'm the attraction."

The physical pleasure Jack had once again been experiencing was suddenly capriciously withdrawn as Laurie pulled his hand away and lit another cigarette.

"I agree. And as soon as the contract comes up for renewal, I'm going to ask for more money and star billing."

"But my own club. That's what I call stardom." Laurie persisted. "Can't you see it, Jack, 'Laurie Christian's?' And I bet I'd take Grosvenor's audience with me and Rory Lake's."

"I'll think about it". Despite the amount of champagne he had drunk, Jack's mouth was dry. "What else did you want to talk about?"

"Christ, Jack, I feel like I'm being interviewed. Three minutes and then we go to a break."

Reluctant to allow the mounting tension to escalate, Jack slid his arm around Laurie's shoulders.

"I'm sorry. I don't want to fight with you. I love you. Go on, I'm listening."

However, Laurie's next question was unexpected.

"How's Elizabeth?"

"She's good. Well, she's had some more bad news, but..."

"What sort of news?'

"Another relative died. Not one of mine, an aunt on her father's side. They were very close."

Flora jumped on to the bed between them, demolishing all hopes of further sexual contact as Laurie started to pet her.

"Poor kid."

Feeling that the dog had made her point, Jack got up and reached for his clothes.

"Yes, she's had a rough time. The good news is at least she's set up for the future. Financially, that is."

"Really? Well, that is good." Laurie shook the last dregs from the bottle into his glass. "I was going to suggest that we had lunch, the three of us. Might be fun."

Jack stared at him, swallowing a flutter of nervous unease. "I don't know..."

"Oh, come on..." Laurie continued enthusiastically. "It's not as if I haven't met her, and..."

"Yes." Jack interrupted. "Thank you for that. She really enjoyed it."

"It was a pleasure. So, how about it then? Tomorrow?"

Jack suddenly felt cold, wishing that he could reward Laurie with the answer he wanted to hear. The odour of illicit sex pervaded the small room and the glow from the fuscia bulbs highlighted the Tunisian colour scheme of chocolate and terracotta, giving it a rather decadent luminance.

"I'd like to, but I really don't think I can."

Laurie's sulky expression returned. "Why on earth not?"

"I don't expect you to understand. I don't really understand myself, but I need time for this. It's such an unusual situation. I have a young girl living with me, my late sister's child whom I don't really know. She has the same name as my mother – the same features – for God's sake. And she's looking to me as someone who will shape her future. Give her guidance." Jack moved to the bedside table and took a cigarette out of the packet, lighting it with Laurie's lighter which he now studied approvingly.

Laurie's expression was scornful as Jack continued.

"I would love to be able to sit at a table in a restuarant tomorrow with you and Elizabeth. There's actually nothing that would please me more. But I know that I can't. I won't be able to look at you or even talk to you without remembering our love making and I know I'll bloody well give myself away. I'll be expected to act normally and make small talk. And all the time I'll be aware of you and how I feel about you, with my niece right there beside me. I know it's pathetic but I just can't do it."

Laurie stared for a moment then, extricating himself from a sleeping Flora, dropped on to the floor in a cross-legged position in front of him.

"I just thought..." He said, rather like a child trying to coax a parent into allowing it to stay up late, "... That if you and I are going to continue as, well, as an item and she's going to be with you for the duration, the sooner we all have some time together, the easier it will be for everybody."

Jack placed his hand under Laurie's chin and cupped his face towards him, bending to kiss him fully on his wine-and-nicotine-scented mouth.

"We are an item. Just give me time. I really appreciate it if you feel like showing Elizabeth around until she starts school and it helps me when I'm working. She likes you and of course that's important to me. It'll all work out somehow. I promise."

—∽—

When Jack called her into the sitting room at eleven o'clock that morning to say that Laurie was on the phone, Elizabeth decided to act super-cool, asking him to hold on while she finished addressing an air mail envelope to Chloe.

Last night she had said her prayers for the first time in ages and, although she felt a bit guilty for having left it for so long, she considered them to be as heartfelt as when she had first prayed for her poor, murdered parents, deeply concerned that such a sudden and violent end might mean they had died in a state of un-absolved sin and could now be languishing in Purgatory.

As her mother had been raised a Catholic and her father, although he called himself a protestant, was secretly an atheist, an amiable compromise had been reached whereby, although Elizabeth accompanied her mother regularly to Mass and took Communion, she also attended the local Church of England Sunday school along with many of her school friends. Still, there had been one incident which had brought her to the edge of a stormy exchange with her mother, when Elizabeth had willfully resisted going through the ritual of confirmation, finding the notion of becoming a child-bride of Christ, a puzzling and slightly unsavoury one.

With her father's support, they had eventually won her mother round, something which was to become more and more common during the following few years.

So, last night, her prayers had fallen somewhere between the traditional, starting with the Ave Maria, and the silently conversational, calling on God once again to bless her parents, along with great-aunt Margaret and her husband Sam, then Chloe and her family and finishing up with Uncle Jack and Hannah. She had thought carefully about voicing her final prayer, thinking that God might find it irreverent, but then it struck her that anyone with the name of Christian would automatically be granted impunity. "Please, let me see him again soon?" she had asked earnestly then adding in a whisper, "he's the only person who makes me feel alive."

Now she was delighted and curious to know why he was ringing her. Taking the phone from Jack, she said in the most grown-up voice she could manage.

"Hello, Elizabeth speaking."

"Are you doing anything today?" He asked.

"Nothing special," she replied. "Why?"

"Have you ever had Chinese?"

She hesitated for a moment. "Chinese what?"

From the other side of the room, sitting at his antique, roll-top desk, Jack heard Laurie's deep chuckle and glanced up.

"Food, silly."

"No," she said, feeling foolish. She didn't remember ever having seen someone Chinese, let alone tasted their food. "Why?"

"How do you fancy a Chinese lunch followed by a bit of Christmas shopping?"

"Just us?" She asked, looking over at Jack, who appeared to be immersed in the process of studying and signing papers.

"I've invited Jack." Laurie told her. "He says he's too busy."

"Alright then."

"Good. I'll pick you up in an hour."

"See you later, alligator," Elizabeth said, not realising that this particular catch-phrase had gone out of fashion in England in the early sixties when Bill Haley stopped making hit records. With little acknowledgement to Jack, she rushed into her room to sort out what to wear, throwing clothes into a pile on to the bed before finally opting for the dress with the colourful squiggles and the deeply unsuitable white platform shoes which she had brought with her from home.

Laurie didn't come up. Elizabeth met him in the lobby where he stood with his back towards her, gazing out of the double glass doors through which she could see his reflection. She thought he looked extraordinarily handsome in tight charcoal trousers, a black leather jacket and a purple velvet John Lennon cap.

"Hello," she said timidly, unable to control the warm blush which was creeping from her hairline across her forehead and down to her cheeks.

"Hello, gorgeous." He turned and smiled at her and she was disconcerted to find that her stomach once again seemed to be lurching alarmingly.

As they crossed the road and got into the Mini, Jack watched them from the window wishing that he had the courage to join them. It was debatable however whether he would have had the physical strength even if he had the courage, for he was almost incoherent with tiredness after arriving back at the flat around six-thirty, fully prepared to explain that he had just popped out for a newspaper, should anyone have spotted him. Then, dozing fitfully until his alarm went off at nine, he had greeted Hannah and Elizabeth looking nothing like a man who had just woken from eight hours sleep in his own bed.

The grey density that had dominated the late November days had now given way to crisp, cold and what Elizabeth had always imagined as seasonal English weather. The sky was an icy blue with bubbly white clouds and Laurie explained that she was now experiencing the West End of London in all its pre-Christmas splendour.

This became evident as they drove along Regent Street, where the windows of all the major stores had undergone a festive metamorphosis which highlighted their wares, in order to seduce every serious Christmas shopper or casual passer-by. Unnaturally green trees shimmered with elaborate ornamental decorations and tantalisingly wrapped boxes. Fairy lights winked and glittered to the accompaniment of carol-singing choirs, and in Liberty and Swan and Edgar, plaster models were arranged to create Dickension and Nativity scenes, uncomfortably reminding Elizabeth both of her embarrassing experience at St.Hilda's and her inner tussle with religion.

When they arrived at the Soho restuarant she realised that Laurie must be a regular visitor, as the rotund and inscrutable maître d', dressed in a white jacket and dark trousers (much to Elizabeth's surprise, for she had expected nothing less than the flowing silk robes of a Mandarin) gave them both a friendly welcome.

"Hello, Mr. Christian..."

"Hello, Michael. Is my usual table free?"

"Certainly, sir."

The manager clicked his fingers and this time Elizabeth was not to be disappointed. A young Chinese girl, her exquisite face framed by ebony shoulder-length hair and wearing a long dress of vermilion and black silk with a slit running down each side, led them over to a table in a quiet corner of the room.

Elizabeth gazed around her, taking in this very unique atmosphere with pleasure and fascination. The wall covering was designed to resemble bamboo and was hand-painted with delicate patterns of willow trees bending over small bridges, where expensively gowned ladies smiled enigmatically beneath their sunshades. Chinese hieroglyphics edged the design and there were gleaming lacquered cabinets on which jade vases sprouted long-stemmed, white silk roses.

Above her head and indeed, hanging from the restuarant ceiling in magnificent profusion, were fringed silk lanterns in the most glorious shades of yellow, emerald green and scarlet.

As before he was her teacher, giving her answers to unvoiced questions.

"The Imperial colours of China. The brightest in the world."

"Have you been to China?" She asked, breathlessly.

He slid a silver lighter from his jacket pocket and lit a cigarette. "Many years ago. I visited Shanghai when I was in the Merchant Navy."

"How wonderful," was all she could think to say, feeling suddenly awkward and inept.

He picked up the enormous menu and studied it briefly.

"I think I'd better choose for both of us. Is that okay?"

"Yes. Yes, please."

When he had given the order to a rather stout Chinese waiter, mysteriously from a list of numbers, he asked if she would like something to drink.

"Um..." She considered carefully. "Perhaps a cup of tea?"

"Good idea. Jasmine tea for two, please Li?"

As she opened her mouth to enquire about Jasmine tea, a tall, white-haired man in a dark-blue business suit approached them, smiling in recognition.

"Hello, Laurie..."

Laurie half rose, then shook the man's extended hand. "Ted. Good to see you."

The stranger gazed at Elizabeth. "Is this one of your young ladies?"

"No Ted, no. This is Elizabeth. She's my agent's niece. From Rhodesia."

Ted once again held out his hand, which Elizabeth took, trying to work out what his question could mean.

"Pleased to meet you, Elizabeth," he told her. "I was in Rhodesia a few years ago. It's all changing now, I gather?"

She nodded, uncharacteristically tongue-tied as the waiter brought the tea, and the man patted Laurie's shoulder and moved away.

"See you, Ted." Laurie turned back to focus all his attention on her as she watched the waiter fill two small bone china cups from a large, brown tea-pot which had a chip on its spout and she wondered why, in surroundings which seemed so finely tuned to oriental delicacy, tea should be served from this ugly old pot.

She took her cue from Laurie as he raised his cup and sipped, then peered into it, wondering whether she should ask for a tea strainer as a few long leaves were still swimming around inside. He didn't seem to notice so she kept quiet, trying not to swallow them and attempting to savour the tea's not unpleasant, fragrant taste. But some of her enjoyment had already been marred by the appearance of the man called Ted. Was Laurie in the habit of bringing lots of girls into this restuarant? And if he was, then why should she be surprised? He was so handsome and clever that it was more of a surprise that he didn't have a girlfriend or indeed wasn't married. But that odd, casual phrase "one of your young ladies" had produced a strange, sour feeling in the pit of her stomach, which she realised to her dismay was jealousy, in all its legendary destructiveness.

He caught her looking at him and enquired, "Is everything alright?"

Without warning, the reticence which seemed to have inexplicably invaded her personality was swiftly swept aside by the old, familiar out-spokeness and, to her shocked amazement, she heard herself almost demanding, "What young ladies?"

He looked puzzled for a moment then burst out laughing, nearly choking on his tea. "Ted was referring to some of the girls – in my show. We sometimes eat in here, as a Company. You should be flattered, they're very glamorous."

Elizabeth stared at him disbelievingly. "He thought that I was a showgirl?"

"He's crazy," Laurie said, dropping his voice. "Even though your hair and the way you dress add a few years on to your age, it's so obvious that you're not. Anyway…" he added smiling, his face close to hers. "I would never have you in one of my shows."

"Why not?" She asked curiously, wondering whether to be pleased or offended.

"Your tits are too small."

He sat back in his chair to welcome the arrival of a massive tray of sizzling food, which thankfully saved the embarrassment of her inability to comment.

Warm-cheeked and pondering on this very personal and perhaps back-handed compliment, Elizabeth watched and listened as the waiter, along with Laurie, discussed, distributed and dissected the enormous volume of foreign-looking food, whose aroma, nevertheless, was beginning to stir her appetite.

"Right." Laurie said decisively, when the waiter had moved away and planted what seemed to be a large bone covered in deep, red sauce on her plate. "It's spare rib of pork and best eaten with your hands. This..." he said, pointing to a small bowl of water with a slice of lemon floating on the top, "is a finger-bowl. Just dip your fingers in here to clean them."

Elizabeth picked up the rib and bit into it, aware that the sauce was covering her chin but noticing that Laurie was also getting messy. Hungry now, she devoured another then rinsed her fingers and sat back as he consumed two more.

"Now," he said, patting his mouth with a large, white napkin. "Let's get stuck in."

She tensed as he reached over to gently wipe a stray driblet from her cheek with his finger then turned his attention to the dishes bubbling gently on the steel hot-plate, folding some dark, sliced meat into something round and soft, resembling a pancake. He then spooned a portion of thick, fruity sauce on top and handed it to her.

"Crispy duck with Hoisin sauce," he said. "Try it."

Again, the flavour and the texture was like nothing she had ever tasted and again she came back for more. He then picked up two of the thin bamboo sticks which lay next to their plates and held them between his fore-fingers and thumb, balancing them within his right hand. "These are chopsticks. You use them like this, see?"

Elizabeth positioned her sticks up carefully, trying to copy the way he held them then blushed again as he placed his hand over hers in order to help her. "Alright?" he asked and she nodded as he tipped more food on to her plate "Sweet and sour prawns and rice. Now, eat them with your chopsticks."

She hesitated, studying closely as he expertly correlated the small, crispy balls of food between the sticks and popped them into his mouth. Tentatively, she tried it and managed to pick one up, crunching on it with pleasure and triumph while he looked on approvingly. Slowly becoming more confident, she dug into a lump of sticky rice and lifted it eagerly, only to let it fall just before it reached her lips. To her horror, particles of rice flew across the table and settled in Laurie's hair. "Oh, no," she said, miserably. "I'm so sorry."

She waited for his reaction with trepidation, for he was once again wiping his mouth, but when he removed the napkin she saw to her deep relief that he was shaking with laughter.

Elizabeth's natural sense of mischief then also embraced the moment and she joined in, helping him to remove the offending clumps of rice. Tears of laughter ran down their faces while their fellow diners, unable to avoid witnessing this genuine display of mirth, observed them with amused interest.

Catching his breath, Laurie beckoned the waiter for water and clean napkins as Elizabeth suddenly stopped laughing and stared at him, the realisation of what she was feeling seeming to explode like a million fire-crackers in her brain.

'I want to tell him I love him,' she told herself with such passionate conviction that she wondered for one dreadful moment whether she had, in fact, uttered the words. As she watched him talking to the waiter, the way he used his hands to express himself, she knew that there was no other man in the world who would laugh with her about something so trivial. Who else would take the time to explain new and fascinating things to her and understood how to make her feel special? The closeness, the tender longing and the sheer heart-stopping excitement which she had experienced while sharing this meal with him was overwhelming and because she had felt nothing resembling these emotions before in her life, more than a little scary. 'I love you, Laurie Christian,' she thought again, 'And I'm going to tell you so one day.'

Somehow she pulled herself together and he asked if she'd finished eating.

"I'm so full, I can hardly move," she said happily as he settled the bill and the pretty Chinese girl helped her into her raincoat.

"You'd better." He stuck his purple cap on his head at a jaunty angle then pushed open the swing doors and led her out into the biting December air. "Carnaby Street, here we come."

—◊—

Jack eased himself into the deep green, pine-scented foam with which he had over-immersed his bath water and closed his eyes.

Although he longed to repeat the activities of the night before, he also longed for sleep and had already made the decision to slip out of the house again as soon as an opportunity presented itself and when his equilibrium had been suitably revived.

Professionally, it had been a good day for he had managed to catch up on a mound of paper-work which Sylvia had sent over and, most importantly had finally closed a long-running and frustrating negotiation, a profitable co-production deal with the States, whereby Sammy Davis Jr. would appear for a four-week season at the Palladium in late March, with Merrick Management providing the supporting acts and receiving a percentage of all television appearances.

He could hear the familiar harmonies of Lennon and McCartney coming from Elizabeth's room played on her decrepit Dansette and was guiltily glad that she had decided to spend the evening in there so that he wouldn't have to entertain her. She had arrived back at the flat with several bulging carrier bags and wearing a sophisticated, salmon-pink coat with military-like silver buttons. Surprisingly, this outfit didn't clash with her coppery hair, leading Jack to admit once again that although the decor in Laurie's flat left much to be desired, his very particular sense of style which he was now bestowing on Elizabeth, was irreproachable.

She hadn't wanted supper, so he had eaten his medium rare steak and chips on a tray in front of the television while watching a couple of his clients in a popular nineteenth-century family saga and reminded himself that as a teenager she would feel the need to be alone and that he would respect her privacy.

Now, lying in the dull glaucous water, for the foam had long dispersed, he forced himself to think about the dreaded forthcoming event called Christmas and whether perhaps he should decorate the flat and buy a tree, something which he had never done in his life.

There was also the little matter of presents, for he had been a creature of habit in that department for as many years as he could remember. A bonus for the dozen or so staff at Merrick Management, Harrods vouchers and Chanel No.5 for Sylvia, a crate of champagne for each of his top artists, extra cash for Hannah and a cheque to Emily. It had all been quite effortless, but now he realised that he would have to give Elizabeth something more tangible, for the gift of money seemed pointless bearing in mind the extent of her inheritance.

He decided to ask Sylvia's advice then thought better of it. He knew exactly what his partner's reaction would be. "Ask her what she wants." Well, he would do that later when he wished her good night. At least, it would give him one less thing to worry about.

He stood up and reached for the large, plum-coloured bath sheet from the heated rail which, as he wrapped it around his wet body, brought back hazy memories of a child's warm, comfort blanket, tearfully depended on very long ago.

Then, of course, there was Laurie. Always Laurie. First and foremost in his mind, waking and sleeping. And he knew then that if events hadn't intervened, they probably would have been spending Christmas together, almost certainly in bed, surfacing for only the most primal functions.

His eyelids felt heavy and he brushed his teeth vigorously, knowing that if he started going down that particular road, sleep would never find him. Slipping into a white monogrammed bathrobe, coincidentally a Christmas present from Sylvia last year, he crossed the hallway to Elizabeth's room and tapped at the door.

"I've finished in the bathroom." He spoke loudly to be heard above the ever-plaintive tale of *Eleanor Rigby*.

He was about to turn away when Elizabeth peered out, cosily child-like in her well-worn, pink dressing gown.

"Uncle Jack, can I have some more money tomorrow?" she asked him.

"Yes, I suppose so. How much?" It seemed feasible that she had spent the five hundred pounds he left with her three weeks ago on all those clothes as well as an expensive hairdresser. "I've got forty in notes. Is that alright?"

"Um..." She thought for a moment, wrinkling up her freckled nose. "Not really. I was thinking of another five."

"Forty-five. Okay."

She made a different funny face and he looked at her in surprise as she said. "No, hundred. Another five hundred."

"Whatever do you need all that for?"

"Christmas presents," she told him, "and one in particular. Yours."

He heard himself spluttering in embarrassment. "Don't be silly. You don't have to buy me anything. Certainly nothing that costs that much!"

Pulling the door further open, she beckoned to him and he was amazed to see how cluttered the room had become since he had last ventured inside, the accumulation of much of the paraphernalia that had arrived from Rhodesia.

The yellow bear, Rufus, had been joined on the bed by a vast selection of fluffy and cuddly toys, as well as dolls; china-white with pink cheeks and flaxen hair and little black ones with large doleful eyes and sprouting corkscrew curls. Not one space remained on the window-sill nor on the densely packed dressing and bedside tables. Photographs, both ancient and modern, were propped precariously on top of various books, which ranged from nursery rhymes, Enid Blyton stories and pictorial histories of Africa to poetry collections and Lambs' tales from Shakespeare.

He bent to study a dog-eared, black and white photograph, recognising himself as a small boy in short trousers with Emily and their parents at the seaside, taken some considerable time before the war, making sandcastles.

"Good heavens!"

"That's you, isn't it?" His niece said, smiling one of her winning smiles. "I could tell it was you."

He straightened up, a little unsettled by this unexpected confrontation with his past. "I had more hair then."

She laughed, whipping a sugar-pink feathered boa out of a carrier bag and holding it up admiringly. "Look what I bought Chloe."

"Very nice," Jack said, softening. "Listen, I'll get a hundred from the bank tomorrow. Your allowance starts after Christmas and that way you can begin to save for personal things."

She knelt down on the floor, replacing records that were scattered across the carpet into their respective covers.

"That's not enough. Uncle Jack, I know there's something you'd like. Laurie told me. He said that if he could afford to buy it for you, he would. And I had no idea what to get you. So I suggested I pay half and we give you a joint present." She looked up and, although her eyes were questioning, he also sensed steely determination.

Flummoxed once again by the mention of Laurie's name and of this unforeseen conspiracy, Jack stuttered. "I don't know what he's talking about. But I don't want either of you spending your money..."

Suddenly she stretched up and kissed his cheek, interrupting his flow.

"Now, now, Uncle Jack. I hope we're not going to quarrel. Please get me my money, there's a poppet."

Jack's overworked brain tried to wrestle with this latest dilemma. If he weakened and gave in to her on this issue, it would be all the harder to put his foot down in future. He had always considered 'start as you mean to go on' a fairly wise policy. But was he being ungracious? After all, it wasn't *his* money and it would be spent on something special for him. A Christmas present, which Laurie thought he would like and which was apparently expensive.

"Okay... Three hundred. That is going to have to do."

She shrugged "I suppose it will, then."

He attempted to lighten the mood. "More to the point, what can I get for you?"

She finished putting her records away and jumped on to the bed, causing the assorted toys to bounce up and down alarmingly. "My room. I'd love a new room."

Jack nodded slowly but was reluctant to see the demise of what he considered a very attractive second bedroom which had only recently been re-decorated. "What do you want to do to it?"

"Everything. More shelves. Different colours. Everything."

"Alright, if that's what you want for Christmas, that's fine.

I'll give the decorators a call tomorrow and you can tell them what you'd like."

"Super. Thanks, Uncle Jack. By the way, I keep meaning to ask – what are we doing for Christmas?"

"Well, we'll be here, of course. Hannah's prepared lots of lovely food. I'll order a turkey from Harrods and a tree, if you like. Sylvia's coming round. She's really looking forward to meeting you."

Empowered by her exhilarating day and the sweet secret to which she had now admitted, she asked innocently, "Is Sylvia your girlfriend?"

Jack laughed, perhaps, he thought afterwards a little too heartily. "Whatever makes you think that? No, I've told you, she works with me. Has done for years. She was my secretary before you were born."

Elizabeth looked at him cheekily. "Well, she could still be your girlfriend?"

"I'm sorry to disappoint you," he told her. "I don't have a girlfriend."

"Oh." Elizabeth decided not to take it any further. "Okay, then."

But she hit him with the stinger just as he had said goodnight and was leaving the room.

"Oh, Uncle Jack, shall we invite Laurie over for Christmas day? He says he's working on Christmas Eve and Boxing Day and isn't doing anything special. I said I'd ask you. Please…?"

—⁓—

Sylvia struggled out of bed trying to ignore the burning sore throat and the headache that felt like a hangover, but most certainly was not. Not unless you could blame one glass of white wine followed by a cup of Earl Grey imbibed on the previous evening as a possible cause.

The sneezing fit that followed convinced her that all the symptoms pointed to a bout of flu, there was some horrendous Vietnamese strain going around, although how any virus could slip across the world, while its country of origin was being bombed out of existence by the U.S. Air Force, was beyond her comprehension.

She recalled the last time she had contracted flu, about three years ago, but had kept going due to the enormous pressure of work and not wanting to let Jack down. That noble effort was eventually rewarded by two weeks in bed with what could only be described as a near-death experience, making her now realise that if she was wanted to avoid that particular unhappy confinement, she should spend today at home on a diet of Beechams and whisky in an attempt to sweat the damn bug out.

At least things at work were reasonably under control. The Sammy Davis deal, closed yesterday, was now to be followed up by the usual paperwork and she and Jack had signed the company's Christmas cards which the secretaries would be getting off today, along with any outstanding contracts. This evening, she had planned to see one of their actors in the Oscar Wilde revival of *An Ideal Husband,* one of the few current West End productions which was putting bums on seats, but that would have to wait. It was possible that Jack might want to take Elizabeth but then Jack, at the moment, was hard to read.

In her small bathroom where a dense array of pot plants nestled against orange and white Conran tiles, Sylvia poured a measure of TCP into a glass, added some water and threw back her head, indulging in a one minute gargle, at the same time wondering if her concern for Jack was misplaced. In Blackpool his usual calmness and expertise were palpable, but beneath the surface she sensed that raging conflicts were bubbling, ready to erupt at any moment. She had also noticed, over the last few months, the number of times he had appeared to be on the verge of tears and that, of course Sylvia recognised all too well as a mark of depression.

She stared at her pale reflection in the mirror, trying not to make comparisons or to allow memories that were long out of season to come flowing painfully back, but if something, somewhere was telling her that this was the time to remember, then so be it.

She wandered into the bedroom and lay down on the unmade bed, closing her eyes. His name had been Peter. Peter Shaugnessy. Irish, charming and the love of her life…

It was in January 1954, that the twenty-six year old secretary took a chance and moved from one of the biggest theatrical agencies in the country with a young agent called Jack Merrick into a one-room office above a camera shop in the Tottenham Court Road.

Her new boss had been cautiously astute in the process of setting up on his own, ensuring that the impressive list of variety artists whom he represented would follow him willingly and of their own accord, rather than his seeming to lure them away from his previous employer. Within six months, most had joined him and, in addition, he had chosen a select few of the acting fraternity to expand the agency's scope.

One of this latter bunch was a young actor from Galway who had cut his thespian teeth in no less illustrious venues than The Gate and Abbey theatres in Dublin and who, on a richly golden, late summer's evening, had strolled into the office just as they were about to pack up for the weekend.

After showing them his list of credits, he asked Jack if he could read for him and, when Jack agreed, mysteriously and wonderfully pulled out an extract from the Budd Schulburg screenplay of *On the Waterfront*, the gripping true story of the stevedores and dockers of New York harbour. Reading the Brando part of Terry, with Jack reading Charley and Sylvia as the Eva Marie Saint heroine, Peter Shaugnessy proved that evening to be a sensitive interpretor, instinctively penetrating the depth of human experience, and an impressed Jack offered to represent him immediately. Within one week he had auditioned successfully for a part in a film starring Laurence Harvey and Stanley Baker and within two weeks he and Sylvia were dating.

The autumn that rolled into winter and then into the following spring gave Sylvia the happiest eight months of her life. She moved out of her parents' home in Middlesex and she and Peter found an affordable little flat just off the Brompton

Road, where he read her Yeats and introduced her to Guinness, while she played him traditional jazz and convinced him of the wondrous vocal technique of Frank Sinatra. During the weeks when he was filming at Pinewood, she lovingly and painstakingly prepared gourmet dinners for his return, accompanied by candles, flowers and wine, before taking him through his script for the following day.

The procedure was reversed when he had finished the film and was spending most of his days at auditions. For her, he would conjure up rich Irish stews filled, it seemed, with every vegetable that had ever been grown, or would roast a chicken in garlic, butter and honey, so that the skin was deliciously crisp and salty-sweet.

Sylvia had parted with her long-protected virginity without a second thought, for their relationship seemed as natural as the elements which surrounded her and, even though their religious differences caused her parents' some concern, David and Betty Lawrence couldn't help but appreciate the happiness this softly-spoken and good-looking young man had brought to their daughter. For Sylvia's sake, they embraced him as one of the family, and he was a regular visitor at their Wembley home for Friday night Sabbath dinners.

In April 1955, Peter was invited back to Dublin for a twelve-week season, to play the demanding role of Christy Mahon in J.M. Synge's *Playboy of the Western World*. Sylvia, devastated that they would be apart for so long, immediately begged Jack if she could take two weeks of her holiday, so at least the separation would be shortened. Her head, however, told her heart that as accommodating as Jack tried to be, this was a challenging time for the agency with a new commercial television channel launching later that year, for which they were poised to supply a healthy number of light-entertainment and dramatic performers.

If the promised contracts were fulfilled, then Sylvia would be made a full partner, another agent would be taken on to look after scriptwriters and they would move into more spacious offices. But at the moment, Sylvia was an all-important lever, helping to steer these components in the right direction for

Merrick Management's future, and taking time off was not a realistic option.

Then, on a Friday evening, when Peter had been in Dublin for two weeks, Jack came over to her desk and dropped a long, white envelope into her tray.

"What's this?" She looked up enquiringly as he gave a non-committal shrug.

Sylvia frowned then began to peel it open, uttering a shriek of joy when she saw the Aer Lingus tickets inside.

"You fly out tomorrow," he told her. "Only until Wednesday, I'm afraid. I can't spare you for any longer. But at least you'll have the weekend and a couple of days."

"Thank you," she said and gave him an awkward hug. This was the first time in the six years she had worked for him that she and Jack had really shared any physical affection.

He became embarrassed and stepped back, saying bashfully, "Never let it be said that I stand in the way of true love."

That evening, Sylvia decided that her trip to see Peter would be a surprise. The plane was due into Dublin at three forty-five and by the time she arrived at the theatre, the matinee would probably just have finished. Throwing her prettiest frocks and her sexiest nightie into a case, she washed and brushed her long, chestnut hair till it gleamed and spent the night in a state of sleepless excitement and anticipation. Even her practical tendancies had been abandoned, for although she knew that Peter was rooming in Dublin with another actor, she simply assumed that there would be space for her, and if not, then they would spend the next few days in a hotel at Sylvia's expense.

The taxi dropped her at the theatre just as the afternoon audience was leaving and, clutching her suitcase, she made her way to the stage-door, standing behind four other people patiently presenting themselves to the custodian, a wild-haired, pixie-faced man of latter years, who was consulting a lengthy rota attached to a clip-board.

"I'm a friend of Peter Shaugnessy, from London," she said with authority. "And I want to surprise him."

"Number one, up the stairs."

The harassed leprechaun looked doubtful, but waved her through the swing doors where Sylvia immediately became absorbed in the unique, skin-tingling aroma of backstage theatre, with all its vibrancy and multiple emotions. She had been around artists long enough to know that it was a drug that lingers in the dust and threatens to get into the blood, if allowed.

Members of the cast, still in costume, pushed past her, laughing. Young men in rough grey shirts, baggy trousers and laced boots, with coloured handkerchiefs knotted around their necks and girls in the dark, peasant dresses of County Mayo draped with carmine-red shawls.

Somehow, although she knew by now she should be used to it, Sylvia felt self-conscious in this atmosphere. It was different when she was behind a desk dealing with actors, for then she was in control. Here, she was an outsider in their exclusive and fiercely guarded space.

Her heart hammering with excitement, Sylvia hesitated for a micro-second before knocking on the dressing-room door marked No.1, where someone had stuck a cardboard star painted gold and which had slid halfway down its worn, painted veneer.

"Come in."

It wasn't Peter's voice but Sylvia opened the door anyway and when she saw the young, auburn-haired woman holding a small child, she turned to leave.

"I'm sorry... I wanted Peter Shaugnessy's dressing room."

"That's right." The girl's accent was West coast, lilting. "He'll be back in a minute."

The child started to cry and the woman soothed it by rocking it gently. "Ssh, ssh Clare. Ssh, ssh now."

Bewildered, but trying not to allow the creeping icy wave of dread to envelop her, Sylvia asked haltingly.

"And... Sorry, you are...?"

The girl extended her free hand and smiled. "Maureen, Maureen Shaugnessy. Did you see the play?"

"No." Sylvia was trembling now, praying that what she feared could not be so. "I've just come from London." She took a deep breath. "Your little girl. She's lovely."

Maureen Shaugnessy's laugh was tinkling, just the right laugh Sylvia observed numbly, to come from such a delicate frame.

"Sometimes she is. Though I'm afraid she's her father's daughter alright! Say hello, Clare."

She held the rosy-cheeked cherub up high in the air till it chortled with joy then, out of the corner of her eye, Sylvia saw Peter coming along the corridor towards the dressing room.

She turned to look at the man to whom she had given all her love and who had just broken her heart.

"Sylvia!" He was still in costume, his hair tousled. In one hand he held a bottle of Guinness, in the other a towel and his face told her all she needed to know. "What are you doing here?"

Wanting to scream and cry and swear at him, but most of all to ask why, Sylvia struggled to maintain her composure. She glanced across at his wife and drew upon all her willpower to force a smile. "Who says your agent can't come and see you? But I've got a plane to catch. I have to go..."

As she ran from the room and hurried down the stairs, she heard him calling after her.

"Sylvia, come back. It's not what it seems. Sylvia..."

For the remainder of that weekend and the whole of a thundery and rain-soaked Monday, Sylvia wandered through the cosy flat she had shared so idyllically with Peter, drinking Chianti and listening to Sinatra singing endless ballads of love found and lost. Her body ached from the lonely rhythm of desolation, her head throbbed mercilessly and when she did manage to sleep, she woke hurting from the deep and torturous agony of loss.

How could she not have known? When the despair and humiliation briefly subsided, the far more positive emotion of steaming anger raged against him and against herself for her naivety. Blindly, and because she had been so in love, she had given him her unquestioning trust. Because she recognised that actors had to be penny careful, she had willingly paid for most of their living expenses. Now, she realised that he had obviously been sending money home to his young family.

But why had she never asked about his past? Was it because that deep down she didn't want to know the truth? "You fool," she said loudly, through mingled gulps of tears and wine. "You bloody idiot, Lawrence!"

On the Tuesday morning with red-rimmed eyes woefully accentuating her blanched face, she went into work where Jack regarded her with surprise, but said nothing until she was ready to tell him what had happened later that week.

Then he had listened in his quietly supportive way, not asking any questions except what could he do to help and when, a few months later, Peter received a lucrative offer from Hollywood, Jack released him from his contract without a fight, his name never again mentioned within the agency.

For Sylvia, work was now the fundamental necessity for her life-support kit. She knew she was good at it and she was fortunate enough to love it, so she regarded herself luckier than most. And work, although often fraught with difficulties, would give her back her identity, for she vowed that nothing and nobody would ever take over or take away her sense of self-worth again.

The following years saw the agency grow and flourish and she and Jack achieved a closeness that was indisputable. Eventually she realised that he was homosexual, although to many in and outside of the business they were often looked upon as a couple, which she felt suited Jack at a time when a nervous phobia towards such inclination was rife. It also, perhaps, Sylvia selfishly reflected, suited her, for although in bleaker moments when she considered her spinster status to be something permanent and choosing never again to experience the thrills and the torment of love, she could at least rely on Jack's agreeable company for most occasions; a man who was intelligent, reasonably attractive and above all, caring and considerate.

Now, she had to admit she was worried about him. Although, as her mother used to say, a Jewish girl always needs someone to worry about. She told herself that she should be glad that he had found a potential partner, for her worries had often centred around the way in which she guessed he spent his weekends, surreptitiously cruising for unsuitable sexual liasons. And her fear of his possible arrest by the police, or worse, being beaten up by some butch navvy approached down by the docks, melted into relief when he arrived unharmed in the office on Monday morning.

Sylvia got up from the bed and turned the thermostat on her heater to maximum, wondering what it was about Laurie Christian that made her so uneasy? Was it simply the bitter realisation that in a coarser, far more basic way, he reminded her of Peter? Aside from similar physical characteristics, the come-to-bed eyes and the perfect, sensuous mouth that most women would die to wear on their faces, there was that same sweet persuasiveness, the flattering tongue from which flowed endless silver blandishments. But most of all, she wondered, was it because they were performers and therefore such credible pretenders? The mask-wearers who possessed a natural ability to present different faces to different people, possibly for their own selfish ends.

Sylvia didn't believe in premonitions. She left all that psychic nonsense to the more susceptible of their creative and artistic clients. But she did believe in her own intuition and right at this moment it was telling her very strongly that not only was Jack in danger of being hurt, but around him hung the gloomy vapour of tragedy.

—⚬—

"It's a Burmese ruby, sir. The finest example of its kind."

The youthful salesman who had delivered the lighter and who was now displaying distinct signs of acne, held the 22 carat tie-pin up to the light, where Elizabeth and Laurie could observe the stone gleaming between two medium-sized diamonds and which set off the piece of antique jewellery to perfection.

She wondered at the way its colour alternated from rosy pale to ox-blood dark and was inexplicably reminded of the rich shade of port wine which Uncle Jack kept in a crystal decanter and which he occasionally drank after dinner, accompanied by a sliver of blue-veined cheese.

"And you are sure this was what Mr. Merrick admired when he came in?" Laurie asked.

"Yes, sir. Most definitely. Said how magnificent he thought it was, and how he might treat himself to it one day."

"Good. Then it should be a nice surprise." Laurie reached in his wallet and removed three fifty pound notes as the jeweller placed the tie-pin inside a small, black velvet box then proceeded to deftly gift-wrap it in green and gold striped paper, topped by a silky gold ribbon.

"Here..." Elizabeth handed Laurie the same amount, her agreed half of the cost of Jack's present, which her uncle had drawn out of her bank account that morning. She had always taken far more pleasure from giving rather than receiving presents at Christmas and was looking forward to seeing the expression on his face the following weekend when he opened his unexpected gift. Now, filled to the brim with the fervour of her feelings for Laurie, she watched as he dealt with the payment and asked the assistant. "What time do you close?"

"Five-thirty, sir."

Buttoning up his leather jacket, he turned towards her. "What else have you got to do today?"

"Um." She hesitated as she had simply allocated the whole afternoon to being with him. "Nothing really. Uncle Jack's at the office because Sylvia's ill. I've got to be back by six as it's Hannah's last day and I want to give her a Christmas present."

"I've got an idea. Why don't we catch the early showing of *Dr. Zhivago* at the Odeon? We can swing by here around five to pick up Jack's gift. Would you like to see *Dr. Zhivago?*"

Elizabeth stared at him, her legs weakening as once again he tore the wind from her sails. Of course she had heard about *Dr. Zhivago*. Everyone was talking about it on radio and television and there were billboards everywhere. The mere thought of sitting beside him in a darkened cinema and watching something which was supposed to be so romantic, was almost beyond excitement.

Aware that he was waiting for her reply, she could only nod

and say, "Yes please," in a tiny voice. If there was one thing that she detested about being in love, it was the way in which she became so shy in his presence. An alien characteristic that her late parents, her friends at home and indeed herself, would never have believed possible.

The cinema was stuffy and she removed her new coat, folding it neatly on to her lap as he passed her a box of Black Magic, with the warning not to get chocolate over her clothes.

For some reason, this made her feel chastised and confused. How utterly stupid she was in believing that being here was anything more than another kind gesture on the part of her uncle's friend to entertain her. In that split second he had reduced her love-lorn fantasies to that of a mundane discipline between adult and child.

"Don't get all messed up, little girl, otherwise you will be scolded."

But as the curtains swept apart and the lights faded, he smiled and squeezed her hand, dispelling all negative speculation and her spirits soared with joy as the stirring sound of a huge orchestra flooded through the blackness surrounding them.

For the next two hours Elizabeth was carried on a wave of visual emotions, the like of which she had never known.

It wasn't just the story of passionate and forbidden love that made her cry, but the way it seductively combined with revolution and rebellion. Something about blood on virgin snow stirred and bewildered her simultaneously. She longed to be as beautiful as Julie Christie and kissed by a man with smouldering eyes.

He passed her his handkerchief and she noticed that he too seemed tearful. Aware of him so close to her, she had fought against burying her head on his shoulder and, during the love scenes, fantasised that it was she and Laurie who were so desperate to be together, never wanting to part.

She was still quiet and absorbed as they walked back to Asprey's and when they reached the flat, she told him she was fine when he asked if something was wrong.

"Elizabeth, do you want me to come up?"

"No, thank you."

Not waiting for the lift, she scaled the eight flights of stairs and breathlessly hurtled through the front door, hearing her uncle and Hannah talking in the kitchen.

"Ah, there she is now." Jack wandered out to greet her then stopped when he saw how flustered she appeared to be.

"Are you okay?" He asked with concern.

"Fine. We went to see a film. *Doctor Zhivago.*"

"Didn't you like it?"

"I loved it." She said tremulously, as Jack looked doubtful.

"Did Laurie see you home?"

"Of course."

Hannah appeared behind him, her uncanny knack of saving a situation once again proving invaluable.

"Oh, it's a wonderful film. Very, very sad. I saw it the other night with my friend. We wept buckets. Come and have a cup of tea, hen, it'll make you feel better."

Elizabeth smiled through her tears. "Thanks Hannah. I'll be through in a minute."

Inside her room, she leaned back against the door and drew in a deep breath which caught on a sob and made her cough.

Firmly ordering her mirror image to pull herself together, Elizabeth opened a drawer where a gift box of Potter and Moore's lavender soap, talc, bath cubes and scent lay covered by her underwear. She then found a roll of wrapping paper patterned with dancing reindeers, carefully cut it to size and, after doing battle with a length of Scotch tape, managed to tie the whole thing up with silver string. The Christmas card she had chosen showed a black cat gazing unrealistically sweetly at a plump robin and inside she wrote 'To Hannah and Betsy, with lots of love from Elizabeth,' drew three crosses beneath her greeting then licked and sealed the envelope.

Jack called to her through the door.

"Hannah's off now, Elizabeth. Are you coming out?"

Wishing that she had some make-up with which to subdue her flushed, tearstained face, Elizabeth emerged to find Jack helping the housekeeper into her coat.

"Happy Christmas, Hannah," she said, holding out the present and the card.

"Thank you, hen. But, you know, it's the New Year that we really celebrate. More than Christmas."

They hugged one another and Hannah reciprocated by handing Elizabeth a package, which felt as though it could be a book.

Elizabeth, remembering her own Scottish relations, enquired of Jack. "Are we celebrating the New Year?"

Jack looked blank as though the imminent approach of another year was something he had never considered "Yes... If you want to."

She couldn't wait to be alone that night to reflect on her intoxicatingly eventful day. Lying in bed with the room lit by the small lamp on her bedside table, the curtains un-drawn so that she could watch a new moon against a backdrop of frosty stars, she realised just how much she had wanted Laurie to kiss her. And not just to kiss her, but to touch her in those most forbidden and secret places.

Elizabeth squirmed restlessly, unable to sleep or to lie still as this new and mysterious awareness crept over every inch of her body. She closed her eyes then slowly raised her fingers to stroke her breasts which, while she imagined they were Laurie's fingers, made her nipples grow harder, springing magically to life with each caress.

She heard herself gasp as tentatively she moved her hand lower, then parted her legs, pushing her forefinger into the warm moistness which she found there. Visualising his eyes looking into hers and his mouth almost on her own, she gasped again, inserting another finger and penetrating more deeply, the excitement which the action provoked giving her the most intense pleasure she had ever known.

"Laurie, I love you," she whispered then suddenly jumped, opened her eyes and swiftly withdrew her wet fingers as a harsh, indistinguishable sound, shook her out of her reverie.

In the now silent room she could hear as well as feel the intense thudding of her heart and she lay rigidly, a shiver passing from the nape of her neck down to her feet while experiencing a mixture of acute guilt and self-consciousness. Also the feeling that she was being observed by unseen eyes.

'God is watching,' she thought despairingly. 'He's watching me being wicked and he's put a stop to it.'

After what seemed like hours her tension began to subside and she stretched and sat up, wondering now what had interrupted that all too brief moment of ecstasy.

The clock showed ten past two and the room was cold when she got out of bed and went to the window, looking down into the forecourt of the building which was quiet and deserted of any human presence. But something was missing, something which she had seen before getting into bed, and it took her only seconds to realise what it was. Jack's car wasn't there. The very conspicuous red sports car was gone from the spot where it had been parked earlier that evening.

Curious now, Elizabeth pulled on her dressing-gown, opened her bedroom door and peered out into pitch darkness. Flicking down the switch, the hall flooded with light, causing her to blink and she stood for a moment outside Jack's bedroom, listening for any sound which might be coming from inside.

But she knew, was practically convinced, that his room was empty. That for whatever reason her uncle had gone out and left her locked inside the flat.

Although she didn't care one way or the other about being left alone, it seemed so out of character and it suddenly occurred to her that perhaps the car had been stolen. It was expensive, she was certain of that. Uncle Jack said it was unique, a collectors' item, so some thief could have fancied their chances and taken it when they considered it to be the safest time.

Uncertain as to what to do next, she steeled her nerve and tapped softly on Jack's door. Gaining courage, she tapped louder then wrapped her fingers around the chunky cut-glass handle and slowly pushed the door open.

The room was half-lit by moonlight which shone on to an obviously undisturbed bed, its navy-blue counterpane and pillows pristinely made-up, and the ticking from the large, brass alarm clock emphasizing the empty stillness.

She had only seen his room when the door had been open as Hannah was cleaning and she looked around now, taking in the shelves lined with books, the trouser press containing a pair of neatly folded, grey trousers and the many pictures dotted over the walls, their styles a mixture of modernist and impressionist, as in the sitting-room.

Suddenly feeling like a criminal intruder, Elizabeth stepped back, closing the door behind her and wondering again where her uncle could be. Gone to a party, perhaps? And had he done this before at this rather mystical hour, when it was neither night nor morning? Usually, she was tucked up and sleeping peacefully by now, not wide awake and burning with love.

Then it struck her that maybe her uncle could be keeping a secret assignation. Perhaps, like herself, he was in love with someone and he would wait until she was asleep to meet whoever it was that he wanted to be with. That was fair enough, Elizabeth conceded, for after seeing *Dr. Zhivago,* she now vehemently favoured secret assignations.

She decided to have another look at the photograph in the sitting-room, the only clue she had to her uncle's possible romantic relationship. The picture of the glamorous blonde whom he had not wanted to discuss. But when she peered into the alcove she saw that its place had been substituted by one of Jack at Buckingham Palace having just received his OBE.

The other silver-framed images were still there as far as she could remember, not added to or replaced. Only that particular one was missing, and she frowned, not wanting to be wrong in her desired supposition.

It would be great if Uncle Jack had a girlfriend. It might distract him enough from noticing how close she and Laurie were becoming, although, she thought stubbornly, it was him that brought them together in the first place so he'd have no reason to complain. Only, of course about the fact that in his eyes, she would appear too young to be thinking of love.

Overwhelmed suddenly by tiredness, Elizabeth wandered back into her bedroom, glancing again out of the window before pulling the curtains and crawling into bed.

For the first time since leaving Rhodesia, her dreams were unconnected to her parents, her home or her friends. The soft blurring heat which hovered over fields brimming with mealies and which she always tried to visualise before closing her eyes, was tonight replaced by the vision of herself in snow-boots and fur, trudging through the winter landscape to be with her lover.

—∾—

"They seem to be getting on well." Mark Dover filled a transparent cup with fruit punch from an elaborate silver bowl and handed one to Jack. "You don't have to have this you know, there's plenty of champagne."

"No, it's alright, I'll stick with what the kids are having."

Three hours of sleep were definitely not enough, he told himself sternly, and he was finding that as he grew older, alcohol exacerbated the fatigue, making him feel as if he were already nursing a giant hangover.

He sipped the agreeably warm citrus and strawberry concoction and studied Elizabeth and Josephine who were talking together in a corner of the room. Well, it seemed that Mark's daughter was doing most of the talking, as he had already noticed Elizabeth cramming chocolate caramels into her mouth, which somewhat impeded conversation.

Mark and Judy's Christmas gathering was mostly a non-pro affair, doubling as well as a birthday party for Josephine and with only himself and Sylvia, who had not yet arrived, invited as both friends and colleagues..

There was also the irritating addition of some noisy little boys of around five and six, who were running about waving balloons and blowing paper bugles, and who had been asked along to keep the Dovers' young son, Sean, company.

Jack wondered what on earth his niece was wearing, for she stood out quite dramatically from the other girls. Apart from one fairly hefty young teenager who should never have been allowed near a mini-dress, they all looked quite conservative in their frilly party frocks or knee length skirts.

Whatever it was, it suited her. He had thought when he glanced at her before they left the flat, that she was looking vaguely comical; a combination somewhere between Max Miller and James Cagney. But the wide, black trousers, brilliant white shirt and spotted kipper tie gave her a look of individuality which made him strangely proud, and she caught him looking across and waved, flashing a dazzling smile.

In a moment, she was at his side.

"Are you having a nice time?" He enquired, as she swayed around to The Monkees belting out *I'm a Believer.*

"Yeah, okay."

"How do you like Josephine and her friends?"

"They're okay."

"Will they all be in your class next term?"

She shrugged. "I think so."

"So this is Elizabeth…?"

He turned as Sylvia came up behind him and kissed his cheek. She was holding a flute of champagne, and, he thought, appeared slimmer than she had for ages in a chic little black dress which he was sure bore an expensive designer label.

"… At last."

Jack made the introductions as Sylvia and Elizabeth shook hands.

"I love the gear," Sylvia told her. "I saw a picture of Twiggy wearing almost the same outfit last week."

"Really?" Elizabeth's eyes widened with pleasure.

Sylvia moved forward to finger the tie. "Where did you get it?"

"Bazaar."

"Of course. I should have known."

"Excuse me, can I borrow Elizabeth?" Judy Dover, the pretty forty-year old ex-dancer interrupted them. "It's time to cut Josephine's cake and do the usual with the candles and the song."

As she drew Elizabeth away towards the group of girls, Sylvia took a long sip of champagne.

"She's something special, Jack. Look after her."

"I'm doing my best."

"I know you are." Sylvia slipped her arm through his in an affectionate squeeze.

From the corner of the room where Josephine Dover was busy blowing out fifteen blue candles to cheers and laughter, Elizabeth watched her uncle and the very nice woman called Sylvia with over-curious interest.

—∽—

Right up until Christmas Eve, although Elizabeth had prayed for snow, it continued to rain relentlessly and, with only a day to go, she had to concede that she was now highly unlikely to get her wish.

The decorators had just finished her room and Uncle Jack had kept his promise and allowed her to have free rein with the colour scheme, although she could have sworn that she noticed his face pale when he peeped in two days ago. The three walls, having been stripped and re-painted in glossy black and saffron yellow, were almost completely covered with posters of the Beatles together with all her photographs and postcards. A white, feathery Biba lampshade hung from the ceiling, with another shading the table-light, and the curtains and bedspread were patterned with spinning black records, which resembled flying saucers. He'd said he approved of the shelves though, which now housed her books and dolls and with only Rufus still taking pride of place on the bed.

A huge tree had arrived and, beside it, Jack had dumped four boxes of decorations. He had suggested that she started hanging the tinsel ribbons and baubles as far up the tree as possible then he would arrange the lights and take over from where she could no longer reach. This was okay, Elizabeth thought, but it denied her the pleasure of planting the beautiful little alabaster angel with the flaxen hair on the top most branch.

She hadn't heard from Laurie since their outing to the pictures last week, and now the anticipation of seeing him tomorrow was both unsettling and thrilling. It was a pity, though, that there had been no opportunity to buy him a present, but she hoped he would understand how difficult it was for her to get to any shops privately and alone.

"Try not to spill too many needles on the carpet." Jack called across to her from his desk, as thoughts of Laurie caused her to lose concentration and catch her hair on one of the branches.

"It's okay," she told him. "They don't come off yet. In a few days..."

It struck her as odd in a country which grew fir trees, that she should be educating him about needle shedding, but she had decorated so many imported ones over the years with her mother and father, and had sat on her father's shoulders with her legs crossed in front of her, precariously hanging paper chains in every room. Joseph and his cousin Sarah, who had been their maid, had helped too, and they all sang carols along to old records of her mother's as the heat of the day took the thermometer swinging towards 100 degrees.

Dear Joseph. He had become almost like a member of the family and it still hurt her to wonder whether maybe he had known who had entered the farmhouse on that terrible day and committed such a violent act.

"Shouldn't we be putting presents underneath?" She asked, determined to push any sad thoughts back into the recesses of her mind where such things should be stored at this pleasant time of the year.

Jack nodded. "Yes, if you go to the hall cupboard, they're in there. Two for Sylvia, one for Laurie and two for you."

"Two for me? I thought I'd had mine? The room?"

Her uncle smiled. "Well, there are a couple of small surprises as well. Something to open tomorrow morning."

She suddenly felt so close to him in a warm, family way, that it was on the tip of her tongue to ask 'Where do you go at nights, Uncle Jack? It's okay, you can tell me. I'm very good at keeping secrets.'

What a lesson in control she had learned over the past few weeks, but for just how long could she be expected to keep it up?

—⚭—

Jack knew that he would have to go wherever the day decided to take him. How, he wondered again as he guided the razor across the thick foam that covered his stubble, had he allowed himself to get into this situation, whereby both Sylvia and Laurie had been invited over for Christmas day?

It was the last thing he would have done. A state of affairs which he would have fought against with every ounce of his willpower, but now it was happening and there was sod all he could do about it. He couldn't un-invite either of them at this stage without giving offence, and he had hoped up until the eleventh hour that one of them might call to cancel.

Why on earth had Elizabeth asked Laurie? Although she wasn't to have known how awkward it would be for him, and Laurie had obviously played the sympathy card to which she would have responded. Certainly his lover had confirmed over these last few days that he was greatly looking forward to the occasion.

Jack splashed warm water on his face and patted it with a soft towel.

His plan was to ply Sylvia with plenty of booze and to have as little as possible himself. That way, she would be less likely to get irritated by Laurie and he, Jack, would be less likely to let his mask slip.

It seemed odd on this Christmas morning not to be placing a call to Rhodesia and waiting for Emily's anxious voice to come on the line, either before or after she had attended Mass. But if it was odd for him, he wondered how Elizabeth would feel, spending her first Christmas without either of her parents. He resolved that he would try to give her the best Christmas he could and that everything and everybody else would be secondary to her enjoyment.

He emerged from the bathroom to be greeted by a hug and a kiss.

"Happy Christmas, Uncle Jack."

"Happy Christmas, Elizabeth."

"Are we opening presents now or later?"

"I thought we'd open them when the others got here, but you can open one of yours now, if you like?"

"Oh, can I?"

He followed her into the sitting room, where he admired once again their joint handiwork on the tree which stood softly glowing in the corner. She positioned herself on the floor and pointed questioningly towards the two gifts he had bought her.

He feigned a difficult decision. "Ummm... The little one."

He watched as she carefully unwrapped the paper and took out the small box containing the present he had chosen.

"What is it?" She asked him.

"You'll have to open it to find out."

With great concentration she lifted the heart-shaped locket out of the box and held it swinging from its fine golden chain in front of her eyes, as though in an act of self-hypnotism.

"It's lovely," she said looking at him appreciatively, then bent her head. "What's inside?"

"Nothing yet," he told her. "I thought you might like to put a photo of your parents in there."

"Yes," she said seriously, slipping it over her head "Thank you, Uncle Jack. I really love it."

"Good. But it will look better on you when you're dressed. That old dressing-gown doesn't do it justice."

Pleased at her pleasure he glanced at the clock.

"Well, duty calls. I've got a date with a turkey."

"What time are they coming?" She asked, still fingering the locket.

"Sylvia said she'd be here by eleven, to help with the lunch."

"And Laurie?"

"About twelve-thirty."

Sylvia arrived as they were arranging the festive napkins and crackers on the table, and sweeping in wearing a long, tartan taffeta skirt and white lace blouse, she kissed Elizabeth, accepted a dry sherry from Jack and looked around the room with obvious surprise.

"Heavens, Jack. I never thought I'd see the day..."

"It's only a few Christmas decorations," he told her.

"A few!" Sylvia exclaimed. "It's like the fairy grotto at Harrods."

"Look what Uncle Jack bought me!" Elizabeth displayed the pendant, now looking far more effective against her electric blue, crocheted mini-dress.

"Oh, Jack, that is gorgeous. Are we opening presents now or waiting for more guests?"

"Only one more guest," Jack tried to keep his tone casual, realising that it had probably been a mistake not to have told Sylvia before the day arrived. "Laurie Christian. He and Elizabeth have become good friends."

He had to hand it to his partner. Apart from throwing him a 'who do you think you're kidding?' look, she took the news in her stride. "Oh... Laurie. Well, it'll be nice to see him again."

"Just the four of us," Elizabeth surprised him by saying, as she carefully placed four Edinburgh crystal glasses on the silver coasters.

"Lead me to the kitchen," Sylvia told Jack. "Let's see what's got to be done."

While Elizabeth and Sylvia began preparing the vegetables, Jack basted the turkey then removed a highly alcoholic fruit and almond pudding covered in muslin from the larder. This was an item which he remembered from previous years as Hannah's *piece de resistance*. Then, as the clock ticked nearer to twelve-thirty, his palate became dry and the palms of his hands started to sweat. He badly needed a drink but didn't dare, as it could excite his emotions further.

"What did Hannah say I had to do with this, do you remember?" He asked Elizabeth in desperation.

"Steam it!" Two female voices replied in chorus then broke into peals of laughter as the door bell rang and all three looked at one another in sudden silence.

"Well, don't just stand there," Sylvia ordered. "Open the door."

"I'll go," Elizabeth said, charging out of the kitchen.

"No, Elizabeth," Sylvia warned her. "Victor isn't on the desk today. Anybody could have come up."

"For heavens' sake," Jack said, ignoring both of them and thrusting the pudding at Sylvia. "I'll go."

The first moment he'd been dreading had arrived and he opened the door to a smiling Laurie, devastatingly good-looking in a jade velvet jacket and bearing gifts beneath one arm, while his beloved pooch nestled under the other.

"Happy Christmas, Jack."

"Happy Christmas."

Longing to greet him with an embrace, Jack stepped back quickly and almost trod on his niece, who was hovering behind.

"How's my favourite girl?"

"I'm fine," Elizabeth giggled, accepting a lick from Flora.

"How did you know I meant you?" Laurie asked with a dead-pan expression then noticing her uncertainty, laughed and hugged her. "Silly, I'm only joking."

"Hello, Laurie."

Sylvia came out of the kitchen and Jack held his breath. This was the second moment he had been dreading, but they both surprised him.

"Sylvia. Happy Christmas."

They exchanged air kisses as Jack cleared his throat.

"Drinks everyone? Come in and make yourselves comfortable."

"Can I have some?" Elizabeth enquired, as Jack started to pour champagne for Sylvia and Laurie.

"Alright. But only half a glass."

"Oh, don't be a spoilsport," Laurie rebuked him. "It's Christmas day."

"Sip it slowly and make it last," said Sylvia, pragmatically.

Jack watched as Elizabeth took a sip then held her nose.

"Bubbles. Up my nose."

Laurie laughed. "Everyone says that the first time they taste champagne."

"Now," Jack said, keeping an eye on his niece who was most certainly not taking Sylvia's advice and had already emptied her glass. "Shall we open the presents before lunch or afterwards?"

"Oh, before, before," squealed Elizabeth.

Jack, whose life-long dislike for Christmas, along with his desire for Laurie was to be well-concealed today, watched as his niece, his partner and his lover unwrapped their various presents and cooed their gratitude.

"Oh, Jack… A Harrods voucher and Chanel. Thank you."

"Jack, this is fabulous," Laurie held the cream cashmere

sweater against his chest as Elizabeth slipped on the other present Jack had given her, a white T-shirt displaying colour photographs of the Beatles.

"Uncle Jack, I shall never take this off," she told him, but he had sensed for a while that the fab four had ceased to be the centre of her universe.

Sylvia had bought her a pretty plastic handbag, coincidentally in the same colour blue as the dress she was wearing. It had large, plastic daisies stitched on to it and the young girl clearly loved it. But Jack wasn't too sure about Laurie's present for Elizabeth, although she seemed ecstatic.

"Look, Uncle Jack. Make-up and nail varnish."

She proffered the Mary Quant palette of powder, blusher and lip gloss, plus a chunky bottle of blueberry liquid.

"So I see." He was all too aware that he sounded like a Victorian grandfather.

"Only to experiment with," Laurie re-assured him. 'Not for school or anything like that."

"I should hope not."

She had already begun to paint her nails and breathed on them fiercely in order to allow them to dry.

"Your turn now, Uncle Jack. Come on everybody."

Jack obediently opened his first present which was from Sylvia, a water colour of Hyde Park showing in the far right corner the block of flats where he lived.

"How very thoughtful. Thank you, darling. " He kissed her as Elizabeth danced around in front of him, waving a small green and gold package.

"It's from Laurie and me," she said as Jack opened it curiously. When he saw what was inside, his surprise was genuine.

"How on earth did you know...?" He examined the ruby pin admiringly then gestured to Sylvia to fix it on to his red, silk tie.

"We did some detective work," said Laurie, stepping back to study the effect. "I must say it looks great."

"You shouldn't have. It must have cost a lot of money. But thank you both. It's exquisite."

He hugged Elizabeth and awkwardly shook hands with

Laurie who threw back his head and laughed. Jack frowned him a warning, then called them to the table for lunch.

The meal, much to Jack's relief, was free of catastrophe and surprisingly convivial and relaxed. And, while no-one would have intentionally brought up the subject of Rhodesia and all that it implied, Elizabeth opened the conversation, talking effusively with warmth and humour about the country in which she had spent her young life and to which Laurie and Sylvia responded with interest. Once again, Jack was forced to admire her courage and her amazing ability to chat and interact with adults whom she had only known for a short time.

She asked for more champagne with her food and, egged on by the others, he gave in while they wanted to know why he was drinking only lemonade.

"I've overdone it a bit lately," he lied. "Maybe later"

"Listen… Listen…" Elizabeth called out, suddenly demanding attention. "When is a door not a door?"

Jack groaned. "I don't believe it. Those crackers cost me a fortune and they give me that old chestnut."

"No, listen… It's not what you think." His niece, flushed now from the wine, jumped up and came to stand by his chair. "When it's a swing. Get it?"

"Oh, I see," Sylvia nodded, as Laurie and Jack looked puzzled. "A swing door."

"Well, it's still pretty dreadful," Laurie said, dismissively. "See if you can get this one? Why did the chicken cross the road to see the football match?"

"Because the referee shouted fowl," Jack and Sylvia yelled, then roared with laughter.

"I'm going to get my money back." Jack picked up the remnants of the torn crackers and pushed their contents – a key-ring, some dice and a pair of cuff-links into a neat little pile on the table.

"I've found a three-penny bit in Hannah's pudding," Elizabeth exclaimed with wonder, holding the rather tarnished coin in the air.

"Keep it, it'll bring good luck." Laurie told her.

"That was a wonderful meal." Sylvia stood up, stretched, then sank on to the settee, kicking off her black stilettos. "I'm bursting."

"A toast..." said Laurie, raising his glass. "To Jack, Elizabeth and an absent Hannah for a great Christmas dinner. Thank you..."

"Hear, hear," Sylvia endorsed. "But I'm not getting up again. Sorry."

Jack managed a smile and began to clear away the dishes from the table.

"Oh, Jack, you're not going to do that now," Laurie chided. "For heavens sake, relax. Have some champagne."

Jack hesitated, his life-long aversion to mess and untidiness as strong as ever, then shrugged philosophically. Perhaps now, when the most dreaded part of the day was over, the sitting down at table where things could have been said which might have caused embarrassment or regret, it was time to ease up.
He held out his glass for Laurie to fill and their fingers touched briefly, igniting his body's craving.

"More for me." Elizabeth placed herself between them, pushing her glass against the neck of the bottle.

"You've had quite enough, young lady." Jack told her. "Have a bitter lemon or a coffee."

"What's on television?" asked Sylvia, as his niece pouted and flopped down beside her.

"Nothing much, just the Queen and Cliff Richard." Laurie giggled and squeezed himself into the small space next to Elizabeth while surreptitiously passing Flora a piece of moist turkey.

"Well, there's a choice!" Sylvia was also laughing and Jack tensed slightly as Elizabeth joined in the laughter. Perhaps he had let his guard down too soon. Elizabeth could not possibly have understood that humorous innuendo. Once again, he was reminded of the dynamics that were at play within this small gathering as he nervously lit a cigar and took his place in the arm-chair facing them.

"What about a game?" He enquired, and Elizabeth clapped her hands.

"I hope you're not going to suggest 'Charades'." Sylvia said dryly, to which Laurie, who was just about to light a Dunhill with his silver lighter spluttered, dropping the cigarette on to the settee.

"What about Gin Rummy?" Elizabeth asked excitedly.

Jack frowned. "I was thinking more along the lines of Snakes and Ladders or Monopoly."

Elizabeth groaned. "Uncle Jack, you are such a square. I used to play Rummy every Christmas with mummy and daddy. It's fun."

"Alright." Reluctantly, he went to the chest of drawers and found two packs of playing cards which he shuffled and dealt on to the coffee table.

His eyes were drawn to her fingernails which shone like bruised fruit as they clipped the edge of the cards. He wondered if perhaps he should allow her to win, and whether the others had harboured the same idea. In the event, he needn't have wasted his sympathetic energy as Elizabeth, either by luck or by skill, and he guessed it was the latter, trounced them all, laying out sequences of the same suits and sets of the same denominations, one after another like a hardened professional until, chortling with delight, she announced that she had had enough.

"You're a dark horse," Laurie told her. "What other secrets do you have up your sleeve?"

This question seemed to quieten his niece and Jack broke the silence by suggesting a walk, which went down like a soprano at a stag night.

"In these shoes?" scoffed Sylvia.

"In this weather?" said Laurie.

The only one who looked interested was Flora, who wagged her tail when she heard the magic word.

"Now, see what you've done," Laurie told him, then was immediately distracted by something hanging above the fireplace, thereby directing Jack's attention to it at the same time. "Well,

Jack," he asked tauntingly. "And just who is supposed to kiss who?"

Jack caught his breath in amazement. However the mistletoe had got there, he hadn't been responsible. He remembered it being delivered with some decorative holly but he thought he had binned it for the obvious provocative reasons. To avoid the sort of incriminating confrontation, laughingly disguised, of which Laurie was about to take advantage.

"Come on, Jack." Noticing his face redden, Sylvia pulled him to his feet. "*Kush kula wush kulah.*"

"What?!" Laurie and Elizabeth looked at one another then doubled up with mirth.

"It's bastard Yiddish," she enlightened them. "If you'll forgive the expression. Roughly translated, it means give us a kiss for Christmas." She held on to Jack's hands, moving closer towards him then, appearing to kiss his cheek, whispered in his ear. "It's alright. Don't worry."

He smiled gratefully and they broke apart, as to his surprise his niece jumped up, dragging Laurie with her.

"Come on, Laurie. Our turn now."

Laurie glanced across at Jack, as Elizabeth wound her arms tightly around his neck.

"Kush kula whatever, Laurie?" Her playful invitation became a command as she closed her eyes.

Jack and Sylvia watched in astonishment as Laurie laughed then placed his lips against her forehead.

"Not like that," Elizabeth opened her eyes and pulled him closer. "Like Omar Shariff and Julie Christie."

Jack's heart began to race, the sensation of warm bile rising in his throat, and he looked on in stunned disbelief as his lover did as instructed. Closing his eyes and holding the young girl's body tightly against his own, Laurie kissed her with a sexual intensity, his tongue obviously exploring her mouth. It lasted no longer than a few seconds, but for Jack who had watched as if in slow motion, it felt like forever.

Laurie gently released himself from Elizabeth's grip and drew back, as Jack continued to stare at them, dumbfounded.

"I'll make coffee." Sylvia's clear voice cut through the uneasy silence. "I'll never be able to drive home unless I sober up soon."

"No." Jack said sharply then made a supreme effort to soften his tone. "You stay here with Elizabeth. Laurie and I will make the coffee."

As Laurie followed him into the kitchen, Jack closed the door and confronted him, a mixture of bewilderment and pain blazing in his eyes.

"What in hell's name was all that about?" His frustration accelerated as Laurie pretended not to understand.

"What?"

"You know damn well what. You and Elizabeth?"

Laurie laughed and Jack clenched his fists.

"Jack, relax. That was nothing. It's just an adolescent crush. That and the champagne."

Jack moved closer, wanting to strike and kiss him simultaneously. "I don't care if she does have a crush. It's how you handle it. That was out of order and… Unforgivable."

"Jack, you really are over reacting. The kid's lonely. I've given her a little fun, that's all. She probably even thinks of me as a father figure."

Jack laughed scornfully. "Oh, yes, that was really a fatherly kiss you just gave her. Listen, Laurie, if anyone's going to be her father figure it's me. I can't allow her emotions to be tossed about any more. She's starting to re-build her life after the most horrific trauma." He drew in his breath as he made his decision. "You mustn't see her again."

Laurie held up his hands as if in surrender. "Okay, okay, if that's what you want. But it's a shame for her."

Jack heard the door open behind him and turned around as Elizabeth came into the kitchen, her eyes questioning each of their faces.

"What are you two talking about so seriously on Christmas day?"

"Nothing." Jack told her, as Laurie filled the kettle. "Laurie will be leaving soon, that's all."

His stomach churned as he saw how much this had upset her.

"Oh, not yet." She stood next to Laurie and touched his arm. "Please stay longer. Please?"

Laurie turned to face her, his expression belying the raw exchange which had just taken place.

"Sorry sweetheart," he chirped. "Got to visit my old mum. You wouldn't like me not to see my mum on Christmas day, now would you?"

"No." Elizabeth shook her head, but there were tears in her eyes.

"Take this in to Sylvia, would you, Elizabeth?" Jack intercepted, handing her a tray containing the coffee percolator and three cups.

"What about New Year's Eve?" She then asked quietly.

Jack observed her with bleak sadness. She'd got it bad, this teenage crush, and he could only blame himself. Why, oh why, hadn't he had the foresight to see this was coming, or even noticed it was there?

"I'm working." Laurie said bluntly, relieving him of an answer.

"Oh."

She wore her disappointment like an open wound, and Jack was poignantly reminded of Emily at the same age when told by their mother that the family dog had died.

"Take the tray in, there's a good girl."

Elizabeth did as she was told, as Jack threw Laurie a look of gratitude, his rage slowly subsiding.

"Thank you."

"Don't mention it. So... I suppose I'd better get off."

He popped his head around the sitting-room door making his excuses to Sylvia and bidding a subdued Elizabeth goodbye, before meeting Jack in the hallway.

"I do wish I didn't love you." Jack said quietly.

Laurie moved as if to kiss him, but Jack held him away.

"See you soon then, Jack."

"Goodbye."

Feeling older than Father Time, Jack accepted a cup of strong, black coffee from Sylvia.

"I've got a headache," Elizabeth announced. "I think I'll go to bed."

"Alright." He wasn't going to try and dissuade her. "You know where the aspirin are?"

"Yep."

"Goodnight, then."

"Goodnight."

They watched her leave the room and Sylvia leaned back into the settee, waiting for him to speak.

"I know, I know. You did try to warn me."

"Oh, Jack, I'm not going to say 'I told you so'. It's not the end of the world. Teenage love. She'll get over it."

A trio of light palpitations danced across his chest but he ignored them, sipping his hot coffee with a frown.

"But why him, Sylvia? Of all people"

"Well, who else has she met? Come on, Jack, it'll all be forgotten when she starts school."

"She's obviously much more needy than I thought. God, I'm hopeless."

Sylvia shifted up on the settee to move closer to his chair. "You're not hopeless. I've already told you, I think you're doing brilliantly. You've taken on one hell of a difficult task. Nobody I know envies you, they all think you've got the hardest job in the world. For heavens' sake, give yourself a break."

"He makes me happy, Sylvia." He suddenly blurted out, as a group of carol singers struck up *In the Bleak Midwinter* in the forecourt below. He had never come this close to revealing the secrets of his heart but the time, the place and the circumstances seemed now to have dictated it.

Sylvia laid her hand on his, as the glow from the Christmas tree, the sound of Christina Rosetti's solitary poem encapsulated in an emotive melody and the cold rain splattering against the windows, filled them both with the comfort of trust and friendship.

"That's alright then," she told him softly.

—◊◊—

Elizabeth barely moved from her room for the next two days. She had pretended to have another headache when Jack suggested they went to the theatre to see *The Sound of Music* and had mooched about playing her favourite records, while trying to work out how she could have allowed such a careless, though undeniably wonderful mistake to happen.

She knew she must never drink alcohol again. That had been the cause, for it had filled her with a different kind of courage than she would normally have possessed. Courage that prompted the audacity to invite Laurie to kiss her in front of Uncle Jack and Sylvia.

Somehow, she had romantically imagined that she and Laurie might have found some time alone together on Christmas day. That was why she had climbed up the ladder to hang the mistletoe in the first place. She shuddered at the memory, realising with regret that it may have spoiled everything. But then, how could she regret giving herself up completely to that moment? If she closed her eyes now she could still taste his kiss in her mouth, smell the tangy, fragrant aroma of his after shave and feel his arms holding her as if he would never let go.

He loved her a little bit, she was convinced of that from the way he had kissed her. And if he felt the same, then surely he would find some way to contact her, for although she couldn't prove it, she was pretty sure that Uncle Jack had warned him off. She lay on her back, gazing up at the frothy lampshade. Fully dressed in jeans and her Beatles T-shirt, she had put on a little foundation and lip gloss from the palette which Laurie had given her. Uncle Jack was in the next room, already getting back to work, making overseas calls and doing deals.

It was a funny time, she thought, this period between Christmas and the New Year, when people who worked in shops and offices were returning for just a few days before celebrating again. It seemed even stranger in such a cold, wet country, when there appeared to be nothing else for them to do but work and drink.

Elizabeth tried to assess the agony she was now going through with the loss of her home and her family. It was pain of a very different kind. Somehow there was something so final about seeing people you loved lying dead, then stepping on to an aeroplane to go and live somewhere far away. It had been horrid and unreal, but she had always known that she would survive it. Get on with life somehow, keep living, for nothing would ever bring them back. Now, because of her feelings for Laurie, she felt as fragile as a dandelion thistle caught in the eye of a hurricane.

The scary truth which she could no longer deny, was that he had become essential to her existence and she was convinced that it was simply her age which was keeping them apart.

She rolled over on to her stomach, grabbing the red felt pen and the lovely, fat notepad designed with wild animals around its border that Chloe had sent her.

She wanted to write him a letter. Words on paper seemed the best thing, for there was something almost supernatural about a person reading words that you had poured your soul into. But finding the right words was something else.

The vinyl rotating on the record player beside her bed drummed out a pop song sung by a man who sounded as though he was being strangled.

"Timin', a ticka ticka ticka, good timin',"

She tapped her pen against the pad, creating soft blobs of red ink then wrote 'Timing'. It seemed that everything in life depended on it, and the few great love stories she had ever read or seen, had ended horribly because of bad timing. She knew that if she were only a couple of years older, the problem wouldn't exist.

But those thoughts were silly and fruitless and she scribbled out the word she had written vigorously, causing four of the under sheets of the pad to be ruined by a red stain. She now had to concentrate on making a realistic plan whereby she could at least speak to Laurie, even if she wasn't able to see him.

"Hush, my darling, don't weep my darling, the lion sleeps tonight…"

Another falsetto male voice was now inviting her to join in with a song that she seemed to have known forever.

"*Wimoweh, wimoweh, wimoweh...*"

Why on earth had they spelt it like that? It was certainly the same song, but the title was definitely not written the way it should have been.

"*Uyimbube, Uyimbube,*" she sang, thinking of the Zulu spelling she had been so used to.

She had to be intelligent about this plan. Think it out carefully. Be... Crafty. She remembered her mother had once called her a 'crafty little madam', when she discovered a skirt that Elizabeth had torn while climbing trees and then hidden, saying that she couldn't find it. She wasn't sure that she really was crafty, but she could be if she had to.

She picked up the pen again then wrote solemnly.

1. Address and telephone number.
    She had already looked him up in the phone book, but he wasn't there.

2. Where he works.

She was about to write 3, when she realised there wasn't any more than that she needed. It couldn't be so difficult, could it? To find somebody like Laurie? A man who knew her uncle.

She sucked the top of the pen. The answers lay with Jack, of course. He was Laurie's agent, which meant that somewhere amongst his files, there had to be an address. And those files would be in his office.

Elizabeth repositioned herself on the bed, her brain buzzing. She had never been to Merrick Management although they had invited her. "Come any time, you'll be more than welcome," Sylvia had said only on Christmas day.

Right then. She would ask if should could go to visit the agency tomorrow, before everyone went off again for the New Year. Jack wouldn't mind. He'd probably be only too delighted that she was taking an interest.

She snapped the pad closed and stood up, facing herself in the full-length mirror and happy to notice that the magical make-up had obliterated the last of any stray freckles.

This was the best solution that she could come up with for now and she prayed it would work.

—∞—

To all intents and purposes, things seemed to have improved between him and his niece and Jack lit a cigarette, gazing across his desk with some satisfaction, as Lesley brought him a steaming mug of coffee, having just escorted Elizabeth on a guided tour of the offices.

He had been surprised by her sudden suggestion that if he wanted to go into work then she would accompany him and not get in the way, and that suited him fine. Working from home was all very well, but there were certain tasks which were best done from the office and he missed being able to check through all his work in person, feeling bad for regularly ringing Lesley and Sylvia for information which he didn't have at hand.

In other words, Jack missed his usual routine. The daily drive in listening to Pete Murray on the radio and the end of the day analysis with Sylvia over a gin and tonic, before they shared a first night or a film preview, or went their separate ways. He was sure that he had spent more time at the flat in the last three months than during the whole of the previous year, and was already wondering whether it was now a suitable home for himself and Elizabeth. Maybe he should invest in a town house which included a small garden, for he could imagine that Elizabeth might find it cramped and claustrophobic after her previous lifestyle. Then there was the little matter of more stuff arriving from her late Aunt's estate. There simply wasn't enough room to accommodate it.

He sipped his coffee, looking through the open doorway into the outer office where his niece was watering a couple of straggly, spider plants which had suffered from a mixture of holiday neglect and central heating.

His routine could now only to be continued when Elizabeth started school and when Hannah was back from her break. And he was looking forward to it, acknowledging that he was too long in the tooth to even want to change the pattern of his working life now.

He heard Elizabeth laugh, and realised that he hadn't been aware of her doing that since Christmas day. If only he could be sure that she was getting over her infatuation with Laurie, but there was no way that he could bring himself to ask her, or to even discuss it. Despite assurances from his lover and from Sylvia that it was simply a transitory condition and would soon pass, the image of her innocent desire continued to haunt him, clawing at his deep-rooted Catholic guilt, along with those precious, occasional visits to Laurie's flat when his ardour could no longer be contained. Once again, he felt a stab of self-loathing. How irresponsible it always seemed in the cold light of morning when he reflected on his weakness. What if there were to be a fire, or, however unlikely, a break-in at the mansion block while he was away?

Jack stubbed out his cigarette, grimly determined that he was no longer able to reconcile this risk. However difficult it may be, he and Laurie would have to find another time to meet, possibly an hour or two stolen during the day when Elizabeth started school.

She came into his office, the laughter lingering in her eyes

"Uncle Jack, I've been so busy!"

"Why, what have you been doing?"

She rubbed her hand over her head, making her recently trimmed, russet hair stick up like an urchin's.

"I photocopied some contracts and I answered the phone and said 'Merrick Management, good morning'... Oh, and I filled the kettle."

"Well, that's very important." He hoped he didn't sound patronising. "Will you do something for me?"

"What?"

He handed her a business card. "Ring these people. They're the caterers for the party tomorrow. Just confirm they'll be at the flat at four."

"Okay." She took the card, glanced at it and walked back into the outer office where he heard her asking Lesley which phone she should use.

He had decided to give a small New Year's Eve party. A few business contacts together with the office gang, including Josephine Dover as young company for Elizabeth.

"You said you wanted to see the New Year in," he had told her, disappointed at her tepid reaction and wondering if it had anything to do with the fact that Laurie wouldn't be there.

"I'm not bothered," had been her shrugged response.

Jack sighed and sifted through his post, finding nothing particularly exceptional. A few late Christmas cards, some party invitations, signed contracts and letters plus photos from various artists who wanted him to go and see them performing in pantomime, with the hopeful view that he would take them on his books.

He glanced at his watch. This afternoon he had made arrangements to go over to the Palladium to meet with the stage staff as technical requirements needed to be sorted out for the Sammy Davis show, and he had invited Elizabeth along, explaining that it was one of the most famous theatres in the world.

"The caterers will be there at four." She told him in her most efficient voice, handing him back the business card.

"Thank you. Better get your coat." He peered over Lesley's shoulder while she finished typing a letter he wanted to sign before leaving.

Following its contents carefully, Jack flourished his signature at the bottom, then when he straightened up and looked around, Elizabeth had disappeared.

Pulling on his overcoat, he wandered out of the room calling her name then noticed her emerging from a door at the end of the corridor, which was the office of Mark Dover.

She smiled disarmingly. "Sorry, Uncle Jack. I just wanted to check that Josephine will be at the party tomorrow."

He felt heartened that she should want to know if Mark's daughter would be going and chalked it up as a definite step in the right direction.

"And will she?"

"I don't know. Mark's gone to lunch. It doesn't matter."

—◊—

A cluster of colourful balloons floated down from the ceiling and she nervously clinked her glass of bitter lemon against a dozen other glasses held towards her, watching as people hugged and kissed, braying New Year's greetings to the accompaniment of popping corks and the last maudlin strains of *Auld Lang Syne*.

"Happy New Year, Elizabeth." Her uncle drew her to one side. "Are you alright?"

"Yes, fine," she lied, so keyed up now by the daring plot which she had concocted, that she was finding it difficult to breathe, let alone speak.

After thinking of nothing else for the last twenty-four hours, she wondered whether, in fact, she could indeed go through with it, for it would take every bit of her courage, and the risks were considerable and high. But then, hadn't she always been just a little attracted to danger? And surely taking risks for love couldn't be as life-threatening as opening the car door while visiting the lion park at Timbavati?

Trying to get Laurie's address from the office had proved more difficult than she had imagined, and it had only been through sheer luck that she was finally hit by an inspiration, moments before being challenged by awkward questions.

Lesley had guarded her address book as if it was as precious as the crown jewels she had seen in the tower and Elizabeth soon realised that she would have to think of an alternative. Thwarted by the fact that the huge, lever-arch files marked 'Artists' were stacked too high for her to reach, she decided to resort to desperate measures. While Jack was reading a letter, she remembered that earlier that morning Lesley had taken her into Mark Dover's office after he had just gone out. Mark, she was sure, was bound to have Laurie's number as Lesley had told her that he dealt with all the nightclub performers at the agency.

As Elizabeth slipped into the empty office and closed the door, she didn't have to look very far. A large diary lay open on the desk and in it Mark had scrawled an entry against the last day of the year, which attracted her eyes like a magnet. 'Laurie Christian – Book table at Grosvenor's – twelve forty-five.'

When she heard Jack calling her name, she had hurried out, trying to decide whether Mark was meeting Laurie at somewhere called Grosvenor's on New Year's eve. But then, that didn't make a lot of sense, because Mark was going to be at Jack's party and Laurie had said that he was working. All Elizabeth could hope for was that she had found out where his place of work might be.

Then had followed the frustration of two hours without knowing, while she'd waited until Jack had finished his meetings at the theatre, desperate to find a telephone directory so that she could check whether her assumptions were correct.

Back at Merrick Management, when Jack became involved in a long discussion with Sylvia, Elizabeth grabbed her chance and crept into Jack's office to do what she had to do.

Now, on New Year's Eve, she knew that Grosvenor's was indeed the night-club where Laurie worked and that he performed twice nightly, at ten o'clock and twelve forty-five. They had told her on the phone that all the tables were booked, but that didn't worry Elizabeth. Neither did the fact that she didn't really know what a night-club was. She would simply stand at the back, watch him sing then wish him a happy New Year and return to the flat. If he kissed her again then that would make the beginning of 1967 even more perfect.

She looked around for her uncle and noticed him sitting beside the Christmas tree, chatting to a group which included Sylvia and two middle-aged men who were festooned in paper streamers.

This would be the most difficult part; making a getaway

while the guests were still in full flow, although, at the moment, quite fortunately, they all seemed to be congregated in the sitting-room.

She touched his arm. "Uncle Jack, I'm tired. Is it okay if I go to bed?"

"Of course." He excused himself from the others and walked with her to the sitting-room door. "I'm sorry that Josephine didn't come. I hope you weren't too bored?"

"Do you know why she didn't come?"

"Apparently, she's staying with her grandparents. Mark and Judy are going on somewhere else from here."

Elizabeth lowered her eyes, not wanting to give away the fact that she knew where they were going.

"I hope we don't keep you awake. I think people will be around for a while longer."

"That's alright," she told him, not sounding quite as natural as she would have liked. "I just wondered if you wanted me to help with anything, that's all?"

He shook his head and smiled. "No, it's all under control. The caterers are doing the cleaning up. We're off the hook tonight."

He bent to kiss her cheek and Elizabeth turned and walked as calmly as she could towards her room. Once inside, she tore open her dressing-table drawer and, with trembling hands, took out five ten-pound notes, half of the money which she had left over from Christmas.

Folding them into the plastic handbag that Sylvia had given her, she applied some lip gloss and eye-liner, checked her securely pinned fake curls, which she hoped made her look considerably older and slipped on her coat.

Tentatively she opened her bedroom door, noticing two of the caterers busy in the kitchen, but it appeared that the hallway was devoid of activity. Seizing the opportunity, and with the dexterous speed of a silent cobra, Elizabeth slid from her room and out of the flat.

Taking no chances, she ran down the stairs, breathing a sigh of relief when she reached the entrance hall, as neither Victor nor the deputy porter were on duty at the front desk.

Hardly able to believe that she had escaped unnoticed, she glanced anxiously over her shoulder and up towards the windows of the flat, where she could see the party guests she had just been mingling with, reduced to silhouettes.

Elizabeth then began to walk purposefully, her heels seeming abnormally loud as they click-clacked against the pavement. She had looked up the address in the London street map and reckoned that if she didn't manage to hail a taxi, then she could walk it in about ten minutes by cutting through the park.

Breathless because of her acute excitement, she noticed a taxi glide towards the kerb and pull up just in front of her, dropping off a dishevelled man in evening dress who had obviously overdone the seasonal cheer.

"Taxi!" she called and the driver acknowledged her, adjusting his meter as the drunken passenger struggled to pay him before reeling off into the night.

"Where to, luv?"

"Grosvenor's," she told him, so confidently that he might have believed it was her second home. "In Grosvenor Square."

The short journey was one which she would never remember, as the destination was all that really mattered. When they drew up outside the brightly-lit, pillared building, a door-man dressed in red, gold-braided uniform and a plumed helmet, hurried forward to open the taxi door.

Suddenly, she found herself starring in her very own fairy tale, an interfusion of Alice stepping through the looking glass and Cinderella arriving at the ball, alighting into what seemed like another world where only she was real.

She caught his name on a poster just inside the foyer and although she wanted to linger to look for his photograph, she knew she must somehow face the enormous challenge of how to get inside this glittering establishment, where a line of men and women, dripping in expensive finery, were seemingly anxious to embark on the night's entertainment.

Elizabeth squeezed through the crowd and, ignoring the main entrance, made straight for one of the side doors where a suave, oily-haired young man in a dress suit held out his arm in front of her.

"You can't go in there, miss. You have to be accompanied by a member."

She took a breath and spoke her rehearsed words "It's alright. I'm with Mark Dover's party. I don't expect he's here yet."

The man creased his face into a dubious frown as he scrutinised her carefully.

"How old are you?"

"Eighteen."

"You don't look it. I'd say fifteen, max."

"I'm eighteen," she repeated defiantly, wishing that she didn't feel so sick with fear. "I'll just have to wait here for Mr. Dover then."

Despondently, Elizabeth wandered into the ladies cloakroom, handing her coat to the bleach blonde attendant, while her head spun with the dilemma of what should be her next move. If the Dovers saw her now, all would be lost.

Her only option was to stay in the toilet until everyone had gone in and then try and sneak her way through the side door.

She sat in the small cubicle, hearing music strike up inside the club and swallowed back tears of frustration. She was going to miss his show. It was a stupid thing to have done in the first place, but she was here now and so badly wanted to see him.

She tried to twirl her fake curls around her finger, as fragmented voices, speaking and singing, floated through her ears. Indistinguishable to her, but obviously well received by the audience, who she could quite clearly hear responding with laughter and applause.

As the intolerable minutes ticked into half an hour, she was finally unable to stand the waiting any longer. Flushing the toilet, she left the cubicle, then combed her hair and touched up her make-up. There wasn't a soul in the cloakroom, not even the attendant, as Elizabeth pushed open the door and ventured once again into the reception area.

Most of the people who had been on duty earlier had disappeared and only one man, tall and thin and dressed in a white, silk embossed jacket, stood behind the desk, speaking on the telephone. Keeping her head down, Elizabeth crossed her fingers and scuttled towards the main entrance, pulling open the heavy door and pausing in the half-darkness, her heart racing and her eyes drawn to the colourful spectacle of movement on the disc-shaped stage.

To her dismay, she felt a hand touch her arm and the same, slick evictor led her firmly back outside.

"I've been in." Elizabeth told him desperately. "I just popped to the ladies."

"Listen…" The young man's voice was softer than when he had first cautioned her. "I don't know what you're up to, and I can't begin to think why a young girl like you is out alone on New Year's Eve. But you obviously want to see this cabaret and seeing that you've missed most of it, I'll let you watch what's left."

"Th… Thank you…"

"You'll probably get me fired, but I'm going to take you to the upper level, where there's a table that's partially masked by one of the pillars. No-one's there. Then I want you to wait for me when the show's over and I'll escort you out of the building. Understand?"

She nodded, feeling vulnerable and exposed, following him up a short flight of stairs and returning to the elegance of black and silver decor where he seated her at a small glass table balanced on a coil of stainless steel.

"If you lean over, you can see reasonably well," he whispered, then was gone and she wiped her clammy hands against her crocheted dress, realising this was the best she could have expected.

She gazed down at the brightly lit stage, where statuesque girls in fish-net tights, spangled costumes and ostrich feather head-dresses were receiving applause and wondered where Laurie was.

She caught her breath as a man in a gold lamé suit bounded forward, but it wasn't him.

"Ladies and gentlemen, sadly we've reached finale time. So

won't you welcome back, the star of Grosvenor's cabaret this evening, the beautiful, the gorgeous, Mr. Laurie Christian..."

Bewildered by the introduction, Elizabeth craned forward as far as she could without plummeting over the balustrade as, from the top of a silver staircase in the centre of the stage, the spotlight picked up a figure descending slowly to the rhythmic beat of bongos and a wailing clarinet.

She stared for a moment then sat back again, disappointed. Another glamorous woman. When was she going to see Laurie?

The audience gasped and burst into applause as the tall brunette wrapped in a clinging, midnight-blue velvet dress covered in star-studded sequins, placed one silver, high-heeled shoe in front of the other, gazed out seductively beneath thick lashes and began to sing in a low, husky voice.

"Don't believe my eyes, they're the coldest eyes...
But they're not so cold, let me put you wise…"

Elizabeth stared hard at the woman, a tingling sensation feathering her spine then reaching the top of her head. Surely she must be wrong…surely…

"Keeping the temperature in mind, this is a work of art…
For there's a fire down below, down below in my heart."

A group of men seated at a table near the edge of the stage, their flushed, wine-indulged faces leering, reached out to the voluptuous figure, who wagged her finger in teasing rebuke as she expertly avoided their touch.

Elizabeth watched with incredulity the eyes she seemed to know so well – the colour of dark smoke – and the mouth painted a wet scarlet. Suddenly, she felt her vagina flutter in an involuntary spasm, causing her to let out a small cry.

It was without doubt, Laurie. Unbelievable and crazy as it appeared, it was him dressed as a woman. Not like the photographs she had seen of Syd Daniels in Jack's pantomime, a comical imitation, but a glamorous woman, oozing with what even Elizabeth knew to be sex appeal.

Her forehead burning, but with icy hands, she sat rigidly, mesmerized by the man she loved who was no longer a man, as the buzz of appreciation followed him between the tables.

"...and my crazy lips, they're such lazy lips,
But they'll come to life, should we come to grips..."

In her frozen trance, Elizabeth watched the audience of men and women rise to their feet when he came to the end of the song, applauding, stamping and shouting in approval.

Then, with a crashing change of tempo which made her jump, the band struck up a Latin beat, and the chorus, dressed in vivid, citrus-colours and seeming to balance baskets of waxy fruit on their heads, cascaded on to the stage behind him, where they each waved banners proclaiming 'Happy 1967'.

When the music stopped to yet more whistles and applause, he silenced them with a wave of his arms and she then heard him speak not in the voice of a woman, but with the virile voice of a man. Laurie's unmistakeable voice.

"Thank you so much... Thanks so much, ladies and gentlemen, for being a wonderful audience, and for choosing to spend the first few hours of ninety sixty seven with me. May I now, on behalf of the company, wish you all health and happiness in the forthcoming year, and if you enjoyed the show, my name's Laurie Christian, if you didn't, it's Rory Lake."

More laughter and applause and, as he bent to gather some of the numerous roses which had been thrown at his feet, he adjusted his fake cleavage provocatively, tossed a kiss to the crowd and, in an instant, the stage was plunged into darkness.

Elizabeth gripped the side of the balcony, trying to assimilate what she had just witnessed.

The cabaret floor was an empty space now and the audience had re-settled at their tables, continuing to eat, drink and celebrate the dawning of another year.

She knew that she should leave. Somehow she should get herself back to the flat and pretend that she had never met Laurie Christian. Forget all about him. That was what she should do.

So why was she still sitting here? Why hadn't she rushed off into the night in disgust, and why did she still feel the need to see him more than ever now? To talk to him and ask him the questions that demanded answers?

The image of how he looked, dressed as a woman, continued to haunt her mind. Words like 'freaky' and 'weird' seemed to describe the experience and yet, couldn't she also confess to some small thrill at watching him? The charismatic pull that he exercised over her as the Laurie she had come to know and love was still there, but in a different guise. She shivered, not wanting to admit that she too must be freaky and weird, if that was the case.

"Was it worth it?"

"Sorry?"

She glanced up quickly at the man who had allowed her in.

"Was it worth all the hassle? Seeing Laurie Christian?"

She was glad that it was too dark for him to notice her blush.

"Yes, thank you." She answered stiffly.

Come on, then." He held out his hand to pull her up from the chair. "Time to go home."

"I don't want to go home," she heard herself saying in her most stubborn Elizabeth voice.

The club employee shook his head. "Oh yes you do. And I'm going to make sure you do. I'll put you into a taxi. Now come on."

She withdrew her arm from his grip, aware that people at the nearby tables were taking an interest.

"I want to see Laurie Christian," she told him haughtily.

He regarded her with amusement. "Of course you do. Come on now, girlie, or I promise you, I'll call the police."

"I know him," she continued obstinately.

He sat down, putting his face close to hers, and the strong scent from the oil on his hair made her recoil. "You're a funny one, that's for sure. I've seen older women wet their pants for him, but no-one as young as you."

Trying to ignore the crudeness of this remark, she decided on what her father used to call 'the olive branch approach.'

"I'm sorry I'm causing you so much trouble. Please tell Laurie I'm here. He does know me, honestly."

He stared at her for a moment longer, then stood up. "Alright. But you'd better be telling me the truth. Wait here."

—m—

Laurie placed the black wig with the heavily-lacquered flick-ups alongside a colourful selection already sitting on half-a-dozen wooden heads waiting like prisoners for the firing squad. He swigged from a bottle of Moet & Chandon and gave a guttural belch. Another night over. In fact, another year over and no-body to celebrate with except Mark bloody Dover and his friends, who had invited him to join them for a meal at their table.

He would have liked a fuck tonight and Lord knew that enough offers were there for the taking. Still, he also knew that having come this far with Jack, it would be madness to endanger that relationship now, for even though the sex was hardly earth-shattering, the agent was certainly besotted and Laurie wanted to keep it that way.

He adjusted the small electric fan on his dressing-table and flopped into a canvas chair. God, he was hot. In more ways than one. That velvet dress and the heavy paste jewellery were sweltering under the lights, and now that he had at last shed them, all that was left was to clean off his face and take a shower.

Naked, apart from a pair of air tex underpants, he tried to cool down, studying himself in one of many mirrors which lined the walls of his dressing-room. At least Jack had arranged all this for him, and what Laurie hoped for now was that he would eventually see sense and put his money where his mouth was. In other words, finance the lease of a venue fine enough for the best female impersonator in the world, a club like no other which would, he was certain, make them both rich and secure his own future.

Taking a long drag from a spliff, he reached for the tin of Leichner cleansing cream and a box of tissues, wishing that Jack hadn't reacted in such a namby-pamby fashion on Christmas day. Now, since his niece's little outburst, he was determined that he wasn't going to leave her alone for one second and would only continue their intimacies when the girl started school, in just over a week's time.

He couldn't help but smile as he smeared his thick eye make-up with the greasy cleanser and the cannabis began to relax him. That had been quite a turn-up for the books. And, maybe, in retrospect, he shouldn't have given her a Frenchie, but she had been begging for it.

The biggest mystery of all was that there had been a definite stirring in his lower regions, but he had put that down to the fact that he had got excited while being watched by Jack and Sylvia.

He drank again from the bottle then took another puff of weed. Well, he'd never know. But it had been something to ponder. The only hard-on he'd ever got from a female was from looking at pictures of Rita Hayworth in film magazines when he was still at school. His maiden voyage, so to speak, at the age of sixteen, had been the rough, yet mutually satisfying kind, from a multi-tattooed First Mate on board a naval carrier, stationed in Gibraltar.

A knock at the door broke into his reflections and he cursed under his breath. Not the bloody public wanting to meet him already. Surely everyone was still down in the club, getting pissed.

"Who is it?"

"Laurie, it's Steve. From out the front."

With only half his make-up wiped away, Laurie slipped on a black silk dressing gown, finely patterned with a Chinese dragon motif, and opened the door to the Club's not unattractive new bouncer.

"Hi Steve. What's up?"

"You're gonna think this weird, Laurie, but there's a kid downstairs. A girl. Under-age definitely. Says she knows you."

Laurie frowned, disbelievingly. "A girl. What's she like?"

"Um... Pretty. Tall, with copperish hair. Why, do you know who she is?"

"I'm not sure," he said, trying to get his mind around all that this news implied. "Did she see the show?"

"Yes, just the end. Not the dirty bits."

"And she's alone?"

"Very alone. That's the problem."

"Okay, Steve. Bring her up. Thanks."

As he left, Laurie tried to gather his thoughts. It sounded very much as if Elizabeth had come to the club without Jack's knowledge. And that she knew what he did. The genie was well and truly out of the bottle and he had to somehow try and salvage the situation.

He finished the joint and batted the pungent air with his hand. This was a development that he hadn't envisaged, and his plan to get to Jack through making himself indispensable to Elizabeth, had now somehow back-fired. The girl was acting out some teenage crush and it was down to him to handle it, for he knew that Jack would go ape-shit if he had any idea that she had been here. In fact, he would most definitely see it as just one step away from her discovering the nature of their relationship, and it would freak him to such an extent that he would drop out of Laurie's life again. At a very crucial time.

The bouncer showed the flushed and nervous girl into the dressing-room and, after thanking him by way of a couple of quid folded suggestively into the palm of his hand, Laurie guided her cautiously towards a chair. He could see the way she was staring at him, more of a sidelong look than fully into his eyes as she always had and he realised how odd it must be for her.

He decided to let her do the talking.

"Champagne?"

"No, thank you."

"You look as though you need something. Are you sure?"

She crossed one of her pale blue stockinged legs over the other and changed her mind. "Alright then."

He poured her half a glass and told her not to rush it.

"Oh, no," she said, absorbing the trappings which made up his extraordinary room. "We mustn't forget what happened last time."

Thrown for a moment by her mention of Christmas day, he cleared his throat.

"What are you doing here, Elizabeth?"

"I came to see you."

"I know that, but why and how?"

She sipped her drink. "It's New Year's Eve. You said you were working, and the party at Uncle Jack's was boring."

He couldn't help laughing. "But how the hell did you get out? Without him seeing?"

She began to look less nervous. "I just did. I said I was going to bed and I came here."

He sat back in his chair and studied her closely. "You are one amazing girl. And was it what you expected?"

At last she raised her eyes to regard him squarely.

"You know the answer to that, I think."

"Are you shocked?"

"I was. I'm not so bad now."

His ego couldn't resist enquiring "Did I look the part?"

"You looked wonderful," she answered without humour, then asked, "but why do you do want to be an imitation woman?"

"That's not what I am, gorgeous. I imitate women, yes, but strictly for my job. The people I would describe as imitation women are mostly those sad devils who feel compelled to dress up in their private lives. And when I say dress up, I mean wearing silk underwear against great hairy bodies and who can't put on mascara or lipstick without smudging it all over their faces."

She stared at him incredulously. "Some men do that? Really?"

"Really. Now I realised a long time ago that I looked pretty okay, and thought I could make a living from it. I've got a good memory for lines and a passable singing voice. That's about it."

"How does it make you feel?" Her questions seemed oddly adult, uncompromising.

"When I've got all the gear on, I feel like the lyrics of that song *Just like a woman*. He looked at her challengingly "More to the point, how does it make you feel?"

She shook her head. "I don't know. Strange, I suppose."

"What... Strange excited or just strange strange?"

He watched her struggling with her emotions. "I don't know."

"You know, Elizabeth, if you feel attracted to me dressed like that, don't for God's sake worry about it. I get so many letters from women who feel the same. They turn up here all the time. It's perfectly alright."

To his alarm, she banged her glass down on the table and jumped up from the chair.

"How can it be alright?" She asked him tearfully, her Rhodesian accent more pronounced than he had ever heard it. "It's... Unnatural. I don't understand."

Instinctively, he moved towards her and took her in his arms, holding her coltish body for a few trembling seconds, before leading her gently over to his dressing-table. As she gave a puzzled frown, he rummaged through the clutter which covered it, then picked up two round pieces of Dunlop foam rubber.

"Do you know what these are?"

She shook her head.

"Well, I'll tell you, baby. These..." He threw back his dressing gown and placed them against his remarkably hairless chest, "are my boobs. Just little pieces of rubber. Go on, feel them..."

Elizabeth hesitated then moved forward to touch and then squeeze the two soft mounds.

"And all I add to that is some paint on my face and a frock and some jewellery." He saw that her complexion had turned the colour of opaline marble, and lowered his voice. "Underneath, I'm just the same old Laurie. So what's the problem?"

She shook her head again and he took her hands.

"What do you want from me, Elizabeth?"

"I'm in love with you, Laurie," she said, dejectedly.

His heart sank. Christ, what was he supposed to do now?

"No, you're not," he said as firmly as possible. "You mustn't be."

"I can't help it. I've tried ever so hard, really, but I can't help it."

Pity for her welled up inside him. "Elizabeth, dear little Elizabeth. My little Eliza. Don't go and get serious on me, please?"

"Don't you love me? Even a bit?" She pleaded.

"Of course I do. I love our times together, the fun we always have. You're the best company of anyone I know. That's why I'm sad that Jack has stopped our outings."

She started to regain some colour and he wondered whether he might be going too far. "...But not in that way, you know..."

She began to sob. "Why not? Am I not sexy enough for you?"

He brushed away her tears with his fingers. "Don't be ridiculous, you're gorgeous. I keep telling you. You'll meet someone one day who will sweep you off your feet. Someone not a bit like me."

The telephone suddenly shrieked causing them to break apart and Laurie picked it up warily.

Mark Dover, rather less articulate than on a normal working day, was ringing from a booth in the night-club.

Laurie tried to keep his voice steady.

"Mark, Hi. Listen, I'm sorry I haven't joined you. I've got one hell of a migraine. I'm lying here just hoping it will go away."

He watched Elizabeth fingering through the line of assorted gowns which hung on a portable costume trolley behind the door.

"...Yes, it is a bummer. No, I haven't had one for months. Well, that's very kind of you. I'll make it if I can, otherwise happy New Year to you and to Judy. Thanks. Bye."

Her tears had stopped and she was wearing a half-smile.

He shrugged. "So, I lied!"

"I'm sorry about Christmas day," she said, taking another sip of champagne. "It was drinking this that did it and now we're not allowed to see each other."

"Hey, it's as much my fault as yours." He narrowed his eyes and placed his hand on his heart in a melodramatic pose. "I didn't have to be Omar Shariff."

She started to giggle and he joined in.

"But I ought to get you home."

She shook her head. "Not yet. I don't think Jack will be in bed yet."

Suddenly Laurie remembered that Jack had said that he would ring to wish him the compliments of the season and wondered when and where that might be. To avoid what would be a further awkward scene, he hurriedly placed the phone on the floor and took the receiver off its cradle.

"Do you want to do this forever?" she asked, not seeming bothered by this action.

"What's forever? I'll do it until I lose my looks, or make enough money to retire. Actually, that's the plan."

He leaned forward, borrowing some of her intensity. "You see, tonight I was the only star of this show, but that's only because no-one else wanted to work on New Year's Eve. Normally, I share the bill with other people, a comic or a girl singer. I don't want to do that anymore."

"But the audience really thought you were good," she told him.

"Sure, I was good. That's the point. I need my own place. Control over my own material." He saw her looking confused and tried to explain in a way that she would understand. "I don't choose what I sing. And other people get to write the sketches, which you didn't see. I change them all the time and get bollocked out. Told off. There's a club in town called "Rory's" which is owned by another female impersonator. He's good, but not as good as me."

"So why don't you buy a club?" She asked innocently.

He gave a wry laugh. "Not enough bread, baby. Simple as that."

"How much would it be?" She enquired, her face serious.

He waved his arms. "Oh, I don't know. Thousands. Nothing I can afford. I need a rich backer who believes in me."

"I believe in you," she said quietly.

He studied her earnest face as the combined effect of dope and champagne began to wear off. "Elizabeth, that's very sweet..."

"Where there's a will, there's a way," she said knowingly, and he suddenly realised what she was suggesting. For a moment, his imagination scuttled away with him. What a gas if he got the money from the niece and not from her manager-uncle. But she

162

was just a kid and he knew that there was no way she could get her hands on the amount he needed, not even from her own, obviously buoyant account. Dismissing this briefly seductive scenario, he then amazed himself completely by asking, as if in gratitude for her suggestion.

"Would you like a New Year's kiss?"

"Yes! No! I don't know," she was looking at him oddly, and he realised that he was still wearing a thick slash of Max Factor's Lady in Red.

"Let me get this ghunk off," he told her, reaching for a tissue, but she put her hand on his arm stopping him, then raised her face towards his.

Pressing his lips on hers and without going into her mouth this time, he kissed her. But she wanted more. Hungrily, she pushed herself against him, trying to find his tongue. Slowly, he pulled away and shook his head.

"No, Elizabeth. No..."

She really was extraordinary, this little country orphan who had been so brutally thrown into the swinging London scene. And certainly not slow to learn. He watched her wipe his lipstick from her face with a tissue and thought that she could probably be quite kinky if given the chance. Forcing such playful imaginings from his mind, he realised that he had to get her back to Jack's flat and pronto, otherwise all hell was set to break loose.

"This is what we'll do," he told her decisively. "I'll drive you back, and I'll ring Jack from the phone-box on the corner, by the flats. Then, when I give you the thumbs-up, that means he's answered and I'll keep him talking. You then try to get back in without him knowing."

He could tell from her face that his crazy plan appealed to her.

"And let's hope, Elizabeth, that he takes the call in his bedroom or the sitting-room, not in the hall."

Laurie quickly showered and dressed and led her down to the street via the fire exit, so that the chance of running into star-struck revellers taking their leave from the club would be lessened.

"Listen," she said, as they tucked themselves into his Mini. "I know you say you don't love me in that way, but you do love being with me. Jack is seeing somebody, I don't know who it is. He sometimes goes out at night, so why shouldn't we?"

Christ, she was persistent. If he'd even considered that knowing what he did for a living might have put her off, that thought was now well and truly banished from his mind.

"Definitely not," he told her. "I'm not going behind Jack's back to see you. I'd get hung, drawn and quartered."

He pulled up adjacent to the park and facing the red-brick mansions where they could see Jack's car sitting in the forecourt, as well as what appeared to be a quiet, unlit flat.

"Right," he told her. "We've discovered two things. Which are that he's there and that he's probably gone to bed."

"That's alright then." Elizabeth said. "I'm sure I won't wake him."

"I'm still going to ring. After all, he's less likely to hear you when he's talking to me."

"He won't be happy at you waking him up."

Laurie smiled in the darkness. "He won't mind. Come on, let's go."

He stepped into the phone-box as determinedly as Doctor Who, leaving her poised on the corner ready for his signal while he dialled the number.

After four rings, Jack's sleepy voice answered. Laurie pressed the button and heard the coins rattle noisily.

"Jack, it's me. Happy New Year."

"Where are you?" Jack asked, struggling to come round. "I tried the club, but the phone was constantly engaged."

"I know. It's broken. I'm in a phone-box on my way back to the flat. Just wanted to talk to you."

"I miss you so much," Jack told him wistfully.

"I miss you too. Where are you, by the way?"

"In bed. Why?"

Laurie looked across at Elizabeth who was hopping from one foot on to the other and obviously experiencing child-like impatience intensified by the damp January chill.

"Well, Jack. You just lie back and relax. I reckon I've got a few more minutes left on this call. Are you wearing pajamas?"

"No" Jack answered, and Laurie could hear his breathing quicken.

"Good. Then I'll begin."

Within exactly two minutes and before the pips curtailed Jack's short, but gratifying introduction to the New Year, his lover had held his thumb in the air and watched as Elizabeth sprinted through the forecourt, tapped in the code that unlocked the main doors of the building and vanished from his sight.

—◊—

When Jack welcomed Hannah back during the second week in January, he realised that as far as his housekeeper was concerned, 1967 appeared to be progressing in much the same fashion as the year she had just seen out with traditional north of the border aplomb. He noted that as usual she scurried around with her usual briskness, polishing furniture and sorting through laundry, but he was more aware of the transition, however slight, in his niece's behaviour and her current pre-occupied state.

It was a state that he was unable to define, for although Elizabeth remained perfectly polite and friendly when they were together, he couldn't help but wonder where she really was behind the far-away look in her eyes, and whether, like him, she might still be re-living those now unspoken events of Christmas day.

On the other hand, it could be put down to half a dozen different things. Nervousness at starting school in two days time, memories of home naturally re-surfacing at the beginning of another year, or simply teenage moodiness, which he kept being told was perfectly common and best ignored.

"Thank you for the diary, Hannah," he heard her say, as she helped the housekeeper prepare an apple pie. "I'm going to write in it every single day this year."

Just the thing for a secretive teenager, he thought to himself.

A red plastic diary with a tiny lock and key. And he allowed himself the brief, voyeuristic curiosity of imagining what she may have already written. Well, at least it wouldn't be about seeing Laurie, even if it were about wanting to see him. That was something he, as her concerned guardian, had drawn the line at and so far, so good.

The phone rang just as he had picked up his briefcase to leave for the office and the caller was unexpected.

"Mr. Merrick, Mackenzie here. Mackenzie & Mackenzie, Rhodesia?"

"Good heavens." Jack stood in the hallway, impressed by the ever-improving wonders of modern technology. "You're so clear, I'd swear you were in the next room."

"Not quite," the solicitor said, prosaically, "but I am in London."

"Oh, well, that explains it." Jack resisted a chuckle. "How can I help you?"

"I've been in Scotland for the holidays – flying home on Thursday and I've got some paperwork for your niece. Thought I might as well bring it with me as the post from Rhodesia's rather unpredictable at the moment."

"Okay. What are you going to do, post it from here?"

The solicitor gave a wheezy cough, which resembled the effect of deflated bagpipes. "Bloody weather. I never get used to it. The point is, I'd arranged for the deposit box to be transferred from Glasgow to the bank's branch in the Brompton Road and they've just told me it's arrived. I can meet you there today if you can make it and I can bring Mrs. Ainsley's inventory of personal property at the same time."

Jack tried to re-arrange his thoughts. He had just made two appointments for this morning that might suffer from postponement, but it was possible he could grab an hour in the afternoon.

"Fine," Mackenzie agreed. "Let's say two o'clock."

Jack looked round the kitchen door.

"That was the solicitor from Rhodesia," he told Elizabeth. "He's arranged for you to see what great-aunt Margaret has left you, and it'll be in the bank in Knightsbridge this afternoon. It might be best to get it sorted out before you start school."

She looked interested. "Alright," she said, expertly rolling out a layer of pastry under a wooden pin. "Shall I meet you there?"

"Yes, at two. It's the Royal Bank of Scotland in the Brompton Road, and you can choose to walk, order a cab, or catch a bus. One leaves from just across the road and stops practically outside the bank."

"Okay."

A sharp burning pain suddenly attacked his thorax and he caught his breath, giving a silent burp. As he rummaged through the bathroom cabinet to find some Alka Selzer, he wondered why his digestive system had been playing up so badly since Christmas, as he hadn't been particularly aware of excessing on the food and the drink.

Perhaps it was time to pay a visit to the quack, for his sleeping pills were running out and he needed another prescription. He swallowed the spuming liquid and grimaced. He'd always hated the taste. That and Milk of Magnesia, administered by his mother to himself and Emily when, after weeks of having endured heavily over-cooked and boring school meals, they had dived far too heartily into her delicious homemade coconut-ice or maple toffee in the holidays.

"Bye then," he called to his housekeeper and his niece, as the latter followed him to the door.

"Don't forget my records, Uncle Jack. If you can?"

"Oh, yes. No, I won't forget. See you at two."

Before the morning was to wrap him up in various duties and decisions, Jack had willingly complied with his niece's request, asking Lesley to order the two records that Elizabeth wanted, to be delivered to the office. One was another copy of the Beatles' *You've Got to Hide your Love Away*, because hers had become scratched and virtually un-playable, the other was a Bob Dylan song, recorded by the group, Manfred Mann, called *Just Like A Woman*.

—◊—

When the cab that they had ordered failed to turn up at five to two, Hannah took Elizabeth down to the bus stop, where a number 19 was fortuitously waiting for its last passenger before trundling off to South Kensington.

"Tell the conductor that you want the Brompton Road," Hannah told her, as Elizabeth stepped on board and climbed the stairs, for this was another first-time experience, seeing London from the top of a bus, however short the journey.

She found a seat, but her eyes almost closed with tiredness as the bus started to move, lulling her within its motion. It was hardly surprising as she hadn't had a decent night's sleep in weeks. As if experiencing those disturbing, impure thoughts weren't enough, the kiss with Laurie on Christmas day and the extraordinary episode on New Year's Eve were now leading her to believe that she might never again submit to peaceful slumber.

His rejection of her had been painful, but the reason why he had done so now struck her as obvious. Laurie relied on Uncle Jack to find him work and they were friends. She couldn't blame him for fearing dismissal from such a big agency, as she now knew Merrick Management to be. And from Jack, who was important enough to have been given an award by the Queen, no less. But still, not knowing when she might see Laurie again was as painful as ever and she felt as though her mind and her body had been weighed down with lead as she made the effort to function normally.

She assumed that Jack must have ceased his nocturnal wanderings for now, as ever since Christmas she had noticed that his car had remained outside the flat overnight. Certainly, due to her unwilling insomnia, she would have been aware of his leaving the building.

She yawned and gazed at the few other people sitting on the top deck of the bus. A woman in a paisley headscarf, reading a paper and smoking a cigarette, a long-haired youth in jeans and a studded jacket and a black man in a Fairisle sweater, drumming his fingers on the steel rim of the seat in front of him.

In a brief flash of disorientation born of fatigue, she almost called out "This is a 'whites only' bus," but luckily checked herself in time. How long ago that other life seemed already. How different a person she had become. In the words of the poet Yeats, via Chloe's father, she had now 'changed utterly'.

And it was all very well having secret and passionate feelings, but at this very moment she wanted so much to share them with someone. To talk about Laurie to anyone who'd listen and understand. If only such a person existed.

She tried to imagine what Chloe might say about it all. Would she be supportive, understanding? She had been her closest friend and in many ways, her only confidante. Closing her eyes, Elizabeth began to silently form the question that she would ask her friend if she was in the bus with her right now.

'What if you met somebody who cheered you up and bought you clothes and make-up and taught you about things like eating Chinese food? What if, as well, he was good looking and laughed at the things you laughed at and took you to see the most romantic film in the world – mightn't you fall just a little bit in love with him?'

Elizabeth sighed and opened her eyes. Well, that was the first part of the question and so far she could imagine Chloe saying yes to everything with enthusiasm and excitement. But the second part was far trickier. 'Then, what if you found out that he dressed up as a woman? That this was his job? That he wore false breasts and beautiful dresses and jewellery and make-up? Would that make any difference, because it doesn't to me?'

She shook her head, causing the youth in the studded jacket to regard her with an expression of sympathy. That was when Chloe would send for the men in white coats. And, to be honest, if her friend had asked that same question of her only two months ago, Elizabeth would have responded in precisely the same way.

"Brompton Road, luv," the conductor's voice called up the stairs and she rose quickly, nearly losing her balance as she began to climb down.

The bus had stopped almost opposite the bank and, as she crossed the road, her thoughts of Laurie were fleetingly replaced by what might lie in the mysterious safety deposit box which her great-aunt had left her.

The solicitor and her uncle were already waiting inside the high-ceilinged mahogany interior and she noticed the anxiety that lined Jack's face swiftly reset into relief as she walked towards them. She felt a stab of guilt for her deception as he bent to kiss her.

"There you are! You remember Mr. Mackenzie, don't you?"

"Of course," she replied, in her best pukka English and, for all her weariness, stifled a giggle. He could be the Beatles' conception of Father Mackenzie with his pasty complexion, fake fur hat and camel hair coat donned for the English winter. And she could certainly imagine him 'darning his socks in the night when there's nobody there'!

"Elizabeth. You're looking very... Yes, well. Very well."

As she accepted his limp hand, she noted with more amusement that he seemed disconcerted by her appearance, so very different since he had put her on the plane at the beginning of November.

"This is for you." He handed her a long envelope with her name typed across it in bold print. "It's Mrs. Ainsley's list of property which you will have to choose from. Anything that is too big, or that you're not sure about, can be put into storage until you find the time to come over and inspect. Other items like jewellery or books, we can arrange to forward on to you."

She folded the envelope into her plastic flowered bag. "Thank you."

"Shall we go through?" Jack led the way along a corridor passing rows of tills attended by queuing clients and towards a door marked 'Manager', upon which he knocked firmly.

When the greetings and introductions had been exchanged and the paunchy, heavy-browed bank manager named Cyril Deakin produced a rather dented tin box from a drawer in his desk, Jack suggested that perhaps Elizabeth would care for a little privacy, and that he and Mackenzie should wait outside so as not to crowd her while she opened it.

"That's alright" The manager told them. "I'll stay with Miss Tarrant. I have to be present, anyway".

Elizabeth glanced at Jack as he left the room, wishing that it could be the other way around. If someone had to stay with her, then she would have preferred her uncle's presence rather than that of a stranger.

She watched as Cyril Deakin took the key and unlocked the box then beckoned her over to examine its contents.

The first thing she lifted out was a thick piece of paper, which looked like a form of some description and, as she unfolded it, she scanned the rather faded typescript, trying to act as though she had immediately grasped its significance.

Her late great-aunt and uncle's names were clearly shown beneath a line which read 'The Henry Charteris Gold Mine' and while her eyes took in a date of 1922 and another figure of twenty per cent, she couldn't be bothered to read the small print included in two columns at the bottom of the page.

"Can I ask Uncle Jack about this?" she enquired.

The bank manager nodded. "Of course. Do you want to see what else is there first?"

"Mmm," she muttered distractedly, peering again inside the tin.

Her curiosity now stimulated, Elizabeth picked up the remaining item – a faded cotton drawstring bag which she could have sworn carried the fragrance of gardenias, a scent called Cape Jessamine, that she always identified with great-aunt Margaret. Almost overcome by tearful nostalgia, she untied the strings and took out something wrapped in cotton wool. From the corner of her eye, she noticed the bank manager observing her movements with interest and she turned to fix him with a hostile gaze, whereupon he averted his attention in order to look out of the window.

Elizabeth then pulled away the cotton wool, holding between her finger and her thumb an object which resembled a small piece of cloudy, rough-edged glass, but which she suddenly knew, without having to be told, was an uncut diamond.

"Can I see my uncle now please?"

"Certainly."

As Cyril Deakin opened the door to Jack and Mackenzie, Elizabeth sank into an arm-chair, visualising her beloved relative when she had been the vibrant force of her childhood, and offering up her own silent thanks for such unexpected generosity.

Jack took the certificate which he studied for a few moments, then addressed his niece.

"This means you own a twenty per cent share in a gold-mine in the Transvaal." He passed it across to Mackenzie. "I presume this is a simple enough transaction?"

The solicitor pushed his spectacles further up his nose and held the document closely to his face. "Yes, I can arrange for the shareholders' names to be changed and for the dividends to be paid into Elizabeth's account at Lloyds." He glanced at Elizabeth. "If you are in agreement?"

'Goodness,' Elizabeth thought, 'I must look more grown up now if he's asking for my approval.'

"Yes, that's okay," she told him, grandly.

Jack was turning the diamond over in his hand. "Well, this is quite a legacy, Elizabeth." He handed it to the bank manager who accepted it with care. "What would you say in terms of carats, Mr. Deakin?"

"To my untrained eye, I would say something between twenty and twenty-five. But it will have to be valued by De Beers. I can arrange to get that done, if you wish, Mr. Merrick?"

"Would you?" Jack looked across at Elizabeth. "And then Elizabeth must decide whether she wants to keep it in the bank."

"What else would I do with it?" she asked him.

"Well, you could keep it at the flat. I'd have to up the insurance quite considerably, but it's your choice."

"I've heard that some people who acquire this sort of property have them mounted, framed, if you like, in a glass case." Mackenzie suggested, nasally. "You may care to look at it on a mantle-piece or a shelf, rather than keeping it wrapped up or locked away."

Elizabeth rose from her chair and moved towards the bank manager, noting mild surprise from Jack as she enquired "Do you have any idea how much its worth?"

Cyril Deakin placed the diamond into the drawstring bag then back in the deposit box. "I'll get a representative from De Beers to look at it tomorrow but, at a rough guess, I'd say around forty-five to fifty thousand." The act of adult caution which Elizabeth had been exhibiting was now carelessly tossed away. "Pounds?" She asked, her voice rising to a squawk. "English pounds?"

"Yes, of course. English pounds."

"Excuse me. Do you have... A toilet?"

Deakin nodded with a smile of understanding. "Yes, it's along the corridor, first on the left."

When she had answered the call of excited necessity, Elizabeth scuttled back to find Jack and Mackenzie standing outside the bank shaking hands.

"Well, Richard, it was good to meet you at last. Thanks for all your help, and don't forget to let me have an up to date account so that a money order can be arranged."

"Will you be coming to Rhodesia?" Mackenzie enquired

"I think we'll have to at some point," Jack told him. "To sort out what's in storage. We'll probably do it in Elizabeth's Easter holiday."

"Have you sold our house?" Elizabeth asked brightly.

"There's no news on either of the farms yet." The solicitor's voice dropped noticeably. "But we'd expect an offer on the Ainsleys' property now that Christmas is over. As for yours... Well..." he trailed off, leaving his sentence disparagingly unfinished.

Mackenzie raised his Krushchev hat and took his leave as Jack led Elizabeth to the Alfa parked on a meter nearby.

"I'll drop you home, but then I've got to go back to work," he told her. "I'll catch up with you this evening."

Inside the car, she yawned again and closed her eyes, falling into a brief doze while hearing him talking about death duties, making the right investments and being sure she was set up for life. Nothing really penetrated her conscious mind until she felt him shake her arm gently when they arrived at the flat.

"Go and lie down," he told her. "You look tired and you've got a big day tomorrow."

Amid all the excitement she had almost forgotten about school, but not about her records.

Neither, it seemed, had Jack.

He handed her the singles with the warning not to play them too loudly. Victor had mentioned that the man in the flat below, a retired publisher, had voiced a moderate complaint about the volume of the music emitting from overhead.

"I won't!" she said and gave him a kiss before jumping out of the car and making her way upstairs.

In her vivid and over-crowded room, Elizabeth switched on the Dansette and lowered one of the brand new forty-fives that Jack had given her on to the turntable. As the twanging chords of a guitar intro enveloped the surroundings, she slipped off her Mary Quant raincoat and sat down on the bed, her expression serious at first, then gradually breaking into a smile as she hugged herself with joy.

"You crafty little madam, Elizabeth," she said and laughed out loud, putting her hand in the pocket of her raincoat and searching for the subject of her humour.

The second uncut diamond, roughly the same size as the one that everyone had seen in the bank, seemed to wink at her conspiratorially. Elizabeth stopped laughing and held the cold lump of pure carbon to her lips, unable to believe that it could be worth so much money.

In the back of her mind, her great-aunt's sweet voice rang out with the clarity of early morning birdsong, her advice the simplest that Elizabeth would ever follow. Of course, she would listen to her heart. How could she possibly ignore it?

—⁓—

Jack continued to sit in his car, even as the last few pupils trailed up the stone steps dragging their satchels over their shoulders, the brims of their grey, felt hats briefly touching, as they giggled and chattered excitedly. These were girls who knew each other. Not the very few, like Elizabeth, who would be wading into uncharted waters today.

His emotions seemed once again to be controlled by some invisible puppet-master, rising and descending rapidly through those doubts and anxieties which come with enforced responsibilities.

And, on the back of those emotions rode the uncanny sensation of *déjà-vu*. He fumbled for a cigarette and heard a hand-bell being rung vigorously inside a corridor or classroom. How many times, when returning to school after the holidays, would he wait until he was sure that Emily was delivered into the safe hands of the Sisters, before making his way to the adjoining boys' building? A sense of duty which became a habit, or had it been the other way around?

His eyes started to irritate and he slid the window down a fraction to allow some freezing air to clear the nicotine fug which had developed inside the car.

Yes, of course there were similarities but, once again, there were also many differences. Elizabeth was such a very contrasting character to Emily. That at least he did know, even if he still didn't really know her. A survivor, if ever he'd seen one. Strong willed and confident. Used to getting her own way, not through any fault of her own, but because of an over protective and delicate mother, and a father too burdened with the problems of running a business in an unstable country, to accept additional stress or conflict in his home life.

A piano thumped out the first few bars of a well-known hymn and then the sound of young girls' voices singing heartily at the first assembly on the first day of term. Another difference. St. Hilda's was a typically English Church of England school, obviously embracing all the ethics which that implied. If Elizabeth was inattentive or answered back, she would not have it drilled into her that Jesus took upon himself all the sins of the world.

In fact, Jack realised that Roman Catholicism might well be verbally denounced in what they called Religious Studies these days. But he could feel no blame for that, not even for Emily's sake, and was pretty sure that Elizabeth was as disinclined as him in matters of theology.

Tossing his half-smoked cigarette out of the window, he

turned on the engine as the last strains of *Oh, God, Our Help in Ages Past* faded away inside the building. She was going to be alright, but he was so uptight now that he knew he couldn't go straight into work.

Just an hour. An hour of trading the chill of concern for the sheer blood-coursing heat of shared desire. For that inevitibility of touch, rough and gentle. Of entwining and pulsating so closely that limbs become indistinguishable. Until, finally, that wash of release, which cures a million woes.

—※—

When he got home that evening, she was lounging in front of the television, chewing on a Crunchie bar, having changed out of her school uniform into jeans and a black polo neck sweater.

"Hi, Uncle Jack," she called, without taking her eyes away from the set. To his relief, her tone of voice suggested that she had not had a bad first day.

He tried to resist the reproachful comments of a parent that hovered on the edge of his tongue. Rebukes such as 'You'll spoil your dinner' or 'Take your feet off the sofa' were replaced by the slightly milder "Don't you have any homework?"

She turned around, wiping chocolate from the edges of her mouth with her knuckles.

"Nope. Today was all about getting acquainted. Tomorrow, it starts for real."

He poured himself a whisky and sat down on the chair beside her.

"So, what's tomorrow?"

"English Lit. and French. Then…" She groaned and rolled her eyes dramatically. "Geometry and Algebra."

He smiled. "Well, two out of four isn't so bad."

The enticing smell of Hannah's Scotch broth reminded him that dinner was almost ready.

"I want to shower before we eat," he said, getting up. "We'll talk more about your day then."

But she didn't tell him as much as he would have liked to

hear, answering his questions sparingly with little volunteered information. Sipping only half of her broth, she declined the ham and salad that followed then rose from the table wishing him good night.

'We've been here before,' Jack reminded himself as he heard her go into her room, and tried not to let it get to him. Sitting at his desk to begin his own home work, he pushed Elizabeth from one side of his mind, only to have Laurie enter the other.

His lover had taken him on a ride of ecstacy as usual. Ill-tempered at first at being woken, Laurie soon displayed his sexual expertise to perfection, causing Jack to wonder just how much juice it was physically possible to lose in sixty-five minutes.

For the first time, a tiny, yet very real resentment of the power that Laurie was exercising over him lodged itself unwillingly in his thoughts. And why, he wondered, again for the first time, was he was allowing such power to be exercised? Defenceless to the arrow which had pierced him, Jack felt everything and yet nothing. Did passionate love always dictate that one party called the shots, while the other remained the more submissive?

Love-blind, he may be, but the narcissism that was such an integral part of Laurie's being could not be pretended away and Jack knew he was being forced to recognise that the only person who really mattered in Laurie's life was Laurie himself.

The technicians' budget for the Sammy Davis show, which was waiting to be checked through and approved, loomed from his desk and into his eye-line almost accusingly as Jack sipped his whisky. He could hear music resonating through the wall from Elizabeth's bedroom and hoped that Ferdy Hyman downstairs wouldn't make another complaint.

Unusually, neither he nor Hannah had drawn the drapes that evening, and he noticed that snowflakes were now falling, gossamer white, some of which brushed the window pane then dissolved, their uncommon beauty reduced to simple droplets as they slid forlornly down the glass.

Once more, out of the blue that pain, further into his chest this time, caused him to lose his breath. He stared at his left hand which was holding the crystal tumbler. Not only was it shaking but it felt as though it was being pricked by a thousand tiny needles. Panic rose inside him and his face felt fire-hot, but when he caught sight of his reflection in the mirror, it was the colour of putty.

Jack carefully placed his glass on the bar, trying now to focus on anything which would take his mind off what he was beginning to fear. He was breathless, but the pain had, for the moment, subsided. The words of the song, he told himself. Concentrate on the words of the song.

It was the same record, played over and over again. He wasn't sure whether she had turned up the volume, but that was now the least of his worries.

"No-body feels any pain,
tonight, as I stand inside the rain.
Everybody knows, baby's got new clothes,
but lately I've seen her ribbons and her bows
have fallen from her curls…"

"That's Manfred Mann," he said firmly and quietly. "I'm standing in my living-room and I'm listening to Elizabeth playing Manfred Mann."

His forehead damp with sweat, Jack eased himself on to the sofa and closed his eyes. "Stay conscious," he hissed, between clenched teeth. Concentrate on the words.

"She takes just like a woman,
She makes love, just like a woman
And she aches, just like a woman,
but then she breaks, just like a little girl."

Dylan's lyrics were teasing him now. Conjuring up a montage of images which floated in and out of his frightened, fevered mind. What was the song about? If only he could tell. In some surreal way, there were three people to whom it could apply, and the mathematics of the triangle was now posing a real problem.

Stay conscious. Concentrate on the words.

"… And when we meet again
introduced as friends,
please don't let on that you knew me when…"

Himself and his own sense of helplessness, Laurie's androgynous magnetism and Elizabeth, a child blossoming into womanhood much too swiftly for his comfort.

"So like a woman, oh yes you are
you ache, you break, you take…"

Jack tried to open his eyes, but the room spun around and he quickly shut them again. "I don't want to die now," he said aloud, hearing the crack in his voice. "I'm not ready to die."

And still more images… Laurie's face, bland of make-up, then superimposed by his well-painted stage persona metamorphosing again, this time into Elizabeth's clear features. Jack heard himself laugh as another insistent stab of pain turned the laughter into a gasping attempt for air.

Why in God's name was Elizabeth playing that particular song so mercilessly? It had been around for a while. What was so appealing about it now?

Something had been eluding him over the last few days. Something which was now forming into a thought to hold on to, however irrational that thought might be.

Elizabeth knew what Laurie did for a living. She had seen him.

As Jack struggled to get up, a far greedier pain sucked at his consciousness, piercing through his chest and into his back. Unable to help himself, he let out a scream, resurrecting harrowing and familiar memories. Memories of his father tormented nightly by the spectre of gun-fire and roughly dug trenches flowing with crimson rain.

—m—

Elizabeth heard his cry just as she was finishing the current entry in her diary. 'Day 54 – still (then she had drawn a heart to signify the word love) LC.'

Snapping her diary shut, she jumped off the bed and ran out of her room, knowing that it must be her uncle and terrified at what she would find.

Jack was lying slumped between the sofa and the bar and

although there was no sign of blood, she was convinced he was dead. His lips and hands were blue and he was very still.

"Not again," she murmured, as she bent down beside him. "Oh God, please not again."

Placing her head against his chest, she could just hear his breathing. Irregular and weak, but there all the same.

Her whole body trembling and her mind a jigsaw where none of the pieces seemed to fit, she rushed to the phone and punched out the number of the front desk.

"Come on, come on," she pleaded, hitting her forehead with her fist as she waited for Victor to answer.

At last he came on the line. "Hello, Reception?"

"Victor, it's me... Elizabeth. It's Uncle Jack, Victor. He's had some sort of heart attack, I think. He's unconscious. Help me, please."

The elderly porter's voice changed from laconic to super-efficient.

"Right, miss. Now you stay with him and keep him warm. I'll call for an ambulance then I'll come up. Alright, miss?"

"Yes, yes. Just hurry."

Elizabeth ran again to Jack's side and knelt down. Desperately, she tried to remember some of her training as a junior member of the St. John's Ambulance Brigade. Screwing up her face, she searched her mind frantically for evocation. "Come on..." she urged herself. "This is Uncle Jack. Try to remember!"

If it was a heart attack, she thought that he should be on his side with his head turned and his chin up so that his tongue didn't block his airway. Praying she was right, she gently pushed him over and positioned his head as she remembered. Her task completed, she couldn't bear to see the upper part of his body looking so uncomfortable, wedged as it was between the two items of furniture, so cautiously she slid a cushion underneath his head and placed her hand on his damp, ashen forehead.

"Please don't die, Uncle Jack," she whispered. "Please... Please?"

She heard Victor calling her name as he used the pass key to open the door.

"The ambulance is on its way and I've left a message for Mr. Merrick's GP." Victor gazed at Jack's prostrate body, then took Elizabeth's arm and led her a little further away. "You did the right thing, miss. Well done."

"Will he die?" She asked fearfully, knowing that Victor hadn't got a clue.

"Not if they get him there in time. They can do wonders these days."

The porter glanced across at Jack's desk. "I think you ought to let Miss Lawrence know. Have you got her number?"

Elizabeth couldn't believe it but she hadn't. Anxiously chewing the inside of her mouth, she tasted warm blood and felt nauseous. "No, no. I don't think so. Where can I find it?"

"Has your uncle got an address book here?" Victor suggested.

"I don't know." She ran across to the desk, pulling out drawers and tossing pens and stationery into the air. Starting to sob, she repeated, helplessly. "I don't know."

Alarmed by her distress, Victor tried to comfort her but was interrupted by the urgent wail of an ambulance as it turned into the forecourt and he hurried towards the door. "I'll show them up." He told her. "Try not to get upset."

For Elizabeth, it seemed that her universe had once again imploded, but she swallowed back her tears as the two ambulance-men moved swiftly through the flat, examined Jack briefly, then placed an oxygen mask over his face and laid him on a stretcher.

"We're taking your uncle to St. Georges," one of them told her as he helped his colleague manipulate the stretcher out of the door. "Do you want to come with him or get someone to bring you over later?"

"I'm trying to get hold of someone," she said as calmly as she could manage. "Please take care of him. I'll be there as soon as I can."

She watched them leave, then heard the siren resume its mournful cry as she tried to grasp the ghastliness of the situation. Her uncle had been transported away on a dark, snowy night, sick and entirely alone.

The phone rang and she grabbed it, but, in her confusion, forgot to speak.

"Miss Tarrant, is that you?"

"Yes. Yes, Victor."

"I think I've traced Miss Lawrence's number in the directory. I remember her telling me where she lived. Try Maida Vale 3049."

"Maida Vale 3049. Yes, yes, I will..."

"Get back to me if she's not there."

"Okay. Thanks, Victor."

With fingers that refused to co-ordinate, Elizabeth dialled the wrong number twice then, when she got it right, it was engaged. Suddenly desperately thirsty, she ran into the kitchen and drank cold water from the tap, then came back to try again. This time, to her deep relief, Sylvia answered.

—⁓—

After she had taken the call, Sylvia realised that she was, from that moment, functioning on automatic pilot. Her initial reaction had been one of primal rage at the injustice of this latest episode in Jack and Elizabeth's lives. And, if she had not been the sophisticated and together person that she had invented, there was little doubt that she would have beaten her chest and screamed at the skies, railing against God or his opposite number for the cruelty they felt compelled to deal out to such undeserving mortals.

Instead, she had calmly packed an overnight bag, called a taxi and went to fetch Elizabeth, who was now sitting beside her in the family waiting room of the intensive care unit where Jack was fighting for his life.

"What's happening?" Elizabeth whispered, as Sylvia held her cold hand, hoping to offer some crumb of comfort to the young girl who had taken on the appearance of an abandoned rag-doll, battered by the elements.

"Someone will tell us soon." Sylvia sipped the milky tea which they had been given by one of the nurses, her eyes once again drawn to the clock. It was ten past eleven and Jack had been in there for almost three hours. Surely, she thought numbly, there must be some news on his condition by now?

In despondent unity, they watched a round-shouldered, grey-haired orderly in a thin, brown coat place himself in front of them holding a mop and bucket. Slowly, he began to rub the blood-streaked area of linoleum where the victim of a road accident had been carried through some ten minutes before, then squeezed the mop and shuffled off, leaving them inhaling the combined aroma of disinfectant and Wintergreen.

Eventually, the double doors facing them were pushed open and a man emerged, his white jacket crumpled and a stethoscope swinging from his hand. Thirty something, with black curly hair, Sylvia recognised him immediately as being Jewish. A web of deep lines spun out around his bright, dark eyes, but he smiled as he greeted them, causing their spirits to lift optimistically.

"Are you Mr. Merrick's wife and daughter?" He asked, motioning them to remain seated.

"Something like that," Sylvia replied, her tone defying further interrogation. "How is he?"

The man sat down beside them and spoke in a mellifluous cream and brandy voice. "I'm David Leachman, a heart specialist. Mr. Merrick's been in my care since he was admitted and he's been very lucky. In layman's language it was a heart attack, but because of early treatment we think, at the moment, that very little tissue damage has occurred."

Sylvia's frayed nerves began to recover. "Thank God. So what's the prognosis and where do we go from here?"

"Well, of course, it's too early to be over-confident. He'll have to remain in intensive care for the time being, where we'll continue to monitor his heart rhythm and blood pressure. Then we have to try and get him moving, walking again. Obviously, he's on oxygen now, which increases the pressure in the blood, providing more oxygen to the heart and keeping any damage to a minimum."

He sat back, and crossed his arms. "I've spoken to his GP, Dr. Beresford, and what is essential when he comes out of here, is the recuperation and after-care. Can nursing facilities be made available?"

"Yes, that can be arranged," Sylvia told him. "Do you have any idea of how long the recuperation period might be?"

"It varies, of course. But I would say that in Mr. Merrick's case, if he does as he's told and behaves himself and if there is no recurrence of chest pain or shortness of breath, then six months should see him resuming fairly normal activity."

"What do you mean behaves himself?" Elizabeth interjected.

The specialist gave a gentle smile. "Well, he'll have to watch his diet, we suggest that he gives up smoking and, of course..." he looked hard at Sylvia. "As little stress as possible."

"We'll make sure of it," Sylvia said, squeezing Elizabeth's hand. "Won't we?"

"I do know what his profession is," he told them, "my wife and I are theatre-goers and we read about his OBE. I presume the job is demanding?"

"It can be." Sylvia tried not to think about what Jack's total absence from business decision-making might mean. "But he's had a particularly anxious few months." She glanced quickly at Elizabeth, hoping that her comment wouldn't make the young girl feel guilty. "Is there any chance we can see him?"

Leachman rose from the plastic padded seat and they automatically rose with him.

"I should think so. But he won't be able to respond very much at this stage and I wouldn't want you to stay too long."

"Of course," Sylvia assented.

He led them through the swing doors where they were each handed a white surgical smock before being allowed any further.

They tried to avert their eyes from other patients, some sleeping, others in obvious discomfort while hooked up to a jumble of tubes and other life-saving equipment. A night-duty nurse sat writing at a desk and smiled at Leachman as he led Sylvia and Elizabeth to a curtained-off area at the end of the ward.

It was as well, Sylvia thought, that she had not deceived herself into believing she could absorb the shock of what faced them behind that curtain.

Jack's motionless body lay on the bed, electro-cardiograph equipment strapped to his chest, connected to a machine which spewed out paper covered in spidery curlicue, indicating his heart beat and pulse rate. There was a drip feed in his arm, which Sylvia presumed was giving a transfusion of glucose or saline to feed the body's shock and loss of fluids, and a plastic bag hung over the bottom rung of the bed into which urine was emptying from a catheter attached to his bladder.

His breathing was controlled through an oxygen mask and a plump nurse was adjusting some small gauze squares which were protecting his eyes.

"This is Mrs. Merrick and her daughter. Elizabeth, isn't it?"

Elizabeth nodded as Leachman continued. "They'd like to stay for a few minutes."

As the nurse left to find another chair, Sylvia cleared her throat and motioned Elizabeth to sit.

"I think I should tell you that I'm not Mr. Merrick's wife," she said quietly. "He doesn't have a wife. I'm his oldest friend and business partner and the only adult next of kin. Elizabeth is his niece – and only relative."

"I see." The specialist studied Sylvia carefully. "Well, it's usually just family members allowed in the unit, but on this occasion I'm prepared to make an exception."

"Is he in a coma?" Elizabeth asked softly.

Leachman shook his head. "No, not at all. He's just resting. We've given him something to help him sleep after the trauma."

He moved towards the cardiograph machine and examined the tracings. "Pretty steady," he told them without looking up. "That's encouraging."

"So you don't think I need stay the night?" Sylvia enquired.

"No, I really don't. We've got things as under control as possible. Come tomorrow, by all means. Dr. Beresford will be here in the morning, and you may want to chat with him."

The nurse returned with a small, canvas chair and placed it on the other side of the bed. As Sylvia sat down, she took Jack's hand which she expected to be clammy, but was remarkably warm and dry.

"We'll give you a little time together." Leachman told her. "I'll be just outside."

"Why don't you hold his other hand?" Sylvia suggested to Elizabeth when they had both gone. "And we'll talk to him. I'm sure he knows we're here."

"Okay." Elizabeth reached across the bed for Jack's hand then looked at Sylvia desperately for conversational inspiration.

"Well, Jack..." Sylvia began, trying to keep the emotion from her voice. "You have given us a fright. But you're going to be alright and home within a couple of weeks."

She stopped, thinking that she could feel his hand move inside hers, but dismissed the notion. A little too much *Emergency Ward Ten* she told herself and carried on talking.

"Elizabeth was marvellous. She knew exactly what to do when she found you, which they say made a big difference."

She smiled at Elizabeth who was looking tearful.

"We're going to go soon, Jack. But I'll be back in the morning when I'm sure you'll be feeling much better."

The snow had stopped falling when they left the hospital and was now being replaced by the much more depressing and unpleasant freezing sleet. As she drove them back to the flat, Sylvia realized soberly that she had to plan a short-term strategy.

"I'm going to stay with you tonight, Elizabeth," she told the exhausted teenager. "If you want to sleep in tomorrow, that's fine. I'll ring the school and tell them what's happened. But you'll have to decide whether you want me to stay until Jack comes out of hospital or if we'd better think about you boarding?"

Elizabeth's sleepy eyes quickly shot open. "Oh, no. I don't want to board at the school. Please, Sylvia, will you stay?"

"If that's what you want, of course I will."

Elizabeth's expression of relief was palpable "And will you tell... People?"

Sylvia maneuvered her car into a space outside the block and turned off the engine. "People? Well, obviously everyone at work will know tomorrow. Who else should I tell?"

Elizabeth had now slid down in her seat, rather than preparing to get out.

"I was thinking of his friend. Laurie Christian?"

"Laurie?" Aware that she sounded surprised, Sylvia wondered at once why she should be. Of course Laurie would have to be told. But what exactly were Elizabeth's motives? Was she enquiring for herself or for Jack? Sylvia knew immediately that it couldn't be for Jack as the girl would have no idea of their relationship. "All in good time," she said, wondering whether her reply might sound too brusque. "Jack won't be able to have visitors for a day or two."

When she had made them both large mugs of Ovaltine and cobbled together wedges of bread with tomatoes and ham, Sylvia wished Elizabeth goodnight and took herself off to Jack's bedroom, her emotional and physical energy depleted. Jack's road to recovery was now the most important thing on her agenda and she would also ensure that Elizabeth was well cared for, as best she could.

As she unpacked her bag, she began to reflect, with a sense of remorse, whether she could have done anything to prevent his attack. It wasn't as if she hadn't seen the writing on the wall. The hectic work schedule, the award celebrations, losing his sister and brother-in-law and acquiring a child, were prominent contributory factors, along with his increased heavy smoking and drinking.

But, at the root of it all, she was still convinced it was his secret and passionate attachment to Laurie Christian that had loosened the soil in which Jack had planted himself. Jack had been raised to experience a sharp sense of sin, so the deception, trying not to mind that it was against the law as well as whatever physical demands were made upon him in the bedroom, would almost certainly have added to the strain.

'What extraordinary times we're living in', Sylvia thought as she closed the curtains on the inhospitable night and slipped into a pair of fleecy pajamas.

They were calling it the sexual revolution. When promiscuity was being exercised like a natural bodily function and young people flipped through a day or night, not seeming bothered about what happened tomorrow.

And she was only too aware that homosexuals like Laurie,

along with the playwright, Joe Orton, possessed the kind of flamboyant and hedonistic personalities that embraced the blatancy of their sexual preference, with little fear of consequence or inner recrimination.

For Jack it was different. He was more complex and comparable to someone like Brian Epstein whom Sylvia had met on a few occasions and liked. Smooth on the outside. Totally in control of their managerial status. And yet, tormented through their sensitive natures by their illicit and often inappropriate objects of desire.

Sylvia noticed the bottle of Seconal beside the bed and wondered how long Jack had been relying on them for sleep. It wasn't hard to see why he would need them. She was tempted to take one herself as her own mind was accelerating with the speed of an express train and rest would not come easy tonight. Jack... The business... Elizabeth... Laurie.

There was no-one else to take them on. It was now all down to her.

He opened his eyes and sucked in a tremulous breath. No pain, just an overwhelming weakness, as though he had been held underwater for hours while fighting for air.

He glanced at the drip feed in his arm, the plastic identity tag around his wrist, and noticed as he slowly moved his head, that the austere little room in which he was lying was filled with flowers, cards and telegrams, spot-lighted by a thin burst of winter sunshine.

What had happened and how long had he been here? He struggled to remember. He knew that the numerous dreams or memories that he'd experienced had been a shadowy mosaic of the past and the present.

Half-glimpsed figures and floating voices. Someone holding his hand. Had that been his mother? And the sound of his father screaming – or had that been himself?

And the pain. Nothing vague or fuzzy about that. That had

been all too real. And now, in the process of remembering, a rush of shock and claustrophobic helplessness wrapped around him like a heavy shroud, along with the realisation that what he had experienced had been pretty serious.

Panic-stricken, Jack tried to call for help, but his throat failed to respond. Then he noticed two buttons on a cord hanging beside the bed. Not knowing which would summon assistance, he somehow managed to press both with his thumb, hammering at them, one after the other in a desperate mechanical motion.

When the door finally opened, he fell back on to the pillows, more enfeebled than ever by his action and wondering how he could communicate with whoever came in; his body sapped of every ounce of its strength.

"Hello, Jack," a moon-faced nurse, her sleek brown hair pinned up under her cap, appeared beside him, greeting him with the familiarity of an old friend. "How are you feeling?"

"Bloody awful," he croaked. "What's happened to me?"

She placed a cool hand on his forehead then popped a thermometer into his mouth.

"A blood clot blocked your coronary artery. In other words, you've had a heart attack. The doctor will tell you more, but you're going to be fine."

He wanted to talk, ask more questions. When she removed the thermometer, he struggled to form them coherently.

"How long have I been in here?"

"This is day three," the nurse replied, studying his temperature. "A bit high. You must watch it, Jack. No worry, no anxiety. Just rest."

Day three. What did that mean? He searched his brain for a clue as to when this could have happened. "What day is it? Of the week?"

"Today's Thursday. You were brought in on Monday night. You were in intensive care and now you're in one of the private rooms of the cardiac ward. Now you really must rest. I'll inform Dr. Leachman that you will be able to see him later. Right, here we go."

Like a vet treating a sick cat, she lifted his head up and before he could object, deftly popped two pills on to his tongue followed by a trickle of water from a plastic cup.

He swallowed hard, tasting the bitter almond flavour of the medication as it slithered down his throat.

Monday. That was the day he had taken Elizabeth to her new school. Who was looking after her? What was she doing?

"But I've got to see him now" Jack could hardly recognize the scratchy rasp that was his voice. "Got to ask him questions now. My niece… My work…"

The moon slid behind a cloud as the nurse's zealous bedside manner turned rather more threatening. "Jack… Mr. Merrick. Right now, you are seeing no-one, speaking to no-one, going nowhere. I'll be back later with the specialist."

Flicking down the Venetian blinds and obliterating the precious rays of sunshine that had acted as glimmers of hope, she left the room as Jack tried to fight the drug-induced sleep which was beginning to claim him.

When he next opened his eyes, they focused on something gold glinting against a fluffy, white background and, as his vision slowly cleared, he realised that it was the locket he had bought Elizabeth for Christmas.

"He's waking up, Sylvia." He heard his niece's voice first and then Sylvia's, which was controlled as always, but with a detectable underlying tension.

"So he is. Jack, can you hear us?"

He felt her face close to his, the familiar Chanel perfume embracing his senses as her lips brushed his forehead.

Suddenly, he saw them both with clarity. Elizabeth in a white bunny wool jumper and blue jeans and Sylvia in a Liberty print blouse and dark green skirt. Relieved, for all sorts of reasons, he attempted a smile of greeting which he hoped would reassure them.

"How are you, Uncle Jack?" His niece asked sounding genuinely concerned.

"I'm not sure." His mouth appeared to be moving in spite of the feeling that it was lined with sawdust.

"Welcome back, Jack," Sylvia was re-adjusting his pillows in a very nurse-like fashion. "Is there anything we can get you?"

Immediately and completely out of the blue, the delicious vision of a peach materialised in his mind. A velvety peach. Ripe, succulent and cool to the tongue. Oh, how he longed for a slice of that tasty, juicy fruit.

"It's winter, isn't it?" He asked, realising that the question might lead them to believe he'd lost his marbles.

He saw them exchange nervous glances.

"Yes, Jack, it's January." Sylvia said, tensely.

"Then peaches are out of season?"

"I'm afraid they are." Sylvia moved towards the door. "But, we've brought some grapes and I'm sure they've got some tinned fruit or something here."

"Where are you going?" He asked her.

"To get your specialist. Mr. Leachman. He wanted to know when you woke up."

At last he was to meet this Leachman fellow. Well, obviously they had already shared some intimate moments, but for the life of him, Jack couldn't remember.

"Is it still Thursday?' He asked Elizabeth, who held a bag of large, purple grapes under his chin.

"Yep, Thursday evening."

Comforted to find that he could move his fingers, he took the fruit gingerly. "Who's looking after you?"

"I'm looking after myself," she replied. A reminder, as if he needed one, of her independent attitude. "But Sylvia's staying over."

"I'm so sorry about this," he said, unable to keep the emotion from his voice... "It's the last thing I would have wished on you."

She laid her hand on his, whilst munching a grape. "It's not your fault. We're managing. School's going well. Lots of homework."

Well, he thought with weak appreciation. I've learnt more from that disjointed sentence on my deathbed, than I would have at home over supper.

When the doctor came in with Sylvia following behind, Jack realised that the man who made people better was as predictable as a pub-comic's punch line. Straight, good-looking, Jewish and most obvious of all capable. He had been in safe hands.

"Hello, Jack." Leachman studied the notes pinned to a clipboard above Jack's head, then perched himself on the edge of the bed. "I'm David Leachman, the resident heart specialist at St. Georges."

"Oh," Jack tried not to sound facetious. "I did wonder where I was."

The specialist gave a wry smile. "You understand what happened to you, I gather?"

"Only that I had a heart attack. How bad was it?"

"Bad enough. Let's call it a warning. The heart hasn't enlarged, so the prognosis is good, but we have to keep you in for at least another two weeks"

"I see." Jack glanced at Sylvia, who nodded. "And then..."

Leachman rubbed his hand over an unruly head of hair. "It will be quite a slow process, I'm afraid. I usually say to patients, even if they don't need surgery, that we have to think about rehabilitation in these terms – bed rest, chair rest, passive exercise and non-stressful mental activity. You are going to feel very tired."

Sylvia interjected. "Dr. Beresford has found an excellent nursing agency who will supply care at home. They don't need to live in, just be there to help you walk and to make sure you take your various medications."

"I see."

They had it all worked out. To his immense sadness and frustration, Jack realised that he no longer had control over his life. And there were still questions to be asked. One in particular – he wished that he knew whether Laurie had been told he was here. But once again, overcome by exhaustion, he had no choice but to close his eyes and sleep.

─w─

At five-fifteen on Friday evening, when Elizabeth, reeling from a double dose of French verbs and right-angled triangles, went into the kitchen for a glass of ginger beer, she found Hannah in tears.

"What's the matter?" she asked, putting her arm around the housekeeper's shoulders.

"Oh, I'm sorry, hen." Hannah dabbed at her eyes with the edge of her apron. "I thought I'd make poor Mr. Merrick a nice cake and take it in this weekend, but they've just told me on the phone that he can't eat saturated fats. Apparently, that means butter and lard. So that's that."

"Don't worry," Elizabeth told her. "I'm sure he'll just be glad to see you."

"Well, there's another thing. They say only close family can visit at the moment. Probably next weekend, they said."

Elizabeth could only look sympathetic. That didn't seem fair. Surely Hannah was practically family.

Wandering back into her room she drained her glass and lowered a Beatles record on to the turntable, then lay on the bed, stretching for her diary from the bedside cabinet.

'Day fifty-eight', she wrote carefully. Then, just as she was about to add 'Still love LC', the telephone rang and Hannah tapped at the door.

"A call for you, Elizabeth."

When she heard his voice she didn't even try to conceal her happiness.

"Where have you been?" She asked, breathlessly. "Do you know about Uncle Jack? How are you?"

He laughed that wonderful, low laugh and she melted. "I know about Jack. Sylvia rang me yesterday. I'm going to see him next week. I really rang to find out how you are?"

"I'm okay," she said, unconvincingly. Then, bored with her recent out-pourings of self-pity and suffering, she summoned up her natural courage. "Please can I see you? It's important."

There was a pause, and then he said "Alright. But where? When?"

She thought quickly then told him. "On Monday. I've got a piano lesson after school. Hannah and Sylvia already know I'll be a bit late. I can see you about four-thirty, if that's alright?'

He paused again, and she could hear him lighting a cigarette. "Alright. I can pick you up, or you can get a cab to my flat."

She grabbed a pen and pad, hardly believing that he had agreed to see her. "What's your address?"

"It's number seven, Rupert Court," he told her. "In Soho. Ring the top bell."

"Got it. See you on Monday, then."

"Bye, Elizabeth."

She wanted to squeal with delight but there was no way that she could. Creeping past the kitchen where a now recovered Hannah was slicing potatoes and listening to the radio, Elizabeth softly closed the door behind her.

As always, her music seemed to fit her mood. She couldn't remember when she had last felt so euphoric. Grabbing Rufus, she held him high above her head and danced around the room, duetting with John Lennon at the top of her voice.

"Hey, you've got to hide your love away…."

"I love you so much, Laurie," she whispered in the toy bear's ear when the music had stopped. How could she possibly wait for two, almost three whole days before seeing him? And then be alone with him, in his flat?

Rufus appeared sad, but she decided that was because his left eye was now hanging down so far that it almost touched his black, snub nose. Poor Rufus. It was time she sewed it back on. He deserved that much.

For a moment she wondered if her mother had ever whispered her own secrets to this little bear and what those secrets might have been.

Elizabeth unclasped her gold locket and gazed fondly at the two photos she had placed inside. Her mother half-smiling and her father wearing his familiar big grin.

She had taken ages to find the right pictures and to cut them so they fitted. Their expressions were as she would always remember them, capturing the essential personality of each. Two people who had loved her unconditionally.

Try as she may, Elizabeth couldn't imagine her mother being in love. Okay, so she knew her father and mother had loved one another, that was how she came to be, but the more she thought about it, the more she wondered whether her mother had ever been capable of passion. The kind of passion that took over your whole being, making you want to dare anything, risk anything, to be with that one person.

And was Uncle Jack the same? After all, they were brother and sister. And most people were married by the time they had reached his age. Perhaps his illness might prompt him into proposing to Sylvia? Elizabeth decided that even if he were not passionately in love with Sylvia, it would be good for him to have someone around who would look after him, apart from Hannah. And Sylvia was okay. She would do.

Over supper that evening, Jack's partner, displaying her admirable knack for organisation, suggested a social schedule for the weekend which would fit in with visits to the hospital.

"I thought that tomorrow we could go to a matinee. It's a comedy called *Arsenic and Old Lace,* which I think you'd enjoy. Let's face it, we both need a good laugh at the moment." Sylvia paused to take a sip of white wine. "Then in the evening, we could have a meal at Trader Vic's. It's Polynesian, and you can have any combination of any fruit drink you choose."

"That sounds good." Elizabeth tried to conjure up some enthusiasm as Sylvia ploughed on.

"Then, on Sunday we can either go to a film, or you can challenge me to a mean game of Gin Rummy. Or both? What do you say?"

"Fine."

Listening to her plans, Elizabeth wondered whether in fact the weekend might indeed pass quickly. It would be wonderful if it did. After all, she really just wanted to go to sleep and wake up at four-thirty on Monday afternoon.

—���—

Laurie strode through the double doors of St. Georges Hospital carrying a large bunch of pink ornamental lilies and shuddered.

He hated hospitals. Detested them, in fact. The smell, the brisk superiority of the men and women who worked there and, last but not least, sick people.

In fact, he had hardly visited his seventy-year old mother last year after she had had her fall. His sister had complained that it was all down to her again and that it wasn't fair, as she was managing a job and four children and could hardly find time to blow her nose.

"Cardiac Unit, fifth floor." The badly permed receptionist told him, without looking up.

In the lift, he stood among other visitors of various shapes, colours and sizes, most of them clutching assorted blooms and, after it had stopped at every floor, he apprehensively stepped out on the fifth.

A blue-clad matron, curiously not unlike Hattie Jacques, was hurrying into the main ward and Laurie deliberately blocked her progress. You could never find anyone to ask about anything, so he would not be put off by her stern demeanor.

Fortunately, she knew the answer to his question. "Jack Merrick? He's in a private ward." She scrutinised him carefully. "Are you family?"

Laurie kept his voice level. "No, but he has asked to see me and the specialist has given permission."

"You'd better follow me, then," she said, marching off with such speed that he almost had to run to keep up with her.

He examined Jack's name on a small card on the door and tensed himself, not knowing quite what to expect. Then, as Hattie Jacques threw the door open, she turned to Laurie before he had a chance to look inside the room.

"Now, I'm afraid you'll have to keep it short. Mr. Merrick must have very little stimulation."

In a second she was gone, leaving Laurie laughing disbelievingly and, as he went in, he saw Jack struggling to sit up in the bed.

Disguising unease at the sight of his grey face and the parched and loosened flesh which hung around it, Laurie gave him a kiss on his lips which he knew was what he wanted.

"Did you hear that?" He asked, attempting to maintain humour. "Did you hear what that old bag said? You mustn't be stimulated and I've got to keep it short. Can you imagine?"

196

Jack nodded and clasped his hand. "It's so good to see you."

"Well," Laurie said, looking around for something to put the flowers in. "It's good to see you too, but not in this condition. Was I too much for you?"

"Probably." Jack stretched out his fingers to touch the lilies. They weren't the Longiflorum variety which he had always thought of as far classier than their over-pollinated cousins. "Thank you for these."

"I thought you would like them." Laurie noticed a cut glass vase nestling behind the horticultural oasis next to Jack's bed and went to fill it with water from the small bathroom area. "Not too funereal, I hope?"

"Not at all. Come and sit beside me."

Laurie finished arranging the flowers and drew up a chair. Jack looked worse than he had imagined and would probably be out of action for quite a while. It was lousy timing for both of them.

"The good thing is..." Jack began, then paused for breath, "I don't have to have one of these new pacemaker things inserted in my body. It's just a matter of taking it easy for a while. I shall find that difficult, of course, but you know Sylvia. Everything's in hand at work. And she's staying with Elizabeth."

"What can I do?" Laurie asked. "Is there anything I can get you?"

Jack managed a wan smile. "You can be the first to pour me a Jamesons' when I get out of here."

"And when will that be?"

"Another ten days or so, they reckon. Then I'll have a nurse or nurses visiting me for about five hours a day. They have to get me walking again."

"God, Jack. I'm so sorry."

"Yes, well..." Jack sank back into the pillow and Laurie could see how much effort the conversation had cost him. "Not half as sorry as I am. What a mess."

"Don't talk any more." Laurie told him, alarmed that he may have another attack while he was in the room. "I'll come back tomorrow."

"That would be great. Sylvia generally comes in about nine and then again after work. So if you could make it around this time…" His voice trailed off and Laurie noticed that his eyelids were fluttering.

Moving closer to make sure that he was still breathing, Laurie almost jumped out of his skin as Jack grasped his hand.

"There's something I've… Got… To ask you." Jack whispered.

"For heavens' sake Jack, don't exert yourself." Laurie's own heart was now beginning to thump like a Ringo Starr riff. It was more than likely he'd have a seizure himself if he had to stay here for much longer.

Jack regarded him through half-closed eyes and held his hand tighter.

"It's just that… And I'm sure I was hallucinating or something. Just before I collapsed, I got the very strong feeling – call it an instinct, that Elizabeth knew."

Laurie shook his head vehemently. "No, no. You mustn't worry yourself about that. She knows nothing about us. Nothing."

Jack squeezed his hand again and Laurie felt that it was taking all of his strength to say what he wanted to say.

"No, that's not what I mean…" Jack coughed and Laurie, terrified now, was torn between running out and calling for help or pushing one of the buttons beside the bed.

"Jack, it doesn't matter. None of it matters…."

Jack drew in a deep breath and continued. "No, what I mean is, she knows that you… That you are a female impersonator."

Laurie was rendered speechless. Why on earth was Jack worrying himself about that now? And what was he supposed to say? Pulling himself together he reassured Jack as best he could.

"Jack, I'm sure that's not true. You almost certainly were hallucinating. Now if you don't rest, I'm calling for somebody."

Jack released his hand and waved his own in the air. A gesture that told Laurie that he had finished saying what had seemed to him so important.

"Alright." He was barely audible, and Laurie let himself out of the room, shutting the door quietly.

Once in the corridor, he began to walk towards the lift but realised that his legs were trembling and he leaned for a brief moment against the wall.

Somehow, he would have to force himself to come in here every day until Jack got home. How utterly terrible that was going to be. And what had made Jack think that Elizabeth knew about his act? Jack was foggy about it, but she must have hinted at something. Maybe it had even exacerbated Jack's attack?

He knew that he would have to be very careful about what he said to whom, particularly in the light of Jack's now fragile condition, and he found himself wondering why on earth he had agreed to meet with that precocious, yet unnervingly likeable girl, later that day.

—∿—

The Chopin mazurka, which Elizabeth had almost perfected before leaving Rhodesia, had now taken on the sonority of a jumble of discordant notes hammered out by a monkey wearing a blindfold. At least, that was how Mr. Feeney, her piano teacher at St. Hilda's, described it. Six foot two, with hair resembling the wire wool used for cleaning pans, and wearing the heaviest and most intimidating pair of spectacles Elizabeth had ever seen, he was certainly not someone to be trifled with.

"I'm aware of your personal circumstances, Miss Tarrant," he told her in a strong Northern Irish accent, "and of course, I sympathize. But I have a letter here from your last teacher, who most categorically states that you have reached Grade 6, and that the mazurkas and waltzes are not a problem for you."

"No, sir. I'm sorry." Elizabeth offered, with a quick glance at the clock which showed twenty past four.

"I am also aware that you do not have practice facilities at your home at present, but for those pupils who are not fortunate enough to have a piano we can arrange those facilities here at certain times to fit in with your studies, if you would like to discuss them with me."

"Yes, sir. That would be fine. Thank you."

"I just feel it's your lack of concentration, Miss Tarrant. That's the problem. Now let's finish with the minuet, shall we?"

The cab was waiting when she dashed outside and as she gave the driver Laurie's address, she suddenly realised what a sight she must be looking. No make-up and far worse than that, school uniform. What a baby she would appear to him. So much for her dreams of shared love now.

She heard Flora barking as she climbed the three sets of stairs that led to his flat and then as she looked up he was there to greet her, opening the door and smiling, sending her tummy once more into a double flip.

Dressed from neck to toe in black, he waved her into his room and immediately started discussing her uncle.

"... Such a terrible thing to have happened. He looks so ill."

She handed him her school coat and hat and he hung them on one of a number of ornamental hooks behind the door.

"Would you like a tea or a coffee?" He asked, and she shook her head.

"I've just re-decorated. Well, added a few more colours. What do you think?"

Elizabeth looked around and was amazed by the seemingly random kaleidoscope that he had created within the small room. None of the colours matched, but it didn't really matter. In fact, they positively clashed. Pink, ochre, apricot and violet. If someone had told her that they were going to design a room using such a mixture of shades she'd have thought they were mad. But somehow it worked. Somehow it was a unique space for a very unique person.

"Golly," she said, blinking. "Uncle Jack thinks mine is over the top. Has he seen yours?"

Not waiting for an answer, which was just as well as none was forthcoming, she sat primly on a rocking chair covered in cerise velvet, trying to avoid looking at the bed on which he had perched. Although his attention seemed focused on her, she felt less at ease with him today. Even less than when she had visited him in his dressing-room. There seemed so little affection or warmth coming in her direction and, in fact, almost a deliberate effort on his part to avoid any physical contact.

"What was so important?" He asked, not unkindly but in a tone that hinted at getting to the point.

She decided she would do just that. Rummaging in her satchel among the school-books, a geometry set and a collection of pens and pencils, she finally pulled out the small drawstring bag and handed it to him.

He took it, looking puzzled. "What's this?"

She returned to the chair and rocked backwards and forwards vigorously. "Have a look?"

He was playing the adult to child role again and she was now determined to confuse him, as she had before.

She watched him untie the strings, peel away the wooly cotton and take out the diamond. After studying it in bewilderment, he looked at her questioningly.

He doesn't have a clue what it is, she thought with satisfaction. Let's see how he reacts now.

"It's an uncut Kimberley diamond. Twenty-five carats and valued by De Beers at fifty thousand English pounds," she recited, having learned the words by heart.

He stared at her and then again at the stone as he tried to take in the information she had just imparted.

"It's a what? By whom? Elizabeth, what are you talking about?"

She grinned at his confusion. "I've just told you. And I'm giving it to you. It's yours."

He started to laugh, but it was a laugh of disbelief more than amusement.

"You can buy your club now," she said, matter of factly. "If that's enough, of course."

Still holding the diamond, he got up and stood in front of her so that her eyes couldn't help but meet what was not so obviously hidden inside his skin-tight, black trousers.

"Elizabeth, if I had fifty thousand pounds then of course I could get my own club. But that's my problem, not yours." He took her hand, placed the precious stone inside her palm and closed her fingers around it. "Thank you, but be a good girl and go home."

Frustrated now that he was not taking her seriously, she stood up, her eyes smarting with tears of love.

"Okay. If that's what you want, I'll go. But you must understand that this diamond is mine to do exactly what I want with. My great-aunt left it to me. And there's another one in the bank. Jack doesn't even know about this one." She paused for breath and wiped her eyes with the back of her hand. "I don't need it, Laurie. I've got money, jewellery, paintings, and there's still more to come. I want you to have it, because... Because I love you. And I want you to be happy."

Angry with herself for crying, she tried to pull her coat from the hook, but somehow it became caught and as she tugged at it desperately, she was aware of him standing closely behind her.

"Come here," he said and she turned around, needing no persuasion as she folded her arms around his neck and hung on for dear life. This was what she had longed for and she wanted it to last forever.

Now she knew what to do. But this wasn't Christmas day and there were no disapproving onlookers. No one to react with shock and horror as the fusion of their tongues warmed her like a furnace on a cold, January afternoon. When he finally pulled away and led her over to the other side of the room, she held her breath, assuming they would now lie down. But this time he sat her down upon the bed and himself opposite in the rocking chair.

"Right," he cleared his throat as she ached to hold him again. "I think we'd better talk, don't you?"

She longed to say 'I don't want to talk. I want you to make love to me', but nodded her head instead.

"If I was to take that... That diamond, it's all a gamble. Jack says that the whole venture mightn't work out. I may lose the money for you."

She shrugged. "I don't care. What you don't have, you don't miss."

"And we wouldn't tell Jack? Is that what you're saying?"

"Why tell him? He's ill and he might worry." She tucked her legs up under her skirt like a practiced gymnast. "It can be our secret."

He ran his hand across his thick hair as she watched lovingly. "But I don't know if I can repay you. That's what I'm saying."

"But Laurie, you can. All I want is for you to love me."

She couldn't be bothered to be subtle any more. That was such a tedious waste of time. She was here with him. In his home and on his bed. He wasn't just a player in her twenty-four hour imaginings. This was real and she had to seize the moment.

He sighed and shook his head. "Elizabeth, let me ask you a question."

"Go ahead."

"Has anyone ever talked to you about what's euphemistically called the birds and the bees?"

She giggled nervously. She got the gist of what he was asking her and shook her head. Her mother and father? He must be joking. And as for Uncle Jack...

"No."

He laughed then, reaching for a cigarette. "And you're looking to me to educate you, are you?"

If that was the way he wanted to put it, fine. "Perhaps."

She studied him studying the silver lighter to which he seemed so attached. "Because, Elizabeth. Because... Because... Because."

"Because what?" She was puzzled but didn't want to appear childish and ignorant.

"Elizabeth, you're fifteen..."

"So?"

"Listen! You're a child. The niece of my... Of my friend and manager. You're too young."

She uncurled herself and sat forward, determined to make him understand.

"Laurie. You think you know me, but you don't. Yes, I've only lived on this planet for fifteen years. No, there are hundreds of things I have no idea about, that I haven't seen. But, in this last four months, I've been through so, so much that I sometimes feel like I'm the oldest person alive." She shivered and rubbed her shoulders, as if chilled by a sudden unwelcome draught. "I've seen death, Laurie. Violent death. I've been uprooted like a young tree and planted somewhere else, with absolutely no choice. And last week, when Uncle Jack had his heart attack, I stared death in the face again. I've been forced to grow up. Very fast."

The smoke from his cigarette spiralled towards the fuscia ceiling and spread into a blue fan as he listened, not interrupting.

"I feel like a woman in so many ways," she continued. "All except one. And I'm ready for that now. But only with you."

He spoke at last, his voice soft, but she could tell that he was still unconvinced.

"How do you know it's not just your hormones reacting? And I happen to be the only likely person around?"

He kept using words that she wasn't sure about. "What are hormones?"

He stared, then started to chuckle. "Oh boy, do you need educating? You really don't know anything about being a woman at all, do you?"

She was embarrassed now. "Please don't laugh at me."

"Oh, Elizabeth, I'm not."

He got up and came to sit beside her on the bed. "Let me tell you a few things about sex. And about what makes men and women tick. It's not straightforward, although a lot of people would like to believe it is. We all have hormones, glands if you like..."

"I've heard of glands," she told him proudly.

"Good. Well, I'm no doctor, so these are the basics. Hormones secrete various fluids in our bodies. The sexual glands do the same. And there are certain times of one's life, like puberty or adolescence, around your age, when these are at their most active. Also, the way you probably feel just before your period, like uptight or emotional, that's a hormone effect too."

"I see." She said slowly, concentrating hard. "So do men feel the same?"

"Well, we don't have periods." He smiled patiently. "I'm sure even you know that."

She pinched his arm and he returned the pinch although more gently.

"And now I'm going to tell you something which may confuse you further. Some doctors and scientists are beginning to believe that we each possess a combination of male and female hormones, like plants where the two sexual characteristics are united."

"Male and female?" She repeated, wide-eyed.

"That's right. And all I'm saying is that some men or women may have a stronger opposite element in their hormonal make-up than others."

"You mean," she twisted her hair around her finger, thoughtfully, "that I could have some male hormones? Is that why I always preferred climbing trees and doing things that boys did, rather than playing with dolls?"

"It may be. Or that could have been just a phase. You feel very female now don't you?"

He leaned towards her and touched her ear with the tip of his tongue then breathed into it, making her whole body tingle.

"Yes," she whispered, but he teased her emotions again by getting up and walking away.

"Got to give Flora her supper," he said, disappearing through a curtain of rainbow-coloured glass.

Elizabeth jumped up from the bed and followed him.

"And what about you?" She demanded, as he scraped dog food into a bowl from which Flora ate noisily. "Which hormone is stronger in you, the male or the female?"

He straightened up and rubbed his forehead. "To tell you the truth, Elizabeth, sometimes I'm buggered if I know."

He took her arm and led her back through the curtain and towards the door.

"I'm going to send you home now," he told her "… And I'm going to do some serious thinking. About the diamond and about having sex with you. And I want you to do the same."

She wrapped her arms around his neck. "But I don't need to think anymore. I know what I want."

Once again he loosened her grip and shook her gently.

"Listen to me, Elizabeth. This is serious. It's not a game. If I fu – make love to you, then I have to warn you that it might not be what you expect."

She looked doubtful. How could it be anything but wonderful?

"You see, when I'm aroused or excited...I might say or do things that could upset you."

"What kind of things?" She asked, curiously.

"Oh, God, I don't know. Things that you mightn't understand, or that might strike you as disgusting."

She laughed, then her hand flew to her mouth quickly. "Sorry, but you look so worried. Please don't be worried."

She could tell he was concerned and she would do him the courtesy of listening to what he had to say.

"Elizabeth. Sometimes the fantasy is better than the reality. That's all I'm saying. Perhaps you've built up our love making in your mind to such a pinnacle of ecstasy, that I could never live up to it. And you'd be disappointed."

She smiled, not even trying to disguise her resolve. "I wouldn't, I wouldn't, I wouldn't. I love you. It will be exactly as I imagine."

She lost herself again as they kissed, hungry for him to touch her and take her at that moment. But he led her downstairs, gave her some money and put her into a taxi, and she waved and touched her lips until he vanished from her sight.

Once again she would have to wait. But this time it was different. This time she knew it was going to happen.

—⁂—

Jack was so glad to be going home that he heard himself whistling "Eleanor Rigby" in the bath that morning. Of course, he would have to pull the cord to get the nurse to help him out, which, even though he was used to it now, was demeaning to say the least. Still deeply tired, he knew that he had come on reasonably well over the last week, managing to walk just those few steps to the bathroom and back. At first, he had dreaded the thought of a structured exercise programme under the control of a professional, but now he was anxious to continue with that routine at home.

Sylvia had said that his body, like a broken television, would soon be restored to normal service if he did not overtax his system before it was properly repaired. He liked the analogy, but he knew it was almost impossible not to be impatient with his progress. And that, according to Leachman and Jim Beresford, defeated the object. With impatience, came stress.

He reached for the cord then soaped himself one more time, trying yet again not to feel swamped with guilt. Guilt about not acknowledging the warning signs that now seemed so patently obvious. And, through his careless disregard for those signs, plunging Elizabeth and Sylvia into pressures that they could well do without. As for poor Laurie, Jack was only too aware that his oversensitive temperament did not respond well to his sickness, or to the hospital environment.

He was also aware that each of the three people closest to him was, in their own way, admitting some liability for his illness.

Elizabeth was being super-sweet as if to make up for her recent taciturn behaviour. Sylvia had told him several times that she had carelessly allowed him to do too much in the lead up to Christmas, given his personal and professional work load. And Laurie had chastised himself for keeping him up all night. And he hadn't meant it as a pun.

A voice called to him through the door and moon-faced Shelagh, the nurse to whom he had now become attached, at least that was the way she put it, strode towards the bath.

"Ready?" She asked, and not waiting for his reply, rolled up her sleeves and yanked him out, then smothered him in a huge white towel. Even though he had lost weight, Jack had to admire her strength.

She was formidable but funny, and they had shared some fights and some laughter. He would miss her and told her so.

"Go on, Jack, pull the other one. You'll be glad to get shot of me."

"That's not true. Can't you come and look after me at home?"

"No can do. Sorry. I'll stick with the poor pay and conditions. Not brave enough to go private yet."

"Pity."

She helped him dress into one of his crisp poplin Savile Row shirts and a soft camel-coloured Jaeger cardigan, then lowered him into the wheelchair which she pushed towards the window, from where he could see a flock of crows balancing on the skeletal branches of the trees that lined a bleak Hyde Park.

He breathed in deeply, beginning to feel alive again. Reborn.

And it hadn't escaped his notice that Sylvia was enjoying some kind of flirtation with David Leachman. As they came into the room laughing together, Jack realised that although that was simply all it was, he was heartened to see her blush and hear her giggle again. In some mysterious way, Leachman was making her feel attractive and feminine, and she glowed, vibrant with the pleasure.

"Well, Jack," the specialist held out his hand. "I'll see you next week for your check-up. Till then, please take care."

Jack shook his hand gratefully. "I don't have much choice."

Sylvia picked up his small suitcase and looked around the room. "What are you going to do with all these flowers?" She asked.

"Jack says they can be taken into the main ward," Shelagh told her. "Which will be much appreciated."

"I'll do the pushing," Leachman said, taking charge of the wheelchair.

"What do we do with the chair?" Jack asked Sylvia. "Can you get it in the car?"

"No need," Sylvia replied. "There's another one waiting at home and Victor will bring it out for you."

With their assistance, Jack managed to tuck himself into the front seat of Sylvia's black Citroen and, waving their goodbyes, Sylvia pulled away from the hospital forecourt and joined a line of traffic making its sluggish way around the Park.

"Are you going to tell me what's happening at work?" Jack

asked her, peering into the paper bag that Shelagh had plopped on his lap and which contained so many varieties of pills. Anti-coagulants, diuretics, pills for blood pressure, pills for sleeping, pills for pain relief. He felt like a walking pharmacy.

"Everything's fine," was all he could get out of her. "I'll make sure you are settled at home then I'll have to go in. If that's alright with you?"

"Of course. But can't you tell me anything? What happened about that Wednesday Play for Justin Norman, and have you heard anything from LA about how many extra musicians I've got to book for Sammy Davis?"

"Yes and yes." Sylvia pulled the car to a halt outside the entrance to the flats. "Now come and meet Adrian."

"Who on earth is Adrian?" Jack asked, in surprise.

"Your nurse. Well actually he's called an occupational therapist."

"That's nice," Jack said, then asked lightly "Pretty?"

He noticed her look of surprise at what she obviously considered to be a diversion from his usual macho bluff.

"Quite cute, as it happens."

He saw Victor hurrying towards the doors, pushing the wheelchair.

"I'm only kidding. I'm a one-woman man. I mean..."

They both laughed then and Jack shook his head. "What a Freudian slip. I can't believe I just said that."

"I can't believe you just did."

After Victor and Hannah had welcomed him back with over-emotional delight, Sylvia introduced Jack to the private nurse who, he was more than aware, would be sharing his convalescence on a daily basis. And it was obvious that Adrian also shared his own sexual persuasion. He looked as if he was used to training, his arm muscles being well developed and particularly noticeable beneath the short-sleeved, pale blue nylon uniform he was wearing. Jack surmised that he was about twenty-seven and that his blonde hair was almost certainly bottle bleached. His skin was clear and tinged with pink like young fruit, and he carried a slight odour of nicotine, all the more discernible to Jack who had been denied cigarettes for three weeks.

"I expect you're tired." The nurse with the fancy title that Jack couldn't remember pushed his chair into the bedroom and threw back the bedcovers. "I just came to say hello, and I'll be back later to see how you feel about a little walk around the flat and to make sure you take your medication."

Jack could feel himself glowering. The exercise was all very well, but did they really think he was incapable of swallowing a few pills?

"I'm not senile, you know." He said grumpily. "I can be trusted to take what I'm instructed to take."

Adrian helped him out of the chair and on to the bed. "I'm just here to make sure. Now… Do you want to undress or stay as you are at present?"

"I'm alright." Jack told him. "I've only just dressed, why would I want to get into pajamas again?"

"Jack, I'm off." Sylvia put her head around the door and looked from one to the other. "You're okay, aren't you?"

He raised his eyes to the ceiling. "Yes, yes, I'm fine. You go and keep the firm solvent. Will I see you later?"

"No. You're in good hands. I'll be by tomorrow. Elizabeth will be home around five. She's doing some piano practise."

"Okay." Jack stretched and allowed Adrian to fuss around with the business of propping up his pillows.

He didn't really want the nurse to return as Laurie had said he would call round at about half-past two. And there was something that Jack wanted to say to him which couldn't wait.

"Could you come back around four?" He enquired.

Adrian checked his watch. "Yes. That should be alright. I'll see you then."

Jack sighed with relief as he left, amazed to discover how thoughts of Laurie had produced a slight, but distinct tremor of movement between his legs.

You old rascal, he mused. Not much wrong with you then.

Hurriedly, he wiped the smile from his face as Hannah came in carrying a tray containing a chicken sandwich and a glass of stout.

"This was on your diet sheet, Mr. Merrick. I hope it's alright."

Once again, he was reminded of his present dependency on others and of how anxious they were to make sure everything was perfect, issuing gentle orders about what he must and must not do. In many ways, it seemed to him ultimately more stressful than going into work.

"It'll be fine, Hannah." He told her gruffly, switching on the radio for a little light music and failing to notice his housekeeper's crestfallen expression as she left the room. Frank Sinatra was crooning a song that advised *"Let's forget about tomorrow, for tomorrow never comes."*

Jack closed his eyes and tried to remember what Leachman had told him. "Try, but don't struggle to try, to find stillness of the mind. Think about something which brings warm and pleasant memories."

Instantly, and as though he had stepped into the Tardis, Jack was transported back to the white-washed stone, semi-detached house by the sea, where he had spent his childhood. One of those cottages where you could smell the salt in the wooden floorboards, and to one of those brief, yet not infrequent periods which his father had spent in hospital and when he and Emily would have their mother all to themselves.

Late afternoon. Possibly a Sunday. And his mother sitting in a cosy chair next to the fire, knitting. He would have been toasting crumpets on a brass fork, looking forward to savouring the taste of the butter and home-made blackberry jam as it dribbled down his chin. Emily would be reading at the table, probably a school girls' annual, or maybe even stories for children from Dickens, and the only sounds were the spluttering of the fire, the click of the needles, and the tick from the old clock on the mantelpiece, as evening lazily crept up on them.

Here he had felt safe. A feeling of 'how it ought to be', before his sick father returned home and a few years before his own life choices did little to ensure such security of being.

When his specialist had first talked about 'stilling the mind', Jack was sceptical, convinced that as far as he was concerned, there was no way such a form of meditation would be able to achieve the desired effect. Warm and pleasant memories, free from tensions and frustrations, did not exist. Until just then. And that particular recollection, he hoped, would allow those feelings of frustration that he was struggling with, to find a shape in which they could be held, so that other realisations, such as why this serious illness had struck him, might be woken.

—⚬—

She knew that he had been in the flat, even before she opened her bedroom door and found the note on the carpet. The lotion he wore lingered like one of the scents from her garden at home when a summer shower had kissed the lime trees. It was the sweet fragrance of forbidden fruit, filling her senses yet again with delicious desire that was crying out to be satisfied.

"Who's with Uncle Jack?" She asked Hannah, hearing voices coming from her uncle's bedroom.

"Oh, that'll be his nurse, Adrian." The housekeeper told her. "Go and say hello. He's very bonnie."

Jack was leaning on the arm of a fair-haired man in a blue tunic who was walking him around the room. They stopped when she put her head around the door and went to greet her uncle.

"Hello, Uncle Jack. Welcome home," she said, pecking his cheek.

"Elizabeth." She noticed that he had slightly more colour but looked exhausted. "This is Adrian. Adrian, this is my niece, Elizabeth."

"Pleased to meet you," the young man flashed a bright smile. "I'm just going to teach your uncle how to take his own pulse, then I'll be leaving. He's done very well today."

"I'll see you later then," Elizabeth said, turning to go. "Are you having supper in your room, Uncle Jack, or with me?"

"Definitely with you." Jack replied, sitting heavily on the bed to re-gain his breath.

In the kitchen, Elizabeth squeezed past Hannah and took a

bottle of milk from the fridge, pouring half of it into a tall glass.

"Has he had any visitors?' She asked casually.

"Aye. Mr. Christian came. Stayed for about an hour. I would think Mr. Merrick will go straight to sleep when he's eaten his supper after all the excitement of being home."

In her room, Elizabeth tore at the envelope and read the note that he had written over and over again, making sure that she understood every word. But her eyes stung with tears of bitter disappointment and her heart, along with her spirits, sank, for it was not what she had been expecting.

'Hello, gorgeous, I thought I'd better write to say that I have been thinking long and hard about your very generous offer. As fate would have it, Jack has also shown me great generosity. He has said today that he will invest in setting me up in my own venue, which is wonderful.

Obviously, I have accepted this, so you can hang on to that incredible rock! Thanks a million and love from Laurie.'

Elizabeth dried her eyes, wondering how she could possibly sit down to a meal with her uncle this evening when she felt, however unreasonable it might be, that he had cheated her out of the opportunity of getting closer to Laurie.

And, obviously unwittingly, Jack had not only denied her the pleasure of giving Laurie a very special present, but everything that went with that arrangement. Her gift of money in return for his gift of love.

Laurie had mentioned fate. And, she thought sadly, maybe it was time to acknowledge that perhaps some higher force was never going to allow them to be together. He had made it clear that he wasn't going to accept either of her invitations and so there was little else she could do. There were no more tricks left to play.

If only, though, this same higher force could quell the bubbling volcano which seemed to be erupting from the very depths of her soul and threatened to overwhelm her. It was all so cruel and unfair.

She had no appetite for supper and even less for attempting an hour's homework on the Plantagenets, but it was her uncle's first day home from the hospital and she knew she must somehow make the effort.

Distractedly, Elizabeth turned over the card on which Laurie had written. She hadn't even noticed what was printed on the back and now she saw that it was a photograph. At first glance it simply looked like a black and white photograph of a glamorous woman. But of course, it wasn't. It was Laurie, his signature flamboyantly scrawled underneath. Although the picture struck her as familiar, this was different to how she had seen him in the nightclub. Feminine, as then. Unbelievably beautiful, as then. A head and shoulders shot of him blowing a kiss to the camera. But here he was wearing a blonde wig and a white fur stole. Suddenly she realised why it seemed familiar. This was a photograph almost identical to the one she had noticed when first arriving at Jack's flat. The one of who she had thought must be a girlfriend of his and which, for whatever reason, had now mysteriously disappeared.

Elizabeth pulled off her school tie and combed her hair. It was all so confusing. And she couldn't say a thing to Jack as she wasn't supposed to know about Laurie's job.

Forget him, she told herself through clenched teeth, as she heard Hannah laying the table for supper. Forget him, forget him, forget him. It wasn't the first time she had harshly commanded that of herself, but maybe if she kept repeating the words like some desperate mantra, she might actually believe that she could.

—∞—

Laurie knew that today would have to be the day, even though Jack had told him to approach it cautiously, there was no rush, and that it would be better to wait rather than to dive headlong into something which wasn't absolutely right. But he had trudged around for over a week now looking for likely properties, and the plain truth was, none of them were in the least likely. That was, until this afternoon.

Added to which, waiting was not a word that featured in

Laurie's vocabulary. Now that Jack for whatever reasons, and Laurie suspected it was because of his near-death experience, had decided to support him in his quest, Laurie was determined not to allow precious time to be wasted.

Jack had given him a budget, which, when he had first made the suggestion, had seemed more than reasonable, although Laurie had to admit that his own limited experience of what leasehold West End real estate might be worth, amounted to zero.

The figure discussed had been £25,000 for one year's rental if the property had already been used as a nightclub and contained the basic stage facilities, sound, lighting, dressing rooms etc. In addition, Jack had offered a further ten thousand for refurbishment, or fifteen, to stretch to the limit, if Laurie deemed it necessary.

The alternatives had been rather less well defined in financial terms. To attempt a complete refurbishment on a property without these existing facilities, and in a good area, would almost certainly cost considerably more, and Laurie, who had just seen such a place, was convinced nowhere else would do.

Set just around the corner from Curzon Street, the substantial, white-stucco fronted building was impressive, even by West End standards. The two lower floors were being offered for lease in early March, wherein the entire ground floor of 3000 square feet housed a massive ballroom with crystal chandeliers and silk drapes, while the basement comprised seven good-sized rooms, including a kitchen.

He knew immediately that this was where he wanted to be. And it wasn't difficult to imagine the chauffeur-driven limousines dropping off the rich and the famous as they flocked to watch him perform in his own show at his own club, where his name was emblazoned above a marble portico in dazzling light bulbs.

The estate agent had told him that there would be no problem with renovation. The elderly owner had died, and his son was working as private secretary to the Sultan of Brunei, rarely setting foot in England, and only interested in obtaining the required amount of money for his property. For the 25 year lease itself, he was asking £30,000 a year and Laurie realised he would have to carefully price the refurbishment through an architect and a team of builders. Even so, it looked as though it would far exceed Jack's budget.

He was certain that if Jack saw it for himself, then he would agree how perfect it would be. But Jack was not fit enough yet, and if he refused to be flexible, then Laurie, unable to exert too much pressure on his sick lover, was convinced he would lose it.

He made his way to the Mini, having decided that he couldn't be bothered to go and view the last property on his list. Some restuarant premises in Piccadilly that sounded singularly unimposing. No, he had seen what he wanted and was going to get it. He would have to try and twist Jack's arm, which before his heart attack might not have proved difficult, but sexual persuasion at the moment was something that the doctors were not prescribing.

By the time he had found a parking space outside Jack's flat, Laurie had already made up his mind what he would do if Jack were to say that this highly desirable property was too expensive. He hadn't heard anything from Elizabeth since telling her he didn't need her money, and that had suited him fine. There were only so many complications he could handle at once and she had turned out to be a major one.

But with Jack's money, together with what his niece had suggested he could get for that amazing diamond, Laurie knew that he would have a venue to die for. And, if her offer were still on the table, then maybe the end would somehow justify the means.

—m—

RHODESIA
FEBRUARY, 1967

Richard T. Mackenzie was not in a good mood. Try as he may, it seemed completely impossible to lay the Tarrant and Ainsley estates, unlike their testators, to rest. And although happily his bills were creeping up by the minute and no-one appeared to be querying them, there always seemed to be some niggling problem which took up a substantial part of his day.

Once again the weather was baking, and once again the ancient ceiling fan was proving inadequate. Strange, he thought, how only a few weeks ago he had been longing for the warmth of the sun on his back as he moved between the cold, damp climates of Scotland and England. But this heat was just too much and it sapped his strength and fuelled his temper.

Pouring himself some iced water from a glass jug, he studied the paperwork in front of him, which was the present cause of his concern.

It simply didn't add up, but then perhaps he was being too pedantic. Some had hinted at this on various occasions and he had ignored it, proud that in an age when standards seemed to be slipping and other people's work often shoddy, he could hold his head high in the knowledge that he had given his best to every task and would never be found guilty of anything which might constitute a dereliction of duty.

Samuel and Margaret Ainsley had been long-time friends of a couple called William and Daisy Campbell, who had owned a jewellers' shop in Salisbury, but sold up in 1948 and moved to

Johannesburg. Here, having invested at a very fortuitous time in a gold and a diamond reserve, they began to reap the rewards of these investments, which ensured them wealth beyond their wildest dreams.

But the Campbells were not to live to enjoy either their old age or their riches, as a car crash on a mountain road in Capetown in 1960 claimed both their lives. Most of their estate and effects had been left to family, but various letters and documents found in Margaret Ainsley's possession indicated specific items that had been willed by their closest and dearest friends.

The gold mine share, now inherited by Elizabeth Tarrant, was accompanied by a document also bequeathing the Ainsleys the magnanimous gift of two Kimberly diamonds yielded by the Campbells' diamond shares, but there had been nothing, and this is what had been bugging the solicitor for days, to prove that these two diamonds had physically entered the hands of the Ainsleys. Until now.

Following the immensely complicated and time-consuming process of clearing out the contents of the Ainsley's farm, had come the whittling down of items to be shared between the servants, money for charities, articles to be kept in storage for Miss Tarrant, and of course his own job of scouring through a volume of cheque books, receipts, and letters.

The recently discovered letter he now held in his hand, was from De Beers in Johannesburg, dated the 14th August, 1961, and partially addressed his concerns.

'Dear Mr. and Mrs. Ainsley,

I find, looking through my files, that my colleague, Henry Cohen, has not replied to your letter of the 12th July, and I would like to apologise on his behalf as he has now transferred to our Durban branch.

I understand from your letter that, at present, you do not wish to accept our offer for the two uncut diamonds and that you are placing them in your bank for safe keeping.

If however, you decide in the future to reconsider our offer, I would be pleased to discuss the matter with you again.

With all best wishes,
Yours sincerely,
David Shalcross
De Beers.'

Mackenzie wheezed out a cough, followed by a deep sigh then very carefully punched two holes out of the side of the letter and placed it inside the bulging file that sat on his desk.

Did it really matter that he had only seen one diamond taken from the deposit box in the Bank of Scotland? The Ainsleys had probably decided to do something else with the other one. But where was the paperwork? The proof that it existed? And, whether he liked it or not, knowing that a stone of such value was unaccounted for would, almost certainly, cause him to lose sleep tonight.

—w—

LONDON
FEBRUARY, 1967

"Now what happened to you since I left this morning?" Adrian demanded, placing his hands on his hips. The over-exaggerated gesture that was reminiscent of a pantomime dame.

Jack shook his head, pretending he didn't understand the question. "Nothing, why?"

"Why? Because after we came back from our little perambulation around the gardens, you had colour in your cheeks. Now you look like chalk."

Jack spread himself out on the sofa and wrapped the mohair rug around his legs, trying to ignore this unappreciated third degree from somebody who, after all, he was employing. "Can you turn the television on for me?"

"What for?" Adrian sneered good-humouredly. "Childrens' Hour? Come on, Jack, sleeve up. Let's check you out."

Obediently, and because he knew he had to stay calm, Jack did as he was told as his nurse tied the black band tightly around his upper arm and pumped away at the pressure.

"So?" Jack enquired, when the equipment had been dismantled.

"A bit high. Not too bad. But I'd still like to know what you've been up to?"

With a sidelong look of accusation, Adrian headed for the kitchen, where Jack heard him gossiping with Hannah who had taken to treating him like a long-lost son.

Jack attempted a few short breathing exercises before, once again, picking up the glossy brochure that Laurie had left behind and which featured the property which he had begged Jack to put in an offer for that afternoon.

They hadn't exactly quarrelled, but there had been a tense exchange, for Laurie seemed stubbornly determined that this unarguably exquisite West End conversion, with its elegant high ceilings, mouldings and cornices, was the only one which he would consider worthy of the investment Jack had offered, and had intimated that he couldn't be bothered to look any further.

Jack realised that while he knew very little about the market himself, his scant knowledge amounted to more than Laurie's. Old cinemas and Edwardian music halls were now being turned into Bingo venues for the masses, and nightclubs were most definitely going out of business. It had been less than a fortnight since he had made the decision to give Laurie something to remember him by just in case he popped his clogs. The fact that he also adored him and didn't want to lose him was another crucial factor, for although he was gaining strength on a daily basis, Jack knew that his inability to participate in their strenuous sexual games posed a dangerous threat to Laurie's delicate notion of fidelity.

He had thought about it carefully in his hospital bed, knowing that if he had died, then his only tangible connection to Laurie would be as his manager, leaving as much lasting impression as a post-coitus stain on his lover's fur bedspread. No, this was the most he could do, and as much as he could do. Allowing Laurie, in his uniquely talented way, to at least be given the chance to achieve his much-desired goal for fame and fortune.

But just how far could he indulge him? Surely it was not too much to ask for him to take a little more time? Even though Jack knew that Laurie was anxious about losing the moment and fretted constantly about losing his looks, with such a huge financial risk at stake it was disappointing that he did not appear to heed Jack's urge for expediency.

Haunted by Laurie's hurt expression, which had changed into one of determined self-control when he took his leave, Jack pondered again on his decision to say no. This building that

Laurie had set his heart on was not going to be a pushover, for the agent had said that only the asking price would be accepted and a year's deposit required up front. But, just suppose they went ahead with tearing the place apart in order to transform it into the worthy venue they envisaged, only to find it didn't pull in the punters? Jack would then be stuck with an un-bankable property and the losses would be considerable.

"You're frowning again."

Jack turned quickly as Adrian stood in the doorway holding a small tray on which a row of multi-coloured pills had been methodically planted.

Practical decisions needed careful planning and Jack wasn't about to break the habit of a lifetime. He would have to try to rein in the haste with which Laurie was now railroading him, and hoped that his lover would take time out to fan his peacock feathers and reflect on the importance of such a commitment.

—⁂—

"The child raised her fingers and stroked her mother's face.
The skin was so soft, so silky.
In the yard, Isaac swore at a furiously barking dog
and waved at the servant who had come from the house next door
wiping her hands on her apron.
The child soon fell asleep, rocked in her mother's arms
and comforted now by the security of having come home."

There was a pause, a cough, the sound of a chair being scraped against the already deeply scratched wooden floor, then the tentative flutter of applause as Elizabeth, her face impassive and unblushing, received the guarded appreciation of her class-mates.

Neil Jenkins, enthusiastically endeavouring to maintain the applause, beamed broadly then picked up her essay and held it in the air.

'Cycles', an essay penned by Elizabeth Tarrant, and I'm sure you will all agree, a mature piece of writing of merit, its efficacy lying in the way she has captured the significance of life's eternal cycle. Everything returns to its beginning. Well done, Elizabeth."

Elizabeth gave a slight nod, neither magnanimous nor modest, as her English teacher turned his class's attention to Jane Austen. She sucked her pencil and gazed out of the window, where a grey squirrel, its bright, oval eyes watching warily, sat on the windowsill nibbling at an acorn.

Was it only a few months ago when she had shed tears at hearing similar sentiments read aloud in this classroom? Now she had expressed, through her own creative skills a story combining many elements of her childhood observations and experiences and yet listening to the words, she felt empty of emotion.

She so wanted to feel something. Anything that would confirm to her that she was alive. How could she be this numb and still be living? That was a puzzle and a half, as great-aunt Margaret used to say.

Without seeing or hearing from Laurie, she had been confronted with the reality of two options. One was to sink into a grey depression and unravel like an old cardigan, driving everyone around her who cared for her, fraught with worry. The other was to throw herself into her school work in order to prove what she was truly capable of.

The problem was that choosing the latter gave her little or no satisfaction and the praise she was receiving seemed hollow and meaningless. It was as though she had become an automaton, programmed to produce stunning essays, perfect translations and a wealth of historical facts. She also knew that for some reason, she had taken to eating far too much chocolate, and her normally flawless skin was now threatened by tiny swellings which she tried to cover with foundation, but was then reprimanded by Mrs. Thomas for daring to wear make-up to school.

She made an effort to retrieve her concentration, for Mr. Jenkins' voice was becoming simply a background accompaniment to the brooding pictures in her mind. But today, all that her efforts produced was a facial expression of false interest, while her mind was once again with Laurie, wherever he might be.

She wondered whether he was at the flat with her uncle. It seemed that he visited most afternoons, but had always left by the time she got home. Would it hurt him so much to sometimes wait to see her? He obviously thought that they could no longer be friends and it grieved her to think that she must have given him that impression.

She became aware of a flurry of movement and realised to her surprise that the class was breaking up, even though she hadn't heard the bell. Trying to gather her thoughts and to remember what she needed for homework that evening, she began cramming things into her satchel as Josephine Dover appeared at her side.

"That was a good story. Was it true?"

"Um... No. Not really."

Josephine released her mass of heavy, dark hair from the grey silk ribbon, allowing it to cascade over her shoulders. "Have you got piano practice tonight?"

Elizabeth shook her head. "No, not tonight."

"Do you want to come home for tea? You can ring Jack from our house if you like."

Elizabeth thought for a moment then nodded. "Okay. Thanks."

It would make a change and hopefully take her mind off its all too-familiar absorption, allowing her to feel less like an alien among the trappings of ordinary, daily life. She liked Judy, Josephine's mother, although Sean, her little brother was a pain, currently obsessed with cowboys and Indians, and adept at playing both roles. One moment, he would be shooting at all and sundry with his toy gun, the next giving the blood-curdling cry of a Sioux chief and attacking everyone with a rubber hatchet.

The girls collected their coats and hats and made for the front door.

"Did you know the Beatles are working on a new LP?" Josephine asked her as they negotiated the steps carefully, having been warned of the dangers of recent black ice.

"No." Elizabeth realised that she hadn't bought any teenage pop magazines for ages. "When's it out?"

"Sometime in the summer," Josephine replied knowledgeably. "It's all about the Maharishi and circus performers."

Elizabeth stared at her as they picked up pace along the pavement. "Golly, I can't imagine that at all."

The glow from the sun was surprisingly strong, an orange light that hung low in a livid winter sky. She squinted and blinked her eyes, thinking that what she was seeing must be a mirage which people in the desert experienced when their minds were wandering through lack of food and water.

Parked across the road from the school was a purple Mini with a psychedelic roof, and inside she could see Flora, her wet nose pressed against the window and barking in recognition. In the driving seat, Laurie sat watching her then raised his arm to wave her over.

Elizabeth stopped in her tracks, as Josephine walked on oblivious to her companion's stunned immobility. When she saw that Elizabeth was no longer with her, she turned around.

"What's the matter?"

Elizabeth thought quickly then blurted out the first words that came into her head. "Josie, I'm sorry. I've just remembered I've got to be somewhere."

"Where?"

"It's alright," Elizabeth ran towards the nearest zebra crossing "I'll see you tomorrow."

Josephine gazed in bewilderment as Elizabeth crossed the road and let herself into the Mini. As it screeched away from the curb she stared harder, wondering what on earth Elizabeth Tarrant, who could write a 'mature essay of such merit', would be doing in the company of a man, whom she had overheard her mother and father say, wore blue lace garters.

—⚭—

"Where are we going?' She asked him finally, as they turned into a busy Kensington High Street.

"To my flat. If that's okay with you?" He said, holding up two fingers at a Mercedes who had dared to cut him up on the inside lane.

Her head was still spinning with the thrill of being with him. "Do you want the diamond, because I don't have it with me?"

He turned to look at her, his face serious. "I just want to be with you."

She took off her hat and laid it on her lap, running her hand nervously through her hair. "How long were you there? Outside the school?"

"I wasn't sure when you'd be out. About half an hour, I suppose." He lit a cigarette as they stopped at the lights. "You'd better ring Jack. Tell him you'll be late. Make something up."

She needed to be sure of the meaning of this obviously planned encounter, anxious not to get things wrong again.

"Well, I was going to Josie Dover's. I could say that."

He shook his head vehemently. "No. Too close to home. Think of someone else."

Flustered as she was, she was almost certain now of his intentions. "Alright."

When they got to the flat, he threw off his jacket, took her coat and pointed her to the phone.

It was all moving so quickly that in a daze she dialled Jack's number, trying to hold on to rational thought, while almost sick with anticipation. Somehow she heard herself speak when her uncle answered.

"I'll be a bit late... Yes, a friend's... For tea. You don't know her. Nicole... Nicole Morris... Oh, I don't know, I'll ring before I leave. Okay, bye."

Laurie was watching her intently, then to her surprise handed her a cigarette.

"Oh no... I don't"

"This is different." He told her. "This isn't tobacco and it will make you more relaxed. Trust me."

Tentatively, she placed the piece of rolled paper between her lips and tried to smoke as she had seen Laurie and Jack do so many times. Not finding it as easy as it looked, she coughed then tried again, inhaling cautiously. The sweet, heavy taste and scent began to relax her as he had promised and she handed it back to him, intoxicated by the fact that his lips were sharing it now.

"Are you cold?" He asked her, gently.

She shook her head. "No, why?"

Immediately she realised that she had said something stupid and immature. Of course she knew why.

Wanting to prove to him how grown-up she was, she started to remove her tie and her gymslip then, standing in only her shirt and slip, she looked to him pleadingly for help.

He moved towards her and, as she held her breath, he slid his hand underneath her shirt and was touching her breasts. She shuddered as he peeled away the rest of her clothes, leaving her naked apart from her panties.

"Lie down" He ordered, removing his shirt and tie. "Lie down and open your legs."

Knowing only that she wanted him, she was confused as to how it was supposed to happen. Part of her needed his kisses and his affection, although the impatience for something her body had craved for so long impelled her now to do his bidding.

As she obeyed, abandoning any lingering embarrassment, she wondered if he could hear her heart the way she could hear it. It seemed to be pounding in her head and gradually spreading its urgent beat down to the tips of her toes. Never in her life had she known such excitement, nor wanted anything so much as for him to touch her.

She watched him drop his trousers and briefs, and for the first time in her life she saw how a naked man looked. How *he* looked. Two questions flew into her mind, one serious and one frivolous, in those seconds before he lay down with her on the bed. Would she have room for him inside her and what did he do with it when wearing those tight dresses?

She became distracted again by the intrusion of a red neon light that suddenly lit up the small room like an alien aircraft hovering just outside the window. Pulsating with hypnotic regularity, it spluttered the words 'STRIP CLUB', illuminating their bodies as he guided her towards the bed and lay beside her.

And then a wave of overwhelming pleasure as his fingers began to very slowly stroke the inside of her thighs.

"Relax." He whispered again and it was impossible for her not to let out a small cry as he moved higher, finally reaching the edge of her panties.

Damp with longing, she spread her legs wider, allowing him to slide her pants down and then push his finger inside her. She cried out again and raised her back, not understanding why, although she felt some pain, she wanted still more of him there. Swiftly obliging, he inserted another finger and she took them both with ease as he worked them rhythmically, her cries reaching a pitch that she didn't even try to control.

This, at last, was real. He really was touching her, about to bring her to her first climax and she was actually on his bed, not lying in her own, touching herself and pretending that her fingers were his.

"You're very wet." He said softly.

"Is… That… Good?" She gasped, then moaned again as he somehow turned his hand, beginning a new rhythm.

"Very good. It means you want me."

Hardly able to bear the sensual headiness that she was experiencing, Elizabeth sat up, pushing him even deeper into her and flung her arms around his neck. "I do want you. And I love you, Laurie."

He kissed her neck, nuzzling her ear and biting her gently.

"I think I might have broken your maidenhood."

She sank back on to the fur bedspread and closed her eyes, surrendering once again to the indescribable ecstasy. "Good. Then I'm no longer a virgin."

He took her hand and guided it towards him and she opened her eyes, fascinated by what he was instructing her to do.

"Just rub me here," he told her. "Up and down, like that. Gently…"

This time she noticed that he had closed his eyes and she hoped desperately that she was doing it properly, able to give him the same pleasure that he was giving her.

They matched their rhythm until it intensified and she was now somewhere far away. Floating in space, her body weightless, her entire being simply concentrated on this duality of passion and how they were pleasuring one another.

She watched as he beat his fist against the pillow, his brows drawn together and a bitter crease tightening his full mouth. Alone on his own planet and perhaps not really sharing this moment with her, after all.

"Quicker," he panted, his hand closing over hers as she continued to rub him. "Quicker, fuck it, quicker."

She tensed slightly. He had said that word. The word you weren't supposed to say. Did it matter? If she was honest, it even heightened her stimulation, inciting a cascade of small explosions which she had no control over.

Her body began to shake with sobs of fierce satisfaction as he exploded too and she felt a warm, sticky fluid cover her hand.

"Christ!" He said, withdrawing from her and opening his eyes. He gazed for a moment at the blood-flecked moisture on his fingers, then as she watched transfixed, he licked it away with his tongue and it was gone. Like it had never existed.

He raised himself on to one elbow regarding her from those amazing, hooded eyes heavily fringed with long lashes which she could have sworn bore traces of mascara. Then he looked enquiringly at her hand.

She hesitated, realizing what he meant and wondering whether she was able to do what he was suggesting.

"It's only me," he smiled. "Like that was only you."

Slowly, she raised her fingers and, hoping that she wouldn't throw up, placed her tongue upon what had come out of him and tasted it warily. It wasn't as smooth as it looked. Warm, but not too unpleasant. In fact, rather like a bland, lightly salted rice pudding. She licked again until her fingers were clean, noticing the intense expression he wore while watching her.

"Good, Elizabeth. That's very erotic. Good girl. You're a quick learner."

He pushed his tongue into her mouth and it dawned on her that their fluids were mingling there, rather than inside her vagina which was now swollen and sore. But to be restored to a living entity once again felt fantastic and the numbness of the past few weeks had completely vanished. He wrapped his arms around her until they both drifted into a state of semi sleep and the thought of leaving his bed was becoming the most difficult thing she had ever had to do.

"I love you with all my heart," she told him.

He bent to lick her nipples, which tickled, stung and rose simultaneously. "I love you too, gorgeous."

Glancing at his watch, he got up from the bed and started dressing.

"Elizabeth, you know I told you about the club I wanted to open?"

"Mmm." She studied his nakedness as it slowly disappeared. "The one Uncle Jack's going to help you with?"

He drew a comb out of his pocket and ran it through his hair. "Yes, well, it's not going to be as easy as we thought. The one I want is perfect, but more expensive than Jack can afford."

She reached over to tug his arm. "But that's wonderful. I can help you now."

He sat down beside her and took her rather cold hand. "Are you sure? It really would make a difference. And it would still have to be our secret."

"Of course." She nodded her head, and threw her arms around his neck, wanting him to do everything to her all over again. "And Laurie?"

"What, gorgeous?"

"Next time...Can we make love properly?"

He rose from the bed pulling her with him then picked up her clothes and handed them to her gently. "We'll see," he said, using one of his most familiar and one of her least favourite expressions. "We'll see."

—⁄⁄⁄—

Jack moved the chess piece abstractedly across the board, causing Adrian to cry out triumphantly "Check mate!"

The young man sat back in his chair, a look of satisfaction having etched itself on his pink and white face.

"I'm sorry." Jack shook his head and stretched out his legs. "I didn't give you much of a game. No concentration today."

"I think you allowed me to win and that's very naughty." His nurse lifted the small folding table on which they had been playing to the other side of the room then came back to sit beside him.

"Jack, do you mind if I say something? It's kind of personal, but also to do with your health."

Jack wanted to say 'If you must," but decided that might sound ill-mannered. The problem was that his natural guard prevented him from discussing anything even remotely personal with Adrian.

He grunted and Adrian, taking it as a yes, leaned forward, dropping his voice so that Hannah, although listening to the radio in the kitchen as usual, couldn't detect what he had to say.

"I don't know whether your specialist or Dr. Beresford have discussed this with you..." He started, then paused as a plane flying low overhead muffled his words with its vibrating drone. "I find that doctors won't volunteer this kind of information, they wait until you ask." He paused again, clearing his throat nervously. "What I'm trying to say is that maintaining a satisfactory sex life is one of the best ways back to health. You might be a bit frightened about... Well... Doing it, but you know, gentle masturbation by your partner wouldn't hurt you."

Jack, disconcerted by this un-called for advice, stared at him in silence as he pressed on.

"I'm speaking as someone in the medical profession, Jack. I hope you understand that. What you do in your own time is none of my business. But there are so many misconceptions about sex after a heart attack and I just wanted to make sure you understand that if you repress your sexuality, it's probably worse for you. I personally think you're strong enough now to indulge carefully."

Jack found his voice then, but it was distinctly tremulous. "Well, thank you for that. I'll bear it in mind."

Adrian got up from the chair and fiddled in the pocket of his nylon tunic, producing a small card. "This is my home number," he told Jack "which I don't usually give out to patients. But if you need someone to talk to about anything, feel free to give me a call."

Jack took the card and couldn't help asking "Why would you think I'd need to do that?"

Adrian shook his head. "Don't ask me why, Jack. Perhaps it's just an instinct. I've come to know you on a daily basis now for several weeks and I can almost touch your isolation, it's so obvious."

He went towards the door while Jack remained seated, having no intention of seeing him out.

"Till tomorrow, then. Don't forget your pills."

"No. Okay. Thanks."

When he'd left, Jack realised that before he took his medication he needed a drink and a cigarette. The former he could manage. A small one anyway. The latter was simply a pipe dream.

Aware that he had to continue to be kind to himself, he poured a careful measure of whisky over a mountain of ice-cubes and tried not to over-emphasise the context of Adrian's unexpected diatribe. "A little gentle masturbation", his nurse had said, without so much as a flicker of his white-blond eyelashes. Well, chance would be a fine thing. Except for a solo performance.

He hadn't heard from Laurie for two days since telling him that he was not prepared to make an offer on that property, and although Jack missed him desperately, he hoped that he had now stopped sulking, had heeded his advice, and was continuing to look for suitable premises in a more realistic price-range.

It really was all down to Laurie to get in touch. But as Adrian's words continued to echo in his ears, Jack knew that he would probably weaken if he hadn't had a call by tonight.

He pulled the silk cord to draw the drapes and noticed Laurie's Mini pulling in next to the Alfa. His heart lurched and he instinctively put his hand on his chest drawing in a breath then letting it out again slowly, as he had been instructed to do, if given cause for sudden worry or excitement.

Hurrying into his bedroom, Jack emptied the six pills that he was supposed to take into his hand. Then knocking them back with half a glass of stagnant water, he checked his appearance in the mirror, patted his favourite Penhaligon's after-shave against his warm face and combed what was left of his hair.

"It's alright, Hannah, it's Laurie," he said when the bell rang. "I'll go."

His lover was wearing a full-length leather coat which Jack hadn't seen before, the collar turned up and the belt loosely tied, leather gloves, and a pair of dark glasses, which were also new. Pursing his lips into a silent kiss, he called a greeting to Hannah and made for the sitting-room.

"Hannah, why don't you get off?" Jack told the housekeeper, meaning it to sound casual. "Leave a bit earlier today. I'm sure there's nothing that Elizabeth and I can't manage."

"Are you sure, Mr. Merrick?" Hannah poured a trickle of stock over two breasts of chicken. "I wouldn't mind, if that's alright. My sister's staying for a few days."

"Sure. Absolutely. You go. Have a nice evening."

"I think Elizabeth said she had piano practice and a lesson tonight so she'll be back around six. You can put these in at about five-thirty."

"Will do. Thank you, Hannah."

When she'd gone, although his immediate impulse was to wrap Laurie in a long embrace, Jack resisted. There were things he was anxious to discuss with him first.

They kissed briefly and Jack poured him a gin and tonic, aware that his own present condition dictated that he was not yet in control of his life. A semi-invalid, whose pathetic, emotional dependence was likely to be obvious now. And he loathed himself for asking, "Why haven't you been in touch? What have you been doing?"

"Questions, questions." Laurie sipped his drink and edged up closer on the settee so that their thighs connected. He was wearing a look of self-satisfaction, which Jack instinctively took to mean that he had something significant to impart.

"I've spoken to the estate agent and said we'll take the lease on that Curzon Street place."

Jack tried to remind himself about control. "What?"

Laurie laid a reassuring hand on Jack's knee. "It's alright. Don't get excited. We've got the money."

"Where from?" Jack asked with bewildered scepticism.

"A surprise investor," Laurie said smugly. "Do you mind if I have a cigarette?"

Of course he minded, but Jack shook his head, anxious to find out what the hell Laurie was taking his time to tell him.

"Well, that's great," he said, carefully. "Who is it?"

"No-one you know." Laurie told him, lighting up. "A woman. Rich. A fan of mine."

"A woman? How much is she willing to put in?"

"Around £50,000."

Jack looked at him in astonishment. "Fifty thousand pounds? But that's incredible. We must set up a meeting. Draw up an investors' contract."

To his surprise, Laurie shook his head. "No, you don't understand. Perhaps I should have said benefactor, rather than investor. She wants to remain anonymous. It'll be cash and a gift."

Jack needed another whisky and this time it was going to be a big one. He got up to refill his glass, wondering whether he had heard correctly.

"Let me get this straight. This woman wants to give you a cash gift of £50,000 and wants nothing in return? There's no such person, Laurie."

His lover's expression was beginning to change to sullen. "Jack, for God's sake, don't let's look a gift horse in the mouth. It's probably some tax fiddle, I don't know. Listen, if you put in thirty, we've got more than enough for renovation. We can even take a holiday in Rio before we open, or buy a place in Spain."

"Thank you, I can do the maths," Jack snapped. "I still don't understand why I can't meet her. Just to make sure it's all kosher. After all, I am your manager. I'm the one looking after your interests."

A thought struck him and as soon as it translated into words, he wished he hadn't said it. "I hope she doesn't believe all that propaganda in Grosvenor's programme. About you being straight and having a son tucked away somewhere?"

Laurie gave a sardonic laugh. "You think I'm fucking her, Jack? Get real."

Unable now to halt the painful tidal wave of suspicion and jealousy, Jack continued. "How the hell do I know what you're doing? We haven't had sex in over six weeks." He downed his drink in one long gulp. "How old is she, anyway?"

Laurie sighed. "What's that got to do with anything?"

"No, come on. Is she old? Young? Built like Monroe or Mama Cass? I only know she's rich. Come on, give me a clue."

He was pacing the sitting-room carpet like a caged animal now, aware that he might be doing himself harm, but too keyed-up to stop.

Laurie rose with another sigh, folding his arms around him in an effort to calm his agitation.

"Don't do this, Jack. You'll make yourself ill again."

Trembling with tension, Jack succumbed to his touch, resting his throbbing head against his shoulder.

"I'm sorry. I just can't help it. Love you too bloody much."

Laurie tilted Jack's face towards him with his hand and spoke seductively. "Listen, I'm doing this for us. This is our vision and it's going to be fantastic. I promise you, we don't have to worry about paying this money back. Trust me, please?"

As Laurie's mouth closed over his own, Jack's anxiety began to rescind. Sexual reassurance was what he needed now and his hand searched for that comfort.

"Hey, hey," Laurie said, pulling away. "Haven't we got to be careful?"

"It's alright," Jack said, tiredness threatening to overcome him. "I'm told I can indulge in a little gentle masturbation."

Almost aborting Jack's passion, Laurie burst into gales of laughter. "Who told you that? Not that blonde slut of a nurse? Jesus, Jack! And you're the one who dares to act jealous?"

Jack managed a smile, allowing Laurie to take his hand and lead him into the bedroom.

As they undressed and climbed into bed, Jack knew that it

was impossible to make any further attempt at rational communication. Whoever this woman was, there was no doubt that she fancied her chances. And, hadn't he always known that Laurie attracted both sexes equally with his looks and charisma? Christ, even his young niece had nursed a crush on him. Life, Jack had recently come to realise, was all too short. And it was no exaggeration to consider that although his heart may only have suffered minor damage from his attack, without Laurie there was little doubt that it would be broken.

—⁓—

Elizabeth finished writing in her diary, locked it and pushed the key into the small cavity behind Rufus's eye. It had been hard enough trying to find a place for the diamond, for although she knew that neither her uncle nor Hannah would dream of looking through her things, that legacy from her great-aunt, together with her diary, were crucial to her mind-blowing secret. Again, she was finding this, the biggest secret she had ever owned, the most difficult to keep. How she longed to write to Chloe and tell her that two days ago she had lost her virginity. But if Chloe's mother got wind of it, then she would fly into a panic and ring Jack, so that was out of the question.

Actually, Elizabeth wondered whether she had really lost it. After all, Laurie had only put his fingers inside her. Although he had said something about having broken her maidenhood which struck her as an oddly old-fashioned phrase to use.

Even now, she was still aching from where he had touched her. How smug she had felt at school, squeezing her legs together under her desk, keeping him with her all through the day, superior in the knowledge that she must be the only girl there who was carrying around such pleasure.

No, she would have to keep this secret strictly for her diary. That day had been the most important in her life and she had written about it with such an outpouring of passion that it left her exhausted, reminding her of a sentence from a Jane Austen novel. Something about 'paying for the overload of bliss by headache and fatigue.'

Now she had received another letter from him. Pushed under her bedroom door as before and saying that he would meet her from school tomorrow at the same time. She loved these secret notes. They were so romantic. But she would have to think up an excuse for being late home. Piano practice was only for ninety minutes and her lesson was only once a week, her uncle being quite aware which day of the week that was.

When Jack knocked at the door to tell her he was going to bed, she knew she would have to say something.

"I'll be a bit late home tomorrow." Her tone was relaxed. She felt some shame in that the lies she was telling him were becoming easier.

"Why?" He asked, predictably enough.

"Nicole's asked me over. You know, I went to her house a couple of days ago?"

To her concern, instead of accepting this explanation and leaving, Jack sat down on the bed, poised to enter into further conversation.

"Where does she live again, this Nicole?"

"Um... Allen Street."

"Why couldn't she come here instead? I'd love to meet your friends."

"No!" Elizabeth replied, almost too sharply. "Not tomorrow anyway. She's got some records she wants me to hear."

Jack squeezed her hand then rose slowly. She thought how much better he was looking, but still how easily tired he became.

"Alright. But next time invite her here. Goodnight Elizabeth."

When he had gone, Elizabeth set out to check everything she needed for the following day. It was so very important. Firstly, she would not be caught dead again in those boring, waist-high cotton pants. Cream embroiderie-anglaise ones, bikini-size with tiny silk bows were laid carefully on the chair with her clothes and she moistened at the thought of him slipping them down over her thighs. Next, she took a small phial of Sandalwood oil, which she had purchased from a little pharmacy near her school

237

and which bore the delightfully Dickensian name of "The Apothecary", ready to be dabbed behind her ears and on to her wrists. Then finally, she reached once again into the stuffed head of her toy bear, taking out the drawstring bag which held her gift to Laurie and which she packed into her satchel, along with her school books and pens.

Deliriously in love and fizzing with happiness, Elizabeth was determined nothing was going to burst this magical bubble which she had worked so hard to create around herself and Laurie. Not even shadows from the past which might have whispered to her that night, echoing her mother's strong conviction that happiness must have its price. That was something she didn't want to be reminded of now.

—∞—

Laurie knew he was playing a dangerous game, but he also knew he had come too far in order to go back. Somehow, and he still wondered how it had all happened so fast, he had become the object of infatuation for two people and they were constantly demanding his presence in what, after all, was only a twenty-four hour day.

But, hey, hadn't that always been what he'd craved for? Love and devotion on a scale that made him feel supremely powerful. Rather like being God. Holding human fragility in the palm of your hand and able to give pleasure or take it away at will. And in return, being worshipped. Not a bad deal, really.

Now, as he lay on his bed beside this young girl who had once again submitted to a cluster of multiple orgasms courtesy of his overworked fingers, he wondered just how long he could continue playing this double game successfully without being rumbled.

She was as insatiable as he had first guessed she would be. But it wasn't working. Begging him to penetrate her with his cock, he had tried to oblige, but his trusty friend had flunked the test, refusing to rise beyond pliant and insignificant. It had been different a few days ago when she had tossed him off. Then, he had closed his eyes and imagined that her hand belonged to that of a beautiful young boy. Probably one of those coffee-skinned Moroccans, whom he had encountered on a memorable trip to Marrakech and who behaved like sexual slaves when dispensing their favours. Now, he thought with some amusement, as his eyes fixed on the small drawstring bag provocatively facing him on the bedside table, he was caught between a rock and a hard place. But, at least he knew for certain that female pussy was obviously not his thing.

"Don't you like me any more?" He heard the poor girl ask, clearly wondering what she was doing wrong.

"Of course I do, silly. It's just that... I'm afraid I'll make you pregnant."

That was clever. That he was pleased with.

"Can't you wear something?" She persisted.

"I don't think either of us would really like that," he told her, playing for time until she had to leave.

To his dismay, her eyes started brimming with tears and, in a child-like attempt to hide them from him, she turned around on the bed so that her back, and more to the point, her buttocks, were facing as well as touching him.

Aware of a stirring, Laurie wildly tried to think of anything that might suppress this unanticipated urge. Determinedly, he forced himself to visualise how the new club would look, and that peppermint green Rolls Royce which he just might be able to afford.

'Go down,' he ordered his swollen member silently. 'Wrong time, wrong person,'

Shit, this doesn't just cross the line, it fucking hop, skips and jumps it. He could never allow his appetite to be satisfied in this way, could he?

Slowly, his hand began to stroke the firm arches, never before corrupted by other human touch, and which she had so innocently presented to him. Then, as she uttered a small cry of delight, he moved closer in order to allow her to feel his hardness. It was what she wanted, wasn't it? She was so crazy about him would she really care about which way he went?

Christ, she could be a young boy! Don't even think about it, Laurie.

His demons were winning the battle. Placing his hand on her small breasts, he caressed her nipples. A boy's nipples. A girl should have mounds there. Soft, squishy mounds. That wasn't fair. It wasn't his fault she was built like a boy.

She cried out again and he pulled her towards him, clenching her body in a vice-like grip.

"Don't turn around. Stay where you are."

"Why?" She was breathless with pleasure, but he could tell she was puzzled.

"Because... Because I want to talk to you for a bit. Okay?"

"Okay."

"Elizabeth, there are two ways I can make love to you. One won't make you pregnant, the other will."

"I don't understand."

"No, I know." He was beginning to perspire. Time was marching on and he desperately needed gratification.

"If I make love to you the other way..." he whispered, tonguing her ear which he knew turned her on. "You might feel a little pain." He waited and when she said nothing, he continued. "How do you feel about me hurting you a little?" There was a silence and then to his heart-stopping delight, she replied.

"I love you, Laurie. Try not to hurt me too much."

"I won't, gorgeous. I promise."

Gently, he turned her on to her stomach and reached with his right hand for where she wanted him to be.

As she moaned, he sat astride her carefully. "Think about what I'm doing to you with my right hand. How much you like that...alright?"

"Yes," she answered, her voice muffled by the pillow.

"Now..." He found the lubricant and smeared it liberally inside her buttocks with his other hand. Going deeper, he heard her cry out but entered her immediately he had drawn his hand away, starting gently then penetrating further.

God, it felt good. Virgin territory. Tight at first, but relaxing nicely.

"Are you alright?' He gasped, knowing that this would be the last sane thing he would say until he burst his seed.

Not hearing her reply, Laurie saw only what he wanted to see. A young, firm male arse. Ripe for fucking. Deeper he went and faster he rode, aware that a torrent of words were uttering from his mouth which were never meant for Elizabeth's ears.

Too damn late. And he had warned her, hadn't he?

All too soon he came. His shouts and her cries harmonizing into a deafening crescendo until an eerie silence descended, hovering above their locked bodies and heavy with uncertainty.

Then another sound lent itself to the highly-charged atmosphere. Flora traumatized by the vocal intensity of passion and pain, began to howl in the kitchen in a way he had never heard before.

He was worried now. The girl was so cold. And still. Also, as he withdrew he realized, so bloody.

"Elizabeth?" He shook her gently. "Are you alright?"

To his relief she turned her head on the pillow, mumbling something inaudible.

He feigned cheerfulness then. At least she was alive. "Was that a yes or a no, gorgeous?"

She still had her eyes closed, but she nodded.

Flora had stopped howling and was now barking shrilly. Laurie stood up and made for the kitchen. "I'll be right back," he told Elizabeth, and throwing on his red silk dressing gown, he calmed his dog and returned with a flannel, towel and a box of talcum powder.

Sitting on the bed, he wiped away the blood and bathed her gently. She winced and he stopped. Time to apologise. Possibly even to try and explain. An hour ago she would have forgiven him anything, but was she able to forgive him this?

"I'm sorry if I hurt you."

She opened her eyes and, to his even greater relief, managed a pale smile. He read pain and some resignation in her expression and could now hardly believe that he had deceived himself into using her as a boy.

"It's my fault," she said, amazingly. "You told me that you

might do things that I wouldn't like. I didn't like what you did. Or what you said. But I love you, Laurie. Please just hold me."

When he took her in his arms, she was still trembling and, as he helped her from the bed, he noticed she had some difficulty walking.

It was clear that Jack would realise something was wrong and he tried to think of the most subtle way to find out how she would handle it.

She anticipated his question and reassured him in the strangely adult voice she sometimes used. "Don't worry about Uncle Jack. I'll think of something." She looked soulfully at the blood stained cloths on the bed. "Did it make you happy?" she asked him then.

He wasn't sure what to say. Sure, it had given him the best orgasm he'd had in ages. But not for the reasons she wanted to hear.

"Selfishly, yes," was an honest enough answer.

She nodded and he helped her on with her school coat. "I just wish that Uncle Jack knew about us. And I wish I could stay here with you and sleep beside you all night and that we didn't have to hide how we feel."

Pulling on his sweater and jeans, he flinched nervously. Surely she wasn't going to be stupid enough to tell Jack.

"Listen..." He said, taking her hands. "Perhaps we ought to cool it for a while. Let the dust settle a bit?"

She shook her head. "I want to be with you, Laurie. The weekend's coming up and I won't see you then. Can we meet next week?"

He asked because he had to. "Aren't you put off at all? By what I did?"

"I'm in pain," she told him. "And I don't want to do it that way again. It's better if you wear something. I won't find a doctor willing to put me on the pill as I'm under eighteen."

He tried not to let her notice his reluctance and couldn't help but watch in admiration as she rang Jack to tell him she was on her way. A performance, he thought, worthy of an Oscar. Then when he saw how she almost crawled into the cab, he began to experience the very real doubt that he could get away with what he had done to her today. Suddenly, the spectre of being arrested loomed large in the forefront of his mind. What would they lay on him first, he wondered? Buggering a man, buggering a female, or buggering a minor? He shuddered as he let himself back into the flat. Whatever? It would still mean the rest of his life viewed from inside a prison cell.

For Laurie, who had always shied away from confrontation and facing the music which he himself had orchestrated, this vision was all too real. He would react in the only way he could, and lie low this weekend. Not answering the phone at home or at the club. What you didn't know couldn't hurt you, could it?

—ᴍ—

When Elizabeth arrived back at the flat, Jack was standing in the doorway seeing a man and a woman out. The man was quite swarthy in appearance and wearing a wide, felt hat and the woman was dark-haired and vivacious with an extraordinarily pronounced beauty spot emphasizing her creamy cheeks.

"Elizabeth, this is Lionel and Alma. Lionel's a songwriter and Alma's a singer."

"Hello," Elizabeth struggled to be gracious, although desperate to shower and get to bed.

"We're so pleased your uncle's doing well." The woman told her, flashing an attractive, dimpled smile. "And you are a heroine, darling, acting so quickly."

Elizabeth gazed at the floor as the three of them lavished her with praise. The last thing she felt like at this moment was any kind of heroine.

They said their goodbyes and Jack ushered Elizabeth into the sitting-room gesturing her to sit. "Tell me all about your evening."

She would not of course sit down. That wouldn't be a good idea. Standing beside him, she suddenly recalled an old Hausa saying which Sarah, their maid, had once called upon in order to scold her. Elizabeth had come in for tea and, when asked by her mother whether she had washed her hands, she replied that she had, drawing her chair up to the table, ready to eat. Sarah had then stood over her, rolling her large eyes and waving a finger. "Miss Elizabeth. Ninety-nine lies may help you, but the hundredth will give you away."

"I fell down," she told him, without batting an eyelid. "On the ice."

He moved towards her, his expression one of parental concern. "Are you alright? Listen, Beresford will be here in the morning. I'll ask him to take a look at you."

"It's okay," Not quite a hundred yet, but certainly getting on that way. "I'm just a bit bruised that's all."

"Have you eaten?"

"Not much."

"There's some kedgeree in the fridge. Go and have some with a glass of milk."

He switched on the television and Elizabeth made her way to the kitchen. She hadn't thought about food, but now she realised that she was ravenously hungry.

While she ate, she tried to come to terms with what had happened that afternoon.

The person she was fated to love was an adult. A skilful lover, whom she had persuaded to initiate her. She, on the other hand was a novice, a childish, inexperienced girl who had had no idea that there were two ways of making love. And, of course, it made sense. As Laurie had said, one way made you pregnant, the other didn't. But the other was not like making love at all. It was so brutal, somehow. Difficult to pass off as love. And she had been unable to participate, pinned down as she was beneath him, too powerless to move.

When he touched her soft area, even though it sometimes hurt, it was so achingly wonderful that she could understand it being described as an act of love. But to be entered the other way? Was that normal? She just didn't know.

She flinched again and went into the bathroom, allowing a jet of warm water to soothe her pain, soaping herself as gently as she could to wipe away any dried blood and to try and ease the soreness.

But afterwards he had been so tender. Then he had given her kisses, and cuddled her and bathed her. If she was honest, she loved him when he behaved like that most of all. But there was no way of explaining the intense sexual hunger which drew her to him and which she simply couldn't resist.

What she hadn't expected to feel was that, although her body now throbbed with the excesses to which he had subjected her, she knew, of course, she would want him again.

And, if she regretted anything, it was that her uncle still believed her to be an innocent child, for no-one had ever explained how you could feel no shame for your actions, yet still be laden with guilt.

She climbed carefully into bed, lay on her side and closed her eyes. She felt light and floating in the stillness, as though the bed sheet were a sheet of silent water. She loved Laurie. He said he loved her. That should be simple. He had warned her about his love making, but not in her wildest dreams could she have imagined that pain and pleasure could come together so relentlessly. And if he hadn't been worried about getting her pregnant, he would have made love to her properly.

Tomorrow was Saturday, and she would spend the day being nice to Jack. Perhaps even accompany him on a little exercise in the park, if she herself, of course, felt able to walk.

—◦◦◦—

Sylvia was glad of Saturdays in the office. They were quiet, she could park outside and apart from the usual bustle of shoppers pounding the pavements, could concentrate on the paperwork which had been steadily mounting during Jack's absence.

She knew how frustrated he must be, having to stay at the flat, and although he insisted on doing as much as he could from home, his concentration was often erratic and he still tired easily. She felt at times rather like a headmistress handing out homework to an under-developed, yet willing pupil, knowing that only a certain amount could be presented and achieved.

But she was delighted with his overall progress. The doctors had reported that he should be able to resume work in about three months, although that seemed a long way off given the accumulation of business that needed attention. She had kept some things from him naturally, such as handing over the offer of staging a huge charity show at the Talk of the Town to Lew Grade, for this was a task that no one at the agency but Jack could have taken on in his role as impresario. Maybe she would tell him of this in the future. In fact, he would be flattered to know that he would have been the Duke of Edinburgh's first choice, but at present it would simply create an unsettling and unnecessary pressure, likely to impede the process of his recovery.

Her position in the agency was much the same as it had always been, although now, of course, there were double the responsibilities, and this new and rather alien task of protecting the man who had been its life force was taking a lot of getting used to.

Sylvia poured a coffee and pulled her chair up towards the desk. Methodical, as always, she began to clean her glasses before taking a piece of paper from the top of the pile and making notes with her gold-tipped fountain pen. To her surprise, she heard the front door open.

"Who's that?"

Mark Dover's genial face presented itself in her doorway.

"Hi, Sylvia. Didn't mean to startle you. Thought I'd put in a little overtime myself."

Sylvia smiled. "What conscientious beavers we are. Want a coffee? I've just boiled the kettle."

Mark loosened his scarf and rubbed his un-gloved hands.

"That would be great. How's Jack?"

"I haven't seen him for a day or two, but I'm going over there later. He's being the model patient, I'm pleased to say."

Her colleague plopped a sugar lump into a large mug and stirred vigorously. "And Elizabeth? How is she doing through all this?"

"Fine, as far as I know."

"Judy and I were talking about her last night."

Sylvia raised her eye-brows questioningly. "Oh?"

Mark positioned himself on the corner of her desk. "We were saying that Jack must have come out at last. What with Laurie Christian and Elizabeth being so friendly."

"Sorry?" Sylvia felt she must be missing something and waited to be enlightened.

"Elizabeth and Laurie. Josephine says that he picks her up from school. So that's good, isn't it? Must be a weight off Jack's mind."

Sylvia, puzzled now, decided that she could only talk to Mark frankly about her own understanding of Jack's situation.

"Mark, I have to say this is news to me. I was of the impression that Jack is still very secretive about his relationship with Laurie. And because Elizabeth had a bit of a crush on Laurie around Christmas, he decided to keep them apart. For his peace of mind and to make sure that Elizabeth could concentrate on her schoolwork. He didn't want her to know about Laurie's drag act and certainly doesn't have any intention of letting her find out about them."

"Even odder then." Mark shrugged and drained his cup. "Well, can't spend the day nattering. Duty calls, and regrettably another two nightclubs are closing down. Jobs to be found for people or we're all out of work."

As he made his way to his office whistling *If I were a Rich Man,* which would normally have drawn a smile from Sylvia, she realised instead that she now felt distinctly uneasy. Jack had been emphatic that he was not going to allow Laurie and Elizabeth to meet again after the embarrassing Christmas fiasco. If things had changed then that was Jack's decision, but it was something that she knew she would have to find out for sure.

Then again, was she repeating her usual pattern of worrying unnecessarily? It might help Jack if his niece was being picked up from school. And Elizabeth had probably outgrown the infatuation that was so patently and poignantly obvious just two months ago.

It struck her that to mention it to Jack may not be a good idea. If, for whatever reason, Laurie and Elizabeth were meeting without his knowledge, then this could be another source of concern. And yet she was aware that Elizabeth could be secretive and defensive. Discretion would have to be exercised in order to satisfy her curiosity.

—⁓—

Jack waited until Elizabeth had gone to her room then dialled Laurie's number again. But, as it had done at eleven-thirty that morning, it continued to signal engaged. He looked at his watch. Now it was three-thirty in the afternoon and Laurie was bound to be at home. His phone was obviously out of order, which was irritating, although Jack felt in such a positive and optimistic mood today, that he would try not to be brought down by the fact that he was unable to speak to him, or that maybe, just maybe, Laurie had taken it off the hook.

He winced slightly as music suddenly vibrated through the flat. Elizabeth was playing that Manfred Mann record again. The same one she had been playing the night he had had his heart attack. He shook his head. His imagination must not lead him down that horribly familiar road. It was simply his own longings that embraced the lyrics and foolishly he had assumed that Elizabeth's did also.

He felt exhilarated by his walk in the park and reluctant to take an afternoon nap. The sun had been shining, the birds vocalising, all indicating promise of an early spring, added to which his niece had been at her most attentive. Although, he reflected, she had seemed different again today, this girl of so many moods and in his mind he tried to articulate why. Then he realised what was missing. There had been none of her usual *joie de vivre*. No sense of mischief, fun or humour.

He wondered if her apathy could have anything to do with the fall she had told him about yesterday, although she strongly declined to allow his GP to examine her when he called round earlier. Jack sighed and closed his eyes. He hoped her familiar sparkle would soon return, for that was what made her tick, and he delighted at the way she often teased him until he finally cottoned on to the fact that she was pulling his leg. Then he would reprimand her sternly, while unable to keep a straight face.

The phone beside his bed rang and he stretched out his hand, certain that it must be Laurie and disappointed when Sylvia's voice fluttered down the line.

"Hi Jack. I'm just leaving the office, going to try and buy a pair of shoes and then I'll be over."

"Fine." He endeavoured to hide his disappointment with a light-hearted quip. "But you don't have to dress up for me."

He heard her laugh then she asked. "Are you alright?"

Sylvia was a marvel, but she was given to fretting. "I'm fine."

"Elizabeth and I will cook you dinner. What's Hannah got in?"

He thought for a moment. "Um, salmon... And steak, I think. Either will do. I'll see you later."

"Okay. Bye."

Now his body was ready for the warm, contented slumber on a winter's afternoon, a custom recently forced on him and so welcome compared to the nocturnal restlessness that he had for so long experienced. Today though, because he hadn't spoken to Laurie, it was not to be, and instead Jack used his all too precious energy on willing his lover to ring.

—✺—

Sylvia knew as soon as she saw Elizabeth that she was too late. But through her mixture of disappointment and dismay, she had to wonder – too late for what?

A warning? Not much use when a determined and resourceful teenage girl believed she was in love. Laurie was amoral, but Laurie was fascinating, and Elizabeth had been ready for an adventure. Ready for something exciting, and she probably hadn't known what, to replace the love that had always been showered on her then cruelly snatched away.

But whatever she and Laurie had done together, Sylvia noticed there was little joy behind the girl's oddly mature demeanor. Her eyes seemed duller and she carried herself wearily. The bright beacon which always lit up a room when she entered had somehow been extinguished, leaving a shadow that remained older but not necessarily wiser.

As the evening melted into night and Sylvia, Jack and Elizabeth performed the motions of dinner conversation each with only one person on their minds, the rage that had been bubbling up inside Sylvia towards Laurie Christian began to manifest into white-hot fury. She forced herself to swallow her food, drank a little too much wine and tried not to stare at Elizabeth too pointedly, unless it might catch Jack's attention.

How could Laurie do something so crass and appalling? Alone in the kitchen, dishing out fruit compote and ice cream, Sylvia realised that the question was not so much how, as why? Why would he want to jeopardise everything when he had come so far? Why put his whole life on the firing line? He was a homosexual, adored by a wonderful and accomplished man on whom he also depended for the success of his promising career.

Then again, why did people like Laurie ever take risks? There was only one motivation, she told herself, and that was money. Sylvia licked a dribble of vanilla fudge from her finger and placed the three dishes on a tray. But how could Elizabeth, as wealthy as she was one day going to be, help Laurie now? There must be something that Sylvia didn't know. Perhaps that even Jack didn't know. She took a deep breath and returned to the sitting room, her mind a shifting tapestry of thoughts and questions.

"I was saying to Elizabeth that in the summer holidays we should take a villa somewhere. Greece perhaps? You could come over for a few days, couldn't you Sylvia?"

"Jack, we've never taken our holidays at the same time."

"No, I know. But just a few days should be alright."

Sylvia turned to the young girl sitting next to her. "How do you feel about that, Elizabeth?"

As she anticipated, Elizabeth did not gush with enthusiasm at the suggestion. "Sounds okay. It's a while off, though, right?"

Jack finished his mint tea, an inadequate replacement for his beloved caffiene. "Of course. Plenty of time to make plans yet."

To Sylvia's relief, he excused himself from the table. "Lovely dinner, girls. Thank you. I'm going to turn in. Didn't get my afternoon nap today."

"Alright, Jack. Goodnight." Sylvia watched him leave the room then heard a tinkle from the sitting room phone as the bedroom extension was lifted. It wasn't hard to guess who he was calling.

She drained her wine glass, wondering how she could have arrived in this most awkward of positions. With no children of her own, she could only base her scant experience of teenagers on her own nephew and niece, neither of whom seemed to have run amok, nor turned her brother and his wife into screaming harpies.

But Elizabeth was from a country which might as well be located in another century. Anything that originated in Britain or America, be it music or other consumer goods, often reached Rhodesia years later and Sylvia had to remind herself that the culture shock the young girl must still be experiencing, from having been raised on a remote farm, would be nothing less than mind-blowing.

As Elizabeth rose from the table, Sylvia touched her arm.

"Elizabeth, I need to talk to you."

The girl frowned slightly, then nodded. "What about?"

Sylvia took her hand, leading her over to the settee where they sat down facing the dancing flames of the mock fire.

"Elizabeth, I know you've been seeing Laurie Christian."

Elizabeth flushed then composed herself, pulling her hand away. "So?"

"Sweetheart, you must know it isn't appropriate. You're fifteen. He's twenty-five and..."

Sylvia trailed off as Elizabeth intercepted "And what?"

Feeling lost before she had started, Sylvia knew she was wading into deep waters and chose her words carefully. Even then they sounded melodramatic. "He's not all he seems."

"You mean he dresses up as a woman?"

Sylvia stared then cleared her throat. "Well... Yes. But..."

"Are you going to tell Uncle Jack?"

"Elizabeth, it's up to you. I'm pleading with you to stop seeing him. I don't want to worry your uncle. It could kill him."

To Sylvia's extreme discomfort, Elizabeth gave a nervous giggle. "Oh come on, Sylvia. That's a bit of an exaggeration, isn't it? Laurie and I don't want to tell Uncle Jack yet, but it wouldn't kill him."

Sylvia realised she was losing control of the situation, and that only being brutally honest would tip the balance. But how could she do that?

"Elizabeth, it gives me no pleasure to tell you this, but I feel I have to, to stop you from being hurt and from hurting others. I don't know how far you and Laurie have gone, but I can guess. Elizabeth, Laurie Christian also likes men."

As total incomprehension blanked the girl's features, Sylvia began to feel desperate. 'She doesn't know what I mean,' she thought, with a heavy heart. 'Any other teenage girl in London in the 'sixties would almost certainly know what I mean. But she doesn't.'

"He sleeps with men, Elizabeth. He's a queer. A homosexual."

She studied the girl's expression closely as it changed from bewilderment to disbelief, then set itself into scowling animosity. Jumping up from the settee, she almost spat her words at Sylvia, while keeping her voice low.

"What a disgusting thing to say." The tears burned in her eyes as she continued. "We're in love and I know I'm young. But girls as young as I am have fallen in love with older men. I'm not the first and I won't be the last. There's no need to say evil and wicked things to try and put me off him."

Sylvia's patience had now run out and the urge to physically shake sense into her was a powerful one.

"God, Elizabeth, who are you comparing yourself to? All the star-crossed lovers you've read about? You may also remember that many of their lives ended tragically. Think about it!"

Elizabeth walked to the door then turned around, staring at her coldly. "I thought you were my friend, Sylvia. Tell Uncle

Jack if you like, I don't care. But if you think it will kill him, then it'll be on your conscience not mine."

When she had left, Sylvia was aware that her whole body was trembling, and she steadied herself for a moment before pouring a dangerously generous measure of Jack's finest cognac. She had thrown caution to the wind and it had blown back into her face. "Well," she breathed, raising the glass to her reflection in the mirror, "You handled that brilliantly, Lawrence. So what the hell do you do now?"

—⁓—

Laurie stood in the middle of the marble mosaic floor and gazed up at the high ceiling of scrolled stucco in admiration and reverence, as city types in bowler hats and well coiffed women in fur coats brushed past him. He hadn't even heard of De Beers until Elizabeth had told him that was where diamonds like the one he was at present carrying were bought and sold. The whole place had an atmosphere that reeked of wealth and he was almost unable to believe he was about to do legitimate business here. His eyes were drawn to a large sign behind the reception desk on which illuminated arrows pointed to the various departments within the building.

Carefully, he bypassed 'Consolidated Mines', and 'The Conservation and Restoration of Paintings', and headed for the third floor, where the department titled 'Precious Metals' was housed. That would be the one he wanted. Laurie's heart began to pound with all the excitement of anticipated orgasm. Soon he would be walking away with £50,000 in his pocket and would go straight to the estate agent to put half of it on a deposit for that West End property, which was destined to become the temple of his art.

As the lift transported him heavenwards, Laurie began to experience a very slight niggle of guilt for not contacting Jack over the weekend. He had deliberately left his phone off the hook, both at home and at the Club, fearing that Elizabeth might have spilled the beans about his little aberration on Friday night. But now, because he was feeling so good about everything, he had decided that when he'd secured the lease, he would go round to the flat and take Jack a bottle of bubbly, in the confident hope that she had kept her promise of silence.

The glass doors leading to 'Precious Metals' were locked and Laurie pressed a bell located on the adjoining wall. He supposed that security had to be tightly exercised in a place such as this, where valuable trinkets were being passed in and out on a regular basis and the temptation for a little daylight robbery might enter many an ingenious mind.

The doors were opened by a man roughly Jack's age, with a sharp nose and equally sharp, dark eyes, which focused on Laurie coolly, although his mouth was smiling and his greeting cordial.

"Good-afternoon, sir. How may I help you?"

Laurie followed him through to an unimposing room containing two red leather chairs, and a low marble topped table. As the man waved him towards one of the chairs, Laurie removed the draw-string bag from his coat pocket.

"I have something to sell," Laurie explained, handing him the bag. "I would like cash please, if possible."

His intrigue well contained, the hawk-faced man took the bag from him and pulled open the strings. As he held the diamond up to the light, he gave Laurie a quick glance and produced a small magnifying glass from his pocket in order to study the stone more carefully.

"May I ask where you acquired this, sir?"

"It was a gift. From a friend." Laurie sat down and took out his cigarette case. "Would you...?"

"No, thank you, sir. And this friend, where did he acquire it?"

Laurie was starting to become irritated by what appeared to him to be an unnecessary form of third-degree interrogation. "She. My friend is a she. She inherited it. From someone in Rhodesia."

"Are you sure it was Rhodesia, sir?"

Laurie considered the question for a moment then nodded. "Yes. Definitely. Why?"

To his further irritation the man rose and, still holding the diamond, went towards a panelled door. "Will you excuse me for a moment, sir? I won't keep you long."

Laurie grunted and checked his watch. What the hell was bothering this stuffed shirt? He tried to remember what Elizabeth had said when she had offered him the diamond. 'My aunt left it to me' came clearly to mind, and then 'Jack doesn't even know about this one'. The last sentence had a slightly ominous ring, but what difference would that make to De Beers? As she had told him, it was hers, and she could do exactly what she wanted with it.

The man returned, still smiling, but it was the tight, set smile of the practiced professional which Laurie knew all too well.

"Sir, I'm afraid I will have to ask you to bear with me for a little longer. Can you please tell me the name of your friend? The one who gave you this stone?"

Laurie frowned. "Yes. Elizabeth Merrick. No... No, it's not Merrick. Give me a minute." Damn, he had forgotten her bloody surname. That was going to sound great. Manning... Garrard. Something like that. "I'm sorry," he said, stubbing out his cigarette. "I've forgotten it."

The hawk looked ready to pounce on its prey. "Perhaps, sir, you could tell me? Does she live in England or Rhodesia?"

"Here." Laurie said quickly. "She lives here now."

"Would it be possible for me to have a word with her? Could you telephone her from here so that I could just ask her a couple of questions?"

"Look, what's all this about?" Laurie was reaching the end of his tether. "I've told you. She was left the diamond. By an aunt. And she's chosen to give it to me. What more do you need to know?"

"All I can tell you sir, is that we have had a communication from one of our South African branches to report that a Kimberley diamond of these proportions is at present unaccounted for. It was last traced to Rhodesia, but they have been asked by solicitors there to investigate anything which answers to its description and might come into our possession."

He straightened what Laurie took to be a public school tie and cleared his throat. "There's no real problem, sir. We just need to know more about its history and if you can let us talk to the previous owner..."

"Alright, alright" Laurie snapped, furious now. "I'll get her to call you."

"As I said, sir. We can clear it up now, if you'd care to get the lady on the phone?"

"I can't. She's at school..." He trailed off, realising how deeply suspicious it all must now be sounding. "Listen," he said, trying to control his anger. "You're making me feel like a criminal, which I really resent. Give me back my property and I'll take it elsewhere."

The man appeared dubious, but shrugged and dropped the diamond back into the bag. "That is your choice, of course, sir. But I'm afraid we will need details and proof of your identification. We are under an obligation to report this back to our Johannesburg branch."

"But it can't be the same bloody diamond," Laurie heard himself shouting. "What makes you think it is?"

"If you would co-operate sir, we can easily check it out and then everyone will be satisfied."

"Jesus! Alright, then." Laurie pulled out his driving licence and slammed it on the small table. "Give me a pen and paper, would you?"

The man obliged and Laurie scribbled his name and address, omitting his telephone number, and shoved it towards him. At the same time he was handed what appeared to be a business card.

"If you should wish to ring us sir, that is my direct line. You don't have to go through the main switchboard."

Grabbing his licence, Laurie pushed open the glass doors and, too irate now to wait for the lift, ran down the stairs to the ground floor.

Out in the street he slid on his Gucci shades, catching his reflection in a store window. Comforting himself that he still looked pretty cool, in fact, if his hair were a few shades darker he could pass for George Chakiris, he made for the nearest pub. He needed to think this one through. Elizabeth seemed certain that the only place to take the diamond was De Beers, and she was the only person who could answer their questions. But the one thing he hadn't wanted was to see her alone again. Now, because of this cock-up, he would have to. His plans for the day completely shot, Laurie walked into the bar of *The Coach & Horses* and ordered a large vodka and orange.

—ɷ—

Jack thought he heard the doorbell, but couldn't work out whether it was all part of his dream; the much-repeated and wishful dream that brought Laurie to him, making amends with caresses and words that soothed and re-assured him.

He opened his eyes as a figure came into the room and stood beside his bed. "Jack, you've got a visitor."

"Who is it?" Jack raised himself up, aware of his nurse's disapproval even through the gloom of the darkened bedroom.

"Your friend," Adrian said flatly. "I really don't think he should stay long. Your blood pressure was very high this morning."

"He's early." Jack got out of bed, put on his dressing gown then drew back the curtains. Peering into the mirror, he rehearsed a grin of artificial cheerfulness but which struck him instead as frighteningly jolly like a crocodile about to be fed.

"I'll show him in here then, shall I?" Adrian asked.

"Yes, please."

Laurie entered amid a flurry of shopping bags, drawing a gift basket of glazed fruits from one that bore the name "Fortnum & Mason". Then, presenting Jack with a kiss that tasted of oranges, he removed his coat and sat on the bed.

Jack exerted the ultimate in self-control as he asked simply and quietly. "Why don't you tell me the truth?"

The flicker of guilt that passed across Laurie's face came and went in an instant, but it told Jack all that he needed to know.

"What do you mean?"

"That you're keeping her happy. Giving her what she wants."

Laurie's face was changing colour now and Jack knew he had not just touched a nerve, but had possibly punctured it.

"Your benefactor? Miss no-name?"

Was it relief that suddenly replaced that first flush of guilty embarrassment? The criminal condemned had been reprieved. Jack was puzzled, but waited for him to speak.

"I'm sorry, Jack. I needed some space at the weekend, that's all. I'm here now, aren't I?"

"Yes. You are." Jack said, cheerlessly. "Did you get your money?"

Laurie unzipped his black Kurt Geiger boots and threw them on the floor, then sprawled on the bed beside him. "Not yet. This week, for sure."

He was as easy to read as a Beatles lyric. Something had gone wrong. The thought briefly crossed Jack's mind that the story of a rich benefactress could all be fabrication. Designed to keep Jack interested and possibly to increase the size of his investment offer, although that seemed a shade too manipulative even for Laurie.

"Laurie, I don't like what I'm becoming. I feel so reliant on you. For my health and for my sanity. And when you don't stay in touch, I feel close to losing that sanity. I can't go on like this."

Laurie sat up and moved closer, his proximity tantalising as always. "What do you want me to do? I know I'm a bad boy. Tell me what I can do?"

Jack shook his head and kept his voice low so that Hannah and Adrian couldn't hear. "Godammit, Laurie. I can't tell you that. You should know. I can't get around much at the moment. We can't live together because of Elizabeth. You don't seem to have even tried to meet me half-way."

He knew he shouldn't have been surprised by the adroitness with which Laurie revolved the onus swiftly on to him.

"Jack, you're always scolding me. I'm the one who's always in the wrong, but I'm not the one who's been treated like shit."

"What are you talking about?"

"You. You tell me you can't live without me and one moment you're including me in your family set up, like at Christmas, then the next I'm banished to an hour in the afternoon when Hannah's still here and there's no privacy. It's not easy for me, either."

"Laurie, how many times do I have to tell you, it's just not possible? At the moment, I'm a virtual prisoner in this flat. People are around all the time, and until I've recovered and can get over to see you, I at least need to speak to you on the 'phone. It drives me crazy the way you disappear. Where were you at the weekend?"

Laurie examined his perfect finger-nails sulkily. "I've told you, I wanted some space."

"Space from what? From whom? Me?"

"No, not from you. From the world, I suppose. I don't know." He lay down again and closed his eyes, halting any further discussion.

Was this checkmate then? Jack wondered, staring at him with an equal proportion of love and sorrow. Had Laurie just made the move that ended the game? What was the point in continually putting himself through this hell, if there was no way out of the straitjacket that he had strapped himself into? There were only two choices available and Jack saw them both as pretty near impossible. One was to finish the relationship completely, or to continue to suffer this careless treatment until he was once again able to give Laurie the hours he needed in order to commit.

"Then perhaps we should call it a day," he blurted out miserably. "I think in the long run its better. It's something I should have done a long time ago."

Laurie's eyes shot open, his expression one of stunned dismay. Then, to Jack's anguish, he clung to him and began to weep.

"Don't." Jack said helplessly, fighting his own tears. "Please don't..."

"Don't say that." Laurie sobbed, rubbing his beautiful face roughly with the back of his hand. "Not now, when we're on the brink of such a wonderful adventure. I know if you were free we'd be living together, Jack."

Jack glanced towards the door, passed him a handkerchief and tried to quiet what appeared to be genuine grief. "Ssh, they'll hear you."

Laurie lowered his voice to a choking whisper. "I don't care. I love you. I want to be with you. Please don't throw me out of your life."

Silently and fervently, Jack began to pray as he held the weeping man whom he was unable to live with or without. He had tried to end it for what would be the final time, but had once again proved himself a slave to his obsession.

"You don't know what love is, Laurie. You have absolutely no idea."

—⁓—

When Elizabeth crossed the road and let herself into his car, her brain was wildly working out how she could explain away another late evening.

"It's alright," Laurie told her in a scarily remote voice. "I can't stay. Got a wig-fitting then a rehearsal."

"Oh," she said sadly. That solved one problem but presented her with another. "I would just love for you to hold me, Laurie. Can we drive somewhere and do that?"

It had been a long and soul-searching weekend, but she needed some time with him alone. She couldn't forget the horrid things Sylvia had said, but she also couldn't make up her mind whether she should tell him that Sylvia knew they had been meeting. Then there were still questions to ask about Friday, which she had been unable to ask at the time.

He looked at his watch and Elizabeth noticed that his eyes appeared swollen, as though he had been crying.

"Okay. We'll drive down to the river. How are you, by the way?"

"I'm alright." She didn't care for the way his question resembled an afterthought. "Why, were you worried?"

He seemed to relax, squeezing her knee with his free hand. "Of course I was. I didn't mean to hurt you."

"I know you didn't." She reached over to kiss his cheek. "I love you, Laurie."

"Love you too, gorgeous."

They drove along the embankment and parked the car close to the Royal Festival Hall on the South Bank. The sky was a streak of buttery salmon on a peaceful late afternoon, and Elizabeth gazed at the barges and other river traffic making their journeys up and down the Thames against a backdrop of illuminated corporate buildings.

"Dirty old river, gotta keep rolling..." he sang softly, wearing one of his lost looks which stabbed at her heart. Wherever he was, she so wanted to be there with him.

He didn't allow the kiss they shared to last as long as she prayed that it would. Releasing her arms gently from around his neck, he was obviously anxious to talk.

"I went to De Beers this morning," he told her. "And there's some sort of problem with the diamond."

Elizabeth's heart lunged into her lace-up shoes. Surely nobody could know that she had smuggled it out of the bank.

"What sort of problem?"

He shrugged and lit a cigarette. "Don't ask me. Apparently a solicitor in Rhodesia has asked one of their African branches to get in touch if a diamond that answers to the description of the one you gave me turns up in London."

'Father Mackenzie's been snooping,' she thought, aggravated by the fact that she would have to tell more lies. "Don't worry. I'll call them sometime tomorrow. There's no problem."

"I wondered if you could try them now? It's not five yet." He nodded towards a nearby phone-box and pulled some coins out of his pocket. "Here's two shillings. That should do."

Frowning, she took the change from him "Do you know who you spoke to?"

Laurie rummaged around again in his jacket. "I've got a card somewhere. Here…"

Studying it briefly, she opened the car door. "Are you coming with me?"

"Do you need me to?"

"No. No, it's alright."

Wondering just what questions she was going to be asked, Elizabeth carefully dialled the number and got straight through to Paul Childs, the name written on the card.

"Oh, er… Hello. I'm Elizabeth Tarrant. A friend of mine is called Laurie Christian. He came in to see you today?"

"Ah, yes." The man answered. "Are you the young lady who gave him the diamond?"

"Yes, and I'd like you to ring Mr. Mackenzie in Salisbury, Rhodesia. He's a solicitor. Tell him that I've given the diamond that my great-aunt left me to my friend. He'll know what I mean."

Elizabeth took a breath and waited expectantly.

"I understand."

She could almost hear him digesting this information.

"Miss Tarrant, our Johannesburg branch is handling this enquiry. I'll give them a ring tomorrow and pass on the information. May I take your telephone number?"

Elizabeth thought quickly. "No. That's alright. I'll come in. In the afternoon. But I want Mr. Christian to be able to sell it to you tomorrow, before you close."

There was a pause as Paul Childs turned this very firm request over in his mind. "I'll see what we can do, Miss Tarrant. Till tomorrow then."

"Alright. Goodbye."

Pleased with herself for saying what she hoped were all the right things, Elizabeth ran back to the car where Laurie was listening to an interview on the radio.

"Brian Epstein…" He told her. "He sounds stoned. Do you want to listen?"

She settled inside and passed him the remaining one shilling piece.

"No, it's okay. I did it. I spoke to the jeweller."

"Everything alright?" He asked, switching off the radio.

"Yes, I think so. They're ringing South Africa tomorrow. We can go in there together after school."

"Okay, I'll meet you. What time will you be out?"

She wrinkled her nose in contemplation. "I can make three-thirty. No lessons or practice on Tuesday."

"Thank you" He gave her a misty smile and this unpredicted tenderness decided her that she could not tell him about Sylvia today. It would spoil the very short time they had together, and tomorrow she hoped he would be back to his old self. On the other hand, she couldn't let him go without saying some of the things that were preying on her mind.

"Laurie, can I ask you something which will probably sound childish and might even offend you?"

He raised one sculptured eyebrow into an arch. "What's that?"

"You know when you told me all about hormones?"

"Yes, I remember."

"And you said you weren't sure sometimes which were the strongest in you, the male or the female?

He looked thoughtful. "Did I say that? Okay, so?"

She wondered how much further she could pursue her point. "So, if you were feeling, um... Female, does that mean you wouldn't want to be with a girl?"

"It probably does, yes. What's all this about?"

Elizabeth began to feel desperate; sickened now by the fact that Sylvia might be right. But she had come this far and she had to know for sure.

"So you'd want to be with another man?"

There, she'd said it, and although the words stuck in her throat, she gazed straight ahead of her, watching a pleasure boat bearing the name Annabelle Lee and filled with the sound of partying, cross their line of vision. She found herself silently praying again. Praying for him either to be angry or to laugh. It didn't matter as long as he denied it.

The silence was crucifying, but when he eventually spoke, his voice was different. Neither angry nor amused, but more resigned. Flat and emotionless.

"Who've you been talking to?"

Still she couldn't bring herself to look at him. Why wasn't he raising his voice in hurt indignation, enquiring bewilderedly why she was accusing him of such perverted things? And why on earth would he say something like 'Who've you been talking to?'

The sound that came out of her mouth was so thin that it hardly resembled a voice. "Nobody."

"Look at me, Elizabeth."

Reluctantly she turned to face him, reading pain and disappointment in his expressive eyes.

"I... I'm sorry," she faltered, hardly able to believe that she could have put things so clumsily. "It was Sylvia. She told me you..." Bursting into tears, she flung her arms around his neck and covered him with kisses. "Why would she say those things? I don't understand."

His response was to frame her damp face in his hands and kiss her both sexually and tenderly. Immediately at peace, she felt comforted and flooded with gratitude.

When he spoke, his voice was lower, more lyrical. "Sylvia is a very sad woman and the reason she would tell you something like that is that she's jealous. It's that simple."

Elizabeth struggled to understand. "Jealous? But why?"

He lit a cigarette and started the car engine. "I'm not saying any more, but believe me, Elizabeth, that's the reason."

She fell quiet as they drove towards the park and Laurie dropped her a few minutes away from the flat.

"I'll be outside the school at three-thirty tomorrow," he told her.

"Alright."

Glad of the walk back, she began to wish that Laurie had gone into more detail, although it was beginning to dawn on her that what he had been implying was almost too absurd to be true. If Sylvia was indeed jealous, then was he saying that the woman was jealous of her? That all this time, when Elizabeth had imagined Sylvia and Jack as a couple, she had really wanted Laurie? Apart from the fact she was so much older than him, Elizabeth had often wondered whether Sylvia even liked Laurie.

The conundrum was one which Elizabeth would ponder for the rest of the evening, the pages in her diary so crammed full of secrets now, that she had been forced to shrink her handwriting in order to accommodate them.

—⚏—

For the first time in her life, Sylvia understood the true meaning of *déjà-vu*. She could almost swear that the stone steps she was climbing now were the same number she had climbed in the Abbey Theatre all those years ago. And when she reached the dressing-room door, releasing that same silent breath of nervous anticipation, she was unsurprised by the tacky and familiar gold cardboard star pinned above his name.

Tired anyway, for it had been a long day, she wondered if she should simply turn on her stilettos and go. Mind her own business, and allow Jack and his niece to wander their singular paths to unhappiness.

But having come this far, she knew she couldn't turn back. Jack was her business. In every sense of the word. And because he was her business, then his niece became so by association. The question was, would she be able to persuade the man behind this door, himself the most skilful of persuaders, to bow out of one or both of their lives?

When she finally knocked, she heard him call, "Come in, Sylvia."

He didn't look up as she went in, but concentrated on applying several layers of mascara to already soot-black, fake lashes. Wearing a high-necked mini-dress blazing with yellow sequins, his shapely and perfectly shaven legs were provocatively crossed as he poised on the padded satin stool.

Refusing to be intimidated by his obvious attempt to disempower her, Sylvia moved towards his dressing-table, addressing him through the mirror within a room lined with floor to ceiling mirrors. "I won't keep you long."

He glanced up and caught her eyes, then began to lightly brush his high cheekbones with a rose blusher. "I hope not. My public awaits in..." He checked the clock on the wall, "... Less than twenty minutes."

265

"Laurie, I've come to beg you to stop seeing Elizabeth."

"I thought you might."

Like an artist approaching a bare canvas, he proceeded to line the edges of his lips with a crimson pencil and she struggled not to allow the amazing transformation she was now witnessing to deter her. She had never seen so much make-up on one table and was unaware that it could be applied in such a manner.

"What gives you the right to control the lives of two people? One no more than a child?"

He unscrewed the top of a lipstick case and once again met her eyes.

"You've got it all wrong, Sylvia. I'm the one who's being controlled. I'm not pulling the strings."

Sylvia hit back, her voice contemptuous. "Oh, yes. A sick man and a fifteen-year old girl are controlling you? Do me a favour."

"What has Elizabeth told you?"

"Nothing much, except that you're both in love."

"And you believe her?"

In her unexpectedly semi-hypnotic state, Sylvia watched him carefully and sensuously apply a moist, cherry-red lipstick to his parted lips, then patting them with a tissue, meticulously cover them with a second coat. This time, a shimmering candy-floss pink.

"I believe she believes it. And for whatever reasons, you've encouraged her. Taken advantage. Can't you see its wrong to rouse the sexual instincts of a little girl so that she falls madly in love with you?"

Laurie sat back admiring his handiwork, then lifted a gleaming, bobbed henna wig from its stand. Within seconds, and displaying all the skill of the seasoned drag artiste, he had fitted it to perfection, fingering, combing and teasing it into life. When his metamorphosis had been completed, he swiveled around on the stool and presented his creation to a discomforted Sylvia.

"What'ya think, honey?"

In an instant, and even though she had never seen his act,

Sylvia realised why so many women found him irresistible. Not only was he the personification of what they, in their secret fantasies wanted to be, glamorous and exuding sultry sexual aggression, but to know that beneath all of that was a man, for Christ's sake, who, with the right woman, could be seduced and who just may be as sexually aggressive as his female alter-ego. What dusty, Freudian corridors of the mind did Laurie Christian explore, each time he walked out on to that cabaret floor?

Unbelievably, it was he who brought her back to the reason for her visit.

"I swear to you, Sylvia, it's Elizabeth who has done all the running. Remember Christmas? She's a passionate and highly-sexed girl. Not at all your average adolescent. I've done everything in my power to discourage her naive expectations, but you know her, she's hard to say no to."

That's too easy, you bastard, the voice in Sylvia's head screamed loudly.

"Laurie, she's fifteen. Have you been to bed with her?"

He crossed his legs again and Sylvia averted her eyes.

"Yes, we've been to bed." Noticing her disgust, he continued. "She begged me, Sylvia. We've been pretty far, but I haven't made love to her and that's the honest truth."

"Will you stop seeing her?"

"I'm finishing it tomorrow. Once and for all. I was frightened, Sylvia. Of what she'd do. And I didn't want to worry Jack. Sometimes she seems a bit, well you know, unbalanced. Probably all the shock of her parents being murdered."

"I've never found her in the least unbalanced," Sylvia said icily.

Laurie got up from the stool and went towards a mirrored cupboard where he removed something that she couldn't see.

"Look at me, Sylvia. Do I look like someone who's gonna fall in love with some kid? Correction. Female kid? Jack and I are happy. We have plans."

"So I've heard." Her head was beginning to throb from tension and fatigue. "So you will finish it? You promise? For everyone's sake?"

He made the sign of the cross over his size forty décolletage. "Cross my heart and hope to die." Glancing up at the clock, he examined the apparatus he had taken from the cupboard. "Now, I really don't think you want to see this, Sylvia. I'm about to put on my 'gaff.'"

He roared with laughter at her bewilderment. "The tightest jockstrap in the world, darling. Well, what do you think I do with it every night?"

Despite her anger, Sylvia was unable to resist a weak smile. For Jack's sake in the future, she knew they would have to get along, but at the moment, concern for Elizabeth still dominated her mind.

As she drove home, Sylvia could feel some relief at the assurance Laurie had given her and prayed that Elizabeth would not be too damaged by what might have already taken place. She knew she would have to talk to her again; take her aside and try a woman to woman approach in an endeavour to assess the degree of her idolisation of Laurie Christian.

He really was the consummate performer; the conjurer of emotions and the juggler of souls. A magician whose sleight of hand transformed his very gender and changed the lives of those who fell under his spell.

—⁂—

"No cheques," Laurie said firmly, as Paul Childs finished counting £25,000 in new fifty-pound notes and laid them in one thousand unit stacks on the marble topped table.

"I'm sorry sir, this is all the cash we have today. If you'd like to come by tomorrow, I can give you the remainder."

"I suppose I'll have to, then." Laurie bristled, now watching the notes being tucked into a brown envelope and sealed by Childs' furry tongue.

Whatever Elizabeth had said had done the trick. Calls had been made and he was now walking away with a fortune, well, half a fortune, and it felt good. He took the envelope from Childs, noticing the way the man was studying the girl in school uniform, then turning his eyes back on him with hawkish curiosity. Smugly, Laurie now regarded this as pay-back time for all the establishment figures who, over the years had treated him like shit. The satisfaction of getting one over on this guy who had clearly hoped that he had stumbled on something irregular, something for which he may well have received the equivalent of the De Beers gold seal of employee approval, was, in Laurie's eyes, some form of sublime retaliation.

It wasn't until they got outside that he noticed Elizabeth's cheeks had turned a high colour and her green-blue eyes seemed very bright, almost glassy.

"Are you okay?" He asked, guiding her into a shop doorway.

"I don't feel too good." Her face strained into a half-smile. "Must have caught something."

"You look feverish. I'll get you a cab." It appeared that the Almighty was being doubly generous today, providing him now with the perfect means of extrication.

He hadn't really given much thought as to how he should handle the severing of their relationship, as obtaining the cash for the diamond had been the utmost priority in his mind. Fearful of another scene, for there had been too many of those lately, he was simply intending to bid her goodbye with the true and convenient excuse that he had an appointment to keep with the estate agent. As far as he was concerned, he planned never to see her alone again.

"Can't we just go to your flat?" She pleaded. "I can lie down for a bit, and I'll be fine."

"No, gorgeous," he said firmly. Just how many more eggshells could he be bothered to tap dance upon? Being cruel to be kind suddenly seemed like the best policy. "I've got an appointment. At Healey and Baker."

"Who?"

"The estate agents. About my club."

"Can I come with you?"

"Elizabeth, you're not well. Besides, I've got to talk business and you'd be bored." There was a raw vulnerability about her now, a state for which he felt only partly responsible.

"But we haven't been together properly for ages." Her voice cracked, and anticipating tears, he waved over a cab and led her towards the door.

"Have you got money?"

She shook her head pitifully. "Only enough for the bus."

He pulled a pound note out of his pocket. "Here, take this."

"When will I see you?" Her whole demeanor was waif-like, pleading. Devoid of her former spirit, she was the puppy he had kicked, the child he had taken to Hamley's then refused a toy.

"When you're better."

Laurie knew it was a hollow promise, but it was the best he could come up with. He didn't want to think about tomorrow or the next day, when she would come out of school, her eyes desperately searching for his car. His mind wouldn't allow itself to entertain the possible bombardment of letters and phone calls or her turning up again at the club. Perhaps even, God help him, at his flat.

He nodded to the impatient cabbie and brushed her lips briefly with his.

Stretching up, she whispered in his ear, her voice taking on a solemn resonance and her message sending an unexpected chill through his bones.

"You mustn't stop loving me, Laurie. There's nothing left for me if you do."

—ɯ—

It was the new words she had learned that day, 'gastronomy' and 'epicureanism', that finally caused Elizabeth to vomit in two neat piles on to her French exercise book, producing giggles and gasps from her classmates and concern from the petite and pretty Mademoiselle Jerard.

Not so much the words themselves, but the context in which her French teacher had used them, for *La belle France*, she had told the girls, is where the cult of gastronomy is a respected avocation and sometimes a full time profession. Mademoiselle

Jerard then went on to describe the delights of frogs legs and snails cooked in garlic, caramel creme and soft, white cheese from the country farms around Provence.

Elizabeth knew she shouldn't have gone into school that morning, but how else was she going to see Laurie? He had met her for the last two days, so surely he would come today? Particularly as he'd known that she'd been unwell. The tablets which she had taken from the bathroom cabinet had kept her stomach stable until around noon, but now they had worn off and, prompted by such colourful reportage of Mademoiselle Jerard's eating habits, she was forced to accept the inevitability of being sent home.

Standing forlornly in the hallway in her hat and coat, she waited for Pamela, the head-girl who had been designated to escort her.

"I've tried to ring your uncle," Anthea Thomas told her, fingering the pearls around her neck with some agitation. "But the phone's engaged. Pam will get you back there. A taxi's been called."

"Thank you," Elizabeth said, once again embarrassed by actions beyond her control. "I'm sorry."

"You can't help being ill," The headmistress said briskly. "Get some rest and keep warm, then you'll feel as right as rain."

As right as rain. Elizabeth wondered in her fevered state whether that phrase, used by someone like Anthea Thomas who was not a stupid person, actually meant what she intended it to mean. How could anyone feel like rain? Or indeed as right as? Particularly the rain in this country which was cold and far too frequent.

Why couldn't people say 'as right as sun', or 'as right as wind'? Or was that simply too un-English?

Puzzling this over, and hoping that she wouldn't be sick again, Elizabeth was silent on the journey home. Her stomach ached, but despite her overall weakness, she felt cross and disappointed that another day would go by without sharing any real intimacy with Laurie. More than anything, she needed to hold him and be held by him. She recalled what he had said about the fantasy rarely living up to the reality, but she knew that for her that would never be the case. Her one wish in the whole world was to lie naked in his arms while she slept, then to be woken by him making love to her. She closed her eyes as the image filled her with compelling happiness, but when the taxi gave a sudden lurch, the nausea returned, centering attention on her sickness.

She was conscious of a hand being placed on her hot forehead, and the head-girl of St. Hilda's saying something that Elizabeth blocked out. She knew she hadn't really felt well since the last time she had been at his flat. Then there had been that dreadful business with Sylvia and the anxiety over whether Mackenzie had found out about the other diamond.

"Do you want me to come up with you?"

"Sorry?"

Pamela was leaning towards her now, studying her face, determined to fulfill the responsibility to which she had been assigned.

"Will you be alright?"

But Elizabeth didn't hear her. She was too busy staring at the purple Mini parked next to Jack's car. Laurie was here; inside the flat. So confused by that fact and how she looked and felt, she stuttered an inarticulate reply.

"Um… No, I mean yes. Fine, thanks."

As the taxi swung round in the forecourt and out on to the road, Elizabeth walked through the front doors, smiled wanly at Victor who greeted her with surprise, and took the lift up to the eighth floor.

She definitely couldn't let Laurie see her looking like this. Somehow she would have to get herself into her room and sort out her face, hair and clothes. But how could she do so unnoticed, even armed with her recent successfully acquired skills of exit and entry?

Elizabeth paused in front of the door, listening to the mellow strains of jazz music coming from inside. One of Uncle Jack's favourite records, played by a trumpeter, and, she always considered this odd, yet another black man called Davis.

To add to her discomfort, the familiar anticipation of seeing Laurie was causing her heart to race, and she realised gloomily that there were too many components present today for any sort of plan to work. Placing her felt hat and satchel on the floor she leaned against the wall and considered her options. Hannah would almost certainly be in the kitchen, where the door was always open, and which she had to pass to get to her room. She didn't know if Adrian was around, but Laurie and Uncle Jack would probably be in the sitting room, talking and listening to music. And had Laurie brought Flora? The small dog would no doubt sense if someone had entered the flat and would bark, alerting everyone to her presence. Somehow, she knew that if she could just get past the kitchen and make it quietly into her room, then no-one would be any the wiser. Once there, she could change and freshen up, and greet Laurie with a show of sparkling, sexy confidence which he would find difficult to resist.

Turning the key cautiously, Elizabeth stepped inside, biting her lower lip in an effort to avoid making the slightest noise. In the hallway, the music sounded loud but she heard Laurie's laugh, followed by Jack's, drifting out of the sitting room. To her surprise and relief, she noticed that there were no other coats on the coat-stand and, as the kitchen was quiet, Elizabeth realised that the housekeeper was not in the flat.

Safely inside her room, Elizabeth set about improving her appearance with meticulous determination. First she scrubbed her face and cleaned her teeth, then flannelled under her arms and applied a roll-on deodorant. Depressed by the sallowness of her skin and the shadow-like bruises beneath her eyes, she made two attempts at smoothing on some foundation before being reasonably satisfied with the result. Paul McCartney's poetry vibrated suddenly through her mind. She really was wearing a face that she kept in a jar by the door.

The tangles in her hair seemed worse than usual, but, after some back-combing and spraying, it achieved a moderate pass for stylish. What to change into was not really a difficult decision. Those wonderful wide black pants, together with the white shirt and kipper tie was the outfit he had talked her into buying almost half a year ago, and which she always enjoyed wearing. She smiled, remembering how he had enthused about her new look. "... Like a little boy lost," he had told her, before sweeping her away on a carpet-ride of adventure, from which she would never want to alight.

Slipping on her shoes, she began to silently rehearse her entrance. There was no doubt they would be surprised to see her home from school so early.

'Hello, they sent me home cos I was sick, but now I'm feeling much better. Shall I make us some tea?' It was dismally unimaginative, but she was unable to think of anything else that sounded natural while Uncle Jack was present. She could hardly walk up to Laurie and kiss him.

Miles Davis was blowing another set as she walked towards the sitting room, but she could no longer hear voices or laughter. The room was empty and, for some reason the blue cushions from the settee were scattered on the floor, while two empty champagne bottles stood on the walnut coffee table.

Disappointed that her rehearsed entrance had been in vain and puzzled as to where everyone could be, Elizabeth wandered once again into the hall.

Hearing her uncle's voice, she noticed that the door to his bedroom was open, and checking her make-up for the last time in the large, antique mirror, she made her way down the corridor.

It took only four seconds for Elizabeth to assimilate the tableau that tore at her heart and assaulted her senses. Although her automatic reaction was to suspend belief, selecting to see only the elements vital to survival, there was little question of its authenticity and those four seconds would be the longest in her life.

One – Jack lying spread-eagled on the bed, naked, his eyes closed.

Two – Laurie, her Laurie, also naked, lying with his head between Jack's legs, his mouth full.

Three – A click and a flash. A photograph being taken from a Poleroid camera which hit her eyes, blinding her with its burning whiteness.

Four – As she blinked and regained focus, the shocked pink face of a naked Adrian, lowering the camera and staring at her numbly.

Jack was the second one to see her, and when he raised his head, she was aware that his face and body appeared completely colourless, like a waxwork in Madam Tussauds. He tried to pull himself up, disturbing Laurie, who drew away frowning, but who then turned and also saw Elizabeth. 'The only one of them who doesn't look horrified,' she remembered thinking. In fact, she was certain that the shadow of a smile passed across his face. A smile that could have almost been an invitation to join them.

Then she heard a howl of anguish. The lamentable sound of a wounded animal and realised that it came from her.

Backing out of the door, her hand held in front of her mouth to catch the flow of vomit, she saw her uncle try to run towards her then fall as he called out, not her name, but her mother's.

"Emily..."

Now, she was convinced that nothing could touch her ever again. There was simply no pain left to feel. Beyond hurt and revelation, she was lost in the storm of her soul's desperation.

As she stumbled out of the flat, she realised that words like 'love' and 'trust' were meaningless. Without those vital ingredients for a joyful life, then was life really worth living?

—⚊—

"Get out!" Jack cried again, pushing a now fully dressed Adrian away from him and causing a shower of pills to spill on to the carpet. "Get out and leave me alone."

"She'll be alright, Jack," Laurie grabbed his arm in an attempt to restrain him from leaving the flat in his dressing gown. "She's got nowhere to go."

Jack broke away weakly, his head throbbing with shame and remorse. How could he have allowed Laurie to talk him into such a compromising situation? The champagne, the celebration he'd organised because he'd signed the contract for the new club premises, to all of these things Jack could attribute blame, but he knew, in his heart of hearts, that he alone held the definitive responsibility. He had been weak and driven by lust. It was nobody's fault but his own, and the heavy burden of guilt was something he would carry with him for the rest of his life.

Speaking in low tones to Laurie, but which Jack could clearly hear, his nurse prepared to leave as ordered. "Remember, call the hospital immediately if he has another attack. Try and get him to take his medication, and he'll need a sedative. That's the lighter of the yellow ones. I'm going home and I'll look out for the girl."

When he'd gone, Laurie poured Jack some water and picked up the pills.

"Come on, Jack. This is silly. What did she see?"

Through his helplessness and pain, Jack swallowed what he was offered then leaned back against the pillows. "If you won't let me go and look for her, then I'll have to call the police".

Laurie shook his head. "It's only been twenty minutes and it's still light. What are you going to tell them anyway when they ask why she ran off? That she interrupted a little orgy?"

Jack took another sip of water, fear and apprehension now added to the list of whirling emotions.

"You know they'll take her away from me, don't you? I'll be considered an unfit guardian. Jesus, Laurie, my own sister's child will be placed in care because of my irresponsible stupidity."

He watched his lover calmly comb his hair and check his watch. "Jack, that won't happen. Listen, I need a drink."

Shivering, Jack followed him into the sitting-room and watched as he poured himself a large vodka. Instinctively, Jack realised that he had to talk to Sylvia. Her cool head and advice were essential at the moment of his biggest crisis yet. Where he was floundering, she would know what to do, although he also knew that, quite understandably, she would be furious and disapproving at the unholy mess that he had created.

He told Laurie who reacted defensively. "Why? Just wait for a while. Don't cause a panic yet."

Jack ignored him. "No, I'm going to ring her and ask her to come over. I can't think straight."

Laurie bent to kiss him. "Of course you can't, and that's exactly why you should wait for a bit longer. Look, do you want me to drive around and look for Elizabeth?"

"Only if I can come with you."

"Jack, you could end up in hospital. No, I'll go. It's not too cold and she's probably gone to the park, or down to the river. I'll be back if I find her, otherwise I'll be in touch later. You don't need to worry Sylvia."

As soon as he had watched him drive away, Jack hurried to the phone and rang the office. Laurie may be the love of his life but Sylvia was his best friend, and that obvious difference made Jack's decision an easy one.

—⧟—

She was so distressed by her partner's haggard appearance, that Sylvia almost forgot the purpose for which she had been called.

"Come and sit down," she said gently, leading him over to his favourite chair as she would her father who was in his eighties. The room stank of cigarettes and booze and she threw open one of the windows, allowing a gust of unexpectedly sweet, cool air to breathe against their faces.

"They've given me a couple of tranquillisers," he told her. "But I don't want to sit around while she's out there somewhere... God knows where."

"Tell me as best you can what happened?" Sylvia asked, not wanting to sit down herself but struggling to maintain an air of calm.

"She came home from school early. She was all dressed up. She saw us..." Jack trailed off, his throat clogged by tears.

"You told me that. But what did she see exactly?'

Jack raised his tear-stained face. "Laurie and me. On the bed. Not... You know... But... Oral."

"I see." Needing to keep a clear head, Sylvia poured herself a tonic water.

"So she saw you and Laurie. Then what?"

"Sylvia, that's not all. I'm sorry..."

277

"What do you mean?"

She was aware that it was taking all of his will power to explain.

"You must understand, we'd had a lot to drink. I'd had a lot to drink. Laurie started messing around with Adrian, the nurse. I didn't like it, but I went along with it. Before I knew what was happening they were both undressed. I went mad with jealousy and Laurie aroused me. Adrian got a camera..." He hung his head as Sylvia closed her eyes, trying to ignore the migraine that now threatened like an angry tempest.

A while passed before she could bring herself to speak.

"Poor little girl," she whispered, then resumed a near normal voice. "Jack, that man has made you into a fool. Now we must deal with the harm that's been done to Elizabeth."

Jack nodded and held out his hand, which she took and squeezed.

"Can you imagine how traumatised she must be, Sylvia? She knows nothing about sex. I wonder if she really understood what she saw."

The desire to enlighten him was almost too strong to resist, but she knew that if she told him now about Elizabeth and Laurie, not only would she have a missing child to find, but probably a body to bury.

"If you tell the police the truth you'll be arrested and Elizabeth will be placed in care. If you tell the police a lie, like it was just a family squabble or something, they'll probe more and you'll give yourself away. You have to hang on for her to come back and then talk to her."

"What in God's name have I done, Sylvia?"

"The only crime you've committed is the crime of infatuation, Jack. You're not the first and you won't be the last. Now, it's not so much what you've done, as what you are going to do. And you know that it starts with you finishing with Laurie Christian, don't you?"

She watched him nod wearily, unaware that he was the last of the fated trio she had warned off.

"I know, I know. She's going to hate me, Sylvia, find me disgusting. Even when she comes back, she won't want to live with me."

"That may be so," Sylvia said, pulling no punches. "But let's jump off that particular bridge when we come to it."

"I've just thought of something," he said, suddenly struck by a memory. "A friend from school that she's been seeing lately. Someone called Morris. That's right...Nicole Morris. Can you try and find out if she's with her?"

"I'll try," she told him. "Any other ideas?"

Plainly defeated, he shook his head. "If she'd gone back to the school, they'd have rung me. She wouldn't be with the Dovers, but if she were, they'd have done the same. Similarly Hannah. And if we call any of them, they'll want explanations. They'll also expect that I've called the police."

She noticed that his eyelids were growing heavy and offered him her arm. "Come on, you're going to get some rest. Where's Laurie now?"

"He went to try and find Elizabeth."

"Okay." Sylvia led Jack into the bedroom, removed his slippers and guided him towards the bed, where she pulled the eiderdown across him and closed the curtains.

"I don't want to lose her," he said, his voice slurring now from the questionable combination of prescription drugs and champagne.

"I know you don't, Jack"

She stood beside the bed until she was sure he was asleep, then quietly left the room. Now, the light was fading and she gazed anxiously into the street and beyond into the park, scanning the faces of strangers while telling herself to keep believing that Elizabeth would return that night.

There were so many things she wanted to know. Had Laurie finished with the girl as he had sworn he would, and if so, how did she react? Why had she left school at lunchtime today, and where in God's name was she now?

Desperate to feel that she was doing something constructive, Sylvia knew the only place that she might find any clue as to where Elizabeth could be was in her room. The telephone number of this school-friend, for instance, would surely be written somewhere. Loathe to intrude into the young girl's very private space, she put it off by making a pot of tea, but when eventually she opened the door, absorbing at first the typical teenage chaos inside, she also noticed Elizabeth's school uniform lying abandoned, obviously in haste, on the bed.

Trying to alleviate her guilt with the conviction that she had no choice, Sylvia searched through Elizabeth's bedside cupboards for an address book, but among the various letters postmarked Rhodesia, packets of chewing-gum, half-eaten chocolate bars and countless photographs, all she could find was a red plastic diary, securely locked, and which almost pleaded to be opened and read.

Sylvia sat on the bed, troubled by her compulsion to commit an act of the most personal intrusion. But she knew, could not deny, that if she could only find the key then there was little doubt she would read Elizabeth's secrets. Not because she wanted to, but because there was just too much at stake. In order to help these two family members whom she loved attempt some chance of a future together, she needed to know and understand everything.

As she contemplated her motives, the phone rang and, grateful for the timely interruption, Sylvia ran into the hall, almost breathless with hope, but hope fizzled into cold disappointment when she realised it was Laurie.

"Did she come back yet?" He asked, not even bothering with common pleasantries.

"No, she didn't."

"How's Jack?"

She wanted to say 'as if you care', but decided against it. What was the point now?

"Asleep."

She heard him light a cigarette and exhale deeply. "Alright. Well, I'm going in to work. Tell Jack to ring me at Grosvenor's if there's any news."

Reluctant to make a promise she had no intention of keeping, Sylvia put down the phone and returned to Elizabeth's room. Unused to the complexity of emotional dilemma or the distraction that accompanied it, she touched and then lifted the battered teddy bear with the black-stitched smile, from its place on the pillows. The most comforting symbol of childhood and maybe the most difficult to leave behind, she reflected, remembering Christopher Robin's attempt to say goodbye to his toys when he felt that he was growing up.

"Pooh, whatever happens, you will understand, won't you?"

"Understand what?" The bewildered bear replies.

As if to heighten her melancholia, one of the bear's eyes plopped out of its socket, only to dangle balefully in front of its face like a broken pendulem.

Guilt now rested like a solid rock on her shoulders as she tried to push the glass button back into the toy's head. But it didn't take her long to realise that something was lodged inside the hole, threatening to push it out again.

The police would have to be informed if Elizabeth was not back by morning.

'Until then, please forgive me', Sylvia whispered in a heartfelt plea to the absent girl, knowing that she would never be able to forgive herself. Then, shaken by her own dishonour and watched by a one-eyed bear, she slowly turned the key in the lock.

—⁂—

The scab on his right ankle had now begun to bleed, and Laurie, furious with the new stilettos which had caused him such an uncomfortable first show, tore them off before he reached the last flight of stairs that led to his dressing-room and padded the rest of the way in stockinged feet.

At least his own club would be designed so that he would have his room on the same level as the stage. No more hobbling in high-heels up and down three flights, twice nightly, and nearly breaking his neck in the process.

Opening the door, he flicked down the light switch but, as if to add to his fury and frustration, the overhead light failed to come on. The switch below it, which lit the bulbs around his dressing-table mirror, also proved ineffective.

"Great!"

Still clutching his shoes, and leaving the door open so that he could see his way to the phone on the table, Laurie raised the long, skin-tight dress he was wearing up around his waist and wiggled across the room, preparing to voice his complaint to the electrician. The wiring in this place was a joke. He would have to have serious words this time.

To his confusion, when he picked up the phone it seemed strangely weightless, and when he failed to hear a dialling tone, he understood why. With creeping apprehension and astonishment, Laurie discovered that the telephone cord was broken. Or had it been cut?

"Don't be a twat," he said loudly, realising that he was in danger of panicking. A darkened dressing room and a cut telephone wire. All the elements necessary for a Hitchcock movie, not for an average night between shows for the world's most sensational drag queen.

But his fear accelerated as he suddenly became conscious of the door closing. Laurie stared for a moment in disbelief, knowing that it couldn't have closed by itself. It was a reasonably heavy door which when it was left open, stayed open. Somebody must have shut it.

"Who's there?" He called out, delivering the question like a military command in order to give himself courage. "Who the fuck's there?"

Only a thin ribbon of light was now visible in the room and he remembered that he would have to be careful, as he'd been shaving before the first show and had left an open razor on the table. His heart pounding, he began to grope his way towards the door, then hearing a sound behind him, spun around, conscious now of a slim shadow whose outline was reflected in every one of the mirrors, making it difficult to pinpoint in exactly which part of the room the figure was standing.

Then suddenly, he relaxed. Of course it was Elizabeth, who had somehow crept into the club unnoticed. She would have come to tell him how much she loved him, and to ask why and how he could have been doing such dirty things with her uncle. Well, he would have to bluff it again in order to get her to turn the lights back on. He'd done it before, and a French kiss would almost certainly work the old magic, or if the circumstances became extreme, his hand inside her knickers.

"Hello, gorgeous," he said, trying to sound composed. "I'm glad you're here. We were worried."

Getting no response, Laurie moved once more towards the door. He knew that if he could only get down the stairs to the dressing rooms below, he would be able to alert someone who would take the girl away. As he edged closer, he spoke again, his tone softer and more seductive.

"I want to explain. About what you saw. Jack loves me. Like you do. There's no reason why we can't still be friends..."

Even closer now to the door, Laurie reached out to grasp the handle but then experienced another sensation which took him even more by surprise and caused him to scream in agony, a sound which was buried beneath the thumping rock music resonating from the speakers. Something had sheared through his arm. A blade. Cutting and slicing. Once, and then again. And, as he tried to hold the damaged arm with his other hand, his fingers touched the warm and sticky, unmistakable texture of blood.

The queasiness passed, but the terror he now felt was motivating him to get out of this fucking room. What the hell was going on? Was she trying to kill him? If so, she wasn't going to succeed.

"Elizabeth..." He whispered, his voice having deserted him. "What are you doing?"

Once again he tried for the door, and once again was driven back, as this time he saw the flash of the blade coming to towards his neck.

Slash!

"Jesus!"

He screamed again, raising both arms to try and fend off his attacker, then fell on to his knees, feeling only hot, searing pain. "Not my face... For Christ's sake, not my face."

He knew she was serious now, and wondered frantically how much blood he could be losing. He was terrified of dying, and to die like this, so young, was not how it was supposed to be. He wanted to live to be rich and famous, to visit Hollywood and to samba at the Rio carnival. He certainly didn't want to lose his life to the mercy of some crazy cunt who believed in the notion of romantic love.

His knees buckling under him, but his heart speeding, Laurie made one final attempt for the door, but the heavy velvet dress impeded his progress, and, as he fell back, he felt a heel kick the side of his head which brought a fresh pain. Numbly he acknowledged that if it wasn't for the thick, natural-fibre wig he was wearing then he most certainly would have lost consciousness.

He started to sob and to call on God. A vain hope, but worth a try, now that he was probably dying.

"Please help me... Oh God, help me... I swear I'll do anything..."

He didn't know how long he'd been crying and praying, but when he lifted his head again, he realised that light was spilling into the room from the landing. The door had been opened. She had gone.

As he clutched the side of the chair to pull himself up, Laurie weakly examined his injuries, almost fainting from the shock of witnessing such a hideous apparition, multiplied around the room in the many mirrors. His face was smudged with blood, lipstick and mascara, and the blonde wig was a lop-sided, blood-matted travesty, the sticky tape which had secured it, hanging around his ears, which were also covered with blood.

Wild, hallucinary imaginings took hold of him as the room seemed to move in and out of focus in blurring cycles. No longer would he be able to earn his living from impersonating beautiful women. He would always be the freak who had somehow wandered away from the sideshow and into the hall of funny mirrors, where it was hard to make out what was distorted and what was real.

"Mirror, mirror on the wall..."

Terrified, Laurie was aware that he needed help badly, but was too feeble to move or call out. Tremblingly, he laid his head on the dressing table, but knew that if he succumbed to sleep, then there was every chance that he could die.

Calling on reserves of energy he had no idea he possessed, Laurie finally dragged himself out of the chair as the door leading to the landing becoming the biggest hurdle he had ever had to face. Sinking down into a half-crawl, which left a blood-stained scroll on the pink carpet, he somehow reached the doorway and maneuvered his body out of the room.

A syrupy orchestral version of *All My loving* was schmoozing from the speakers as he staggered on to the stone-floored landing and raised his un-injured arm to grip the iron banister in a desperate attempt to attract attention.

"Help me..." His voice cracked, and then petered out. "Somebody help me."

The cloudiness which filled his eyes momentarily cleared, and he was able to distinguish the figure of one of the chorus boys leaving the communal dressing room below and making his way towards the payphone on the wall.

Frantic to be noticed now, but in intense pain, Laurie pulled himself further up on to the railing, precariously leaning the upper part of his body across it and calling hoarsely. "Chris... Chris..."

In the time it would take a greyhound to react to a gun-shot, Laurie Christian then, unsurprisingly, lost his balance and hurtled over the banister like a grotesque, crumpled mannequin, bypassing the horrified chorus-boy on level two, and crashing on to the stone steps of the ground floor below. His life story, short but often excruciatingly sweet and accompanied by a soundtrack of applause, projected itself in glorious Technicolour onto his mind's screen in those few moments before impact.

—∞—

285

CORFU
APRIL, 1970

Jack sipped from a glass of ice-cold Chablis and gazed past the rich olive grove beneath the terrace towards the blue opaqueness of the Aegean Sea, undisturbed except for the few white boats that bobbed serenely on its glittering surface.

On the beach below he could see Elizabeth, startlingly beautiful in a simple cream cheesecloth dress, her coppery hair still wet from swimming, and bending like a dancer to pick shells from the fine, warm sand or from between the rocks and boulders that rose dramatically, every so often, along the curving shoreline.

Jack placed a straw Panama on his head and strolled towards the edge of the terrace, hoping that she would remember that the pigmentation of her delicate skin, like that of any redhead, was no match for the heat of an unseasonably fierce Hellenic noon.

As if reading his mind, she drew a silk scarf over her hair, shielding her face, then looked up and smiled.

The villa he had rented was cool and white, curtained with yards of billowing voile, and sparsely furnished with heavy, cane furniture and lush plants. This was the fourth year that he had brought her here, since they first made the trip in 1967 in order to recover from the events leading up to that March night, and from their aftermath.

He watched her climb the steps towards the villa and, because, at this time of the year his mind was programmed to wander uneasily back to those events, he realised once again that he would be grateful till the end of his life for the maturity she showed in her understanding and forgiveness.

He had tried, in his embarrassed, clumsy way, to apologize and to explain to her about a certain kind of love. The kind that could be destructive because it was all consuming and invariably one-sided. This, he had told her, was how he had felt about Laurie, and that love had been the biggest mistake of his life.

Calmly, she had listened. Poignantly, she had wept. Soon they had clung to one another, crying for so much that had been lost. After that they set out to repair the damage, gradually picking up the pieces of their shattered lives, and starting again.

Laurie's name was never mentioned now, but Jack knew that the sheer force of him could not be forgotten. Now, for the first time in years, he felt at the right place in his life, strong in his relationship with his niece, supported by his long-time friend, Sylvia, and physically and emotionally cleansed of the sicknesses which had gripped him, allowing him to face the future with clarity and hope.

"Look, Uncle Jack," she said, spreading out her hand to reveal a collection of pearly sea-shells gleaming in her palm, and more childlike now, at 18, than she had been then.

As she removed her scarf, he noticed with pleasure that she was wearing the gold locket he had given her.

"Have we got any Coca-Cola?"

"In the fridge."

She seemed to glide towards the kitchen, trailing her scarf behind her, and Jack experienced again the warm swell of pride which came from being her only living relative.

She had developed into a brilliant and dedicated student, her A-levels were going well, and Oxbridge, he had been told by Anthea Thomas, was more than just a possibility. She had also expressed a desire to spend a year studying art at the Sorbonne, along with two other French speaking students from St. Hilda's, after getting her degree. At 21, she would be financially independent and could make any number of life choices, and Jack was confident now that those choices would be carefully planned and accomplished.

The only concern to which he could admit, was one that made him wonder whether he might bear the blame. A missing factor, which, at her age, he felt should be a natural and normal preoccupation. Beautiful as she was, she seemed to have no interest whatsoever in boys. Continually invited to a diverse selection of grown-up parties, she always returned home alone, and whereas a few of her schoolmates were now dating, she showed none of the symptoms of dreaming about, or being, remotely in love. Even certain pop stars and actors, swooned over by many of her contemporaries and whom she had even met through his agency, appeared to leave her un-moved.

She came up behind him and pushed his hat playfully down over his eyes.

"Aren't you reading?" She enquired.

"We can't all be book worms," he smiled, reminded that he probably uttered the same words to Emily, so many years ago.

"I thought I'd take the opportunity to study some mythology," she said seriously, and he almost choked on his wine. "Seems like the right time and place."

"Good luck," he told her, closing his eyes and sinking back into the wicker lounger. "I'll take the opportunity to sleep."

—w—

Elizabeth rested the book on her lap, listening to her uncle's gentle snoring, as the sun rose higher in the afternoon sky. Last night, maybe because there had been a full moon, or perhaps because it was simply that time of the year, she had dreamed of those few fateful days when she had stumbled upon the second shocking discovery of her short life.

How clear the dream memories had been, re-invoking that whole period which had changed her forever. The sickness and despair that had driven her to run blindly through a town that seemed to mock and accuse, before the world that inhabited it finally stopped spinning around.

Waking in a strange bed, her ears had echoed with questions fired from copious hospital staff. There had been no identification found on her, and they were on the point of contacting the police.

"No!" She protested, hating the thought of returning to the flat, but also not wanting to talk to the police. "My name is Elizabeth Tarrant and I'll give you my telephone number, where I live."

Sylvia had picked her up and Elizabeth spoke neither to her nor to her agitated and sick-looking uncle, until the phone call at midday once again drew them together.

Laurie had been attacked at Grosvenor's the previous night and left for dead. The police had drawn a blank. Did Mr. Merrick have any idea why anyone would want to kill him?

Dazed by the onslaught of such continuous shocks, Elizabeth met her uncle's eyes, feeling an instant rush of pity for him, for herself and for Laurie. Each of them was powerless now to change the past and, although she realised that she would never see Laurie again, such intensity of feeling couldn't simply be blown out at will, like a candle's flame. He hadn't been a bad person, just someone incapable of giving or accepting love.

Soon she was to discover that Jack, whom she suspected possessed the family trait of keeping pain well hidden, was opening out to her in a plea for forgiveness.

At first, Elizabeth had longed to do the same, but a mixture of embarrassment and cowardice plus concern for her uncle prevented it. Where he had been so honest with her, she could contribute nothing but her understanding. And, as time passed, although she saw them both as casualties of a shared romantic passion, revealing her secret became less of a compulsion. Unless Sylvia, with however little or much as she knew, chose to enlighten him, then it was a chapter of which he would always be unaware.

A fat bee buzzed around the saucer of black olives on the small table between them, then attracted by the heady scent of grape, plopped into Jack's wineglass.

Picking up the glass to toss both wine and bee on to a patch of hot grass, Elizabeth reflected that in a way, both she and Jack had each suffered a fate similar to the struggling creature.

Continuing to be drawn towards the same glass, they had nevertheless relished the bliss of drowning in wine.

But now, three years on, the world wasn't disintegrating for either of them without Laurie Christian, after all. The only question that remained to be answered, perhaps never would be, was how could she help but forever compare the exquisite heights of eroticism to which he had lifted her, with that of any far paler satisfaction?

—m—

LONDON
APRIL, 1970

The headline on the cover of *The Stage* caught Sylvia's attention unwillingly, causing her to push her work aside and examine the story in more detail.

So, Grosvenor's night club was closing down. After twenty years as a top London venue, it had been served notice for bankruptcy and was now in receivership.

Although the last thing in the world Sylvia needed was for his image to form in her thoughts, it was impossible to read the article without making the observation that without Laurie Christian as a popular draw, the club had been floundering for years.

"Damn," she said under her breath, for now it was too late, and the shadows of that night had already awoken her deeply buried recall.

She needed to clear her head, get some air. For once work could wait.

"I'm going out," she told her secretary through the intercom. "Take any messages, will you?"

The Easter weekend had come and gone, and these were the last days of the break before the kids returned to school. In the park, standing beside a woman and a small boy who were feeding a group of mallards, Sylvia noticed that more mothers and children were starting to materialise, and the formation of a herd mentality, determined by the women's common bond, urged them to coo politely over each other's offsprings.

Far from being filled with regret for something which she

hadn't experienced, Sylvia realised for the first time that this way of life was one which would have never fitted in with her conception of a fulfilling day. Satisfied with the dawning of this conclusion, she wandered the foot-path that twisted around the Serpentine, until, with great reluctance, her train of thought abruptly changed gear, drawn back to the night of which she had just recently and so unpredictably been reminded.

After reading Elizabeth's diary, Sylvia knew that her emotions had never had to endure such a nerve-splitting embodiment of sorrow and revulsion. Every word had risen from the pages to plant themselves forever inside her troubled soul, making her a victim of her own discovery. Impassioned, bittersweet, and laced with tragic hope, the young girl had travelled the short, yet all too easy journey from romantic puppy love to sexual obsession.

Pacing the flat for an hour, streaking fast and frequent tears across her face with her hands, and nursing the terrible menstrual pull of a period brought on early by the trauma of that discovery, Sylvia had paused for a moment outside Jack's bedroom, before picking up his door keys and hurrying away into the night.

What do you do when two addicts refuse to surrender their addiction? When whatever you advise makes not the slightest difference, because they are so hopelessly and blindly hooked?

Sylvia was lucky. There was a parking space close to the fire exit beside the artists' entrance and she turned off the engine, shivering with indecision.

What you do is remove the cause. Destroy the drug. Then, and only then, can the people you love be set free.

She wanted to kill him, but had no idea how or whether she would be able to do it. She certainly meant to hurt him. And frighten him. There was no other way. Mere words, he could twist and sugar so brilliantly that she would be seduced, as they had been.

Sylvia wasn't to know, but only after each performance did a club bouncer turn up for duty backstage. Offering silent gratitude for being able to enter the building unseen, she climbed the steps to the star dressing room for what would be the final time. The sound of applause and laughter told her that the first show was well underway and, when she pushed open his door, her confidence suddenly returned as instinct took over.

Acting totally against character by not thinking beyond the moment, Sylvia checked the landing, then with gloved hands swiftly and silently removed each of the bulbs that surrounded the mirrored dressing table. Balancing on a chair, she reached to take another from the light which hung on the ceiling.

Dew moistened her forehead as she frantically considered her next move. This would puzzle him, entering a darkened room, and she tried to imagine what she would do in similar circumstances. Of course, she would go to the phone. Laurie would almost certainly walk in and call for someone to solve the problem.

With the open door still providing light to the area around his dressing table, Sylvia searched for a pair of scissors, while almost laughing from near-hysteria. What a predictable whodunnit scenario she was about to create. But one thing at a time. Confuse him first. Don't be seen and then...

Unable to locate any scissors, she began to sweat again, the cramps from her period almost doubling her in two. Through the speakers, she could hear him performing his act and it unnerved her, even though he was way below her on the stage.

"... I've got a query for you, Laurie."

"Well, don't bring him in here."

Hearty laughter.

Something glinted on the table, amid the pots and boxes of foundation and powder, and Sylvia picked it up cautiously then stared at it with a quickening heart. Perhaps she had found the perfect tool to cause him pain and fear; a weapon almost symbolic of his trade.

"Let's see how sharp you are," Sylvia whispered, surprised by how easy it was to slice through the telephone wire. Then, satisfied that the razor would serve her purpose, she closed the dressing-room door, having counted how many steps she could safely take in the dark in order to position herself as near to it as possible.

Fear and exhilaration thundered through her body as she heard the applause die away and the band strike up the play-off music. Perhaps the madness to which she had been driven had been a mistake after all. She had always considered herself incapable of violence, but he would soon be here, and it was far too late to back out now.

As if her rough plan had taken years instead of minutes to formulate, Laurie Christian performed the entrance that Sylvia had scripted to perfection.

Standing in the doorway, holding a pair of high-heeled shoes, he had cursed at the lack of light and limped across to the phone, where he soon realised that it wasn't working, and why.

Bewildered, he had stood for another moment contemplating his situation, as Sylvia moved quickly towards the door.

She had succeeded in at least part of her scheme. He was most certainly frightened, and his voice shook as he called out, "Who's there?"

Then, unexpectedly, he began to address her as if she were Elizabeth. Laurie thought she was Elizabeth and his voice became cajoling and sweet.

Flooded now with a revenge nothing less than that inherited from her Old Testament forefathers, Sylvia lunged forward and lashed the razor into his right arm. Then, as his scream lent her renewed energy, she tore at him again, and watched as his sadly dilapidated, curvaceous outline made for the door.

Her unspoken thoughts came easily enough.

' ... That's for Elizabeth's lost innocence. For her trust and generosity of spirit. And for the mental and physical abuse you put her through, you bastard.'

As he slowly approached the door, Sylvia caught her breath, then wildly brought the razor down once more, this time slicing into the back of his neck. Screaming again, he swayed forward, then jerked himself upright with great effort.

When he turned, she would cut his face; disfigure the looks that ruled his life, and perhaps allow him to live. Surely the sweetest revenge of all.

'... That's for Jack's dependence. For all the cheating and the lying...'

But then, as Laurie sank to his knees and begged in the

darkness for her to spare his face, she knew, without any doubt, that she couldn't finish what she had started out to do.

To her bitter dismay, Sylvia realised that if she concluded her task, it would no longer be just for Elizabeth or Jack. It would almost certainly be for herself; for all those dreams and plans shattered long ago by a charming imposter whom she had once desperately loved.

Tearfully, Sylvia kicked out her foot in frustrated anger at the now ludicrous and pitiful figure struggling to reach the door, no longer excruciatingly sexy and no longer in control of his situation. Then as he cried and lowered his head, she dropped the razor and ran from the room almost praying that she would be stopped, in order to allow this nightmare to end in her own well-deserved punishment.

Perhaps he would die, anyway; bleed to death in his dressing room and not be discovered until someone called him for the second show.

Hardly able to believe what she had done, Sylvia drove to her west London home and tore off her blood-stained trouser-suit and silk shirt, throwing them into a heap on her bedroom floor. Catching sight of herself in the glass, her hair wild and her face gaunt, she ran a steaming shower and scrubbed her body with such force that her skin took on the appearance of undercooked meat.

Swilling from a bottle of Courvoisier, she changed into different clothes and, by the time she arrived back at Jack's flat, although more composed, she was still nursing the uneasy sensation of being a character in someone else's dream; unable to leave until they chose to wake.

The anxious and sleepless night ahead would be spent waiting for Elizabeth's return, as well as reliving her own actions, and Sylvia was soon to realise during the weeks and months that followed, that nobody possessed even the slightest clue as to who had attacked Laurie Christian.

Only time, as ever, could dictate and aid the healing process, and Jack and Elizabeth had each gone cold turkey and somehow survived.

A sudden April shower caressed her face and Sylvia took it as her cue to return to work. Please God, she had now exorcised that particular ghost once and for all.

A new decade had begun and there had been many changes since those lamentably evocative days. Gay was now the word, and it wasn't simply the title of an Ivor Novello musical comedy. Orton and Epstein were dead, both victims of their sexuality and fame, while the homosexual bill finally became law, ending a century of intolerance and shameful blackmail. Now Jack and others like him were released from further years of nervous repression, allowing him to choose how and when to love again.

Because their pain had become her pain, Sylvia would continue to be bound to him and his niece by the strongest embryonic kinship outside of close family, and in many ways that was all she ever wanted.

—⁘—

PARIS

The female impersonator did his best to ignore the Levi-clad buttocks of the young make-up boy who bent down to retrieve more lip gloss from his box, then stretched his deliciously muscular body in order to apply it with meticulous care. The photo-call had been arranged in the Luxembourg Palace Gardens which now, at 8.00 a.m., were becoming inconveniently busy, even though he had made a huge effort to get out of bed to be on location by 6.30.

To his mind, Jacques, the photographer, seemed to have been farting around for over an hour, setting up what appeared to be a mass of unnecessarily complicated equipment, and was currently expressing gruff, Gallic astonishment at the way the sky alternately darkened and then shone, as though it was the most unusual of phenomena for this time of the year.

"Are we nearly ready?" The impersonator enquired petulantly and in English, for although he had lived in Paris for seven years, he still declined to speak in anything other than his mother tongue, unless absolutely forced to do so.

"*Oui, Dieu merci.*" Jacques rocked on his heels and scrutinised him through the lens, while make-up and wig were once again assessed by the dish in blue jeans.

It had been a difficult decision as to what to wear. A one-piece pantsuit in soft, black leather, with phallic-style silver studs was a present item of clothing of which he was especially fond, but then again, he had spent so much money on the hormone injections for his new and conspicuously elevated bosoms, that it would have been sacrilege not to have worn the low-cut, aquamarine number on which he had finally settled.

A look of ferocious concentration crossed Jacques' face as he began to click his brand new imported Japanese camera, and the impersonator smiled and pouted as instructed, while allowing himself a moment of reflection.

His latest show in Pigalle was going to be a sensation and he had been told by management that they were accepting bookings for at least the next six months. Since arriving in this city, every show he had performed had been a sell out, but the new tits, together with some plastic surgery on his nose, had ensured not only a renewed following, but he had been able to negotiate a salary which placed him on the same level as stars of the famous extravaganzas staged at "The Alcazar," the "Moulin Rouge" and the "Folies-Bergère."

Changing his position so that he could lean seductively against the Medici Fountain, he became aware that the photographer had diverted his attention away from his current task and towards a group of young women who were making their way down to the lake, carrying books and exchanging laughter and animated conversation.

Feigning boredom, he gave a loud, exaggerated yawn, but his full, red mouth forgot to close in surprise as they passed his line of vision.

At first, he wasn't sure, but then as he stared harder he knew it had to be Elizabeth. The only girl who was unconscious of the effect she was producing and of the lusty whistle that followed her. The one with the tall back who held her head high as she took the lead with a stride that indicated confidence and freedom of spirit.

Her mass of hair was brighter than he remembered it, titian and pre-Raphaelite, pulled back on the nape of her neck, from where, straining to be unleashed, it sprayed into an undisciplined wreath of curls.

Disturbed and apprehensive, Laurie turned his head away in the primitive hope that if he couldn't see her, then she wouldn't notice him.

When the girls had gone, the action around him continued

much as before, as Jacques changed the film in his camera and the make-up boy looked at him now with presumptuous curiosity.

"*Qu'est-ce qu'il y a, Lauree?* 'Av you seen a ghost?"

How could he tell these people whom he hardly knew that one of those girls had tried to kill him? That one of those pretty young things had been so sick with love for him that she had lost her reason?

What the hell was she doing in Paris? He hoped that it was a holiday and that she wasn't studying here. His top-floor apartment, located on a winding street in Montparnasse, was in immediate proximity to areas frequented by students from the Sorbonne.

He shuddered, instantly reminded of the terror of that night and his long and lonely road back to health.

There was no way that he could have told the police who had attacked him, as Elizabeth had known far too much for him to risk a retaliatory accusation. Nursing two cracked ribs, a broken leg and a fractured shoulder, not to mention the array of stitches holding together the flesh on his arm and the back of his neck, he had indicated through bruised lips that it had been an unrecognisable stranger. Probably a burglar or some homophobic nutter who thought he was doing the world a favour.

Apart from the CID who regularly attended his hospital bedside, he had been visited only by his sister, the kids in the show and once by Mark Dover, who brought flowers on behalf of Merrick Management.

When he had tried to ring Jack, he was informed that his private number had been changed and, when he was pronounced strong enough to go home, Jack was back at the agency but not taking his calls.

Realising then that the time had come to make a fresh start, Laurie considered his options. Might as well kiss goodbye to his own club in London, for without Jack's financial input and clout, he would be unable to afford it now, and equally unable to retrieve the twenty-five grand deposit.

However, the other twenty-five grand was still stashed away in a wig box under his bed, and he was damned if he'd offer it back to the girl after her savage attack on him which could have proved fatal. While struggling to think straight through a blur of pain, there came the offer that was to save him. Whether or not he had been instructed to get shot of him from the agency, for Laurie would never know, Mark Dover had suggested that he consider a lucrative six-month contract at a famous drag night-club in Paris. Just a tryout of course, but if both he and the punters were happy then it might lead to something more permanent.

Only just fit enough to work and still bearing scars, Laurie gave notice on his flat, packed up Flora and, five months after that horrendous night, took himself, his costumes and his wigs across the Channel to star in his own cabaret in the heart of the French capital. He was surprised to learn that his scant knowledge of the language made little difference to his act. The references to parts of the male and female anatomy could be translated through gesture, as likewise allusions to homosexuality and the sex act itself. His musical numbers had to be French and he learnt these phonetically, pleased that he could exercise his choice of some of the classic torch songs made famous by Piaf and Hildegarde.

It also became clear that, unlike England, where caricatures abounded, really attractive female impersonators were not uncommon on the nightclub circuit. Few relied on foam rubber for their ample chests, many had risked the highly controversial sex change operation and Parisian nightclubs were often staffed by stunning transvestites working as waitresses as well as chorus girls.

But when he thought about it, and this could have been a line from his act, he was more than able to hold his own. The competition had been hot and often bitchy, but the customers soon voted through their return visits and their money for the beautiful impersonator from London, Laurie Christian.

One of those customers, in particular, had made himself known to him during those early days. A silver-haired banker with a penchant for good wine, in which he indulged at his chateau in the Loire valley where he lived with his wife and two children. Meanwhile, residing during the week in his apartment in Le Marais, the respectable businessman indulged in another of his passions, young men who wore lipstick and frocks.

Being kept in the manner to which he had always hoped to become accustomed brought Laurie security and wealth and, when the weekends threatened to stretch beyond long and lonely, he chose not to go short of company. Screw being faithful. Monogamy was strictly for Catholic wives and undersexed romantics.

So why at this particular moment was a tight knot of discontent lodging itself in his stomach? Could it have anything to do with seeing that girl again?

Perhaps it was fear? It didn't feel like fear. And, come on, was she really likely to have stalked him to Paris seven years later to get her revenge?

Jolted out of his reverie, he heard Jacques signalling the end of the shoot by announcing *"Fini!* We are through," and saw a driver in grey uniform and cap appear at the top of the steps.

"Your car, *monsieur."*

Oblivious to the stares and giggles from camera-toting tourists who had gathered next to the fountain, Laurie accepted a cigarette from a crumpled packet of Gauloises proffered by the photographer, then hitched up his dress and followed the chauffeur to a peppermint Rolls Royce convertible parked near the entrance to the gardens.

They had had fun, he recalled, before she got silly and imagined she was in love. He had told her once that she was the best company of anyone he knew and, as he reflected on his life so far, that still held true. They'd laughed at similar daft things and, remembering *Dr. Zhivago*, had cried together too.

As he stepped into his Rolls, Laurie wondered whether he might be losing it. Why in God's name was he having these thoughts now? Why was he even thinking about her at all, the murderous little cow?

Jack and Sylvia had worried themselves sick about her, but how good a girl had she really been? After all, she had offered him money in return for sex. Nor was she a slow learner. How much further would she have allowed him to go, given the opportunity?

Bewildered and wearied by his emotions, he leaned back against the cream leather headrest as the car sped along the tree-lined banks of the Rive Gauche.

The early chestnut blossoms stretched defiantly towards a stormy sky, their rebirth somehow forcing him to once again consider his future.

Throughout his life, Laurie Christian had created the dual role of the wanted and the wanton, and control had become an acceptable substitute for love.

Perhaps he was just beginning to understand why so many men and women, far wiser than he, drew their inspiration from this city he now called home.